TALES OF MANTICA

EDGE OF THE ABYSS

Edited by

BRANDON ROSPOND

ZMOK
BOOKS

Cover Art by Michele Giorgi c/o Mantic Games
Tales of Mantica: Edge of the Abyss Edited by Brandon Rospond
This edition published in 2018

Published by Pike & Powder, LLC
Zmok Books
1525 Hulse Road, Unit 1
Point Pleasant, NJ 08742

ISBN 978-1-945430-42-8
LCN 2018943426

Bibliographical References and Index
1. Fantasy. 2. Action. 3. Adventure

For more information on Winged Hussar Publishing, LLC, visit us at:
www.wingedhussarpublishing.com
www.pikeandpowder.com

CONTENTS

INTRODUCTION

The dawn brings a new day to the continent of Mantica. The sun brings warmth from the mountaintop of the Howling Peaks, across the Ardovikian Plain, whistling through the trees of the Forest of Galahir, and through the cities that make up the Successor Kingdoms. Over the years, life has grown in every corner of the world; countless races and cultures have sown their roots and spread out, creating vast territories. No one race reigns king over the land, as each is the ruler of their own domain. Each leader of every army fights to be his own king on the field of war.

Mantica exists in a constant state of turbulence. There are those that seek more than just their own domain; they wish to destroy all that would oppose them and conquer the whole land for their own desires. As of recent times, the land itself cries out in pain. Mantica has been rent by dark forces, creating a chasm filled with hellfire and nightmarish creatures. The people of the realm call this place the Abyss. From this pit of darkness emerged winged stone gargoyles, baleful horned demons, and elementals of hellfire called efreets. They torture and taint the earth with every step they take, every breath they breathe.

All hope for Mantica is not lost, though. Heroes that stand on the side for the forces of good take the guise of various statures. Whether they come in the form of forest dwelling elves with their understanding of the land, dwarfs who dwell deep underground and bring with them their knowledge of craft and technology, salamanders whose fiery tenacity knows no bounds, or men who are born and bred to fight wars, the darkness of the Abyss shall always have someone to contend against.

This anthology is a collection of ten short stories that span the *Edge of the Abyss* campaign in the *Kings of War* universe, covering as many factions as Mantic has put rules out for. Each story has been tailored to fit into the overall lore of the universe, having worked closely with Mantic, as well as unified under my guidance to create one overarching universe for our fiction. Some of the stories we have adapted directly from the *Edge of the Abyss* campaign book, while others may seem very close, but we've changed the armies to put our own spin on the battles. Even though the stories can be read in any order, we've purposely ordered them as so that the first is the earliest in our narrative, while the last brings the most recent developments. This is but the first of many works we plan to publish in the *Kings of War* universe!

The Brotherhood is a mysterious order of men that can commune with the power of water through their most highly trained and elite warriors, the Order of Redemption. In Duncan Waugh's story, "Unfamiliar Territory," a unit of Brotherhood soldiers, led by a Redemption Knight named Aldous, scout the area by the Abyss, unaware of what horrors have begun to leak onto the world. They stumble upon a bizarre ritual site and are ambushed by Varangur soldiers. Their leader, a man named Gunnar, states that there is a greater evil coming for them; that the men of the Brotherhood must either run and flee the Varangur, or stay and face the darkness, reluctantly, together.

Some cannot rest, even in death. The pharaohs of the Empire of Dust use the dark powers of necromancy to reanimate the dead to do their bidding, as is the case of C. L. Werner's story, "The Sea Does Not Give Up Her Dead." Djwet is a former plunderer who was killed by the hands of the Empire of Dust, only to be brought back to life to serve the bidding of High Priest Nekhbet. Having brought Djwet's fleet up from the bottom of the sea, Nekhbet orders the skeleton to sail him toward his former home of the Fang Isles so they can build their army. Not willing to let such dark magic sail through their waters, the naiads of the Trident Realm of Neritica board the ships and attempt to stop the dead from reaching their targets.

The Abyss has twisted many creatures, but perhaps none so much more than the dwarfs. Perhaps it is the fact that so many of them live underground, or perhaps it is that there are those that are so easily tempted by the dark whispers. Whatever the case may be, the Abyssal Dwarfs capture the ingenuity and craftsmanship of the dwarfs and combine it with the sickening, dark power of the Abyss. In C. W. Conduff's story, "Kinship," Lord Yurec has created a group of dwarfs known as the Traduciators to try to divine the truth behind the dwarfs that go missing to see if they've truly succumbed to the corruption of the Abyss. When the latest to go missing is his brother, Durok, the dwarfs travel deeper underground than they've ever been. Whatever the case may be, Yurec is ready to face his brother; to bring him back or to strike him down.

Orcs pillage and destroy; it is as much in their nature as it is to breathe. Such behavior could be blamed on the Celestial known as Kyron, who was responsible for taking the members of the group, collectively known as The Herd, and corrupting them into the beasts we now know as orcs. In Andrew McKinney's story, "The Beast Within," the two cousin races collide on the field of battle once more. Many different groups have come to answer the call of the longhorn, Malgar, to stand and defend their land from the destruction of the orcs. Dragyr, his apprentice, has only known his master and is amazed at how many creatures come to protect their wilds when threatened. Can the unity of The Herd defeat the villainous orcs, or will they triumph in burning down the longhorns' forest?

To the salamander known as Lukhantl, his brother, Lorquan, is all that he has left. When the latter is taken by Twilight Kin slavers, after losing a bloody battle at Hokh-Man, Lukhantl and his captain take to the seas. While salamanders are often thought of fighting best on the land, Robert E. Waters fights the salamanders against the Twilight Kin in a fast-moving, action-packed naval battle in "Into the Straits of Madness." Will Lukhantl succeed in finding his brother, or are the ships all going down in flames?

It has now been several months since the Brotherhood and Varangur fought the Forces of the Abyss. News has spread across Mantica of the darkness that the demons bring with them. The Kingdoms of Men have begun work on a giant wall that they hope will act as a first line of defense for their lands. In Michael McCann's story, "Emerald Eyes," Commander Cassandra Agrias has been put in charge of overseeing the work, but they have been met with obstacle after obstacle, impeding their progress on the wall at its tail end of construction. After fending off efreets that had bombarded the wall, the men find that the orcs have begun to move on them. Agrias has sent word back to the Kingdoms, requesting more aid, but the response she gets disappoints her. Instead of sending men, ogres have been hired to aid her army. Agrias is hesitant to put her faith in these mercenaries, and her brash lieutenant, Sir Ewan, does nothing but help to antagonize that nagging feeling. But as they bicker, a force begins to move in on the wall…

Dunstan Rootwell is a halfling that resides in the League of Rhordia. Once a rat-catcher, Dunstan now trains his halfling troops in preparation for whatever uses the League has for them. When they are called upon, Dunstan is surprised to find their task is something he has quite a bit of experience in. Hunting rats. In Scott Washburn's story, "Rat-catcher," the halfling army travels to the city of Norwood to find that it has no ordinary rat problem; the ratkin have infested the tunnels under the city and have begun striking against civilians. The duke is concerned if this goes on much longer, their entire town will be overrun. Dunstan turns to the aid of his friend, Paddy Bobart, to see if they can find a way to deal with the infestation, and things take off with a bang.

It takes a powerful source of magic to affect a dragon to the point of lethargy. In Bill Donohue's story, "The Last Stand," Commander Sindfar Greenspar is a leader in a group of Dragon Kin. Even though he does not ride one of the beasts like his exalted brethren, he is tasked with scouting the land ahead to find out why the dragons act as if their flames have been extinguished. Their target is a fortress that was once used by elves of yore as a defensive point, but when they arrive, they find that an old priest is living there, harboring children. The priest, Anselmo, speaks of a great evil that is plaguing the land, destroying the children's villages as they go. Meanwhile, the undead are on the move. Led by a necromancer named Zar and a vampire lord name Yarik, their crusade against the living grows ever more powerful. Even though Zar seems a pitiful necromancer, he seems to have stumbled upon some power that even makes the vampire shudder with worry.

Out of all of the Celestials that have split into two personas, one of the few that has remained intact is the Green Lady. Under her tutelage, the Forces of Nature protect the land from any that would threaten prosperity of natural life. In Marc DeSantis's story, "Eyes Unblinking," Dillen Genemer is a part of a Basilean army that is in search of the Lady's aid; knowing that the powers of Basilea and the Green Lady combined would stop any foe, they search her to forge a truce. However, before they can reach her, they are set upon by Abyssals, who seek to destroy both forces before they can unite. Dillen is sent forward by his allies to try and find the Green Lady, and when all hope seems lost, he is led to her by the sylph named Shaarlyot. Can he still make it back to his allies in time to save them?

Almost a year has passed since the Abyss split Mantica apart. Someone must unite the people to stand against the darkness. Prince Talannar Icekin has established the wintery capital of Chill, and with it, an army to unite the people of all nationalities, known as the Northern Alliance. Gavin Stalspar is one of the many warriors who fight under the prince's banner, but his purpose for being there is unclear. While thankful for being given a place to fight and sleep, his thoughts and heart seem distracted. In "Crimson Winter," by myself, Brandon Rospond, Gavin seeks a purpose, while others around him question what secrets Prince Talannar has laid hidden within Chill.

With these ten stories, we hope to run the gamut of battles for all of the different factions. We hope the gamers appreciate the tales written and can either use these to come up with new ideas for their own armies, recreate the battles described, or even use these as inspiration to come up with tales and adventures of their own. Keep on reading, writing, exploring ideas, and sharing with other players of *Kings of War* to prepare for the next anthology!

UNFAMILIAR TERRITORY

By Duncan Waugh

The perpetual twilight covered the men's progress as they quietly and carefully made their way through the dense treeline. The pair acted as if they were a single entity, each anticipating and mirroring the other's movements, their instincts honed through years of experience together. Although not born from the same parentage, they may as well have been brothers, so close was the bond between them. When one looked in any given direction, the other would cover his blind side. Slowly, the lead man stood, before quickly dashing to the next point along their path, the other following in his stead. Each had their role to fulfill, and they operated like a well-oiled machine.

A loud cracking sound made the two drop down into crouched positions, their eyes scanning the horizon in the murky darkness. The wretched, ash-laden forest floor made for little in the way of vegetation or ground cover, leaving a landscape predominantly covered by thin, coniferous trees. The plants' sickly, twisted forms, bereft of much of their needle-like leaves, provided little nourishment to the rest of the area's ecosystem. And yet despite the relatively barren terrain, the cloying, dank air was filled with swarms of incessant, biting insects, whilst the ground was home to writhing piles of worms and beetles feeding off any fallen detritus.

The rearmost man gently lowered his two swords, noiselessly placing them on the ground, and slowly pulled back his garb's brown, woolen hood. He waited silently, rotating his head in either direction, trying to place any further noises. In the quietness of the lifeless terrain, the sound of his ever increasing heartbeat became an unnecessary and uncomfortable distraction. As irrational as he knew the fear to be, he still worried that the mere sound of it might give their position away to any unknown threats lurking beyond his vision. No follow up noise was forthcoming, and yet still they remained stationary, the tension at odds with their seemingly placid, barren surroundings.

After several minutes, satisfied that anything which might have caught their scent would have acted by that point, the man tapped the lead ranger on the shoulder and softly whispered. "Falling bough."

A nodded acknowledgment was all it took, and the two continued on their way. Deftly sidestepping any obstacles or hazards in spite of the low-light conditions, their feet rolled onto their outer-most edges with every stride, spreading the weight of the men and reducing the impact and sound of each step. Eyes flicked between the forest floor and the horizon, constantly wary of any movement that seemed odd or out of place for the environment.

Having covered another hundred yards or so, the front-most ranger, bow in hand, called a stop with a quick flick of his wrist, and turned to his comrade. "Randall, how far do you reckon?"

Letting his swords fall to his sides, the man mulled the question over. "A mile and a half, maybe two? You thinking it's time to head back?"

"Yeah, I don't want to push out too far from the rest of the column," the first speaker answered. "A safe perimeter is one thing, but if we run into anything out here, we'll be too far from the others for support, and then we'll just be alerting any enemy to our presence."

"No complaints from me," Randall smiled at his friend's response and raised one eyebrow. "Sainted Ones, Warner, you would think after all this time we would be used to this place by now."

Warner chuckled. "The day I get used to the lands of the Abyss is the day I truly fear for my soul. You really want to feel at home next to that gateway of hellfire?"

The other ranger shrugged his shoulders indifferently. "Not when you put it like that." As they turned to retrace their way back to their camp, he muttered to the archer. "I swear though, if Denner has been at my food again, I will personally throw him into the pit myself."

*****

Aldous stood alone, staring skyward at the billowing plumes of toxic gas and filth that spewed forth from the Abyss. The deep crevasse may have lain far beyond the reaches of his sight, but its effects could be felt for vast distances in every direction. Like all of his fellows within the Brotherhood, Aldous had spent his entire life working against the forces of the Wicked Ones - the ancient fallen deities who had had all goodness ripped from their very souls. Long ago they had been cast down, trapped within the very tear in the world's core that they themselves had caused. Nevertheless, for untold generations, both their demonic minions and their sickening allies had harried the mortal races, a constant threat from which few were safe.

And so it was that his people, bereft of home and hearth in the wake of the great floods, had made their pact – to stand guardian over the Abyss and all its foul ills, to do what others lacked the strength or will to do themselves. They were not alone in this task, but while others, like the Basilean Hegemony, were ruled by self-interest and mired in political machinations, the Brotherhood remained true to their cause. It was a burden, one he had been born into, but one that he carried proudly. Men could spend their whole lives searching for a sense of purpose, but he, along with the rest of his people, could stand firm in the purity and righteousness of their cause.

Behind him, the knight could hear the sounds of his retinue as they broke camp. They had been on the march for several weeks, patrolling the periphery of the Wicked Ones' domains, and during that time, Aldous had felt a growing sensation of unease build within him. In spite of his natural gifts, he had been unable to divine the cause of his apprehension, and that fact weighed heavy upon his shoulders. Removing one of his heavy gauntlets, he traced the course of its delicate, engraved filigree work with one finger. Such ornate ostentation was not commonplace amongst the knights of the Brotherhood, but his armor was a precious relic, blessed in ages past by the great mage Valandor and imbued with a portion of the man's immense power. Very few of his knightly brethren would ever be called upon to wear the plate-mail of his order. None could predict who would be chosen, and few were even able to speculate as to what caused the ancient suits to react to one person and not another.

Pulling off the leather glove beneath, he exposed the burned and scarred hand within. Life within the Order of Redemption carried with it certain expectations and commitments. Their knights were ever at the forefront of hostilities with the forces of the Abyss, regularly tasked with some of the most dangerous missions their people were called upon to undergo, and they were even required to work alone on rare occasions. Flexing his fingers, Aldous felt the itching fire spread along where they had restitched the skin of his palm, its constant irritation flaring into one of outright pain. Over time, he had learned to manage it; keeping the disfigurements that marred his body hidden from view helped when it came to interacting with others. His skills with the sword were superlative, and his armor granted him great prowess in the field, but even these could not protect one from the flames of the Abyss indefinitely.

The knight plunged his hand into the small stream next to him. Feeling the cold water soothe the injured flesh, he tried to banish the memories of how the sorcerous fire had bathed him in pain and agony, finding its way through the seams of his armor and tearing at his muscular form beneath. Closing his eyes, Aldous concentrated on the texture and smell of the liquid. His enhanced connection to the life-giving element, bestowed upon him by his armor, allowed the knight to detect even the smallest of particles that flowed through the medium between his fingers. Normally, this far from civilization, the water would feel clean and pure, but something about this particular flow felt sickly and strange.

Reaching out with his mind, Aldous pushed against the current, slowly feeling his way back up the tributary toward the river's source. The further his spirit traversed from his body, the darker and fouler the sensation became. It started to overwhelm his senses, the fetid stink filling his nose and mouth as he ventured on. The knight started to feel dizzy and thrust his other arm out to stop himself falling forward into the watercourse, all sense of his true position utterly fleeing him. In his mind's eye, he became surrounded by a deep ocean of blackness, its viscous nature clinging to his body, pulling him down. As his flailing attempts to stay afloat weakened, he could feel something vast and terrifying, an entity that had lain deep below the surface, starting to rise upward, attracted by his ineffective struggling.

The knights of the Order of Redemption had indeed been bestowed incredible powers, but they were a far cry from a true master of the mystical arts. The abilities that Valandor had gifted to Aldous's ancestors were largely martial in focus, and he could feel himself being swept under by the sheer force of the being he had encountered. Whatever he had disturbed was far beyond his capacity to understand, and the knight could feel his ability to resist its strength diminishing with each failed attempt to escape its inexorable pull. The man tried to focus on thoughts of home, his people, and their noble undertaking; but the shadows were too all-encompassing, their pall binding his spirit to the damned place.

Suddenly the world turned sideways, his inner ear sensing the falling movement of his body in spite of the pitch blackness. Aldous panicked, certain that whatever presence had been lurking below was finally seizing upon him, dragging him down into the soulless oblivion that lay beneath. He tried to reach out and strike it, but instead he felt a hard, inert surface greet his flailing limbs. His hand came back bloody and cut, the metallic smell of the slick fluid triggering an unusually visceral response from his senses. As if awakening from a long slumber, he began to pick up other smells and scents too. The darkness began to fade, and he noticed the air becoming cleaner; the strength was returning to his muscles and his lungs were able to breathe once more.

"Aldous!" A voice that he recognized punched through the haze clouding his mind. "Aldous, get up."

An armored man stood over him, someone familiar, someone trusted.

"Come on, slow your breathing now. Steady yourself," the other man turned to a figure beyond Aldous's sight. "Grant, you keep an eye on those hills. You see anything move, anything at all, call out."

The reassuring sound of a steel blade scraping against the metal locket of its scabbard cut through the air. It sounded dimmer and further away than the man who had spoken to him, yet Aldous could tell his hearing was beginning to return. Slowly his awareness of his surroundings also began to recover, and he struggled to suppress the heavy shaking that rattled through his strained musculature. Realizing that he was lying sprawled out on the bank of the river, with an immense effort Aldous rolled over onto his back, hauling his arm out from the insistent pull of the stream's current.

The knight forced himself to take a deep, heaving breath, his voice sounding ragged and drained. "Quaid?"

The face swam back into focus, its owner's concern evident, even in Aldous's disorientated state. "I'm here, brother." Quaid started to reach for the fallen knight's helm, attempting to release the strapping that held the faceplate in place. "Aldous, what on earth..."

Before he could finish his question, the Redemption knight slapped his fellow's hand away. The sheer physical effort of the act caused Aldous to burst into a coughing fit that pained his already ravaged throat.

Quaid recoiled from his cohort, his voice failing to suppress the emotional pain he felt at the surprising rebuke. "I did not mean to... I just..." He faltered, striving to find the right words for the man that he had once been so close to, and yet now seemed so utterly distant. "How did this happen?"

Aldous tried to compose himself, attempting to breathe life into a body that had seemed close to shutting down. His nerve endings sparked semi-randomly, limbs gradually responding more and more to his own control as their feeling returned, but every part of him felt unbelievably cold. A pervasive echo of dread still filled the knight's entire being, impairing his cognitive functions and making it difficult for him to pull himself up, out of the mud.

At last, after what seemed a pain-filled eternity to Aldous, he managed to summon sufficient strength to answer his one-time friend and compatriot. "I cannot explain it. Not to someone outside the Order." His words came out slow and labored, interspersed with heavy, rasping breaths; and even in his injured state, Aldous could see the hurt they caused the other man. The knight struggled to find a less harsh way of explaining himself. "I just mean that you would not be able to comprehend the significance of it. Here, help me up."

Quaid lowered a leather-wrapped forearm and, bracing his back leg, heaved the fully armored warrior to his feet. His voice and demeanor having hardened in the face of Aldous's slight, Quaid coldly addressed the man before him. "If you do not wish to explain events to me, you can at least provide some reassurance that you are fit to continue leading this force, and perhaps inform me as to whether we should be concerned of any immediate threats."

Aldous's expression was unreadable, hidden behind layers of hardened, tempered steel, the whites of his eyes being the only things visible through the darkened recesses that were cut into his helm. Tension filled the air as he stood silently appraising Quaid, and when he spoke, it carried the full weight of his authority as a member of the Order. "Grant can rest easy for now. And with regards to my efficacy when it comes to command of these men," his tone took on a deep, threatening growl. "Never bring that into question in my presence again."

"Brothers," both men turned at the warning inflection within Grant's voice as he approached the pair. "Remember that we all walk the same path, each and every one of us. Do not let our proximity to the wicked twist what and who we are."

"Hmph. Well said," Aldous's gravelly reply had lost much of its venom, but undercurrents of anger still swirled below the surface. "Too long out here can... *wear*... on a man's soul. In any case," he gestured upstream of their current location. "There is something out there, something immense and powerful. I have never come across anything like it in all my years. Whatever it was felt utterly different to any Abyssal power I have encountered before, and I do not believe that to be a good thing."

Upon hearing Aldous's words, both of his compatriots developed looks of deep concern. As the silence dragged on, it was Grant who eventually spoke. "Is this something we can even handle? Our troop is not equipped for a pitched combat."

"It will have to be," Aldous turned to each of them in turn. "The Brotherhood does not flinch in the face of evil. We cannot let something of this magnitude go unchallenged so near to our lands."

As the three men paced back to camp, the fiery pits of the Abyss continued their endless burn in the distance, leaking sickness and corruption out into the world, poisoning the surrounding earth, and seeding their malady for leagues around.

*****

Warner finished wolfing down the last of his meager scraps of meat. The food's stringy texture, a result of the corrupting influences of the Abyss on nearby fauna, left an acidic, rank after-taste in the mouth, despite any attempts they made at seasoning it. He and Randall had been the last of the rangers to report back in, leaving them little time for rest before their group would once more be on the move. His compatriot was slumped next to the fire, catching what brief moments of sleep he could manage, a trait that Warner had always marveled at. This close to the home of the Wicked Ones, he could never quite shake the restless irritation that crawled its way beneath his skin. It was not unknown for the ranger to go days at a time without proper rest, and similar effects could be seen in many of the other men as expeditions dragged on.

The three dozen or so other villeins that made up their party busied themselves stowing the camp's baggage and securing their own personal armor and equipment. The majority of the men comprised a spear company that had been pulled from one of the defensive watches at the Brotherhood's fortress, called the Crucible. They were capable fighters but lacked his men's experience when it came to operating out in the wastelands far from any support. As such, Warner's rangers had been tasked with accompanying them at the direct request of the Redemption Order.

He watched as the three Brotherhood knights walked back down to their encampment, the men's armor glinting through the weak rays of light that fell between the threadbare trees. The villein could not help but marvel at the ornate, ancient relic that was Aldous's suit. It stood in stark contrast to the more easily manufactured, utilitarian plate of his other knights; a sad indication of the toll this endless conflict was taking on their small nation's industrial capacity to keep their forces armed and in the field.

Warner shook his head bitterly at the thought of their neighbor states, always happy to let the Brotherhood stand watch over their boundaries, yet rarely to be seen whenever the call for aid went out. His loved ones, the people he cared for, had to die out here while the pompous Basileans politicked and debated in their ornate temples, so desperate to curry favor from what little, fickle goodness remained within the Celestials. And the dwarfs, so content to bury themselves in their dank tombs, unwilling to take responsibility for the pain and suffering caused by their twisted cousins upon the peoples of the world. It was such weaknesses that had allowed the forces of the Abyss to propagate unchecked, and if it was necessary for the Brotherhood to bear the burden of responsibility for all, then they would do so. Because as far as Warner was concerned, they were the only ones with the strength to face such a challenge.

The one known as Quaid approached the center of camp, and the assembled soldiery came to a respectful hush, awaiting further instruction. "We have discovered some," the knight faltered, trying to find the right words, and, glancing briefly at Aldous, a look of concern momentarily flashed across Quaid's rugged, battle-scarred features. "Some new *information*. If this is as serious as we expect, then we cannot allow the Brotherhood to remain ignorant of such a threat. This will, however, be an undertaking of information gathering only. Our goal is not to engage whatever we find out there. Is that understood?"

As the men around him nodded in understanding, Warner could not help but wonder who that last part had been directed at. Having worked alongside the knights of the Order of Redemption before, he knew they were prone to sometimes reckless, independent behavior, but the codes of knightly honor and conduct were a complete mystery to him. With the surrounding camp suddenly energized, he gave a sharp kick to the unconscious form of Randall lying next to him.

"Urgh. What the hell?" His bleary-eyed compatriot was not at his best upon awakening.

Warner bent down to pick up his gear. "Come on, we're getting ready to move out."

"Fantastic," Randall's humor was as dry as ever. He stood, dusting himself down and stretching out the taught muscles of his upper back. "When do we leave?"

The other ranger laughed, indicating the spearmen already falling into a marching column. "Now, from the look of things."

Randall looked around, staring at the camp's detritus with confusion. "But what about all this?"

As his friend gestured at the discarded remnants, Warner easily caught the man's meaning. Any foe that came across such a large swathe of debris as the one that they were leaving would find little difficulty in picking up the group's trail.

Pointing to the wide tracks being left by the soldiers, however, Warner shrugged his shoulders with resignation. "Doesn't really make much of a difference when we're dealing with that, does it?"

"Bloody lead-footed clods," Randall grumbled under his breath as the pair moved to rejoin the rest of the men.

*****

The small Brotherhood patrol force wound its way along the gravel-strewn riverbank, heading toward the tributary's source. At some point along their journey, in spite of all his misgivings, Quaid did expect to find whatever unclean presence had so unsettled Aldous; he just had no idea what they would do when that moment came. His horse whinnied suddenly, the animal spooked at nothing in particular, and he pulled sharply on the reigns to settle the creature once more. The diseased air around them was taking its toll on everybody, and he ran one hand down the beast's neck to try and help calm her, receiving a half-hearted flick of the tail in response.

Still lost in contemplation, he barely noticed as Grant pulled his mount in beside him. "So, are you going to tell me then?"

Snapping back to the present, Quaid barely heard the other man's words. "Hmm?"

The knight raised one eyebrow inquisitively. "You and Aldous, I need to know what history exists there. If this thing is as dangerous as he suggests... Well, this is hardly a crusading army that we have at our backs."

Quaid sighed, knowing that this moment had been inevitable. "We were initiates together." The knight's gaze became unfocused as his thoughts reached back into his own history. "We were both born on the very same day, if you can believe that. And then we grew up together, so, naturally, we ended up starting our training alongside one another too. During those years, we walked every step of the Order's path as if we had truly been brothers."

"We all share a bond, you know that," Grant interjected, his tone mollifying. "Any one of us would die for another."

"Not like this though," Quaid grimaced. "From all those years we spent together, we were utterly in sync with each other's thoughts and movements. Fighting became like a symphony to us, an intoxicating mixture of bladed precision and martial prowess. I knew everything about that man; every fear, every dream. I knew his very soul, Grant. And he knew mine."

The other knight's mood softened upon hearing the pain in his friend's voice. After a moment of silence, he eventually spoke again. "What changed?"

Quaid was staring down at his own gauntleted hand, unable or unwilling to make eye contact. "The calling."

"Ahh," a look of understanding crossed Grant's face, his tone somber. "I have never known a knight on a personal level before he donned the Armor of Tides. For one of us to be chosen is such a rare event in and of itself."

"He changed almost overnight, pulling away from everything and everyone that was important to him. For the last few years, it has been rare for him to spend any length of time at the Crucible, always out here in the badlands. I know the trials he has been through must weigh heavy upon him, but it does not help ease the void left by his sudden absence," with a look of resignation, the knight pointed to Aldous. "That man over there, I do not even know who he is anymore, or what he has become."

*****

The areas surrounding the Abyss were far more than just a desolate wasteland of destruction and devilry. Existing so close to the home of the Wicked Ones could change a being all the way to their core. Entire nations had been known to fall to the will of the dark demigods, turning from their past deities to find renewed strength in service to the twisted, broken shadows of what had once been Celestian souls. Unless one had hardened their resolve against such depredations, it could be all too easy for any sentient creature to fall under their sway, let alone the simple animals of nature that still remained.

As the armored column moved through the constant, quasi-darkness of the region, their passage did not go entirely unnoticed. Their observer was clad in plates of blackened steel. A myriad of rough gashes on the surfaces exposed bare metal beneath, the mixture of oxidized rust and stained blood lending the armor a faint, reddish hue in the dim light. Vicious-looking spikes adorned many of the jointed panels, turning the man's every movement into one of potent lethality. A large, double-handed axe was chained to a vambrace and hung, resting against his side, the edge dulled to better suit its role as a tool of violence. Cold eyes stared down the rocky incline at the troops below, black ash-paste hiding what little of his skin would have been visible above the helm's cheek-guards. His unmoving vigil failed to mask any of the man's capacity for murderous brutality, his body's absolute stillness a testament to the muscular strength it contained and the focus with which he could wield it.

From his vantage point upon the steep, craggy flanks of the valley, the warrior continued to watch in silence. Whilst he waited, the rising winds whipped at the fur-lined cloak that hugged his shoulders. Finally, having satisfied himself as to the strangers' course and their ultimate destination, he turned and headed back along the winding path that led between the peaks and over the ridgeline.

*****

Warner sat with Randall on the uppermost boulder, the two having spent the last hour climbing the steep incline together, unprotected from the chill wind that cut through to their bones. From their elevated position, they looked out over the wooded valley below, Randall still reeling in the last of their rope lines. It had been a difficult climb, and not something the rest of the armored column would be able to make. Warner hoped that the other scouts had had better luck in their exploration of the surrounding area, otherwise they would be forced to follow a far more time-consuming, roundabout route to get back to the river; and every day spent out in these lands reduced the odds that a person would be returning home. After taking a big swig of water, he handed their canteen back to the swordsman, and turned around to eye the terrain ahead of them.

The ground sloped upward, leading away from them before returning to the gentler inclines that they had been traversing prior to encountering the cliff face. More of those sickly, ailing pines lined the horizon, obscuring whatever lay beyond from view. The men had stayed fairly close to the steep, falling rapids during their ascent, and he could make out the river no more than a few minutes' walk away; its path ultimately disappearing into the distant, silhouetted tree line.

The archer had started shouldering his pack when a shrill bird call broke the eerie silence of the mountainside. Both rangers' hands immediately went to their weapons, Warner ducking down, palming an arrow from his waist-mounted quiver and immediately nocking it into the bow string without a moment's thought. The two remained completely silent, each straining intensely to pick up any further sounds.

After a brief pause, they both made eye contact with one another,

Randall using his free hand to sign the direction that he thought the noise had come from. Warner nodded back, concurring with his comrade's judgment, and delicately lowered his bow to the ground. The ranger placed each hand to his mouth and whistled back an almost identical call, ever so slightly higher pitched, using both of his cupped palms to induce a characteristic tremolo effect.

Almost immediately, a similar, deeper warble was carried back to the men over the cold air, confirming their earlier suspicions as to the source's bearing. Toward the end of the bird song, the sound suddenly pitched back up, hitting the higher notes and creating an altogether unconvincing impression of the local wildlife.

"That's got to be Denner," Warner chuckled, retrieving his weaponry from the ground. "He never could manage the proper calls."

Randall grinned back at him. "What do you reckon, good news or bad this time?"

Warner smiled wryly at the pair's regular guessing game. "When was the last time it was ever good, Randall?"

*****

Fellow ranger Denner and his partner, a swordsman by the name of Gareth, were waiting at the tree line for the two men as they jogged across.

"I swear, Denner, if you weren't such a good shot, you'd be booted from this outfit after unleashing a cacophony like that," Randall greeted the slovenly archer good-naturedly. "How your wife puts up with it is truly beyond me."

Denner smirked. "We can't all have your dulcet tones, Randall. If only our surroundings were more suitable to appreciate the full extent of your auditory brilliance." The men laughed as they locked arms in a welcoming gesture.

"Yeah, yeah, don't encourage him," Warner cut the conversation short. "So tell us, what have you found?"

This time it was Gareth who spoke up. "It's bad, boss. I don't know if it's what that knight was talking about, but it's a pretty big damn coincidence if not." The fear in the man's eyes and the earnestness of his voice cut through the fraternal geniality from mere moments before.

Warner's features took on a serious cast. "Go on."

"There's a church or something down there. I've never seen anything like it before, filled with these horrific statues and carvings that were just... just..." Gareth went quiet.

Denner was left to finish the man's thoughts. "The whole place had this aura about it too, just being near it felt nauseating." He grimaced. "I'm telling you, Warner, it has to be linked to the Wicked Ones somehow, there's just no other explanation for the feel of that place. There's also... the..."

"The what?" Warner's tone had become increasingly anxious.

"The bodies," Gareth's shock-laden voice cut the air like a knife, utterly emotionless and cold. "There are a lot of bodies."

*****

Night fell as the men of the Brotherhood made their way slowly up through several of the narrow breaks in the rocky cliff face. Weapons were holstered as members of the garrison bent and helped their comrades up and over the more difficult obstacles in their path. Warner and the other rangers, their packs lighter and armor more maneuverable, clambered easily across the rough terrain, leading the rest of the group toward the temple site. The way the skirmishers hugged the craggy outcrops, their eyes never leaving the dark horizon ahead of them, was not lost on the other soldiers.

Seeing such experienced fighters rattled had caused a deep, stifling silence to descend across the rest of the infantry. The only sounds to be heard along the rise were the muffled, angry curses emitted whenever an ill-advised step caused loose stones and scree to bounce noisily down across the slabs below, coupled with the soft clinking of the knights' armor. Having been forced to leave their horses at the base of the rise, the unmounted knights struggled under the weight of their suits, but they continued on nonetheless.

Several hours later, the main body of the patrol finally finished traversing the ground that the scouts had taken such a comparatively short time to cover, and they were able to move out across the plateau toward the location of the unidentified temple. As the remaining distance to the isolated site decreased, the atmosphere within the group became increasingly tense and fractious. The men had heard the rangers' dire reports of the massacred worshipers and seen the fear in their eyes as they recounted the scene to Quaid and the other knights. In spite of the usual military rivalry that existed between the two groups, the men of the watch still held a grudging respect for the experience of the hardened irregulars, and the concern amongst the skirmishers' ranks had become contagious.

The remaining distance to the shrine was passed in silence, the mixture of the unforgiving surroundings and utter darkness conjuring a myriad of horrific nightmares to run through the soldiers' minds. But none of their scouts' reports could fully prepare the men for the devastation they were to discover as they began their descent into the clearing that ringed the ruined structure.

*****

The soldiers picked their way through a scene of utter slaughter and destruction. Smoke rose in thin plumes from the cooling, burnt out remains of the building's wooden supports. The once large beams were now nothing more than twisted and brittle, crack-ridden lumps of charred timber. Altars had been pulled down and numerous dark stone statues smashed, the men unable to make out whatever bizarre scenes the crudely ornate sculptures had once depicted.

Quaid wandered through the broken remains of the smashed and desecrated religious site. It seemed that around every corner lay yet more of its dead inhabitants, their bodies mutilated and burned, piled up in small groups for some purpose that he could not fathom. The church had sat in the middle of a small clearing, its low, single story hiding the grounds from prying eyes. There was a stream flowing through the center of the compound, running directly underneath the main building. Had it not been for Aldous's vision, Quaid doubted that they would have ever come across the peculiar site.

When they approached the outer edges of the perimeter, Warner and some of the other rangers had come across several of the more intact corpses, and from what he could tell, they did not belong to any group known to the Brotherhood. Entirely male, they had worn unusual robes of midnight purple, free from any form of lavish decoration or ostentation, in stark contrast to the level of effort put into the imagery adorning the structure around them. Each man had marked their face with some kind of charcoal paste, many of the designs mirroring the symbols that had been inked across much of their exposed flesh, the letters and numerals utterly unknown to any of the soldiery.

As far as Quaid could make out, it appeared that none had survived whatever attack had reaped such devastation, so complete and total was the destruction to their surroundings. The fact that such an established culture had managed to secure some kind of foothold in this region without anyone in the Brotherhood being aware of its existence caused him a great deal of concern, and it would no doubt trigger much debate when presented to the Captain's Council upon their return. He allowed one hand to linger on the bas-relief inscribed into the stone pillar in front of him, a chill running through his bones at the touch.

There was indisputably a sick malaise hanging over the whole area, and he managed to gain some measure of understanding as to what Aldous had felt by the river earlier that day. Whether it was linked to what had existed within the fallen walls before recent events had turned the space into a charnel house, or instead was simply the result of such a brutal massacre, he could not say. Was the presence that his brother-knight had felt merely an echo, or had something truly terrible once resided here?

Before him, the carved stonework depicted a large, almost featureless face. Its forehead disappeared into a swirling mess of tendrils, and where the left eye would be was nothing but a blank void. The mouth twisted and turned, one side smirking in an exaggerated depiction of mania, the other frowning, almost a mirror image of the other facet. The image was dominated by a curving mask, swooping up and over the manic cheekbone before curling back on itself above the creature's nose. It was lined with concentric stretches of the same kind of text he had seen tattooed onto the worshipers, and within its eye-hole lay a single overly diluted pupil that seemed to stare into his very soul as he watched it.

Turning away from the ghoulish visage, Quaid took in what remained of the rest of the room. Circular in shape, it resembled one of the larger antechambers from the Crucible's monastery, easily able to hold a couple dozen practitioners; although portions of the wall had subsequently fallen in from the heat of the blaze, leaving the ceiling open to the cold night sky. Set within the inner portion of the room, two more pillars stood, each one laid out to form the points of a perfect triangle. Letting his gaze take in the scene in its entirety, Quaid soon noticed that all of the stone uprights featured a different design wrought into their surfaces. Each depicted a face, but they varied significantly in both design and demeanor.

One of the other columns showed a man's head tilted back, screaming toward the heavens. Where the first had featured a comparatively plain expression, this guise was covered in crisscrossing scars, the ligaments taught and stretched in a grotesque exaggeration of complete and utter rage. The look of hatred in the sculpture's eyes seemed so real to Quaid, that the lack of any sound being emitted from its mouth almost felt more unreal to the knight than if it had been shouting.

Turning to take in the last of the three figures, he gazed into a countenance that appeared utterly indifferent in its attitude toward the viewer. While the others had disconcerted him with their intense depictions of raw emotion, this face felt all the more perturbing for its detachedness. Unfocused eyes stared back at him out of features that looked hardened and weathered from a life spent in the outdoors. The paths of various celestial objects were tracked across a background depicting the night sky, with the man's eyes seeming to reflect their light back towards the viewer. Quaid had never felt so small in his entire life, and it took significant effort for him to break eye contact with the carving, having to remind himself that it was nothing more than a piece of inert rock.

The knight had no idea what the meaning of his surroundings were, but he could sense that nothing good would come from lingering in such a place. Taking a step back, his foot caught against a raised section of the floor, and looking down, he realized that a winding series of shallow channels had been carved into its surface, linking all three of the bizarre pillars. The weaving paths appeared to be stained with splashes and rivulets of deep ocher, alluding to the kind of primitive sacrifices his kind had forsaken millennia ago. Alone, he felt a strange chill run down his spine, and, sure that whatever the worship site was it had to be linked to the Abyssal forces in the region, he made his way back to find Warner and begin the ordered dispersal of their men.

*****

Brotherhood soldiers hurried around the site, pulling the fallen rubble into doorways and corridors to create choke-points and defensible fallback positions should they be needed. Any spare weaponry was collected and stashed behind the makeshift emplacements, while torches were lit and scattered around the grounds. Warren was not sure that advertising their presence would prove to be the wisest of moves, but the unsettling knight from the Retribution Order had overruled him, apparently confident that they could expect company before whatever he was working on was complete.

The archer headed over to the other rangers who were gathered in a small group just inside the main courtyard. "Come on, lads. We've got a job."

Denner looked up, sour-faced. "Picket duty?"

"Picket duty," Warner nodded back to the sound of much sighing from the assembled men.

Slowly, the tired soldiers got their gear together and started to head out in their pairings. Randall looked over at him, wrinkling his nose and smiling cheekily. "Ah well, you know I love a good walk in the fresh, country air."

Warner smiled and slapped his friend on the back as they paced out through the arched entranceway, making their way toward the tree line.

*****

When Quaid found him, Aldous was standing in what appeared to be the main altar room of the shrine complex. He was bent over, studying what appeared to be some kind of plinth placed into the floor at the midpoint of the space. Inlaid in its center lay a tablet, made from some kind of ancient metal. Cracked, and with some parts missing, it clearly predated the rest of the structure that was built up around it. Its surface was adorned with more of the raised symbols that none of their group had been able to discern the meaning of.

With the other man's footsteps snapping him to attention, Aldous addressed his fellow knight. "This is it, Quaid. This thing here is linked somehow to what I sensed before by the river."

Quaid came to a stop next to his one-time brother and looked down at the strangely hammered motifs. "How do you know?"

Aldous hesitated. "This gift I have… It lets me feel other magics. Only in the crudest sense, you understand. But every instance of malign energies that I have encountered has left its own distinct aftertaste. And this... Well, it is unique. After a fashion."

"So, what is it?" Quaid failed to keep some of the bitterness of the past from creeping into his voice.

Aldous turned his helm to regard the other knight. "That is a good question. There is undoubtedly a presence tied to this place, and this artifact does rest at the very heart of whatever it is I felt. But whether there is an entity that is being bound to this location by the magic here, or is merely being connected to the shrine through it, I have absolutely no idea."

For the first time in years, Quaid heard real emotion underpinning the man's words, and it filled his stomach with dread.

*****

Gareth and Denner stood, leaning against the trees at their allotted picket point. The rangers had made sure to position themselves between cover, with the torchlight illuminating the shrine behind them, so as not to provide any telltale silhouettes that would give away their location. Gareth could hear Denner idly stroking the fletchings of his already nocked arrow, a nervous habit that the man had sported for the whole time he had known him. As much as the dark shadows of a forest could reach in and tug on the primal fears of a man, he was grateful to be away from that eerie shrine and its dead bodies.

The swordsman preferred enemies that he could fight with his blades, and the unwholesome witchcraft that had infused that cursed place chilled him more than any natural phenomena could have. Shivering in the cold night air, he pulled up the collar of his leather jerkin and breathed deeply into his hands in an effort to warm the freezing digits. The woodland appeared completely still and devoid of life, not even a breeze stirred the branches or their thin, waxy needles. Nevertheless, he still strained to see into the dingy pools of light being cast by the intermittent moments of moonlight breaking through the cloud-covered sky overhead.

From the corner of his eye, Gareth saw Denner's stance harden, his body going rigid as the man rose to a fully upright position. With his weapon still pointing down at the ground, the archer slowly pulled back the string of his bow to the midpoint, the tensioned limbs groaning softly under the additional strain they were bearing. Gareth immediately stood and silently slipped forward, positioning himself against a fallen bough that lay angled between Denner and the potential threat that lay ahead.

Gently peering from around a protruding section of rotting wood, he scanned the ground in front, trying to identify what it was that Denner had spotted. Suddenly, he felt the back-draft of an arrow as it flew past his face, no more than a foot away from his head. Unperturbed, he stared into the distance, following the projectile's path as it disappeared into the gloom, the serrated metal point glinting in the starlight. Unable to see what Denner had been shooting at, Gareth turned back to the archer to seek confirmation, just in time to see the man's body fall limply to the ground.

He barely had time to cry out a warning before an axe buried itself in his back. As he collapsed to his knees, he could not help but wonder at how he no longer felt cold anymore.

*****

Hearing Gareth's scream, Warner and Randall spun around to face the direction of the noise, only to be greeted by the sight of three half-naked men, caked in thick layers of black warpaint, closing on their location. The small group was mere yards away in the darkness and would have caught the pair completely unawares. Randall swung into action, freeing his second blade and taking up a defensive posture between the oncoming assailants and his partner. Seeing that the element of surprise had left them, the unarmored men separated, with the two on the edges breaking away to either side, encircling the pair of rangers.

Randall could not help but marvel at the speed and silence with which they moved through the undergrowth, easily rivaling the skills of the best scouts the Brotherhood could produce. Sharp teeth glimmered in the half-light, their predatory smiles betraying the attackers' confidence. Each wielded a pair of mismatched hatchets, their crude, battle-damaged edges waving dangerously in their owners' hands. The swordsman began edging backward, trying not to let any one individual pull him into an engagement and lock him in place. To do so would leave Warner defenseless and vulnerable to the rest of the pack; and once the archer was gone, it would be only a matter of time before they brought him down too.

With a sudden blur of movement, the quickness of which stunned Randall, the man to his right flung one of the axes toward him. Desperately pivoting on the spot and leaning his body back, the ranger narrowly managed to avoid the spinning weapon; but before he had time to pull himself back into a ready stance, the enemy was on him. Savage blows rang down one after another onto his dueling blades. The man attacking him may have been reduced to a single weapon compared to Randall's two, but the warrior's momentum combined with his own poor positioning lent his foe a tremendous edge. The sheer downward force of the strikes threw Randall's arms wider with each and every parry, making it even more impossible for him to regain his positioning, the feral aggressor's crazed fervor utterly unrelenting in the face of the savage melee.

*****

Warner's eyes were wide with a mixture of fear and surprise. The shock of having been so nearly set upon without any warning whatsoever was so completely unfamiliar to the experienced soldier, that for a moment, he was utterly fazed by it. But seeing Randall jump into motion snapped the archer out of his daze and his right hand unconsciously fell to the quiver hanging from his belt. Grabbing hold of the first arrow shaft he could find, Warner tilted the bow into the motion, and with practiced speed, fitted and nocked the arrow onto the string.

The bow was already at mid-draw by the time Warner had switched to an aiming stance. As he pulled his right hand in below the chin, drawing the arrow back, he felt the habitual sensation of the string's rough fibers dragging across the lower portion of his face. With practiced speed, he took in the full scope of the skirmish before him. Randall was struggling under a flurry of brutal blows from one of the painted wild-men, while another of the snarling ferals closed on Warner himself. In the background, he could also see the third man pulling some kind of primitive, short-length bow from behind him. Three threats, all of them potentially fatal.

Warner was not unaccustomed to hand to hand combat, but he could not fight and shoot at the same time, one leaving him terribly vulnerable to the other. Randall was staggering back under the ferocious onslaught of his attacker, losing ground every second. If he did not help him, it would only be a matter of time before his friend was cut down, and he needed Randall to keep his own approaching antagonist at bay. The archer had no other option than to hope his opposite number was either slow, or a poor shot.

Lifting his feet high to avoid catching them on any unseen obstacles, he quickly sidled around the tumbling free-for-all ahead of him, trying to find a clearer angle on the enemy. Randall, unable to see his comrade's movements, but trusting to the pair's training and experience, tried to open up some space between himself and his assailant to allow his partner to take the shot.

Warner, starting to feel the burn set in across his chest from the effort at keeping such a high poundage bow at full draw, focused intensely on the two men in front of him. He had no time to check the rest of his surroundings, any opening in the frantic brawl would be momentary and gone within an instant.

Suddenly, Randall twisted and threw himself bodily beneath an incoming blow, leaving his back exposed to the enemy, but crucially placing the axeman between him and Warner. Instinctively, and without any hesitation, the archer let his arrow fly, the force of the released energies rippling along the limbs of the bow, his arm shaking slightly as the load it had been bearing suddenly dissipated.

At a distance of only a few yards, the projectile hit the target at once; its lethal, triangular broadhead tip slamming into the man's unarmored torso and smashing through the bone, burying itself deep in his core. The enemy's attacks were halted instantly, his body too concerned with the catastrophic damage it had suffered from the bolt's impact to pose any threat to them. As their foe fell to the forest floor, Warner could see Randall back-pedaling to avoid being trapped under his bulk. Satisfied that his partner was safe for the moment, the archer reached for another arrow and looked to his sides, trying to locate the other raiders.

Without warning, a steel-capped boot kicked him in the lower back, sending sharp signals of pain shooting up the rest of his spine and throwing the archer down onto his front. After hitting the ground, Warner felt a knee slam down hard, pushing him into the dirt. With the pommel of his blade caught beneath his own weight, he struggled futilely against the sheer mass pressing down on his body. Laboring to breath under the crushing pressure, he was unable to call out, and, pushed face-first into the mud, the villein never saw the downward blow coming.

*****

With his initial assailant incapacitated, Randall rounded on the enemy archer and rushed forward in an attempt to cover the intervening ground before his foe could draw him in his sights. The other man pivoted on the spot, trying to get a clear shot on the Brotherhood soldier, his vision obscured as the swordsmen maneuvered behind a nearby tree trunk whilst still closing the gap between them. With a growl, the maddened wild-man cut the string of his bow, letting it fall to the ground in the process, and hefted one of their group's characteristic short-hafted axes from his belt.

As Randall cleared the tree, he was caught flat-footed by the archer, who, having thrown himself forward, immediately lashed out with his crude axe in a wide sweeping blow. With no time to think, the swordsman stepped inward into his opponent's guard, taking the flat of the axe blade against his chest. He could feel the sheer strength of the hit cracking several of his ribs, but the larger surface area of the axe's bit bounced harmlessly off his gambeson, the thick, padded-linen fibers preventing its edge cutting down into his flesh.

With the pain in his chest making him roar in frustration, Randall slammed the pommel of the sword in his right hand hard against the axeman's forearm, the reflexive shudder running up and down the injured enemy's limb, causing him to lose his grasp on the primitive weapon. The whites of the enraged man's eyes shone in stark contrast to the cracked black paint that encircled them, and Randall tried to push the other warrior back so that he could exploit his blades' longer reach. But before he could put the full force of his weight into the action, the enemy landed a quick flurry of punches on his uninjured right flank, throwing the whole movement off.

Quickly recovering from the ham-fisted blows, Randall lashed out with a forward kick, planting his foot firmly into his adversary's lower core, finally driving the man backward. Grinning wickedly now that he had the upper hand, the swordsman started to slowly circle his prey, simultaneously working some movement into his upper arms to loosen up the musculature that was beginning to cramp. The wild-man, rather than showing concern at his own lack of weaponry, rotated his head almost quizzically, appearing to be appraising Randall with curiosity as opposed to apprehension.

Sensing the end of the fight coming, Randall let out a low growl and made to move toward his rival, only to find himself staggering more with every step. It felt as if his energy was draining away, and the surprised swordsman pitched forward onto the ground, digging his blade into the earth in an attempt to stay upright. He looked up at the painted man in confusion and watched as his foe revealed a left hand holding a thin, bloodied, dagger-like length of steel. It took several seconds for Randall's increasingly oxygen-starved brain to process what he was seeing; and as his head collapsed under his own weight, he at last saw the gore-soaked puncture wounds down the side of his gambeson.

Collapsing onto one side, he tried to cough up the blood that was flooding his respiratory system, his vision slowly fading away as he watched the unknown attacker walking off into the distance.

*****

The men pulled from the Crucible had heard the desperate screams echoing out of the darkness and were all on edge, a fact that Quaid could not fault them for. There was something about this place that crept into a person's bones, and, being so close to the source, even he could begin to feel what Aldous had spoken of. Pacing along one of the stone-lined passageways, he finished checking in on the last of the garrison's deployments and headed back to the central courtyard to reconvene with Aldous and Grant.

"Everyone is in position," Quaid nodded to the other two knights. "Whatever is coming, there is not much left that we can do to prepare for it."

Grant nodded glumly and turned to Aldous. "Have you managed to glean any more information about this place? You may not get another chance going forward."

Aldous's scarred and burned face stared hopelessly into the distance.

"That altar back in there, the one that I sensed earlier; I dare not delve too deeply into it. Whatever presence it is linked to is waiting, always just out of sight. I will not be able to defend myself against something that powerful. And from what we have seen here," a sweep of his gauntleted hand encompassed their surroundings, "all I can tell you is that it is not in fact Abyssal in nature, or at least is not tied to any individual Wicked One that we have dealt with before."

Cruel, guttural-laughter came emanating from a darkened alcove set into one corner of the enclosed space, causing all three men to recoil noticeably. "And it took you that long to come to this realization?"

A powerful figure clad in layers of black plate and moving with deceptive ease, despite the weight of his armaments, stepped into the light. In one hand, he clutched a large, brutal looking axe that immediately put all of the knights on alert. "You are all truly ignorant. And none of you should be here."

Aldous quickly shifted into a bladed stance, resting a hand on the grip of his sheathed sword. "It would be wise for you to tell us who, or what, you are."

The newcomer's eyes locked balefully onto the Retribution knight, all sense of humor lost. "Really, it would, would it?" The dark warrior's tone took on a more threatening note. "You have no right to even set foot in these grounds, and yet here you stand. The only reason that you are still breathing is because I will need every one of my men for the coming battle." The stranger's volume continued to rise. "You will leave, now! While I am still feeling generous."

Undaunted, Aldous's body language hardened noticeably as he stared the other man down. "Whatever strength you think the darkness that you serve may have granted you, be warned that –"

Grant stepped forward, interposing himself between the two and cutting off his compatriot, his voice more ingratiating, but still firm. "Wait, you said a battle." He pointedly made eye contact with his fellow knights. "Who are you expecting to come here?"

More harsh laughter, the chain of the dark warrior's axe clinking with the heaving movement of his chest. "Come now, don't tell me that such esteemed paragons of virtue as yourselves, members of the Brotherhood even, could possibly be so uninformed as to the true nature of the Abyss."

*****

A man daubed in black warpaint sprinted shirtless through the trees, his breathing rough and ragged. Alongside him ran a blur of white, a creature raised in the far north and unfailingly loyal to its master. Fear got the better of him, and he turned, in spite of himself, to see if his pursuers had closed the gap. A ball of burning incandescence nearly blinded him as it flew by, mere inches from his face, ultimately smashing into the dead, rotten husk of a nearby tree trunk. The fiery projectile immediately set the tinder-dry wood alight, and he raised his arms to ward off the unnatural heat of it.

The bright light coming off of the blazing tree ruined the man's night vision, causing him to trip and stumble over the many rocks and unseen roots that lined the forest floor. His pace slowed, and he heard his companion growl dangerously at a threat that lay just behind him. Gripping a pair of axes, one in each hand, the man turned to face his fate, knowing full well what was about to befall him.

*****

Even the ever diplomatic Grant bristled at the insult. "What do you mean?"

The knights watched uneasily as the armored warrior's grip alternately tightened and loosened on the haft of his axe in a random, but seemingly increasing, frequency. "This is a holy site of the Varangur, and it has stood here since the Reckoning itself. It encompasses more knowledge about the truths of this world than can be found in all of your libraries combined. And yet you have the arrogance to presume that your path is the righteous one? You cannot begin to fathom the powers that exist beyond the pathetic struggle that you dedicate your lives to, so consumed by your own people's limited importance."

Aldous drew his blade first, followed shortly by Quaid. Grant, still trying to glean whatever information he could from the man before them, moved to interpose himself between the knights. "If that is the case, then why not enlighten us?"

The man's significant bulk twisted to face Grant, bringing with it an intense and entirely unwelcome focus. "Is your faith so shallow? Are you so weak that you would turn from your beliefs and bend a knee to a stronger patron?" Even with his features hidden behind the helmet's brutish faceplate, it appeared to the other knights that the stranger was enjoying playing with their discomfort. "Very well, perhaps my words can enlighten your blinkered souls. I am Gunnar, one of the chosen Sons of Korgaan - the only truly whole deity still left, whose magnificence surrounds you right now. And for time immemorial, we have fought against the –"

The man's words were cut off by the shrill howl of a nearby, canine-like creature, which was soon picked up by more and more of its breed.

Breathing in deeply, Gunnar closed his eyes, savoring the cold air as it filled his lungs in anticipation for what was to come. "It would appear you have missed your opportunity to leave. They are here."

Quaid stepped forward, his voice earnest. "*Who* are?"

The other warrior looked at him, his eyes shining with mirth. "The slaves of the Abyss, of course."

The three knights shared shocked looks between themselves, events spiraling beyond their control.

"One question remains, however," Gunnar began. "Do you want to die on your feet, fighting, or running, like an animal?"

*****

"I do not like this," Grant stated matter-of-factly as the knights walked down the corridor.

"None of us do," Quaid grimaced as he stopped and looked the man in his face. "But what other option do we have?"

Grant shrugged. "It just does not feel right. We know nothing about these people, we simply cannot trust them."

Aldous rounded on the other two, anger flushing his face. "Our job is to kill the Wicked Ones' servants, and that is what we are going to do. If these Varangur help to serve that goal, then so be it!"

Grant looked to Quaid pointedly. "And if they turn on us?"

"Then we kill them too!" Aldous snapped. "But right now, we have a known enemy to deal with, understand?"

The two knights eyeballed each other for a drawn out second before Grant begrudgingly turned on his heels and headed off in the direction of their men.

Quaid waited until his friend was out of hearing range. "What the hell was that?"

Aldous seemed surprised by the question, nodding in the direction in which Grant had left. "He forgot his place."

"His *place*?" Quaid was incredulous and drew close to the Retribution knight. "Have you forgotten what our order stands for? Every man has his say, you know that as well as any of us. What is really going on here?"

Aldous gazed off into the distance, his hand instinctively going to the burn scars running across his once handsome face. When he spoke again, his voice seemed different, softer; it reminded Quaid of how he had sounded all those years ago.

"I am sorry, truly. Sometimes... I..." The knight struggled momentarily to regain his composure. "It has been a long time since I have worked alongside others. With everything that has happened, it can be difficult."

Seeing the sincerity in his brother-knight's face, Quaid nodded in acceptance, gently laying one hand on the other's shoulder. "Then let us prepare to fight them. Together."

*****

The black-clad warriors, or night raiders as Gunnar had called them, came streaming out from the edges of the clearing. Alongside them ran small packs of tundra wolves, their large size and sheer physical presence more than making up for their conspicuous white pelts. As the men poured into the temple, the Brotherhood soldiery watched them engaging in strange observances and rituals before the desecrated idols. Some even began collecting together the chunks of the broken statues in an effort to sort through them and return the fragments to their respective effigies.

The two groups kept largely to themselves, the fact that these strangers had mere moments before been fighting and killing his brethren made Aldous feel sick to his stomach. He could see that the same thought had not been lost on the other Brotherhood soldiers, with a number of men having to be held back by their fellows to avoid any acts of outright violence being committed against their new allies. Some of them shouted out angry taunts at the newcomers, who, for their part, merely stood staring back impassively at the Brotherhood men in response.

He and the other knights had agreed with Gunnar to keep the two factions as separated as possible, but some contact between them was inevitable. His hand flinched reflexively around his weapon's grip at the very sight of the savages. Necessity might have made them allies for now, but the Brotherhood's numbers were small compared to other nations, and no one could be allowed to kill their people without recompense.

With the last of the Varangur having made their way into the compound, their combined force did not have long to wait before the vast wave of Abyssals came screeching over the rise. Consisting of scores of lesser demons, and being led by the towering, hulking form of a far more powerful moloch, the baying horde bore down on their ramshackle position with a sheer, murderous glee. Aldous smiled; at last it was time for the true battle to begin.

*****

Quaid turned to look down the main corridor, trying to gauge the casualties his men had sustained in the early throws of battle. As he watched, one of the already damaged walls was suddenly smashed inward, sending sizable lumps of stone and mortar flying out across the space. Bursting in with the cavalcade of destroyed masonry came one of the feral minions of their enemy, a craven but incredibly vicious gargoyle. Baleful red eyes glowered from a twisted female form, the creature's skin the color of burnt charcoal, with each hand ending in a set of four contorted claws. The disgusting thing locked its eyes on Quaid, unleashing an ear-splitting scream, whilst simultaneously seizing upon an unfortunate Brotherhood soldier who had still been reeling from the collapse of the wall beside him.

Snarling at the knight, as if it was warning off another predator from its kill, the gargoyle continued along its trajectory, slamming into the back wall with its prey. Before Quaid had any time to react, it had barreled through the obstruction with equal ease, carrying its prize off into the night sky, screeching triumphantly. The entire scene had taken less than a couple of seconds, a man's life snatched away before the dust had even begun to settle, his body to be used for god knew what purpose.

Abruptly, he was snapped back to his more immediate surroundings as one of the sergeants of the watch grabbed him, screaming into his ear. "They've overrun the west nave, we have to get back to the chancel now or they are going to cut us off from the others!"

Seeing how many dead and fallen bodies lay around him, men of the Brotherhood and Varangur alike, the idea of retreat railed against everything in Quaid's being. But he was equally loathe to throw away yet more lives in a fruitless holding action that had no real hope of success.

"Alright!" He shouted, trying to be heard over the noise and chaos of the violence. "Get them back, and I'll cover our retreat."

*****

Gunnar stalked through the halls of the Varangur shrine, his fury rising with every instance of defilement and sacrilege that he came across. He cared little for the dead holy men, they were the ones who had allowed this blasphemy to happen after all, but such desecration of one of their holy places at the hands of the Abyssals was unconscionable. He picked up the pace, deftly switching between a number of different handholds on his axe, a barely controlled manifestation of the man's impatience to return to the fighting. His armor sported new rents and burn marks from the conflict, but he remained unharmed, his martial prowess undiminished.

The Son of Korgaan turned a corner at speed, only to be confronted by a lower Abyssal in the midst of yet more debasement. The demonic creature's beastly face was distorted with laughter as it slammed a giant, double-handed axe into a wall-mounted icon that depicted his god in the form of the Reaper. The sacred effigy was shattered into a dozen pieces and, roaring in apoplexy, Gunnar leaped forward, covering the distance in a matter of heartbeats.

Turning its horned head to face him, the Abyssal's long, lizard-like tongue seemed to leer in his direction. A handful of the small, imp-like beings that had gathered around the larger demon's feet scattered at the sudden assault, leaving their master to weather the onslaught by himself. Regardless, at the last possible moment, the lower demon managed to swing its weapon back around, blocking Gunnar's lunging strike with an ease that belied the creature's comparatively diminutive form.

The Varangur's axe, a powerful relic dating back to his people's first holy wars against the Wicked Ones, bit deep into the metal of the enemy's, carving a large cleft into the head of the inferiorly crafted weapon. Pushing with the immense strength in his legs, Gunnar managed to force the demon back against the corridor wall before employing the huge length of the beast's own axe to pin it in place.

Using his formidable weight, which he positioned centrally behind a one-handed grip, Gunnar leaned forward onto the bound weapons, keeping his opponent trapped. With his other hand freed up, he tried to reach the large, serrated dagger that was attached to the cuisse covering his thigh. However, before he could release the blade from its sheath, he felt several of the small imp creatures climbing their way up his legs and torso. The irritating beasts scratched and tore at the joints in his armor in their attempts to get at the human flesh within, all the while cackling incessantly.

Grabbing one of the diminutive wretches by its neck, he twisted it round to look at the ugly demon's features. Its body was brittle and weak, and he despised the cowardly thing. Throwing it away from him with disgust, the Abyssal slammed into the wall with such force that its neck broke, instantly killing it and leaving its broken carcass to fall limply to the floor. As pathetic and powerless as the imps were individually, there was no way he could keep all of them off him with just the one arm.

Gunnar bent to one side and heaved, letting his axe fall to the ground and throwing the lesser demon down with it. Finally, able to release his smaller blade, he came down on top of the Abyssal's body and punched the dagger's point downward into its torso just behind the creature's clavicle. Frenziedly wrenching the ragged knife back and forth with his upper body, Gunnar managed to sever the foul being's head from its shoulders. As the decapitated corpse fell to the floor, he stood back and ripped the remaining imps from his armor.

Free of their grasping talons, Gunner bent to retrieve his axe, lodging the Abyssal's weapon into a damaged section of mortar and levering his own to release it from the binding bite. Just as he was about to leave, the man heard the scraping sounds of movement and turned back to see the lower Abyssal rising upright once more. A leering face had formed where its chest had once been, and, upon seeing the look on Gunnar's face, the grotesque thing burst into evil laughter.

With the Varangur shrine once more burning at the hands of his infernal foes, the Son of Korgaan hefted the weapon in his hands and stepped toward the Abyssal, grinning evilly beneath his helm. "I'm going to enjoy this."

* * * * *

Grant struggled to breathe through the cloying smog, the stink of burning flesh filling his nostrils. The surrounding nave was on fire, but he had little time to ponder their situation, so numerous were the foes streaming toward his small group of men. Switching to a two-handed grip, he cleaved left and right, the last of his guardsmen pouncing on the enemies as he struck them down, ensuring they were left with no chance to regenerate from their injuries. He could hear Aldous shouting over the din, but given the chaos, any attempt at coordination between them was utterly futile.

He brought his elbow up and slammed it into the sternum of the Abyssal in front of him, causing it to stagger backward. Stepping into the open space, he swept his sword around in a wide, arcing cut that sliced through its lower torso and buried itself in the creature's spine. Quickly placing his boot against the howling being's chest, with one mighty heave Grant kicked it backward, freeing his weapon. Before he had a chance to recover, however, the knight was immediately bowled over by a massive impact from one side.

Grant's body was sent spiraling through the air, and he slammed heavily against one of the colonnades separating the nave from the south aisle. The force of the hit traveled through his armor and the padding beneath, and Grant fell to the floor with the deadening crunch of breaking bones. Momentarily blinded, by the time his vision returned, he looked up to see the vast, ruinous form of a moloch stomping through the battle toward him.

Easily as tall as two fully grown men, and with a mass more than double that, its horned, hellish visage sent fear racing through his heart. Struggling to rise, he could feel his left arm no longer responding to his brain's commands, and a dreadful certainty filled his soul. Picking up his sword one-handed, with the other left dangling limply at his side, he watched as the demon closed on him, its huge, clawed feet crushing both men and Abyssals with every step.

The moment the beast was within striking distance, Grant tried to deliver a lunging stab directed to the moloch's heart, but with so little strength behind the movement, the beast easily slapped it to one side before violently slamming its trident-like weapon into his chest, crushing the armor like it was made of nothing. So strong was the strike, that the three-pronged spear was left protruding from his back and became wedged fast in the column behind. The Brotherhood knight's last moments were spent staring in shock into the otherworldly grimace of the monster's snorting, animalistic face.

*****

Aldous saw Grant go down but was incapable of reaching him, so overwhelmed were the remaining survivors by the sheer number of Abyssals. He watched, helpless, as the other knight was butchered by the hulking moloch, and he felt the rage rising within him. He had held off from employing his mystical gifts out of fear of leaving himself open and vulnerable to this Korgaan being, the one worshiped by the deranged heathens they now found themselves allied to.

Not that their erstwhile partners were faring particularly well in the conflict either. From what he had been able to ascertain, it seemed like they were some kind of light raiding party, ill-equipped for manning an entrenched defensive position. The night raiders were undoubtedly skilled fighters; both vicious and fast, they had killed many of the enemy, but they lacked the discipline and cohesion to hold out for any prolonged period against a horde of this magnitude.

Too often he observed them exposing themselves unnecessarily to the attacks of their targets' compatriots. And the wolves that the Varangur bore alongside them fared little better, at times saving their masters from an unforeseen strike, but all too commonly this came at the cost of their own lives. His patrol was facing the minions of the Wicked Ones, and, rather than soldiers, they had found themselves left with only a bunch of feral warriors to aid them.

Seeing the last of the nearby Varangur fighters break and run, he retreated back into the northern transept, using the small, enclosed space's solid walls to protect his sides and rear. It was a desperate move, cutting off any hope of retreat, but Aldous was coming to the growing realization that he was not going to survive this fight. It was, after all, inevitable for a knight of the Retribution Order to ultimately die in the throes of combat, and such an eventuality was something that he was well prepared for.

Watching the remaining Brotherhood soldiery gradually being worn down, each man resolute to the last, ultimately forced Aldous's hand. Reaching far down into his soul, he began to feel the stirrings of the deep-rooted, elemental energies that he had been taught to harness. The knight let his mind follow the course of the stream below them, feeling his way along its winding path through the mountain's gullies until he found what he was looking for.

The obstruction, an accumulation of collapsed earthworks and fallen trees, had created a small basin that had filled with water over the years. Barely cognizant of his body's real surroundings, Aldous swerved to avoid a downward strike from one of the enemy's minions and forced it back with a savage backhanded blow across the face. Attempting to keep his mind focused on the distant dam, he began slowly to manipulate the water pressures within the lake, agitating the usually fairly placid creek. Gradually, parts of the river blockage began to break away, until finally its structural supports became completely undermined and collapsed.

Aldous could feel the huge power unleashed as the river broke its banks and the huge body of water came crashing down the hillside, completely beyond his ability to control. Reaching out and grabbing a nearby stanchion for support, there was no time to warn the others before the torrent of muddy water came smashing through the church windows, the massive power of it hammering into those inside. Many of the building's occupants were immediately thrown off their feet and sent spinning downstream in the torrid flows until they came to a stop, crashing hard against the church's thick stone walls. Some sections of the structure were even washed away, leaving great, ragged holes in the exterior walls.

While the moloch's incredible mass helped anchor it against the oncoming deluge, it still bellowed in pain as large tree roots and displaced rocks picked up along the watercourse hit its armored hide and threw the creature off-balance. Seething in frustration, it looked around the wrecked remains of the nave, soon identifying Aldous, the only fighter still standing, as the source of the shockwave. Roaring in fury, it stamped its way toward him through the lessening flood surge, each massive step kicking up large sprays of water into the air.

Aldous rolled his shoulders, loosening up the tense musculature of his upper torso and prepared to meet the behemoth. The demon grinned menacingly, the chance to test itself against another of the Brotherhood's knights clearly appealing to the monster. Before it could close the remaining distance, however, Aldous cast his unencumbered arm up into the air, using his magical gifts to raise a huge wall of the dirty, brown water between them. With the beast's vision obscured, the knight seized the opportunity to cover the ground quickly, advancing up and around to the side of it. Thanks to his affinity with the element, the waters directly surrounding his legs calmed with every step, aiding the man's movements, rather than impeding them.

When the sheet of filthy river water fell away, the moloch seemed momentarily confused as it faced the empty side-room where the knight had been standing prior. Suddenly appearing to the thing's side, Aldous stabbed his sword into the Abyssal's unprotected underarm, pushing on the blade with all his might. Against any other creature, such a strike, falling as it did above the protection of the ribs, would have been fatal. But the towering demon merely bellowed in pain and anger, and swung its weapon round, nearly taking the knight's head off with the wild blow.

Desperately, Aldous struggled to free his sword from the monster's body, but it was stuck fast into whatever bony structure had saved the Abyssal's life, and the knight was forced to relinquish it, lest he be crushed by the moloch's flailing follow up swipes. Leaping back, he threw up yet more intervening walls of water in an effort to hide his movements. He ran over to one of the human bodies that had been thrown against the shrine's walls. The blunt force trauma that it had sustained had ended the person's life instantly, and he felt a momentary pang of guilt when he noticed the dead man's Brotherhood livery. Nevertheless, he snapped up the soldier's hefty spear and turned back, ready to make his stand against the huge beast.

Facing himself in the direction of the moloch's last position, the knight made to circle around it for another strike. With the distance to his target closing, Aldous raised his spear, preparing to launch it at the lumbering brute when it reappeared from behind the pillars of water in front of him. The knight was so pre-occupied with the ground ahead that he had no time to react as the creature's long trident came slicing out from the wall of water to his flank, its pronged head emerging in a wide, all-encompassing arc. Caught off guard by the monster's cunning, Aldous had no chance to evade the vicious weapon and was lifted off his feet as its sharp cutting edge ripped through his armor, breaking the spine and causing him numerous severe internal injuries.

With the moloch stepping through the visual barrier of muddy water, Aldous looked down the length of the weapon's pole and stared into the grimy, dirt-caked face of his killer. The magics around the two faded as his life energy trickled away, and the Abyssal threw him down to end his final moments drowning under the waters that had once been his ally.

*****

Gunnar, having watched the entire struggle from the shadows of one of the nave's alcoves, silently stalked up behind the demon. His movements appeared impossible for a man of his bulk, particularly one that was equipped with such substantial weaponry and armor. However, the warrior had met with great distinction through his long, dedicated service to Korgaan, and his lord had favored him accordingly with many unusual gifts and abilities.

The Abyssal remained ignorant of the Varangur man's presence up until the point where Gunnar brought his massive axe down across its ripped, muscular back. The dark fighter smiled as he heard the monstrous chest snap and crack beneath the weight of the axe. Reaching round, he took hold of the Brotherhood knight's sword that was still wedged in the cavity underneath the thing's shoulder and wrenched hard, splitting the demon's compromised bones and subsequently driving the blade on into its heart.

The giant Abyssal came crashing down to the floor, with Gunnar watching curiously as it writhed in its death throes. The lesser demons that still remained cried out in horror, aghast at the great creature's destruction. And as Gunnar turned to face them, the cowardly devils turned and ran, leaderless and disorganized. Aldous's body, somehow still breathing and barely clinging to life, floated back to the surface.

Gunnar regarded him, the warrior's faceless mask revealing no emotion. "You never should have come here, you know that. You have transgressed upon one of holy places, and there always has to be consequences."

Slowly, the Son of Korgaan put his boot on Aldous's chest, and then gradually, but firmly, pushed him back beneath the roiling surface.

*****

As the morning light dawned on the Varangur shrine, its cold rays piecing the palls of smoke that still hung over the area, the men of the Brotherhood took in the devastation of the night before.

Quaid felt as much as heard Gunnar's arrival as the large man came up alongside him, the Varangur warrior staring off into the distance as he spoke.

"You will go now." His voice was hoarse from recent events, but still firm nonetheless. "This place is ours, it always has been and it always will be."

Quaid felt bile rise in the back of his throat. He wanted nothing more than to drive a blade down the sickening man's gullet, silencing him forever. But their losses had been heavy, barely a dozen of his men were left in any shape to fight, and both his brother knights were gone. He was tired, so unbelievably tired that he feared he might collapse from exhaustion at any moment. The heady rush of battle was electrifying, but it took a severe toll on the body's faculties; and when it passed, it left an empty shell behind it.

The knight turned away from the Son of Korgaan, unable to stomach a reply, and went to help his men prepare their wounded and the bodies of the dead knights for their journey back home.

*****

That night, Quaid wandered the halls of the fortress, unable to sleep. Whatever differences had existed between himself and Aldous in recent times, they could not undo the years of kinship the two had shared. The knight had lost friends before, everyone in the Brotherhood had; it was the unavoidable cost that came with their purpose. This time, it hit him harder than usual.

Pausing his meandering, he stepped up to one of the open, Gothic arches that lined the passageway and stared out of the gallery at the moonlit courtyard below. For a moment, he allowed himself to once more enjoy the feeling of the clean, cool breeze as it kissed his face. The only sound in the early morning air was the gentle lapping of the courtyard's fountain, its surface slowly sparkling as it reflected the moon's rays.

Quaid stood, watching its continual, almost rhythmic patterns, and allowed himself to close off his feelings of guilt for a time. In many ways, what the Brotherhood did, throwing themselves completely and utterly into a cause that was larger than oneself, gave them all a way to avoid dealing with the pain of reality. It occurred to him how easy it was to disappear into the obligations of duty, to push down other feelings and hide from their true impact.

In that instant, Quaid felt that perhaps he had gained some measure of understanding for the way that Aldous had kept a distance between the two of them over the intervening years. Every member of their society had had to find their own ways to cope with the constant stresses. Still restless, the knight continued his aimless wanderings. It was not until some time later that he was surprised to find himself in the council chamber next to the laid out armor of his fallen friend. It felt as if waking from a dream, with no knowledge of why or how he came to find himself there.

For a long time, he remained still and unmoving. Dust motes danced in the beams of light that were being cast across the open space by a number of the higher windows. Quaid did not know what it was that had brought him here to the altar on which Aldous's armor was neatly arrayed in honor of the dead knight. Seeing the ancient plate-mail still sporting the wounds of battle caused the emotions of loss and failure within him to return once more.

For some unknown reason, the knight found himself unable to divert his gaze from the armor, and Quaid could swear that he saw a faint movement within the intricate, cut designs that spanned the metal's surface. Bending over to take a closer look, he could see what appeared to be faint trickles of water moving along the delicate channels, albeit in apparent disregard for the forces of gravity. He had no idea why, but he could feel himself lifting one hand, bringing it ever closer to the strange phenomenon that he was seeing.

The nearer he got to it, the more the armor seemed to react to his presence. What had started as mere droplets became a continuous flow, mesmerizing in its beauty and complexity. Without thinking, he placed his hand fully on the remarkable cuirass before him and was immediately blinded by a searing flash of light. His head roiled as his senses were momentarily stolen from him, but in that instant, Quaid finally understood what his friend had been through, and what trials he himself would go on to face as an inductee of the Order of Retribution.

THE SEA DOES NOT GIVE UP HER DEAD

By C. L. Werner

A briny breeze moaned across the barren shore. Djwet could hear it whistling through his fleshless ribs, rippling the tattered remains of his vestment. He raised his bony fist and stared at his skeletal fingers, at the crust of sand embedded in each joint and crack. There was a strange detachment as he gazed upon the horror he had become. The fear and repugnance felt by the living had been stripped away from him, along with his flesh. All that remained was a tormenting sense of weariness.

Djwet let his hand drop to his side. There could be no rest for him now. Not unless he was released, and that was something he knew his masters would never do. He had dared to offend them, and this undying slavery was their revenge upon him. They had damned him with their obscene magic, condemning him to the ghastly borderland between the living and the dead.

The sea breeze continued to blow against his skeletal frame, but Djwet could not feel its caress. He could not smell its crisp scent or taste the salty tang in the air. The only sensations left to him were those of sight and sound, and even these were but an arcane semblance of what he had known in life. Just enough stimulation to allow him to perform the tasks demanded of him by his masters.

The revenant slowly turned his skull and looked toward the half-sunken tower that jutted up from the shoals. The Pharos of Karkus, the great lighthouse raised by the ancient Ahmunites. It was all that remained of the once mighty city. The rest lay drowned by the Infant Sea or buried beneath the desert sands. Only the monolithic Pharos had endured, rising up into the sky, a gravestone for a vanished people.

Or so Djwet had thought when he brought his pirate fleet into the shallows with the intention of plundering the Pharos. He had not feared living kings, he scoffed at those who feared the kings of the dead. But death and the Ahmunites were strange bedfellows. He discovered that when he dropped anchor and led his crew into the crypt-like corridors of the Pharos.

Djwet did not linger upon the memory of his destruction. If only that had been the end for him. Instead it had merely been the herald of a strange and terrible beginning.

He could not see the imperious gaze that watched him from the ramparts of the distant lighthouse, but he could feel their scrutiny just the same. The royal mummies of Karkus had gathered to see he fulfilled the purpose he had been given. Perhaps, Djwet hoped, it would be enough to atone for what he had done. Perhaps they would banish the necromantic energy that coursed through his bones and allow him to rest.

"For those who would profane the dominion of the Ahmunites, there can be no rest." The words were uttered by a dry, rasping voice; a tone devoid of all empathy. Djwet looked away from the half-sunken tower and found the withered form of Nekhbet standing beside him. The high priest's mummified body was swathed in strips of resin-coated papyrus, each fold inscribed with eldritch hieroglyphs. A frayed robe of faded blue fell around his shoulders while a tall headdress of gold and sapphire adorned his head. Nekhbet's countenance, such as remained, was locked behind a golden death-mask, a fabulous representation of his features in life. They were harsh and imposing, warning Djwet that undeath had not inflicted these qualities upon the high priest, but had simply magnified them.

"There is only atonement," Nekhbet stated, removing the golden mask and exposing the desiccated features beneath. "Service to the great empire of the Ahmunites." He raised a bony hand, each finger festooned with a ring cast in the shape of a beetle. He gestured to the bay. In response, the waters began to churn and bubble.

Djwet's desiccated heart could no longer feel the awe of horror the sight should have provoked. He watched as the boiling waters began to slide away and shapes rose up from the bottom. They were shapes known to him, despite the corrosion and decay that caked their hulls. Ships! Nor just any ships, but the pirate fleet he had brought to plunder the Pharos so long ago.

"Your fleet rises once again," Nekhbet said. "Only this time to greater purpose than base thievery. They serve the empire now... as does their admiral."

Djwet wanted to reject the high priest's declaration, but such will as had been left to him was unequal to the task. The revenants raised by the Ahmunites were allowed only so much initiative as was deemed necessary by the necromancers. All he could do was simply bow his fleshless skull in acceptance.

"Your skeletons have labored long to restore my fleet," Djwet said. "Rebuilding them beneath the very waters that swallowed them." He turned his gaze toward Nekhbet. "Your magic can conjure dead men from their graves. Now I understand it can do the same with ships as well."

Nekhbet gestured toward the ghostly fleet with its encrusted timbers and splintered hulls. "This is but a small part of what we shall achieve," he said. The undead priest fixed Djwet with his cold eyes. "We will raise a still mightier armada. An armada that will sweep across the Infant Sea and bring vengeance down upon the kinslayers of Ophidia."

Djwet looked across the pirate galleys now floating in the bay. Lean, wasted shapes with encrusted hulls and ragged masts. The banks of oars, however, were sound, as were the rudder and prow. The undead had focused their labors upon making the vessels seaworthy, not restoring them to their old grandeur. Pragmatism, not pride, was Nekhbet's intent. The tomb-robbing pirates were simply a utility for the nobles of Pharos.

Skeletons climbed up from the depths, scrambling up the chains which dangled over the sides of each galley. Dripping, their bones caked in brine, the undead who had worked tirelessly to rebuild the sunken ships now took their places at the banks of oars. In unison, each leering skull turned toward the shore and looked toward Djwet. He could sense the skeletal sailors awaiting his commands.

"Where will we find such an armada?" Djwet dared to ask. The question quivered in his mind, as though dreading to hear the answer.

Nekhbet's withered flesh pulled back in a grisly smile. "We sail for the Fang Isles and the little pirate republic that sent you to plunder the Pharos. Much will have changed since you walked their shores, but the vessels caught in the Cobra's Coils will still be there."

Djwet felt a cold sensation when he heard Nekhbet state their destination. He would have resisted if there were still any power within him to do so. "This is why you did not leave me as those," he said, pointing to the mindless skeletons on the galleys. "You needed me to navigate a course through the Cobra's Coils. You needed me to lead you back to my people."

The high priest's smile curled into a cruel sneer. "Many a ship has been sunk upon the rocks that guard your pirates. The waters around the Cobra's Coils are littered with the wrecks of those who pursued your sea-wolves. They will rise again, this time to serve the Ahmunites."

"And the Fang Isles?" Djwet asked.

Nekhbet shook his head. "The wrecks will be there, but who can say the drowned crews remain? Hungry fish may have picked them over long ago." The priest brought the butt of his staff cracking down on the beach, its tangle of charms clattering against its sides. "On the isles there will be bodies enough to man the oars." A dry, raspy excuse for laughter whistled across his blackened teeth. "Fret not, Djwet. You have been long under the Pharos. Whoever we find on the isles, they will be no one known to you."

Djwet bowed his head in submission to the high priest. When he lifted his face once more, he saw gangs of skeletons wading out toward the ships, long planks raised up on their shoulders. As the planks were brought to the galleys, troops of armored undead marched out from the Pharos. Their coats of copper and kilts of bronze glistened in the light as they walked to the crude piers and made their way to the ships. Sword and shield, spear and bow, the undead soldiers moved with eerie precision to take their places on the decks and in the holds. Some of them carried great urns which they set carefully near the prow of each ship. One group of skeletons bore a massive jar, its sides painted with cabalistic symbols and the most arcane of hieroglyphs. The bearers paused near Nekhbet, waiting until the high priest gestured with his rod toward the largest of the galleys.

"That will be your flagship," Nekhbet told Djwet.

"There must be a most potent magic in that jar," the revenant observed as he watched the bearers pick their way across the planks.

"Dust," Nekhbet replied. He looked back at the crawling sands beyond the beach. "The dust of death," he hissed, and in his words there was both a forlorn regret and a merciless promise.

*****

Psarius darted down between the gnarled, stalk-like coral growths. From the corner of his eye, he could see the sleek, dagger-like shape whip its tail to the left and bring its gray-white body turning about. The shark's black eyes stared from either side of its broad head. Its gaping jaws exposed rows of triangular teeth, each one keen as a knife and serrated along the sides. Morsels of meat fluttered about the fangs, caught between them during the creature's frenzied feeding.

The shark had his scent. Of that, Psarius was certain. It was no good simply trying to hide from the creature's vision once it took notice. Some uncanny instinct allowed a shark to hone in once it had selected its prey. The fish circled around the coral pillar, its powerful tail lashing from side to side as it zeroed in on its prey.

Psarius darted up toward the surface. He knew the sudden motion would bring the shark charging toward him. There was no question of outpacing the creature, for raw speed the fish was more than his match. What it lacked was agility. Before the shark could reach him, Psarius suddenly twisted around and turned his ascent into a dive toward the bottom. Leaving the bright surface far behind, he plunged toward the debris-ridden sea floor.

The gills along the sides of his neck fluttered as Psarius watched for the shark to come again. His webbed hands clutching the sides of a corroded anchor, the naiad waited for the creature to pick up his trail and come rushing after him. From the corner of his eye, he caught a flash of motion. The huge shark was diving toward him from the left rather than straight on. Psarius quickly shifted his position, putting the heavy anchor between himself and the predatory fish.

The shark's eyes rolled back, showing only white as it moved to the attack. The massive jaws stretched wide, displaying their razored rows of teeth, as the creature surged forward in a burst of frenzied excess.

Psarius pushed from the anchor, propelling himself a dozen yards away. The blind shark kept coming, gnashing its teeth against the corroded metal. The jaws clamped down, teeth scrabbling at the anchor. With mindless rage, the shark lashed about, trying to destroy this object that refused to sate its terrible hunger.

The naiad swam around the enraged shark and darted for a piece of barnacle-ridden wood. Psarius groped around the wood before his hands found what he was looking for. Brushing away the obscuring sand, he withdrew a long cross-shaped metal device. Ropes ran along the sides of the weapon, while at its forefront there protruded a sinister spike of bronze. Swiftly bringing the harpoon-gun up to his shoulder, Psarius aimed at the amok shark. While the fish continued to worry at the anchor, he squeezed the trigger and sent the barbed spear hurtling into the creature.

The shark jerked as the harpoon slammed into its body, shearing through the gills on its right side. Blood gushed from the injury, and the fish erupted into a frantic spasm as it tried to pull itself free from the spear and the heavy ropes that connected it to the naiad's gun.

Here was the most dangerous part of the hunt, Psarius reflected. Blood in the water had drawn this shark to pursue the naiad. Now the shark's own blood might bring more of its kind to the scene. Psarius had lost a few catches in his time to such cannibalistic frenzies. He swiftly drew his knife. In a flash of motion, he launched himself at the shark. Distracted by its own pain, the fish failed to react to Psarius until the bronze blade was raking across its belly.

Psarius clutched at the shark's gritty skin, feeling its sharp edges digging at his scales. He dug the knife deeper, stabbing up into the creature's body until he brought the blade ripping into its heart. He felt the splash of sticky gore on his fingers as the organ ruptured. The shark flailed about in one last spasm of agony, then floated limply in the harpoon's chains.

The naiad looked about anxiously, eyes peering through the depths for any sign of more sharks. Satisfied that none had caught the tang of blood in the water, he started to secure his catch. Lord Ichthyon would be pleased. There was no game in the sea the noble savored half so well as that of sharks.

Psarius was binding his catch in a web of seaweed when his every sense became alert. There was something close, something that awakened in him an almost primal agitation. He swung around, ripping his harpoon clear and holding it at the ready.

Only a few yards away, drifting above a mass of kelp, was an uncanny figure. It had the general shape of a human, but the body was almost impossibly lean and covered in a rubbery gray hide. The feet were clawed and with great spurs jutting from the calves. The hands were long and webbed, the fingers grotesquely stretched. It was the thing's head that was most alarming; a lumpy mass of tissue from which a tangle of short tentacles projected. Above and behind the ropy tendrils, two oversized amber eyes glistened.

The naiad had to fight to keep hold of his harpoon as a sudden urge to cast it aside swept over him. He knew it was no inclination of his own, but an alien impulse seeking dominance.

"Relent, mythican," Psarius snarled. "Ere your spell can subdue me, I will make my cast."

At once, he felt the urge abandon him. A voice that was not his own echoed through his mind, intoning its excuses. "Speak," Psarius told the cephalopod. "Keep your magic out of my head."

The cephalopod's eyes turned a cold blue and its hide transitioned into a mottled crimson. The thuul lived at the bottom, far from the richer waters of Lord Ichthyon's domain, but Psarius knew enough about them to recognize that this shift in color denoted irritation at best and rage at worst. He tightened his hold on the harpoon, ready to react at the merest hint of wizardry.

Instead, the thuul's tentacles fanned outward, exposing the fanged beak hidden behind them. Slowly, as though out of practice, the cephalopod's mouth formed words. "I bear no harm to you, Psarius Sharkstalker. I bring warning. All the mythicans have ascended into Ichthyon's shoals to alert you."

"Alert us of what?" Psarius asked, slowly lowering his harpoon.

"Invaders come," the thuul declared. "We have seen them in our scrying pearls. A fleet of the landborn, more black and evil than anything before seen in these waters."

Psarius threw aside the chains that held his catch, forgetting entirely about the prize shark. The mythicans were known for their magic, among them the art of prophecy. For them to arise from the depths, the threat must be great indeed.

"Lord Ichthyon must be told!"

The thuul waved one of its hands. "Ichthyon has been warned, but he will need time to muster his army. By then it may be too late." It pointed a clawed finger at Psarius. "You must rally the others who prowl these reefs. Gather the hunters who swim through these waters. It is they... and you... who must defy the landborn until Ichthyon's warriors arrive."

Psarius fluttered his gills in agitation. "What can we do? All told, there may be two or three score naiads in these reefs. How can we defy a fleet such as you describe? Is it not better to let them pass us by and strike them with the rest of Ichthyon's forces?"

"The landborn will not pass you by," the thuul said. "It is here they will come." It gestured at the decayed shipwrecks littered around the coral outcroppings. "This is what they seek. They intend an abominable profanation, an atrocity we cannot allow." Again, the mythican pointed at Psarius. "It is your burden to take on this responsibility. There is none other who can."

The naiad bowed toward the thuul. "I will seek out the other hunters and discover what kind of defense we can make ready."

"You will not defeat the landborn," the mythican said. "But if they can only be delayed, the victory will belong to Psarius Sharkstalker even more than Lord Ichthyon of Ceticia."

*****

Djwet felt a strange sense of unreality when he recognized the jagged snarls of rock that peaked above the rolling waves. To him, it seemed eternities had passed since his disastrous raid on the tombs of Karkus, yet here were the Coils just as he remembered them. He wondered if the settlements on the isles would still be familiar. Would the people recognize his ships? Would they appreciate the horror he was bringing with him?

The revenant looked down on the decks of his flagship, at the bony ranks of rowers seated on their benches, tirelessly propelling the galley across the Infant Sea. A macabre gesture was the skeleton seated on the raised platform amidships, its fleshless claws pounding away at a rotten drum, beating a rhythm for the crew. A dirge for the undead.

"All is the way you remember?" Nekhbet asked. The high priest stood beside Djwet on the elevated quarter deck. His tattered robes and funeral bindings fluttered in the sea breeze while the charms that hung around his neck clattered against his shriveled chest.

Deep inside Djwet there was a tiny ember of resistance, a spark that made him want to lie to the mummified creature and divert the destruction that was sailing ever closer to the Fang Isles. Instead, it was the truth that rattled from the revenant's mouth. "Little has changed," he said, unable to resist the necromantic power of his master. "The rocks are where they have always been. We will not share the fate of the pirate-chasers and bounty hunters. I will bear us safely to the islands."

Nekhbet nodded, his leathery lips pulling back in a black-toothed grin. "Those who fell victim to these rocks will rise again. The drowned dead will have their revenge upon the thieves they sought." A fanatical gleam shone in the high priest's eyes. "Then they will be bound to the Ahmunites, thralls of the empire evermore."

Djwet imagined that ghastly scene, the undead marching out from the surf in answer to Nekhbet's magic, converging upon the settlements in a merciless campaign of massacre.

"No longer are you any part of these people," Nekhbet told Djwet, guessing the turn the revenant's thoughts had taken. "Their lives were forfeit when their ancestors sent you to plunder the tombs of Karkus. More, it is with their blood that the drowned legions will be called from their long sleep. Their blood will become the chains that bind their killers to the empire."

Again, Djwet felt the faint flicker of resistance. If he could but reach out and seize Nekhbet and snap the monster's scrawny neck, he could end all of this. There would be no massacre. His people would be spared the annihilation the Ahmunites intended for them. Even as the thought took shape, it crumbled away. He was Nekhbet's creature now, enslaved to him in body and soul more completely than any mortal thrall. To defy him might not be unthinkable, but it was impossible.

"Then the sunken wrecks will be rebuilt," Djwet stated. He stared at the flotilla of galleys that accompanied his flagship, each one scarred and pitted by the many years they had spent beneath the waters around the Pharos. "A graveyard armada."

"A fleet to bring doom upon the kinslayers of Ophidia," Nekhbet gloated, contemplating a revenge that would be far more horrible than what was intended for the Fang Isles.

Djwet could just make out the outlines of the Fang Isles on the horizon when the flagship suddenly bucked violently in the waves. Many of the skeletal rowers were thrown from their benches, a few cracking apart as they slammed into the gunwales. The drummer's hand stabbed through the rotten skin of its instrument as its cadence was disrupted. A grotesque grinding sound rose from the prow of the ship.

Nekhbet steadied himself with his staff, his eyes ablaze with fury as he looked at Djwet. "You have run us upon the rocks!"

"Back!" Djwet called to the skeletal crew. "Keep her from pushing any higher on the rocks!" Vividly he could picture the fate of a pirate hunter he had long ago led into the Coils and how rapidly that ship had sunk once the rocks ripped away at her hull.

With unquestioning obedience, the skeletons carried out Djwet's command. The galley slowly pulled back against the waves. As it started to move, the ship was again shaken from stem to stern, even more violently that before. Djwet marched forward, intent on seeing for himself the extremity of their predicament. How badly were they caught upon the rocks?

When Djwet drew near to the prow, he was surprised to find that their dilemma was caused not by submerged rocks, but by a great length of chain that was stretched between them. Drawn taught, the chain had ripped across the hull, digging deep into the wood. Unless great care was taken, the very act of freeing the galley would send her to the bottom. He started back to explain as much to Nekhbet when the groan of splintering wood drew his attention to port-side. One of the other ships in his flotilla was caught upon another stretch of chain. Hurriedly, he called out to the rest of his vessels to stop their advance. Put into harmony with Djwet, the captains obeyed as unquestioningly as the skeletal rowers had.

Water spilled across the decks as angry waves pounded the stricken ships. A third galley was caught upon a submerged chain, swinging around until its prow was dashed to splinters upon one of the rocks. The galleys that had thus far retained their freedom gradually pulled away, retreating from the Coils.

"Cut us free!" Djwet commanded the skeletons of his crew. Several of the undead rose from their benches to retrieve bronze-headed axes. Showing no sign of hesitation, they climbed over the gunwales and climbed down the side of the rocking galley to come within reach of the chain. When the crashing waves ripped one of the skeletons free and sent it plunging into the depths, the others gave no notice to its doom but assiduously continued to hack away at the chain.

"What treachery is this?" Nekhbet demanded as his withered figure stalked toward Djwet. "One of your piratical traps you thought to keep from us?"

Djwet bowed his head in submission to the high priest. "These chains were not here when I sailed from the Fang Isles, master. Someone has put them here while I was gone."

Nekhbet's smoldering gaze held Djwet, as though peering into his spectral essence. "They will not stop us," he snarled, deciding that there was no treachery in the revenant. "All of them will die. Their islands will become dust and their bones will serve the Ahmunites." He gestured with his staff and a ghoulish light flickered about its head for an instant.

A groaning rattle sounded from the chains that gripped the galleys. Djwet could see the dark patina of decay that spread across the links. With the next blow of the axes, the flagship was free, leaping forward like a stallion plunging from its stall. The other trapped galleys were likewise freed, though the vessel with the smashed prow began to ride low in the water. Across the maze of the Coils, other lengths of chain came whipping upward, the links rotted by Nekhbet's magic snapping under the strain of the pounding waves. They flared upward into the sky, then went spiraling back into the sea.

"To the Isles!" Djwet called out to his skeletal rowers. The echoes of kinship he might have had for the islanders were suffocated by the sting of failure that now gripped him. His masters had entrusted to him the duty of bringing this fleet safely through the Coils, but the trap had caused him to fail in that purpose. To the revenant, there was nothing which could forgive such an offense. He would bring Nekhbet through and then watch his descendants pay for their temerity.

A flash of metal in the waves drew Djwet's attention to starboard. At first he thought it was another chain snapping and then snaking away down to the bottom. Then he caught the glimmer again and saw that it wasn't something sinking, but rather it was rising to the surface!

Memories flashed through Djwet's mind, recollections of terrifying encounters between his seafaring kinsmen and a race even more at one with the sea than they. "Boarders!" Djwet shouted as he ripped his sword from its scabbard.

The warning came too late to prepare the skeletal crew for action. A great wave rolled across the deck, sweeping some of the undead off of their feet. The wave carried more than mere water onto the ship. As the flow receded, a dozen blue-skinned creatures were left behind. Manlike in shape and proportion, each of the invaders bore in his webbed hands a hooked sword or a barbed spear. Their wide, dark eyes gazed across the skeletons, the gills along their necks fluttering in what might have been a trace of fright. Then one of the mermen aimed a bulky box-like weapon at the ranks of rowers and sent a harpoon crashing into them. One skeleton was cut in half as the harpoon sheared through its rib-cage, while a second was impaled on the point and transfixed to the bench behind it.

The harpoon's havoc spurred the rest of the mermen into action. Croaking out their glottal war cries, the blue-skinned invaders charged into the undead crew.

"Kill these vermin!" Nekhbet howled. "They must not interfere with my ritual!"

Djwet bowed his head and his bony fingers tightened about the grip of his sword. "As you command, master," he replied as he started toward the melee. If the mermen had lost their fear of the undead, he would soon remind them of it.

*****

Psarius brought his sword crunching down through the decayed skull of his adversary. The skeleton toppled backward, spilling its bones across the rolling deck. Other undead lurched toward him, spears and axes clenched in their fleshless talons. A slash from his blade sent the forearm of one foe spinning away into the sea while a backhanded drive of the sword's pommel tore the lower jaw from the creature's head. The maimed skeleton plodded onward, relenting only when Psarius kicked it in the knee and sent it crashing to the deck.

"Lord Ichthyon will have no need to stir from his palace," the naiad fighting beside Psarius exulted as he shattered the rib-cage of a skeletal spearman. "These things go down easy enough."

Psarius stamped down upon the head of the skeleton whose arm he had cut off, pressing the undead back against the deck as it started to rise. "It is not enough to put them down, Narian. They have to stay down." He ground his heel against the creature's skull, finally cracking its bones and collapsing its structure. Only then did the bleached bones fall still.

"They will stay down," Narian swore. He met the sweep of an undead sword with his own blade and used his greater strength to push the skeleton back into the ranks of those following close behind it. "We will send this cursed fleet to the bottom where gigas larva will nest in their skulls."

The thought of the undead ships sinking down beneath the waves sent an eerie chill through Psarius. It was not comforting to think their victory over the intruders would see these vessels polluting the waters that closed around them with the black magic that kept them afloat. Better by far to capture them and run them aground on the islands, let their evil taint the land rather than the sea.

A burbling cry of anguish sounded from behind Psarius. He swung around to see a naiad warrior spitted on the end of a sword. The merman's killer wore pieces of ancient armor strapped to its bones, and the hollows of its skull glowed with an uncanny light. There was an impression of wrathful scorn on the fleshless head as the revenant contemplated its dying victim. With a brutal twist of its curved blade, the undead ripped its weapon free and sent the mangled naiad crashing forward.

Psarius darted aside as the dying naiad pitched and fell. "Narian! Golatha! Behind us!" he shouted to the closest of his companions. Then there was no time for shouting. The revenant was bringing its heavy sword smashing down. Psarius blocked it with his sword, but the impact sent a shiver trembling through his body. There was an infernal power inside the revenant, a strength far beyond that exhibited by the skeletal crew. When the creature struck at him again, the force of the impact almost knocked the blade from his hand.

"My ship, and you shall not have her," the revenant hissed, the words spoken with archaic intonations that Psarius scarcely recognized.

Psarius brought his sword whipping around, catching the hilt of the revenant's weapon and spoiling the side-wise thrust the creature made. He staggered back as the monster smashed its bony elbow into his face. Blood spurted from a cut cheek. He risked a glance around him, wondering where his fellow hunters were. A sick sensation boiled inside his belly. Narian and the others could not come to his aid because they too were beset by armored revenants with glowing eyes.

"You should not have interfered," the revenant said, again striking at Psarius with its curved sword. "The living are foolish to incur the enmity of the dead."

Psarius lunged at the undead creature, his sword crashing across its armored shoulder and raking a sliver of bone from the side of its arm. "You trespass upon our waters with your profane fleet. Psarius Sharkstalker will teach you the folly of your invasion."

The undead responded with an angry sweep of its sword that smashed into the naiad's breastplate and sent him sprawling onto the deck. "Your waters!" it snarled down at him. "I am Djwet of Tarsa! I am a son of the Fang Isles! It is you who trespass upon my domain!"

Horror seized Psarius when he heard the old names echo from the fleshless mouth. Stories so old they were almost legends even to his grandfather swirled through his memory. How old was this creature he was fighting? "The Tarsains died long ago. Those the plague did not kill were exterminated by the avenging tridents of the sea! There are no more Tarsains! There are no more sons of the Fang Isles!"

Djwet came toward Psarius, ready to bring his heavy sword chopping down, but as the naiad shouted to him the doom of his people, the revenant hesitated. In that moment of uncertainty, the naiad kicked a webbed foot into a bony leg. The blow was not enough to trip Djwet, but it did cause him to stagger. The descending sword slashed down into the deck instead of Psarius.

Psarius seized the chance. Rolling to the side, he brought his blade stabbing into Djwet as the revenant tried to drag his sword free. Ribs shattered under the blow and bony fragments jounced across the deck. The naiad surged up from his prone position, adding the impetus of his rise to the attack. Djwet was bowled backward, the revenant's sword left shivering in the deck.

"Your people were an evil and unscrupulous race," Psarius accused Djwet as he drove the weaponless revenant back. "Piratical hagfish, they earned their doom. I will send you to join them in their graves."

The cleaving stroke Psarius sent whistling toward Djwet failed to strike the revenant's neck. Instead, it was blocked by the creature's upthrust arm. The sword smashed through the skeletal limb, but the blow was deflected enough that the edge merely glanced off the revenant's helm. Before he could recover, Psarius had his sword-arm seized in Djwet's remaining hand. The undead pressed close to him, the glowing eyes staring into his own.

"There can be no rest until the masters are finished with me," Djwet moaned. His jaws opened wider as he leaned toward Psarius's throat. The naiad struggled to free himself from his foe's grip, but the unnatural strength he'd felt before was like a steel vice around him.

Psarius was certain he was about to die when a shimmering wave swept over the ghostly ship's deck. He knew it was too freakish to be any natural caprice of the sea. Like the one that had borne the naiads onto the galley, it was a conjuration of the thuul mythican. Only this time, there was far more power within it than simply a magnification of its force. An arcane energy permeated the water, at once emboldening the naiads while staggering the undead. Wisps of black energy steamed off the animated skeletons as the shimmering wave washed over them. Djwet's bones gave off a greasy fog, rank with the stench of the tomb.

Psarius could feel the abrupt slackening of the grip around his arm. With a fierce effort, he wrenched himself free from the skeletal talons and lashed out with his sword. Djwet was thrown back as part of the revenant's ribcage broke under the blow.

Before Psarius could pursue the crippled revenant, he glanced across the deck around him. There were only a few of his raiders still standing, the rest were scattered about the deck in bloody heaps. Though many of the skeletons had been struck down, there seemed far too many still to face. Off to the starboard, he could see the mythican levitating just above the rolling waves, its hands raised in esoteric gestures that mirrored the ritualistic writhing of its tentacles. Whatever magic the thuul was conjuring, Psarius hoped it was swift in coming.

Then, off in the distance, Psarius saw one of the other undead galleys pitch upward and then plunge down beneath the waves. For only a moment, he thought he saw something red and massive closed around the ship's keel.

"Courage, brothers of the deep!" Psarius cried out to his remaining warriors. "A little longer and there will be no escape for these fiends!"

*****

Djwet swatted at his steaming bones, trying to wipe away the burning scum that coated them. He could sense it eating away at his strength, lessening the necromantic spell that gave him power. All around him, he could feel the undead crew wavering, their unnatural animation flickering like a candle in a strong wind.

The naiads pressed their attack, striking down the reeling skeletons while they were disoriented. Djwet fought to retain his own focus. Turning about, he pulled a bronze-headed axe from the grip of a nearby skeleton and readied himself to meet the charge of his late antagonist.

A dark shadow wafted across the galley. Djwet could feel new energy pouring into him, reinvigorating his spectral essence. He could see Nekhbet with his staff raised high, a black cloud swirling about it and sending tendrils of necromantic force into the crew. The shimmering scum was rapidly burned away.

Djwet brought the axe crashing against the naiad's sword as Psarius rushed him. The revenant leered into his enemy's face. "Your magic will not avail you now," he hissed. "Behold the power of the Ahmunites and despair."

As Djwet spoke, Nekhbet shifted to a different ritual. Ghostly lights now flickered away from the high priest's staff, sparks of sorcery that shot down into the cracks and holes that marred the galley's hull. From each depression, a pallid shape crawled into view, the withered husk of beetles that had bored the holes long ago. Animated by Nekhbet's magic, the ghastly insects surged across the deck in a quivering swarm.

"Devour!" Nekhbet commanded. With an imperious sweep of his staff, he pointed toward the levitating thuul. In perfect harmony of motion, the undead beetles opened their wing-shields and took flight.

Grim satisfaction smoldered in Djwet's mind when he witnessed the panic on Psarius's face. The naiad's eyes were wide with alarm when he saw the direction in which the swarm was flying. "Yes," Djwet snarled as he brought his axe cracking down once more, denting the bronze breastplate. "Your sorcerer has cast its last enchantment. With it, dies your last hope."

The swarm of beetles fluttered above the waves. The thuul was not so lost in its conjurations that it failed to notice the danger that had arisen to challenge it. At a gesture, it sent a swirling spout of water soaring upward to drag most of the swarm down into the depths. The few beetles that escaped continued onward, flying straight toward him. The thuul might have obliterated them as it had the rest, but already it was forced to divert its magic. The swarm from the flagship was not the only one called by Nekhbet's necromancy. Each of the galleys had disgorged its own mass of undead insects. The mythican was forced to attend to each in turn, hastily raising water spouts that were increasingly ineffective at drowning the masses of beetles.

Disaster struck the thuul when the last few beetles from the flagship reached it. The insects landed on its gray flesh, stabbing their mandibles into the rubbery skin. The mythican's conjurations faltered as it ripped the gnawing insects from its body, crushing them in its webbed hands. By the time the survivors from the first wave had been removed, those that had endured the second water spout were landing on the thuul's body and tearing at it with their jaws. The survivors from the third swarm arrived before the last from the second had been destroyed. Then those of the fourth and fifth swarms reached the mythican. A horrible wail of agony rose from the deep-sea wizard as its entire being vanished under a mass of devouring beetles. An instant later, and the thuul plunged into the depths, bleeding from hundreds of bites and still encased in a mantle of undead vermin.

The death of the mythican brought new fear to the naiad raiders. Their morale shaken, the mermen became desperate; and in their desperation, they lost the determination that had allowed them to resist their undead enemies. The skeletons, invigorated by the spectral energy Nekhbet had poured into them, charged into their foes, dragging them down one after another.

The power that swept through Djwet made him not only stronger, but quicker than he had been before. He slipped around the guard Psarius had established and brought the axe sheering down across his wrist. Psarius howled in agony as his wrist was severed and his hand went tumbling across the deck. While he was overcome with shock, Djwet pressed home his attack, smashing the flat of the axe into Psarius's face and knocking him down.

"No," Nekhbet's voice rolled through the revenant's mind. "Do not kill him. I have better use for his blood."

Djwet cast aside the axe and closed his skeletal fingers around Psarius's throat. Savagely, he pulled the naiad up off the deck and carried him toward the high priest. Other revenants were doing the same with raiders they had subdued in the fighting, dragging them to their shriveled master.

Nekhbet stood upon the raised quarterdeck, watching as the prisoners were brought before him. His withered face pulled back in a scowl as Djwet brought Psarius forth. He pointed a mummified finger at Djwet. "It was decreed by the lords of Karkus that this thief's descendants should spill their lives to fulfill our purpose." He glared at Psarius and raked a nail across the naiad's forehead, drawing a stream of blood. "Your ancestors have made that plan impossible, but the great ritual will not be abandoned."

Djwet could see the skeletons that came lumbering up from the galley's hold. They had their arms wrapped about a stone urn. The undead filed past Nekhbet. As they did, the high priest struck out with his staff, driving a crack into the side of the jar. A stream of dust spilled out, spreading across the platform. The dust was foul with the necromantic energies of the desert, the ancient sorceries that had long ago consumed the Ahmunites.

"The rites to raise the ships lost in the Coils demand blood," Nekhbet stated. "If not the blood of humans, than it will claim the blood of naiads!" Nekhbet started toward Psarius, then abruptly spun around and lashed out at the captive to his left. There was a copper arthame hidden in the high priest's hand,

and as the blade raked across the merman's neck, a welter of gore came gushing forth.

Exultant, Nekhbet stepped back, eyes agleam with a fanatic light as the blood splashed across the corrupt dust. Dark energies began to bubble up from the ancient dirt, ghostly emanations that swelled as the high priest reached out to them.

Djwet could feel the loathly power that was now rising, sensed its vibrations pulsating through his bones. Nekhbet turned toward a second captive, ready to send more gore down onto the planks to feed his spell.

Then, from across the waves, there came a loud tumult. Djwet turned his head to see one of his galleys breaking apart, splintering as a tremendous force lifted it out of the water. Another galley was beset by what looked to be a swarm of giant crabs. Still a third was in the grip of a great sea serpent, its scaly coils wrapping around the hull and splitting its keel.

"Master, we are attacked!" Djwet called out. Angrily, he threw Psarius down. "These were naught but a distraction to delay us until their full army could be brought to bear!"

Psarius glared up at the revenant. "Lord Ichthyon will scourge his domain of your evil."

Nekhbet laughed at the naiad's defiance. "What matter the army of your lord when soon all those drowned in these waters will arise to do my bidding? I will spare none of your people, naiad, and when they have been slaughtered, they too will rise again to serve the Ahmunites."

The high priest brought the arthame slashing across the throat of a second captive. Blood sprayed across the ensanguinated dust. The dark, bubbling manifestation of arcane power intensified, tendrils of black magic streaming out across the deck, seeking the sea and the wrecks far below the waves.

Even as the necromantic energies began to spread, a great wave came smashing down upon the flagship. The undead and their prisoners were sent sprawling. Nekhbet shrieked in rage when he saw the corrupt desert dust washed overboard, its evil spell disrupted by the fury of the sea. He scrambled toward the side, trying to prevent the last of the dust from slipping away. The high priest had only taken a few steps before he realized his mistake. The wave that had washed away the dust was still aboard the galley, undulating like some great eel. The writhing mass of water reared up as Nekhbet started to move, standing as a great wall of white-capped water. Dark eyes glowered at the high priest from the living wave before the water elemental came smashing down and obliterated the Ahmunite sorcerer.

Djwet staggered as the impact of Nekhbet's destruction sent a shockwave through the undead crew. Some of the skeletons collapsed instantly, crumbling into fragments. Others began to splinter, flakes of bone sloughing from their bodies. The more intact of the undead, particularly the revenants, retained their substance, though a crippling lethargy afflicted them.

The naiad captives were loose now. Most ran to the side of the galley and dove overboard, but Psarius hesitated to join them. Glancing back at Djwet, he caught up a sword from the pitching deck and ran for the revenant captain.

"Join your pirate kinsmen!" Psarius shouted as he struck at Djwet. The revenant rammed the jagged stump of his missing arm into the naiad's face, ripping through one eye and gouging his jaw. The naiad staggered back, the sword falling from his stunned fingers. Djwet reached down and caught up the blade.

"I do not go to the grave alone," Djwet vowed. He started toward the stricken Psarius.

The galley suddenly shook violently. A hideous grinding sound rumbled from below. The clamor of breaking wood rose to a thunderous din as the ship abruptly broke in half. Stalking toward Psarius, Djwet found himself plunging down through the wreckage of his flagship. The cold water of the sea closed around him as he plunged below the surface.

Through the mess of debris that surrounded him, Djwet could see a colossal red shape standing below the water. Titanic in its proportions, the thing was no reef or sunken rock, but a mammoth humanoid shape seemingly carved from one vast enormity of coral. The giant's arm was upraised, its huge fingers clawing at the galley from below, ripping the ship to pieces.

All about Djwet, he could see the glowing eyes of other revenants as they sank toward the bottom. There was no risk of drowning for the undead. They could endure the chill depths as easily as they could the chill of the grave. No, it was a different kind of menace that dove in to assail the sinking revenants. Clusters of naiads, their scaly blue bodies encased in golden armor, swam through the water and struck at the undead with vicious tridents. Unable to buoy themselves with their skeletal bodies, much less swim, the undead were unable to dodge the attacks. Perhaps they could have matched the fury of the naiads with solid ground under them, but their attackers gave them no chance to settle on the bottom.

Djwet had escaped notice of the naiads until a lone figure came speeding toward him. The maimed Psarius, gore streaming from his mangled face, dove at him with a crooked sword clenched in his fist. Djwet tried to angle away from the enraged avenger but was unable to react in time. He felt the flashing blade strike him in the neck.

There was a disorienting moment when Djwet briefly felt as though he were floating rather than sinking. Then he was plunging back toward the bottom.

He could see Psarius swimming above him. Below, he watched a headless body vanishing into the depths, a body he distantly recognized as being his own. Drifting away from the rest of his remains, the revenant's head clattered down a fissure before finally coming to a rest.

Great timbers encrusted with barnacles and anemones fell into view as Djwet's skull raced to the bottom. His gaze finally came to rest on the naked, barren crossbeams of an ancient hull. There was a terrible irony that one of the ships he had brought Nekhbet so far to raise from the deep should now serve as the revenant's grave.

In the cold dark of the ocean deep, Djwet wondered how potent the high priest's magic had been. How long before the curse of eternity was lifted and his spectral essence would dissipate. How long before Djwet's awareness faded into oblivion.

How long before Djwet could finally rest.

KINSHIP

By C. W. Conduff

The Ironguard descended through the tunnels in pitch blackness, their eyes having long since adjusted to only the faintest traces of light many leagues behind them. The softer races from the world above would have never made it as far in their expeditions under the firmament, instead turning back in fear when their torches began to sputter from the thin air, or when the tunnels shrank so tightly that a grown man could but barely squeeze through… but dwarfs were a hardier sort, at home so far beneath the world.

The path they followed, old and untraveled for hundreds of years, had narrowed and forced them two-abreast, their armored pauldrons leaving runnels in the walls beside them on occasion. So far below the surface of Mantica, deep within the bowels of the northernmost reaches of the mighty Halpi Mountains, the walls gave off a dry heat; the traveling warriors had grown so accustomed to their sweat beading beneath their heavy helms and running down into their bushy, ash-crusted eyebrows that they hardly noticed the discomfort any longer. They marched on, clanking like so many parts of some steadfast machine, knowing better than to deceive themselves at the notion of a stealthy arrival. It was no secret they were coming, and it was best to be prepared for ambush in the unfamiliar crawlspace. Worry of a sudden attack was not at the forefront of their thoughts; it would be a fool who should attack an armored column of Ironguard in so cramped a space. No, the battle would come when they found the caverns housing their dark kin.

A simple bark of command issued from the front of the column and all at once the dwarfs halted, the practiced veterans selected to be Lord Yurec's Traduciators for this endeavor so experienced with one another that they operated almost as much on instinct as voiced orders. They had come upon the abrupt end of the tunnel, but where an opening should have stood before them was only a smooth barrier, as though of polished stone. Their rummaging and clanking seemed to absorb into the glossy wall before them rather than reverberate back in the usual fashion, warning the dwarfs to the power of the magic in the wall's creation. There could be no mistaking it now; they had at last come to the end of their long march.

The column parted and the warriors flattened themselves behind their shields – as best as they could, at least – with their backs to either side of the tunnel and holding their beards away from their chests. The driller crew, kept in the relative safety of the middle of the marching column alongside their hulking commander, shuffled single-file through the gap to the front wall. A deafening bang signaled as the machine came to life, sputtering in its struggle to burn fuel at such a depth, and tore into the barricade in their path.

Within moments, the drill still barely freed from its housing, it broke through with force enough that it threatened to tear itself from the strong hands wielding it. Orange light poured in from around the edges of the hole, nearly blinding the dwarfs in its suddenness, and the superheated air that washed through caused the driller's exposed flesh to begin to blister. Wrestling it back into position with a curse and a grunt, the driller made one quick circle around the perimeter of the hole to widen it before pushing the device through and letting it fall unseen, then shuffled backward through the ranks to his place in line. The Ironguard wordlessly locked back into formation, each warrior now holding his shield firmly with both hands, braced against the back of the dwarf ahead of them. Pushing forward with all the strength their combined number could provide, the dwarfs at the front of the column pressed into the newly drilled opening and forced it apart, breaking through into the space beyond.

As they piled out of the tunnel onto a steep hillside, Lord Yurec took the lead position in his mighty Steel Juggernaut, an overlarge suit of fire and steel, careful of his footing on the craggy, sloped ground. Behind them, the hill climbed sharply above the tunnel's exit, stretching up and away like a mountainside, the top disappearing so far above that the blackened ceiling resembled roiling clouds of soot through the haze. The Ironguard had not made that observation yet, however, because the ground stretching away before them was unlike any the veteran combatants had seen before. Where the hillside ended to meet level ground, the floor of the cavern was comprised of blackened sand. That sand formed a beach, extending forward fifty paces or more before reaching the edge of a sea made entirely of roiling magma. At a glance, the lava seemed both to flow and yet have no pattern, to churn and yet sit entirely still, and gave off an unnatural orange light of such strength that it caused pain to look upon its mocking reversal of the noonday sun. The heat of it was nigh unbearable, even for those stout sons of the forge. The sandy beach stretched away to their left and right as far the horizon, the shape of the world above completely hidden so far below its surface. Hundreds of yards above the sea, the ceiling of the cavern looked like a desert made of charcoal, nearly free of stalactites except a group clustered around what might have been the inverse of a proper, old-fashioned dwarfen keep, its spires snaking down from the ceiling toward the magma below.

Venturing out upon the broken beach of black sand, their heavy boots crunching into the fine black powder, Yurec's heavier footsteps sent up small clouds of dust as they fell. Near the cliff wall, the beach was clustered with what might have been stalagmites in a different cavern, but here looked like trees surrounding a body of water, only cut down to dirty, blackened stumps. Beyond the stumps, the beach of molten, grainy slag extended cleanly to the sea's edge, where liquid magma washed up and receded ever so slowly, leaving swollen patterns of hardening lava with each crawling wave. There was an entrancing motion to it; a current, even, when they could find it, and it swelled away across the cavern for as far as their keen dwarf eyes could follow. The light emanating from the liquid rock seemed to somehow grow in intensity as they approached it, the orange glow managing to simultaneously permeate every nook and cranny of this new world and yet still create dancing shadows between the dripping rock formations in the ceiling far above.

His gaze transfixed upward as they neared the land's edge, Lord Yurec wondered at the glossy black stones hanging above, conjuring the image of glittering stars in a night sky capable of guiding a ship across that molten sea. The heavy clanking noises of the Ironguard, so loud in the cramped tunnel before, seemed to disappear in the shimmering waves of heat, transformed into something they could feel in the air more than catch with their ears.

The stretching expanse made the dwarfs uneasy, all of them acutely aware that their number, which had seemed more than adequate in the tunnels before, seemed insignificant in their new surroundings. Stifled from the heat in his armor, Yurec took off his helm for a moment's respite as they walked, confident he would have plenty of time to replace it should a threat manifest against them. His heavy iron-shod boots hissed with each step, their soles beginning to score and brighten from the intense heat they protected him against, the gears and servos whining in protest. It was like walking through the fires of the Abyss itself.

It is beautiful here, brother; I'll concede to you on that. But damn is it hot!

Unrelieved, he placed his helm back atop his head, finding no joy in the typically satisfying -click- as it settled into place.

As their eyes finally adjusted to the searing brightness of their strange surroundings, the form of a single stout dwarf became visible near the sea's edge. He sat with his legs crossed, clad only in a tattered and blackened loincloth, his matted hair and scarred back facing them almost serenely. Miraculously, he seemed completely unbothered by the intense heat of the ground upon which he sat. Yurec halted at the sight of him, the Ironguard stopping a few paces behind their leader.

"Lord Yurec, is it him?" Joshurn loosed from the line of Ironguard, his voice betraying only the slightest hint of the worry etched so clearly into his eyes. This quest had been Joshurn's first selection to join the Traduciators in their hunt. The more seasoned veterans around him grumbled at his outburst.

Yurec stepped ahead another several paces to gain a better view, his encyclopedic mind racing until recognition dawned within him. "Nay. That is not our former Lord Durok… that would be one of his suspected companions, a former champion of our clan named Andreu. He's been on the council's list for many years now."

The scarred abyssal dwarf before them stood slowly and turned to face the Ironguard with an almost feline grace, his presence intimidating even at the distance between them. The craggy face bore none of the hate the Ironguard had expected to see, his expression instead that of cold indifference. His deeply set eyes appeared solid black with the backdrop of the glowing lava behind him.

"Hmph." Andreu grunted, turning his neck slowly, the bones within crackling loudly.

Breaking ranks, Joshurn burst free of his fellow Ironguard before they could stop him, running forward with his weapons held wide. Joshurn turned his head and spat upon the ground as he ran, where it sizzled away almost immediately. "You'll be mine, betrayer!" He was shouting, but his voice fell flat in the heavy air. "You'll pay for the dishonor you placed on our clan!"

Rage commanding his features at the sudden insubordination, Yurec held his position as Joshurn raced past him. Yurec roared, "Joshurn, *no!* Stand *down!*" His words fell on deaf ears however, as the fool dwarf began to gain speed in his headlong rush.

Andreu stood stock still, his expression nothing more than detached boredom; not so much as a single muscle twitched as the armored dwarf bore down on him. As Joshurn reached the point of no return, his hammer swinging in a beautifully executed crescent aimed precisely for the berserker's skull, Andreu's eyes seemed to light up as though an internal fire had been stoked. A sudden and disarmingly bestial scream escaped his chapped lips as the hammer arced down, and he began to move alongside the projected force of his yell. In the span of a single heartbeat, his hand shot up to the descending hammer and pushed, using the charging dwarf's own momentum to slip deftly from beneath the blow and simultaneously bring a rock-hard elbow crashing into Joshurn's armored cheek. The faceguard crumpled as though made of paper.

Joshurn howled with embarrassed fury, spinning himself around rapidly to gain extra power in a bone-shattering cross hand swing. Contorting his unarmored body to allow the hammer an unobstructed path, the berserker launched an open hand strike into Joshurn's exposed chest the moment the swing was clear with enough force to stumble the dwarf back a step. Andreu followed in a leap, reaching out with both hands to grip Joshurn's helm before arching back and delivering the most violent headbutt the Ironguard in audience had ever witnessed, the percussive waves of the impact visible as they spread away in the heat haze. Joshurn's face melted into his helm with the force of it, and the dwarf immediately went slack, dead before his body crumpled to the sizzling ground.

Andreu turned slowly to face Yurec, his eyes having faded again to a depthless black, only now he wore a smirk. Blood dripped from a fresh cut on his forehead somewhere above the hairline, running down into his eyes and resembling the oil of some foul machine in the glowing cavern. The Ironguard raised their shields in unison, maintaining their discipline where their shamed cousin had not, and prepared to crush the lone berserker.

*****

3 Months Earlier

You have always known that he would come for you. It was inevitable that the council would place you on his shortlist.

Durok shook his head, shook it hard, the voice in his mind feeling like an incurable itch beneath the surface of his skull, ever at a simmer and threatening to bubble to the fore.

"Of course I knew, I've been expecting it… Just hoped we had more time. He isn't ready to listen, yet." The dwarf spoke aloud in his cavernous chambers, alone except for the cowering goblin slave by the doorway attempting to sink unnoticed into the ground.

The plan you've concocted may work. By Her light, I am to know only what was, and what now is, but not what yet may be. I believe that h-

"YES I KNOW!" Durok shouted, interrupting the gravelly voice within his mind, the dwarf's words sinking into the warm walls of blackened stone. The inky, darker-than-black walls of the chamber always seemed to steal his words from the air quicker if there was anger in them. The laws of the Abyss were not so rigid as they might be in the world above, after all.

Ahem.

Durok hated when his 'guide' acted as though it were performing on a stage, voicing actions in that manner, as though it actually had a throat to clear. Its dramatic pause only succeeded in frustrating the dwarf further.

I was simply attempting to inform you, Lord Durok, obvious and evident master of his domain, Durok's brow furrowed unconsciously into a grimace, *that I could allow you to see it as well, if you would like. I could show your eyes the sight of your kin in their hunt for you. They ransacked your private study only a short while ago.*

"So they've broken the seals, then. That speaks highly to their desperation. I'd wager they've finally taken notice to how few orcs roam their northern tunnels. How many went in, then? Was Yurec there himself?"

Of course he was. One does not investigate a traitor lightly.

"Traitor!? *Traitor!?* I am her Chosen! The Bearer of the Torch! You have grown too bold, creature. Perhaps She would raise concern at your delight in delaying the progress of Her plans by troubling me so!" Durok's fist seemed to glow with an inner light as though magma itself coursed through his veins, and he soundly struck his chamber wall with explosive force. The room suddenly grew brighter – and quite a bit hotter, as well – as orange and red light from the molten sea below spilled in through the chamber's new window.

This had proven to be a common degradation in their conversations as of late, the chamber already having several of the fist-sized windows throughout. Durok and the guide assigned to him, a formless creature of energy named Ka'Ryl, had steadily grown more and more frustrated at their slow progress during their time together. They had been bound during Durok's second century in a secret ceremony, on a day now many years behind him. Initially he had felt hesitant of the binding, but he could not deny that Ka'Ryl had indeed helped to guide him in seeing the true way forward for his people. The responsibility of it had lost him a great many things, but it would all seem a trivial cost soon enough, of that he was confident.

Ariagful had said that all dwarfs were rich when beneath the world. It was their kingdom to rule; their seat of power. Durok had learned the truth of such statements.

Finally, he calmed enough for Ka'Ryl to continue.

Close your eyes, groundling, and look upon your brother's Traduciators which hunt us, like so many before.

*****

The Traduciators had been at it for hours, their frustration growing with each passing moment. They were ripping through the furnishings of the former Lord Durok's grand apartments, pulling all manner of adornments from the walls or off of shelving in their search. It had taken the fire priest nearly five solid hours to breach the outer seals and access the abandoned portion of their family keep. Yurec was beginning to fear the seals had been nothing more than a distraction, though. The abandoned chambers had been largely ignored after the initial search, but Yurec's gut had lead him back one last time, and finally he'd discovered the seals. It had been so obvious that he'd missed them the first time, but it would be just like Durok to have left a seerstone secreted away in his very chambers.

Breaking through the seals, Yurec and his men had discovered a grand set of rooms extending immediately below the primary rooms, the architecture and styling within shaped from glossy obsidian. Adorning the walls throughout and typical in their design aesthetic, pieces of finely crafted gold had been fashioned into unnerving and embarrassing organic shapes. The vast majority of them now riddled the floor, obscuring the lush red carpets with their heavy golden swirls, seeming to invoke both flame and flesh when looked upon. Stone dressers filled with lavish cloths and trinkets were overturned as well, their contents spilled before them. One of the chambers had contained a humongous bed with a tall headboard of the same black stone found throughout, but Yurec's men had cracked it when trying to yank it away from the wall, leaving it to lean at an unnatural angle as they continued their search elsewhere. Numerous sitting chairs were overturned, the stuffing from their slashed cushions strewn across the floor. Hundreds of leather-bound tomes had been pulled from the abundant shelving throughout the apartments, many of them in languages that would invoke madness should anyone attempt to read the words scrawled within, and now sat in piles from which they would be collected at some later time and fed to the fire priest's cleansing flames.

Yurec found himself fretting, yet again, that this latest dishonor would be impossible to keep secret for long. The former Lord Durok, the influential eldest child and Lord of Grunn Keep, formerly in good standing with the Council of Free Dwarfs, had been discovered to be as traitorous as the other villains seeking power beyond the natural means. And it would be his own brother, now Lord of Grunn Keep in Durok's absence, that would be the Chief Traduciator to drag him before the council for judgment. It would have struck Yurec as ironic, had it not felt so ridiculous.

The Traduciators always tended to err on the side of caution and be more thorough in their investigations than not, but the manner in which they shredded and ravaged here, their rage evident, bothered Yurec more deeply than he would have cared to admit. How easily their hearts had turned against a former lord of the clan; how fickle the hearts of dwarfs, that the lure of the Abyss had become an issue at all. Perhaps these few had simply been too close to Durok, their former admiration now fueling their ire? But no, they had allowed their newest inductee, Joshurn, a recently promoted member of the Ironguard and now the youngest among them, to accompany them on this search, and he ravaged with no less enthusiasm than his companions. Yurec thought, *could their hearts turn so easily against me, as well?*

"Ol' Durok decorated more like the pointy-ear folk than one of us, eh, fellas?" The ginger-haired veteran, Kristoff, exclaimed as he enthusiastically ripped through an embroidered pillow laced with delicate metals to depict a sea of fire beneath a mountain.

"You'll not speak of Lord Durok that way again and keep that tongue in your head, Kristoff." Yurec spoke with a calm and confident tone, at odds with his discomfort for the deed at hand. "Suspicions be damned, he was still a lord of this keep."

A tense moment of silence passed before Broyleson muttered something from the next chamber, but Yurec couldn't quite make it out. Kristoff seemed to collect himself at it, though, and dropped the pillow before turning to address Yurec more formally. "Aye, sir. Forgive my outburst. I forget sometimes he was your kin. The two of you are just so different!" The warrior spread his arms to indicate the artifacts littering the ransacked chambers with a smile.

Yurec sighed. "…It is forgiven. These are hard days for the House of Grunn. If we can retrieve the seerstone, though, we can prove Durok's ties to the Abyss and get approval from the council to use it to find him and haul him back." Yurec's fists clenched tightly. He shook his hands out with an exasperated grunt. "I have every confidence we'll find it this day; we know that he never came back to his chambers before he fled, and the keep has been under constant guard ever since. It *must* be here."

Nodding in mute agreement, the golden trinkets in Kristoff's beard clanged against his breastplate like coins spilt onto the paving stones at market. "We will find it," he said, before moving to continue his search along the far wall of the spacious underground chambers.

It was high upon that same wall, from a tapestry comprised of thousands of glittering gemstones, that Durok himself watched the ravaging dwarfs through the molten orange seerstone hidden within the effulgent eye of a magnificent fire beast. Yurec's head shot up, his attention suddenly drawn to the tapestry as a wave of unfiltered rage and disgust and frustration and disappointment radiated from it, lasting no longer than the blink of an eye. He cursed at how obvious Durok had made it; it had always been games within games between them, and this had proven no different.

"Stop the search! It's right there, for Fulgria's sake!" he exclaimed, gesturing to the tapestry upon the wall. "He's been watchin' the whole damned time!"

Grumbling profusely, Yurec tore a small black pouch from his belt; no larger than a coin purse, the glossy metal links were woven so tightly that no light could penetrate it. He moved toward the tapestry, intent upon tearing it down, but caught himself and thought better of it, the image of Durok laughing soundly as his sibling scrambled for the stone clear in his mind. Finally, he tossed the bag across the chamber to Broyleson.

Broyleson caught it deftly, having anticipated Yurec's decision and already moving to pull the tapestry from the wall. The dwarf had witnessed the brothers' relationship for many years while serving under Lord Durok, but he had been one of the few to remain loyal to the council when his lord had fled.

Just as he reached it, however, Joshurn grabbed the bottom corner and yanked, ripping it from wall in a single swift tug. "I've got it!" he exclaimed excitedly.

As it fell, the eye of the beast seemed to flare with light, the seerstone brushing against Broyleson's face on its way to the ground. It burned like a touch from magma itself, searing away the facial hair on his cheek and scorching the flesh black instantly. The dwarf howled, his hand shooting up to cover the mark while simultaneously shoving Joshurn fiercely into the stone wall with his free hand. "Fool youngling!"

"Youngling!?" Joshurn's face contorted in fury, the title clearly hitting a sore spot. "I've earned my place here an-"

"You're a gap filler and a waste of good armor! Get away from me!" Broyleson shoved the other dwarf again with finality, gritting his teeth and squinting his eyes at the fresh wound on his cheek. Turning back to the fallen tapestry, he committed his hands – steady, despite the pain – to carefully wrapping the black pouch over the seerstone before firmly tearing it free.

Yurec, wanting nothing more than to get away from the ravaged chambers, held out his hand expectantly. "I'll present it to the council before the week is through and get our final orders. See to your face, friend, then ready the others; we'll depart as soon as we're given approval."

Grumbling his acknowledgement, Broyleson shouldered past Joshurn and put the pouch into Yurec's hand before stomping out of the room, sending an unfortunate chair in his path flying into the nearest wall for good measure. Kristoff moved to help Joshurn up from the floor, but the younger dwarf shrugged out of it, staring bitterly after Broyleson.

Gauging the stone's weight in his hand, Yurec waited for the other two to shuffle out before taking one last look around at his brother's chambers and following silently after them.

*****

Present

A voice boomed down at the dwarfs from the structure above, reverberating from the rocks, the magma, and even the ashy sand itself. "*SEEK NOT WAR HERE, BROTHERS.*"

The voice drifted off crazily, the constant heat maddening enough to convince them it had only existed in their minds; the looks passed between the companions, however, proved it must have at least been a delusion they'd experienced together.

Fires burst into life far above, shooting down from the dripping spires of the ashen keep in the ceiling toward the roiling lava below. An immediate sense of dislocation overwhelmed the Ironguard as they stood upon the scorched shoreline, their minds struggling to reconcile the vision of fire burning down instead of up in this deep and twisted world. As the madness wormed deeper, it became difficult not to envision the myriad of stalactites above as burnt mountain ranges. The peaks of those hanging mountains stabbed like sharpened spears against an inverted skyline, with the valleys between reveling in their shadowed existence below a writhing magma sky, brewing its storms of ash and soot. Their stomachs churned as they wrestled with the imbalance of such a thing.

The feeling only worsened when the former Lord Durok himself, clad in blackened steel lined with immaculate golden inlay from head to toe, stomped purposefully from within the now obvious inverted citadel as though the ceiling above were the ground and they were the ones upon the ceiling, that they were in fact the unnatural occurrence in that vivid hellscape.

"Seek not war," he repeated. "We've naught to fight about. What kind of host would that make me?" Durok's voice had taken on a sweeter tone, calm even, and though he spoke at a regular volume, none on the beach struggled to his words. His tone brought a grimace to Yurec's face, though, his sibling recognizing the familiar and friendly mannerisms from the many years spent in his company. It was not a grimace at his deceit, however; it was a grimace born from knowing Durok to be completely sincere in his words.

Partially obscured by the wavering heat, the dwarfs below watched silently as two glistening protrusions from the ceiling came to life on either side of the abyssal dwarf and unfurled into ghastly mockeries of life, only with shiny obsidian wings protruding from their backs. The living gargoyles grasped hold of Durok's still-extended arms, and the trio released their hold from the inverted world above to glide toward Yurec and his Ironguard.

The gargoyles landed without so much as a whisper, the glossy black stone of their bodies shifting unnervingly to the observers' eyes; that such dense stone could move with life seemed impossible. Durok, in sharp contrast, landed as though the weight of the world bore down upon his shoulders, as though the ground had sought his reconnection and pulled at him greedily. His impact sent tremors through the shins of the Ironguard, and the ground cratered around him in a wide circle; the lava at the shore behind him rippled outward before slinking back toward the beach.

Looking at the fallen Joshurn, now unrecognizable with the blood pooled where his face had been moments before, Durok only made a chiding 'tsk, tsk' sound. "Is this how you would have me treat guests to the new family keep, little brother? Are you no longer teaching your men respect?"

The Ironguard stood with their weapons before them, sweat pouring from their faces, and watched as the broad abyssal dwarf walked calmly to the body of their fallen comrade without budging. The gargoyles were still, crouched at the lava's edge. "Pity, really. Perhaps he should have crafted a better helm? Shameful how poor the metalwork of the so-called 'Free Dwarfs' has become." Several of the Ironguard bit back sour retorts at the slight against their craftsmanship. Durok reached down, grasped Joshurn's armor at the neck, and tossed him the dozen paces through the air into the burning tide at his back without so much as a grunt of effort. The heavy corpse sank quickly, rivulets of steam popping free to rise with a hiss as it boiled within its encasing armor.

"Durok! You know the dishonor you would show his fami-" Yurec began, but he was cut off by his imposing abyssal counterpart, a sudden and unnerving fury in his words.

"*Do not, brother!* Do *not* mean to tell *me* of *honor*," Durok emphasized each word with sharp jabs at the air, "when you have entered my home and mean for *war!*" Durok's eyes had begun to burn the same angry red as Andreu's had before, and the Ironguard collectively crouched in preparation for the strike sure to come.

"It was you that abandoned our house… You've known since that day we would come for you. It is our way." Yurec's voice was strong but filled with the pain only born from surviving absolute betrayal. "You do not stand with us, brother." Yurec gestured stiffly in his mechanical armor at the blackclad dwarf. "You stand against us; against the whole clan. You've become a slave to the Abyss, and I'll see you free from it!" The armorclad dwarf stood stalwartly, the joints in his Steel Juggernaut armor clicking as he positioned himself for violence.

Durok's head nodded slowly before he shared a look with Andreu. The quiet berserker walked to his side and began to unbuckle the armor plates on the Abyssal Lord's back. "Standing here, in this place, you see it, don't you? You must have felt it by now, at least." The abyssal dwarf's rage was gone again, his tone unexpectedly mantic. "This is our true realm, Yurec. We are made for it, grown and forged in Ariagful's magnificent light to reign in this land and receive her blessings." Andreu tossed Durok's heavy pauldrons to the sand at their side, their considerable weight loosing a slight *thud* as they struck the ground. "Our kin have spent too many years with the softskins from above, adopted too many of their ways. We dwarves have become too focused on the steel without," Durok waved dismissively at Yurec's impressive armor while himself removing his gauntlets. "While we've forgotten the steel *within*." He tapped his fist against his chest for emphasis.

It was clear Durok's impassioned speech was beginning to affect several of the Ironguard, their resolve diminishing as they found themselves wondering at the Abyssal Lord's words.

Andreu stepped back as Durok pulled his own black mail shirt clear, his pale skin immediately beginning to redden from the extreme heat. Stripped down only to coal grey slacks and heavy dragonhide boots, he continued, "It is *you* who are the slave, Yurec. Your traditions, your orders, all of it! There is no power there, no freedom. You're just the council's pawn. Have you never wondered why *they* have developed such an interest in the strength we can gain from the depths of the world?"

Durok began to walk slowly, never taking his eyes from Yurec, his pacing somehow both casual and anxious as it followed the edge of the magma's tide. "Our people are those born for something greater than the other races of this world; it is why we survive where they cannot." He gestured grandly, spinning in place. "Just *look* at our realm, brother! Look, *all* of you! *We are ALL kings*. It is our place to rule over the weak humans and fancied elves, the beasts of the forests, even the fishmen in their realms of water, and it is their place to bow to *us*. Your precious council knows the truth of it, too… but they would rather keep that power for themselves alone."

Yurec lost all pretense of composure, his voice raised to a shout. "That's ridiculous! The clan is strong because of our unity, each of us a cog in the great machine. You speak with madness, and would see us fall into a state of chaos the likes of which we should never recover. The Abyss whispers only madness in your ears." The mechanisms in his gauntlets squealed with strain, the warrior gripping his hammer with such force as would warp a lesser-made weapon.

Durok laughed, but there was a sadness in it. "Madness? I would see us serve a unified purpose. The purpose. Together. It is not too late for you, brother; nor for any of you." Durok included the nervous warriors at Yurec's back with a sweep of his hand, their minds reeling from the effects of the cavern and from Durok's words. "We are the masters of the very firmament upon which all others tread. The abyssals are our only kin here, in the heart of the world. The fire to our steel." Without warning, his countenance again turned dark, as though blackened with soot, and his eyes blazed like the molten lake behind him. "But I can see now what a fool you've become under the tutelage of the council. They nearly blinded me to the truth, too. But I'll show ye the light of the Black Flame of Ariagful… and you'll see as clearly as I do!"

With a rocketing burst of speed, the shirtless abyssal dwarf shot forward into his brother as though from a cannon. His bare fist rang loudly as it struck Yurec's breastplate like a hammer on an anvil, slamming his heavily armored sibling off his feet to stumble back several paces before he was caught – but only just barely - by his Ironguard companions. Durok smirked as he whispered, "Some lessons are harder than others, of course."

Loosing a bestial yell filled with years of bottled fury, Yurec's armored form came to life. Propelling himself forward with impressive power provided to him by his suit, he swung his hammer down into the space Durok had occupied a split-second before with enough force to bury his hammer in the rocky ground as debris sprayed outward like an explosion. His peripheral vision blocked by his helmet, Yurec never saw Durok's second blow coming. The wind rushed from Yurec's lungs as his brother's fist made contact just below the ribs and crumpled the thick steel plate. A burst of impossibly black light flashed when the strike connected, and Yurec was propelled up and away before crashing into the scorched ground, his hammer left behind and still sticking from the sand.

"You've come all this way to fight me, haven't you?" Durok rolled his shoulders backward, and his eyes again shone a bright red-orange. "*So fight me, whelp!* You've always been nothing more than a servant to the council. Learning of my defection must have been the best day of your miserable *life.*"

Yurec scrambled to his feet, unsettled at how powerful Durok had become in such a short amount of time. His previous dealings with iron-casters had always been challenging, but he had never before faced such raw power directed internally as to amplify the iron-caster's own strength; the typical student of the Abyss preferred to express his or her power on an unwitting subject and then point *them* toward Yurec's Traduciators, instead.

Durok continued, his voice suddenly revealing the duality of his new power as another voice chorused with his own, "*I am indeed different, little brother. All those you've hunted before were fools, playing like children with powers beyond their comprehension. Allow me to show you the true strength of our people!*"

Yurec's face betrayed the shock he felt, but his stout Steel Juggernaut frame would not allow any more of his fear to telegraph through. In that moment, he knew that he had likely brought his Traduciators on their last hunt of the fallen, his only regret in that moment that he would never be able to warn anyone, even the overbearing and secretive council, of the powers they would soon face.

Moving in unison, the unnatural sounds of their bodies alerting the Ironguard with just enough time to raise their shields, the gargoyles launched themselves into the armored dwarfs. Andreu stood apart, squinting his eyes at the steep cliffside some distance away, seemingly unconcerned with the violence.

Durok again shot forward at Yurec with incredible speed, ever the aggressor, this time Yurec only just managing to bring an armored gauntlet up to repel the first attack before falling back under the iron-caster's rapid-fire punches. The Steel Juggernaut armor was some of the most powerful kit to be found within the realm of the collective Free Dwarfs, though, absorbing the worst of Durok's assault. Yurec could only hope to survive long enough for Durok to burn through his energy reserves, and leave him unable to pursue any surviving Ironguard. Rallying his strength, Yurec loosed a single powerful blow, his amplified strength sending Durok sailing through the air toward the lava's edge.

Durok snapped to his feet in an instant, his eyes still glowing with the red light Yurec had seen before, only brighter. Much brighter, in fact. Durok's muscles seemed to swell with yet more strength, the veins bulging sharply as his skin stretched to accommodate, his fists clenched.

Yurec spat blood and loosed a sharp laugh. "You'll kill me, true. But know in the days to come that it was me that freed your slaves, me that brought your ruin! Haha!"

Durok's brow creased in confusion, but before he could speak, Andreu's voice cut through the chaos. "Lord Durok… it would seem our stables have indeed been emptied."

Kristoff smashed the obsidian skull of the final gargoyle with his axe, the glassy chunks blending seamlessly with the sand at their feet. Breathing hard, he became aware of the immediate silence from his comrades, and looked around at them curiously before following their gaze.

The steep cliffside wall stretching away to the horizon writhed with movement, the bodies of hundreds of orcs scrambling across it, resembling nothing so much as the side of a disturbed insect hive. Many were headed away, which the dwarfs knew instinctually to be south, but several dozen were making their way rapidly toward the conflict at the lava's edge.

Durok's voice escaped as little more than a whisper. "…What have you done?"

"While you focused on me through that stone of yours we kept with us as we traveled, another unit made for your slave pens," Yurec countered triumphantly. "You're stronger than me, sure. But you can't take on the likes of the Rhyn Dufaris without your army."

"You *IDIOT!*" Durok shouted. "Have you truly paid so little heed to the world around you while hunting the servants of the Abyss? The world has changed while you chased me, little brother. Our former clan has already begun evacuating and heading south to seek the aid of the fat King Golloch. The armies of Tragar are pressing into the Halpi Mountains even now as we stand here and spat like children."

Several of the Ironguard shifted uneasily, uncertain whether to believe the words Durok spoke. Now it was Yurec that appeared unsettled and confused.

"This bunch will push south and grow stronger, maybe, but more than likely they'll be picked up and their number added to the slaver's ranks among the gilded horde of Tragar itself. What you've done to weaken *me* has only made it worse for your precious council. Do you even understand what you've unleashed here? It's no wonder Ariagful chose me instead of one as shortsighted as you!" Durok's bulging form moved to place himself between the confused Ironguard and the approaching orcs, the lone berserker joining him. "If you want any chance at surviving the day, we'd best make friendly-like real quick."

The orcs were coming toward them at a run, their fangs bared, the beasts seemingly unaffected by the heat against their naked flesh. Even a handful of orcs would have been a challenge, but in such numbers it would be a slaughter.

Their decision made, the Ironguard stepped forward next to Durok and the berserker, with Broyleson and Kristoff at the lead. Yurec felt the years of confusion reawaken within him, the many times where Durok had seemed so right and so clear headed in his arguments for pursuing the powers sure to be found at depths unexplored, at the notion that the dwarfs could only grow in power the closer they came to Mantica's core. The notion that to capture and use the ever-present orcs as weapons, in the manner of their abyssal cousins, would simply be fighting fire with fire. But always, always the council had rebuffed his brother and sent him away with shame. Had cast away his ideas as blasphemous, as tantamount betrayal… but had it not also inspired the council's further investigations, and even their creation of the Traduciators? They had claimed the creation of such a group, a militant faction fulfilling clandestine missions to track and hunt those dwarfs whom had fallen to the sway of the Abyss, was kept secret only to insure it could operate independently. Yurec was no longer certain that had been their intentions at all.

Seeming to read his thoughts, Durok stated, "There is more than one god of the Abyss, after all, little brother."

But before he could internalize any more, the haze lifted, and the orcs were upon them all at once. Fighting tooth and claw, the press of bodies tore into the Ironguard, the tangle of limbs ripping the life from the valiant Kristoff as Broyleson screamed his rage at his side, beheading the orc which slayed his companion before shifting to the next in line. The screams of the dying filled the air from both sides. Andreu vaulted past his kin into the midst of the green horde, his countenance again that of rage incarnate, his movements making the orcs look slow and dull in comparison.

Durok howled, and a burst of light blinded those few surviving orcs closest to the iron-caster as a bolt of lightning shot forth from his blackened hand to strike through a line of the beasts, the sour smell of cooked orcflesh filling the air. Yurec regained his composure, the flash reawakening his brain, and he hurriedly collected his hammer from its impact crater, smoothly transitioning the motion into a wild swing and intercepting a humongous orc and crumpling its chest inward just before it connected with Durok. The iron-caster immediately returned the favor, his thick arm sweeping into another orc intent on Yurec and batting it away, its neck broken. Awarded several seconds of respite before the next wave crashed against them, Durok saw his opening.

"Keep 'em off me for a moment, brother!" he shouted, and with a nod of confirmation, the iron-caster crouched and placed his naked palms against the sand, where they began to glow as brightly as the sea of lava at their backs. Yurec took up a defensive position in front of his brother without a second thought, his confusion and uncertainty swept away with the clarity of battle, facing the grotesque horde bearing down upon them.

The dwarfs were holding them off, but only just barely. The Ironguard had been few in number, and each loss they suffered made the situation exponentially worse. Andreu slayed with reckless abandon, the gore splattered around him so thickly it was impossible to tell if he had suffered any wounds at all. Yurec could see, though, that it would prove pointless in the end. His brother had been right, no matter how much it pained Yurec to admit it to himself. He had wildly underestimated the sheer amount of slaves Durok had possessed, and his own orders to open their cages had unwittingly loosed a floodgate upon this part of the world. The warriors he had sent to open the slave pens were certainly slain, and as this battle raged on, this conflict on the beach would only draw more attention from the fleeing orcs. The bloodthirsty creatures would pour down upon them, and that would be the end. The tide of greenskinned beasts would then flow south unopposed, just as Durok had said, and bring great hardship for years to come.

Yurec's hammer swung widely and found purchase in another orc's skull, but he wasn't fast enough to stop the next beast in line. The orc collided with him like a battering ram, taking the Steel Juggernaut from his feet. His eyes squeezed shut instinctively as he awaited the killing blow, but after several heartbeats passed without consequence, he slowly opened his eyes once again. Yurec looked up to see the orcs backing away, an expression of unmistakable fear clear on their hideous faces. The ground had begun to rumble, and from behind him where Durok still crouched, glowing tendrils of bright orange magma were worming through the sand toward the orcs.

Yurec clambered back to his feet and stood stock still as the channels of magma splintered and multiplied, the sea of lava behind Durok fueling their advancement. Stretching between the feet of the confused orcs, the tendrils rejoined into a single point, where the pool they formed began to sink rapidly into the blackened sand. The ground rumbled more violently, and with a howl from the iron-caster, a huge hand made of blacked stone shot up from the pool of lava, the splash from it searing off the face of the nearest orc. Following that hand was an obsidian arm, the breadth of it as thick as an entire dwarf all by itself. Another hand then followed, and grasping solidly at the surrounding sands, a massive obsidian golem pulled itself free from the ground as the surrounding orcs stumbled over one another in terror. Its massive hunched form reverberated from the power used in its creation, rivulets of brightly glowing magma coursing through the shiny black stone of its body. Taking a single gigantic step toward its enemies, it swung its gauntlet in an arc that splattered three orcs effortlessly, their bodies flying through the air before tumbling to the beach some distance away.

The orcs surrounding the fallen form of Durok's faithful berserker locked on to the new threat, the dwarf's twitching body no longer important, and their combined guttural howls rang out in challenge at the massive stone creation. Slaying the last of the orcs in his immediate vicinity, Broyleson, the only Ironguard still on his feet, cradled his mangled shield arm as he backed away towards the lava's edge. Durok stood breathing heavily, sweat pouring down his body, his form clearly diminished back to normal from the energies spent in the golem's creation.

The three surviving dwarfs watched, exhausted, as the nearly indestructible obsidian golem absorbed the full onslaught of the horde and butchered several in return with each sweep of its mighty arms. The orcs which had been eagerly heading for the battle across the beach had turned back and gone with their fleeing fellows, their numbers still continuing to pour from the hillside and follow the sea's edge.

Durok finally broke the uneasy silence between the wounded dwarfs, the golem clearly capable of handling the rest of the immediate threat on its own. "The Council has told you many half-truths I'm afraid, little brother. Perhaps they thought to slow the armies of Tragar, but they've greatly underestimated that bunch. There are many among that green horde I'd kept imprisoned that will make mighty slave champions at the hands of Tragar's slavers."

Yurec could only grunt in response, his world shattered. The Council had sent him on this mission knowing the chaos it would cause in freeing Durok's slave pens, just as his brother theorized, of that he was confident. They had wanted this madness, hoped even for it to save their own skin, but clearly had been too foolish to consider it potentially strengthening the foes knocking at their door. And he had blindly followed their orders. How much blood would stain his hands for this?

"Looks to me like we've got our work cut out for us… eh, Lord Durok?" Broyleson spoke uneasily, his allegiances clear.

Yurec couldn't bring himself to raise his head in response, his failure heavy upon him, his shame too great.

"That we do." Durok replied.

THE BEAST WITHIN

By Andrew McKinney

The scent was on the wind.

It was the smell of war.

Dragyr sniffed at the air once again, taking in the heavy scent of blood and fire. It was unkind; smelling of ploughed earth and felled timber. If he waded through the mixture of scents deeply enough, Dragyr could detect hints of an even darker, unnatural nature. These strange things raised the hair across the beastman's body as the instinct to hunt down those responsible rushed through him.

"Do you smell that, brother?"

The other longhorn shifted his posture, irritated at the interruption. "I don't need to. I have felt it coming in my bones. Would you but pay more attention, you would notice a great many more things." Malgar shot Dragyr a pointed look before closing his eyes and relaxing back into his meditations.

Dragyr, unfazed by the admonishment, wandered closer to his mentor. "How can you relax at a time like this?"

"With age, one finds reason to enjoy any moment of peace, young one. You will see conflict soon enough. Calm yourself, I can sense your aggression even now. Save your fury. Look around you and see what is here and now."

The younger beastman took a deep breath, visibly trying to calm himself. Malgar was right, he was too excited for what was to come, and part of him was ashamed by that. He tried doing what the older longhorn asked and looked around himself. They sat beside a swift moving stream, the surface a mirrored shell of currents and ripples that distorted his already bestial features. Only the blended outline of his man-like appearance mixed with his spiraling horns and shaggy fur could be discerned clearly. Tiny drops of water slipped from the branches above, but the morning's drizzle seemed to have finally ceased.

The cold, wet day only drove his desire to get moving. He didn't understand how they could just leave the despoilers to their predations. His mentor should be enraged, rushing to join the fray even now!

Malgar grunted again as though he could read Dragyr's thoughts. Or perhaps he simply had enough of his apprentice's pacing and snorting. "We must wait for the herd to gather, young one. Would you go face them all alone? Then you would die. Needlessly. Pointlessly."

An exasperated growl slipped from Dragyr's throat before he could stop it. The elder longhorn's eyes blinked open with another hard look deep within them. That look said enough, there would be no more argument. Dragyr dipped his head in a show of submission, beads of cold water dripping from the points of his curling horns. The elder seemed to calm at the display, and his voice was soft once again when he answered. "Go, young one, leave me to meditate and find us something to eat. The others will be hungry when they arrive."

With another dip of his head, Dragyr rushed from the stream, happy to have a task to give him something to do. It didn't take him very long to fell a half-dozen of the flightless jackersnipe, but by the time he had cleaned the great bipedal birds and returned, the herd was already beginning to assemble. What had been a quiet clearing near the stream that morning was now rapidly filling with the commotion that a gathering of his kin often brought along with it. It was times like this he could see why his mentor preferred his hermetic lifestyle wandering the wilderness, rather than stay with a herd as most of his people preferred.

There were nearly a hundred of his kin assembled, at least four distinct herd groups gathered against a common threat. Their nomadic lifestyle dictated that they roam about in smaller groups, separated and scattered across Mantica. Any large gathering over a prolonged period would see them unable to sustain themselves, and they would strip the environment bare trying. Only in times like these, under the direst of situations, did they unite together.

The majority of those gathered were much like himself, bestial featured satyrs and fauns. They stood upon two goat-like legs ending in cloven hooves, with horns sprouting from their heads and fur covering their bodies. Supple corded muscle rippled under their fur, a testament to their lifestyles as nomadic hunters. Some among them were more beast than man, others could pass as a human with only minimal mutations that marked them. Many even possessed features of boars, reptiles, felines, and any other beast of nature that could be imagined.

Then there were those rare tribes to harbor humans among them; completely 'normal' in their appearance, these oddities chose to accept the herd way of life and were accepted into the Green Lady's favor. As a people, the herd had learned to celebrate and prosper from their diversity. Long ago, their race had only been the broken castoffs of a dark god's scheme, and they were thankful for the lives they now had, no matter what form that took.

As Dragyr walked through the camp, he saw satyrs and fauns locking arms as they shouted about how long it had been; there were also looks of great tension exchanged as what it appeared to be rivals meeting eyes for the first time on equal ground. Dragyr stayed far away from the latter. But it was not like he even knew most of them! Sure, there were some such as Lokin of the Raventree tribe, who he had encountered with Malgar in the past, but most of these longhorns were strangers. Looking around the assembled gathering, the half-dozen jackersnipe he carried in the net slung over his back seemed a paltry addition to their provisions.

He found Malgar among the gathered chieftains in the middle of the throng. He sat quietly while the other chieftains bellowed and snorted, renewing vows and refreshing competitions much like the rest of the gathering was doing. When he saw Dragyr approach, he motioned for him to put the birds on the nearby fire to cook and then stood to assemble the gathered leaders. As a revered elder, he was awarded a place of respect and honor among them. Dragyr assumed that must be the reason for the immediate hush that fell over the group as soon as Malgar began to speak.

"Brothers and sisters. You have my thanks for answering the call. Our forest, our home, has been violated. Our dark cousins come again, and it looks like they intend to stay this time. They rend the earth and uproot even the ancient willows of Galahir. This trespass cannot be allowed to go unpunished."

The others snorted and nodded in agreement. He could see their bristling anger in the shake of their horns and the way the hairs along their spine stood on end. The orcs were never something they wanted to encounter, even at the best of times. They served as a reminder of where they had come from, what they could have been. They were the darkest countenance of themselves seen through a warped mirror. Only narrow chance separated their races, if the legends of their past could be believed. They stood opposed now in basic tenants; the herd protected the natural world as their sacred and inherit duty, whereas the orcs merely sought to destroy anything that lay before them. Neither of them lacked in savagery or strength. That common bond could see any encounter between their forces become very bloody and costly. It was little wonder the elders here were so on edge.

Malgar looked around those collected before him, his eyes searching each in turn carefully. Dragyr could not see any hesitation in the crowd as his eyes scanned the assemblage. Even those who were rivals among them would lay aside their grievances. An accord was in place for gatherings like these, they knew they had a threat to take care of before settling any rivalries; that would wait until the great seasonal feasts. Nothing would stand between them and upholding their duty to protect this land.

"We stand together." One by one, the assembled leaders stood and pledged their support. Even those who had known disagreements shook hands and swore the oaths.

Dragyr watched the scene cautiously; it was not his place to be so involved, but he could not help but be marveled by the connection that linked their people together. Even so, he nearly overcooked the meat, an easy thing to do since most of his kin preferred it so rare. He had never observed a council of war before, and to see such highly regarded chieftains making peace here before they went off to war was a rare and moving sight. Everyone knew of the animosity between Goxul and Kvim. The two had fought on and off for years over the affections of a faun, nearly killing one another on multiple occasions. But now they gripped each other tightly, pressing their horns together and swearing oaths like brothers.

A low snort beside him brought Dragyr back. He glanced around to realize Malgar had broken from the group and now stood beside him. They watched together as the other leaders resumed their seats and began making plans for war. Dragyr lowered his eyes, embarrassed to have been caught watching so closely. He knew he should have been paying closer attention to his duties. The elder motioned back toward the group. "That is one of the most important duties of any chieftain. Being able to lay aside your own pride and desires for the good of the herd. The day we cannot come together will be the day we fail in our sacred duty."

*****

They came to the forest, ripping and tearing. Destroying and burning. And building. The fortress they had thrown up was an abomination of twisted wood and metal. Their fresh fortification sat a few hundred yards distant from the edge of the tree line, in what had a short time ago been a pleasant meadow at a place where the hilly forests gave way to open ground. It was clear they were digging in. Southward, they would encounter the towns and empires of men, so it was likely they meant this place to be their camp for a time while they raided and pillaged. They would not have that chance; they clearly hadn't anticipated the response of the inhabitants of this wild land.

Anger was getting the better of the young satyr. The twisted fort before Dragyr reeked of death, its walls made of fresh timber crudely felled and hurriedly stacked. The scent of blood and refuse streamed from the place, a testament of the orcs' treatment of the local animals. Even the elder longhorn beside him had a snarl curling his lips to bare the sharp fangs beneath.

The orcs had set up this location too boldly near the herd forces; it was within an hour's march from where they held council. There had easily been several dozen orcs patrolling the perimeter of the crudely fabricating fortress. It had not quite been finished yet, as there were still plenty of wide openings and gaps where their dark cousins were still building, as well as the fact that there were no watchtowers. They were not expecting to be attacked, especially not so soon; how haughty of them.

The two of them slunk forward from the west, being careful to stay crouched so that the foliage at the wood's edge would keep them concealed. Here, Malgar paused and spoke. "Stay close to me, and pay close attention to everything going on around you."

A raucous noise went up from the forest to the south. The greenskins loitering about the fortress shot to their feet, suddenly alert, and rushing to meet the threat. They responded much faster than Dragyr thought they would. "Would it not have been better to try to get closer and take them by surprise?"

Malgar shook his head but did not take his eyes away from the battle unfolding from the south, where the first wave would come from. "Too much open ground to approach in secret, and many of our kin can't move as quietly as us. But we still have our surprises."

The orcs, seeing the host of satyrs and fauns rushing across the field toward them, must have gauged them little enough threat. In an effort to trounce their enemies quickly and defend the hastily assembled unfinished fortress, they gave a great cry and altogether abandoned their fortifications to rush forward and meet them in open battle upon the fields. The orcs looked to outnumber the beasts nearly thrice over. Dragyr chewed the inside of his lip nervously as their lines crashed together. He bristled, wanting to burst from the tree line to rush to the aid of his kind. They needed to hold.

As though the sound of impact was a signal, a second, even larger band of beastmen burst forth from the forest line just north of where the two perched watching the battle unfold. The orcs seemed totally oblivious as the horde advanced rapidly across the open ground, interposing themselves between the greenskins and their abandoned fortifications. By the time the enemy realized the threat that approached them from the rear, it was far too late.

"Now we go." Malgar was brusque, radiating an intensity that Dragyr had rarely seen the elder exhibit. He leapt from the tree line and burst into a run that the younger satyr was hard-pressed to match. The battle was fully joined now against the outnumbered orcs that were pressed from two sides. Still, they showed no fear as they fought back; if anything, they seemed to push harder, working to break through the press of bodies that assailed them. For a moment, it looked like they might even do it.

Then Malgar reached the point where the line had begun to break.

A huge brute of an orc was leading the push, knocking down two or three foes at a time with sweeps of his massive shield. His shout of defiance was cut short as Malgar leaped through the ranks, swinging his axe in a deadly arc that ended with the brute's head sailing through the air. The massive shield thunked to the ground, followed by the toppling corpse. The elder waded into the press, his axe moving back and forth, exacting a bloody tally with each step forward. Dragyr followed closely behind, doing his best to protect himself and watch the elder's back.

Dragyr quickly lost the ability to focus on much else besides keeping up with his mentor and staying alive. Though he favored the bow, he had been trained for many years to fight his enemies face to face. His blade met those of the orcs' in desperate clashes, their blows almost too much for him to deflect at times. Dragyr was forced to halt acting as Malgar's shadow as an orc threw himself between the two. The young satyr ducked and weaved with superior speed, but he could not find the right opening to attack. He parried and blocked the relentless axe swings, until eventually he could strike true, stabbing his sword through the windpipe of his enemy. He had no time to think about what just happened; another was on him in a moment. He yanked his sword out just in time to parry another flurry of blows. As he staggered back, doing his best not to trip over the fallen or bump into another duel, the orc finally let up, falling dead. Malgar stood proud behind the body as it fell, staring balefully at the younger satyr.

Dragyr nodded his thanks and followed his master's trail of carnage once more.

Being so close to the enemy, it was easy to see the relation between them. Their leathery green skin did not hide the similar cast of bestial features, and the savage look behind their gaze could have been mirrored in the eyes of any one of his own people. Even as strong and willful as the orcs were, the forces of the herd were still gaining ground, pressing them harder with each step.

Before he knew it, Malgar's pace slowed, and Dragyr realized that the orcs had thinned out to the point of nonexistence. They had been slaughtered; every last one of the orcs. The herd had prevailed, but as the longhorn looked more closely at the ground, he could see the price his people had paid in gaining such a victory. This foe was more tenacious than anything Dragyr could have ever thought to face.

Dragyr sighed as he began to clean a shallow wound in his leg, that he had not remembered getting, when Malgar's growl brought his attention back to his surroundings. His kin were already tearing down the enemy's hastily wrought fortifications, while another group tended to the dead and injured, carrying them back to the safety of the treeline.

"Why the rush? The enemy is defeated. We should let our forces rest a moment. That battle was hard fought."

The longhorn snorted. "Now you want to rest? What happened to the haste you possessed earlier?"

Before Dragyr could inquire further, a pair of satyrs approached dragging a smaller form between them. They dropped the figure in front of the elder before the one on the left spoke. "This one was a prisoner in the camp. The orcs' pet goblins weren't very kind to him."

Malgar nodded his thanks to the satyrs and they stood back behind the man, eyeing him carefully. The elder turned to the outsider, and he paused for a moment. It was hard for longhorns' tongues to form the words of men, and Malgar could speak their language much better than Dragyr thought possible for any creature of the wood. The elder's words, when he spoke, were delivered after a small growl. "What do you in this place human?"

The man's face was full of fear, and the stink of it reeked from him. Dragyr could feel little but pity as the scrawny human answered in a shaking voice. "I was returning to the Hegemony, to warn them of what comes for us, but I was captured. The great citadels of the Brotherhood have been cast down and the Abyss grows! Orcs and goblins are streaming down from the north, rushing straight toward the lands of men, but they will first pass through your forests. You must let me go and allow me to deliver my message, for the protection of my own lands as well as yours."

The longhorn shook his head, mane bristling. "Land is protected already. From orcs. From humans. From any who seek ruin or defile. We protect homes, we protect Lady." He raised his arm to indicate the crude fort being torn asunder about them, clearly hoping it would help to illustrate his point through the language barrier. "You see? Flee from place. Tell kin of your kind to come in respect or not at all."

The man sagged slightly as he understood they meant to let him go, a small bit of fear and tension fading from his posture, and his voice thickening slightly. "There are many more orcs and goblins to the north. I don't know that even your strength can face what is coming."

Malgar's eyes narrowed, but he nodded. He gestured to the satyrs that had brought the man, and they led him away.

"Are you certain it was wise to let him go? They may return."

"Mankind is not our true enemy," Malgar spoke in the tongue of the longhorns once more, Dragyr no longer having to listen to the rough tones of the humans. "They are easily mislead, but they should not all be judged so harshly. Do not ignore the strength of compassion, lest we become just as dark and twisted as they believe us to be."

"He was right though? More orcs come this way even now? And could the Abyss truly be spreading? What evil could come of that?"

"I see little reason the human would lie about such a thing. But we will meet any other threats, just as we met this one. No, the enemy is not defeated. This was the chaff sent ahead of the main force; they merely awaited the host. This was not the true threat we face. I suspected as much from the beginning."

Dragyr could feel the color drain from his face. "That can't be. This battle was already hard fought. How can we face another force even larger than this one?"

"This was just a skirmish, young one, a taste of what is to come. The real battle is before us. But fear not, we've known this would come for a long time. We are not unprepared."

The confidence in his elder's voice gave him hope; of course they would face the threat. He hadn't realized how much seeing the orcs close up had unnerved him. He was learning many lessons today. He straightened up and shook his horns hard.

"That's better." Malgar smiled upon seeing the renewed determination. "Now, listen closely, young one. I have a task for you; it will be dangerous, but I trust in your ability to see this through. The Lady has many allies. I must gather the herd."

*****

Silence and the ability to remain unseen were highly valued traits in the natural world. Predators used stealth to sneak up on their prey, while the prey used it to avoid predators. The best confrontation was one that ended before one party was ever aware of the other's proximity. There was wisdom in nature, and this hunter knew that. This predator came not in search of prey, but information. He sought knowledge of the enemy's size and location, or so Malgar had reminded Dragyr repeatedly before he set out toward the mountains bordering the eastern reaches of the forest.

It was strange to be so far away from his mentor. He had been by his side for many years, ever since the old longhorn had taken him away from his tribe as a youngling. But now it seemed the elder had learned to trust him, or perhaps the situation was merely that dire.

Three days of travel brought the hunting satyr to the northernmost reaches of the forests, where the craggy landscape finally gave way to the rise of a vast mountain slope. Dragyr slowed his pace considerably from there, knowing he was much more likely to be seen by the orc patrols beyond the cover of the trees. His patience and careful approach was rewarded when he encountered a patrol of greenskins, a diminutive breed the orcs called goblins, his first evening beyond the forest.

These foes were much smaller than those he had encountered so far. The sharp-faced goblins were riding on mangy beasts that looked like wolves, but these mounts seemingly lacked any sense of nobility that animals of his forests possessed. They had patchy fur and flattened maws that opened too wide to look natural, even on their over-sized heads. The goblins must have brought these mawbeasts with them from the cruel lands to the north.

He barely had time to find cover as they came from around a bend in the canyon ahead of him. Dragyr crawled into a small crack between the rocks, pressing himself deep within and covering himself in the loose dirt and mud. The goblins' mounts sniffed around the outside of the crack, snarling softly as they picked up his scent. Before the lead beast could advance further, its goblin rider gave it a kick to the flanks, apparently eager to be on his way.

That group was but the first of many. With each patrol encountered and avoided, Dragyr waited to be found, his anxiety causing him to tremble more with every new patrol. Every time they passed, he said a silent thanks to his mentor for teaching him the value of patience. He craved battle with the orcs, but he knew he could not face them alone.

After another two days of travel, he knew he was growing close to the orc encampment. The deep cadence of drums boomed through the narrow canyons seeming to come from all around him, but there was only one direction to travel. He climbed the canyon wall as the sun dipped below the horizon, knowing it was the only way he could get any closer without being seen. The climb was difficult, even for one of his kind, finding tenuous handholds and digging his hooves into grooves within the rock-face. He wished dearly he'd been born with wings like those of the great eagles that made their homes within the forest when he made the mistake of looking down.

The moon was a hazy blur beyond the clouds, and the sun had long since departed as he finally pulled himself upon a high ledge to rest. He took a few deep breaths and soaked in the incredible view around him. The clouds seemed so close he could touch them; it would almost be beautiful, if not for the awful sight below.

Fires were appearing in the valley below as the orcs lit fires within their camp. Malgar had taught him to count the flames to estimate the enemy's strength, but this didn't seem right. There were too many fires springing up. Then he noticed the glow rising throughout the rest of the valley. In the west, where the Mammoth Plains stretched out into the horizon, here too was the ruddy orange glow. They covered the plain as far as the satyr could see. This force of orcs wasn't some raiding party striking out from the north, this was an exodus of many tribes banding together and striking southward. Dragyr wanted to turn and run back immediately to warn his brethren in the forest, but he couldn't. Not yet. Malgar had given him one other task.

Creeping along the canyon wall, trying to be very careful not to lose his footing in the dark, he approached the closest of the camps. From here, he could make out individual orcs, massive and feral forms mixing with the smaller greenskins that ran about beneath their notice. The big ones settled about their fires, feasted on raw meat, and drank of foul smelling grog; while the smaller ones ran about engaging in all manner of vicious sport among themselves and the captive beasts they carried with them. The roars of these brutes was constant, and it was only elevated by the way they fought between one another, sometimes even bringing about bloodshed.

Through it all, there was a single spot of quiet calm within the chaotic maelstrom. Like the eye of a terrible storm, one immense orc sat quietly brooding in the shadows at the center of the encampment. He watched while all the others went about their nightly ritual. Dragyr had heard talk about this kind of orc – he was called a Krudger among their kind, a leader possessing the strength and cunning to unite fearful armies under his singular command. This orc was the real threat.

A diminutive figure broke from the throng into the island of calm surrounding the Krudger. This one wore a dark heavy cloak, but the long thin nose sticking from beneath the hood marked him out as a goblin. The orc watched the goblin approach with a lack of fascination, bordering almost on boredom. Dragyr's interest was piqued, so he risked climbing down closer to the odd meeting between the two.

The rock shifted underhoof, dislodging a small stone. It bounced down the cliffside, clattering as it went. Two dozen pairs of eyes turned suddenly in his direction as he hugged as tightly as he was able against the sheer face of the rock. One of the sharp-faced goblins walked over to the fallen debris, looking directly into the shadows where the satyr concealed himself. It picked up the rock and opened its mouth as if to cry out. With a sudden motion, the goblin turned and hurled the stone back into the head of one of its smaller fellows.

The entire group of them broke into laughter at the cruel joke and returned to their own entertainment. The satyr breathed a sigh of relief and carefully shifted himself to a more secure resting place to listen to the conversation between the orc Krudger and the goblin. Even as close as he dared to get, only bits of their conversation could be heard, carried along by the wind. He was surprised at how easy the orcs' language was to understand, as it was very close to his own; another unfortunate similarity.

"Two more days till we will arrive at the forests, then your sniveling gits had best get to work. We will need those war machines as quickly as possible if we are to make much headway against the enemy in the south. The race of men is weak, but their weapons and walls are strong."

The goblin's high pitched voice carried better upon the wind. "We have the greatest minds of the engineer's guild among my horde on the plains. The forests should provide us all the raw materials we need to see to the construction of enough war machines to destroy anything those pitiful pinkskins put in our way."

The orc gave a nod of his head, followed by a guttural grunt. "Do not keep me waiting. I expect to be past this forest and sweeping toward the human kingdom of Basilea within the week. Your war machines should be behind me by the time I have cleared their rabble from the fields and ready to press into their cities."

"Oh, the things we will make. We have been hard at work for many years waiting for this moment. The wait will be well worth it."

With a wave of his hand, the Krduger dismissed the goblin. The grin the creature gave as he turned his back told Dragyr the goblin held more in mind than the Krudger realized, but that would be something to worry about another time.

The goblin departed and the orc rose to his full height, the burble of the crowd fading to a low rumble and then to silence with surprising quickness.

The Kudger's voice could be heard clearly across the main camp of his inner circle as he made his declaration. "This is our time, come finally. No gods stand in our way, nothing shall bar us from taking what is rightfully ours. We were made with purpose, and it is time to fulfill it. This is our age. The age of orcs!"

The cheer went up. A booming chorus echoing from all around him. "Age of orcs! Age of orcs!"

The satyr slipped his hand to the bow that was strapped to his back, feeling the familiar grain of the wood beneath his fingers. He stopped before he drew it. Though it was tempting, he knew he would never make that shot from where he perched, not with the cold gusts of wind that threatened even now to dislodge him if he were to drop his guard. He would have taken the chance, were it just about him; but he knew his mentor would expect him to return with the information he'd been sent to retrieve. He needed to warn his people of the storm that would soon blow over them.

*****

Desperation fueled Dragyr's return to the forests. The human's words had been truth after all. It was not only this threat from the orcs in the eastern reaches they had to worry about, but an invasion of all their lands. The forces of nature must be rallied across the whole of the forest of Galahir, not since the old days when the broken Celestials still battled across the realms had they ever faced such a threat.

As he moved through familiar forests, he was relieved by the fact that he was home. Coming back to the camp where he left his allies, he was awestruck seeing even more of the longhorns' various allies assembled. All of the Lady's forces had to work together to protect their wilds in this age of strife, lest all the great wonders of the natural world be felled. When they were threatened, they reacted as any beast would, not in half measured responses as is the way of men. A beast turns to face a threat and makes its choice in a moment. To flee, or to fight.

While he was gone, it seemed the choice had already been made; and if he had to guess, it was probably a unanimous one. This fight would be waged with all the force their combined tribes possessed. Many of them had already assembled, more than Dragyr had even seen at one place, even during the great feasts. Not only had the satyrs and fauns gathered in their entirety, but countless others of the forests' people had also decided to heed the call.

Even the mighty yet stubborn centaur tribes had decided to show themselves, standing prideful atop a nearby hill, deep in conversation among themselves. Their bodies were those of fleet four legged creatures such as deer or horses, but where their necks would normally be, they instead sported the torso of a man, often covered in ritual markings.

The lycans were not nearly so hard to attract. Tall, lithe, powerful. They personified the best traits of wolf and man. While they resembled the dark and unnatural werewolves that made their home in the Kingdom of Ophidia to the south, they were nothing alike. Lycans still had their humanity, their sense of morality and duty to the land. Among all the beasts, none seemed to revel as they when it came time to kill, and they were almost zealous in their devotion to protect their territory.

Dragyr threaded his way through the camp, passing gatherings of sparring tribesmen and walking by the legs of monstrous chimeras that stood patiently waiting while their bizarre combination of three heads each – ram, lion, and dragon – chewed on lumps of strange vegetation. Harpies, avian creatures with the face and torso of a woman, thronged the canopy overhead, making the branches sway and groan. Strange smells emanated from the tents of the shamans as they brewed the concoctions the spirit walkers would imbibe to connect them to the honored ancestors and strengthen them prior to the coming battle. It was a surreal experience to see the army preparing for war, something he was sure he would remember for a long time to come.

He found his mentor sitting on a fallen log, drawing a stone across the rough blade of his axe. Even after witnessing Malgar's ferocity against the orcs, the weapon in his aged mentor's hand still looked awry; but from the way the old longhorn handled the weapon, it was clear they were familiar as old love. The relic was roughly crafted, as were most of his people's weapons. They were not artisans or craftsmen, especially when it came to metal working. The weapons they forged were often crude, but despite this, in the hands of a longhorn, these blades were as effective as any human-crafted steel. His master's axe did not look extraordinary; the only thing that set it apart from the roughly beaten head and marred shaft were the bestial runes, clearly painstakingly carved into the head.

"You return," the elder called out without even looking up.

Dragyr snorted in response. "Of course, you gave me a task. I know how you get when I don't complete them."

Malgar laid aside his blade and looked up at the younger beast. There was a look in his eyes Dragyr had never seen before. "Tell me then what we face."

*****

For the last day, they had made their plans. Dragyr had sat in the war council of assembled warriors and delivered his report. The elders did not despair as he suspected, but instead they calmly began to make decisions on how best to defeat the approaching threat. He was truly amazed to see the different beasts of the forest working together as they devised a plan, but the talks and strategizing was all too much for Dragyr to keep up with. The day went by in a blur of activity that he could scarcely remember.

Now was the time for action; their scouts reported that the greenskins spilled from the mountain pass, making their way toward the forest. The herd's best chance to stop them would be to bottle them up against the pass before they could bring their full weight against them. Dragyr only hoped their plans would prove sufficient. A brightly blooming purple flower caught his eye, and he bent down to enjoy the aroma, however bittersweet it was. The idea of what the orcs would do to their vibrant homeland was worse than the thought of dying.

Hunters already waited above the pass. They had spent the last day priming their trap, but against such numbers, it would probably afford them little advantage. The rocks they had dislodged would fall into the pass, cutting off the forward elements of the orc horde. The greenskins wouldn't be slowed by the rubble for too long, he was sure, but it might be enough to do the damage to their forces they needed to even the odds.

Malgar knelt before one of the herd's shamans. The revered satyr priest dabbed drops of sacred oils onto the elder's horns before making markings with blue woad dyes in his pale fur. A low soft chant finished the blessing, calling for the aid of the Lady as well as their ancestors in the coming battle. Dragyr watched in silent awe, trying to mentally prepare himself.

Branches swayed overhead as they accompanied the fluttering of wings.

The harpies had sighted the oncoming horde and rushed forward to sate their insatiable hunger. Immense birds of prey departed their nests in the topmost branches closely behind the avian beastkin.

"They are almost upon us." The shaman stepped back as Malgar rose. He picked up his massive axe and strode down the hill.

The satyrs paused at the edge of the forest and watched as the orcs loped along in no particular order. They weren't an army on the march, they were a wave of destruction, not expecting any sort of trouble. Their fight was many days to the south. Expectations changed as soon as the first elements of the herd broke from the woods, the tribe's elite spirit walkers leading the way. The orcs spotted them almost at once, and with a surprising coherence, their pace increased, immediately charging toward the satyrs emerging from the trees. Fearsome shock troops wielding large axes in either hand led the way, while orcs wielding two-handed greataxes and bearing gore stained banners followed close behind. Orclings, similar to the ones they had first encountered, were pushed aside as their larger brethren surged toward their enemy.

The two forces met with a mighty clash any human army would be hard pressed to imagine. Savagery met ferocity and the lines of battle instantly dissolved into a whirling melee as orc and spirit walker alike were catapulted well into the enemy's ranks by the force of the charge. The orcs outnumbered the spirit walkers many times over; their mighty few were hardly a fraction of the size of the orc army. But they led the way knowing the battlefield was to be their gravesite. Seizing the power of the longhorns mighty ancestors, Dragyr found it hard to watch as they moved like fire through the battlefield; tearing and destroying with a swiftness that could not be matched.

The battle was wild, and it was hard to tell who was getting the upper hand; but most importantly, the orc surge had been halted for a moment.

Malgar raised the signal horn to his snout and inhaled deeply. The tone shifted through octaves, loud and piercing enough to be heard even over the din of the battle raging before them. Moments later, a rumble answered the call of the horn as immense boulders broke away from the cliffs overlooking the mountain pass.

If the orcs noticed the falling rocks behind them, their tenacity remained undaunted. The greataxe wielders continued pushing their way to the front of the battle as though nothing had happened, even though the rocks killed hundreds of their brethren and cut off any chance of reinforcements. Mighty hooves pounding against the forest floor echoed through the dense foliage as the centaurs thundered into the flanks of the combat, intent on pushing the orcs back against the cliff sides.

Trolls came bellowing from behind the front ranks of the horde, appearing from the mass of green like mushrooms in a bed of moss. Dragyr wondered how he had missed them before. They pushed through a tide of diminutive orclings and charged into the ranks of the longhorns, flinging them aside like leaves in the wind with their massive clubs and brute strength. It looked like the push of the trolls might break a hole through their line and ruin the battle plan entirely.

A line of mighty beasts charged in to face the trolls, plugging the gap left as the longhorns pulled back to regroup. These benevolent guardians of the forest's sacred places joined the fray now with unexpected violence. Minotaurs put their heads down and led the way with their long bovine horns; owlbears following close behind, eager to get at the enemy with their sharp beaks and furry claws. The trolls fell back as they were pierced by massive horns and trod under ironclad hooves; their remarkable regenerative abilities had trouble standing up to the onslaught that beset them.

The clash of the brutish warriors spilled into the rear ranks where Dragyr held his ground, picking off targets with his bow. He dove aside as one of the massive owlbears tackled a troll to the ground, nearly taking him with it. Acrid blood flew from the struggle as the owlbear tore with its razor-sharp beak and rended with the ferocity of its giant bear-like paws. Another of the orcs' lumbering brutes came bellowing out of the haze and sent the beastkin flying off its fallen comrade with a sweep of its massive club. The fallen troll picked itself up from the ground, strips of its flesh hanging raggedly from its torso. The satyr found himself standing before the pair of trolls alone with little hope of winning this combat on his own.

With a savage roar, he drew his blade and charged toward the lumbering enemy, hoping to take the initiative. His quick movement succeeded in surprising them momentarily, and his blade managed to strike home against the already injured troll. His sword could do little against their overwhelming might, and the return blow of the troll sent him tumbling into the dirt and struggling to breathe. He rose to his knees, one of the trolls reaching for him apparently believing he looked like he might make a good snack.

A ground-shaking impact rocked the earth and even the trolls seemed to hesitate. From the dark forest behind Dragyr, a creature even more massive than the trolls appeared as if from nowhere. A towering beast that looked like the combination of a cyclopian giant and a scaled, horned reptile came striding forward, and with a swipe of the uprooted tree it carried as a weapon, one of the trolls simply vanished in a spray of blood. His people called these vast warriors brutox, and they terrified even their own kind when they were riled for battle. But at the moment, he had never been happier to see one.

He rose and followed the brutox as it waded forward into a renewed press of the orcs, these bearing immense axes in each hand. It was hard to imagine anyone being able to wield such weapons effectively, but they seemed to be doing it with far more skill than he had imagined possible.

Over the din of combat, there was a warning cry, followed by the sounds of beating hooves. The satyr paused just long enough to look over his shoulder and caught a glimpse of the hunched forms charging their way. Orcs sitting atop massive boar-like creatures known as gores roared as they thundered across the open ground. Their raiders must have been away when the attack began and were now returning to find a fight they were eager to join. Orc spears and gore tusks gleamed in the pale sunlight before the battle turned to complete chaos.

A gore rider flashed past him and a bright flare of pain sent him tumbling back to the ground. The spear had missed him by inches, but the beast's tusk had caught his shoulder, drawing a bright crimson streak across his arm. He picked himself up, trying to wipe away the pouring blood that threatened to cause his blade to slip from his grip.

Before he could recover, he found himself face to face with another foe. The gore's fanged maw was so close, the putrid stench of its foul breath filled Dragyr's nostrils. Before he had a chance to escape, the orc atop it leapt down, swinging his bloodstained blade at the satyr. Dragyr staggered a few steps back, and the blade just nearly missed him. The orc brought his blade to bear once more, and Dragyr mustered the strength to bring his own sword up to parry. The orc was stronger, and Dragyr watched as the blades came closer and closer to his throat. A swift rush of air was the only warning before a solid shape slammed into the orc from above, ending their struggle. Dragyr stumbled away, realizing that one of the hunter's bodies lay atop his foe. He looked upward to see what had happened.

Goblins were overwhelming the hunters that had dropped the rocks into the canyons. The harpies were doing what they could to help them, but the tide of goblins swarming toward them seemed endless. Bodies rained down from above, impacting hard into the midst of the swirling battle. One by one, they were forced from the cliffs above, bleating defiantly as they fell. But even in death, the hunters had helped save at least one of their kind. The orc that had attacked Dragyr was dead beneath one of those fallen hunters, leaving their broken forms entwined in a cruel mockery of embrace.

Finding no others foes in his immediate vicinity, Dragyr pulled back from the battle lines for a moment's rest. He found his mentor similarly pausing and gazing carefully at the onslaught before him.

"Their leader is not among them," mused Malgar as his pupil came to his side. The elder's eyes scanned the enemy ranks, but it was obvious his target was not among the lead element. "I had hoped he would be closer to the front and we could end him here."

"Still, our plan worked. We have thinned their ranks considerably. If we could hold them in the mountains like this, we could win."

Malgar gave a shake of his gray mane. "We have lost many, young one. We are not as thinned as they are, but our numbers are less than favorable. As well, this Krudger is no fool. He will spread out his forces now that he knows that we pose a threat before him. They will backtrack and stream from every pass for miles around in such numbers that we will never be able to bottle them all up. They will overwhelm us. We would not make a suicidal stand, and he knows that as well. It would be best for us to fall back into the forests, striking as they travel, taking bites out of him even as he tries to lash back at us by despoiling and defiling our forest. It would turn into a long and bitter fight where neither side could truly claim victory. Unfortunately, it may be the best option we have left to us."

"Then, what now? What choice remains?"

"They will return, but their leader will be sure to be at the head this time. He will not let this insult go unheeded. We must remember they are not so different from us. Can you think of a single chieftain that would not look to recoup his honor after losing so many warriors?"

Dragyr nodded gravely in understanding. The battle before him seemed much less significant now. True, they had struck a mighty blow today, but against the forces that would soon stream out of those mountains, it was nothing. The only enemy that would defeat the orcs now would be themselves, prone to infighting as they were. Only their Krudger held them together in such numbers. "Single combat might be the only way to effectively end this… Could we possibly goad the Krudger into such a plan?"

The orcs on the field before them were fully cut off now. Their left flank had already unraveled beneath the hit and run attacks of the centaurs, and their right flank still struggled against the savage assault of the lycan packs. Only the center still held strong, thanks to the support of the resolute trolls, but that would change once the flanks broke completely.

"Come, let us join our brothers and help where we can. The fight will be over soon, and then preparations must be made." Malgar set out at a trot to join the final press against the center, his apprentice eager to finally be joining the fight at his heels.

*****

Seeing the broken forms of his kind, Dragyr understood now his elder's reticence when it came to shedding blood. It wasn't for lack of fury, the longhorn had shown him that he held plenty of that. It was to avoid this tragic scene that now unfolded about him. The orc dead were piled high before the pass, almost forming another barrier themselves, but there were plenty of his kindred among the bodies as well. Each still form was a tragic loss, a price paid in blood to uphold the sanctity of their realm.

"We are beasts, inside and out. There is no avoiding what we are. But we are also more. There is something greater inside us, and we cannot forget that." Malgar's voice was grave as he took in the dead surrounding them. He knelt before one still form almost as gray as himself and arranged the body into a state of dignified repose. "They died protecting their herd and home. They deserve all the honor we can manage, but there is little time for ritual."

Night had fallen and the sounds of the orcs clearing the rubble within the pass had grown louder. It would not be long before they broke through. The herd's army set watch fires on the slope before it, and they attended to their wounded and dead while they waited. Sadly, there were far too many of both. Others reformed their ranks just beyond the tree line, ready to meet the orcs head on if they did attempt to break out from the pass again.

With a resounding crack, the last of the rubble was cleared and dark hulking forms lumbered from the canyon. These greenskins were much larger and more fearsome looking than any that he had seen before. These were the elite of their tribes, the personal bodyguard of the host's leader, and their master the largest form among them. His bulk made the others look small in comparison, and his silent approach was far more terrifying than the screaming hordes had been earlier in the day.

Dragyr knew that someone must challenge the orc champion, but still he was surprised when his mentor was the one that stepped away from the group. Malgar called out, insulting the enemy leader. "Finally done hiding behind your underlings? Come and face me, if you are not afraid!"

Tension crackled in the air like lightning before a storm. Time slowed to a crawl as Dragyr took in all the details. The Krudger paced forward, lit by the glow of the fires; his arms raised in gloating invitation. Malgar strode forward to meet his challenge, the head of his axe glinting along its sharpened edge. Embers drifted along on cold winds between them. This dark cousin of theirs had to be ended here for the sake of any future chance at peace. This combat of champions could all but end this war before it began.

Both combatants seemed eager, both of them increasing their pace the closer they drew. A slow measured walk turned to a brisk step, and then they were running full sprint until it seemed there would be no stopping either of them. Malgar sprung into the combat at the last moment, swinging his axe from above and kicking out with his powerful leg strength, but the orc blocked the axe with his own weapon and barely stumbled back from the force of the kick. The satyr landed, rolling aside from the orc's counter blow, and came up to his side with a sweep of his own axe.

To see Malgar now was to see his truest form. He was primal fury made manifest, a rage-filled howl bellowing from his lungs as he met blades with the massive orc. Sparks flew as beast axe met orc cleaver, both weapons moving faster than Dragyr believed possible for such large blades. He'd seen Malgar fight before, spent years learning how to fight and hunt from the elder satyr, but he never realized that he was capable of this sort of showing. The sheer speed, strength, and ferocity of his fight was breathtaking.

The herd's champion seemed to be delivering the majority of the blows, but the orc just continued to shrug off every cut as though he didn't feel them. Malgar was hard-pressed to keep ahead of his foe's vicious sweeps, parrying or dodging aside at the last moment. But as an eternity of time passed, both combatants were slowing down, exhausted by the intensity of their fight. They broke apart for a moment, circling, watching the other for weakness. All it would take would be one clear opening and this fight could be over.

The two came back together in a clash of blades. The orc put a little too much behind his own swing, allowing Malgar to surge forward past his opponent's guard. The beast kin gave up a cheer as they saw the blade cleave deep into the orc's neck, right where it met his shoulder. Blood sprayed, and the orc staggered.

But the orc did not fall, he just gave a triumphant grin and clamped his hand around the haft of the axe. Malgar tried to jerk it back, but it was stuck fast in the bone. Before anyone could react, the orc swung his cleaver in a wild sideways cut that impacted the graymane across his ribs as he struggled to free his blade. His hands came loose from the handle, and he fell back onto the bloodied rocks. The Krudger pulled the axe from his neck with a grunt and tossed it aside, standing triumphantly over his foe. He raised his cleaver for the blow that would end the fight.

It broke every convention that his people had to interfere in such a way during an honorable contest. But against such a sight, Dragyr found it impossible to stand idle. The arrow flew into the night with hardly a conscious thought. He did not even realize the bow was in his hand until the sharp thwip of the bowstring split the tension in the air. With a sickly wet sound, the projectile found its target, and the orc staggered back from his fallen opponent, the shaft protruding from his eye socket.

The orc's bodyguard surged forward to protect their leader and exact revenge, and the beastmen champions did not hesitate in meeting the charge. Before him and behind him, Dragyr could hear more forces rushing headlong toward the fight. He had ensured the battle to come would be long and bloody. Could it have ended any other way?

"You cowardly goat!" The orc warlord screamed as he was harried away by a pair of his bodyguards. "You will pay for this! This land, and all of your gods damned kin will suffer for this transgression! We will slay all of you! No mercy!" Perhaps he was a coward and a half dozen other things as the great orc claimed, but that hardly mattered now. The battle surged back into life around him as Dragyr stumbled toward his fallen mentor, his steps faltering with sorrow and disbelief.

Malgar lay on the hard ground in a pose that might almost make it seem he was merely sleeping, were it not for the great rends in his flesh. Dragyr grasped the still form tightly, absently brushing at the blood-soaked fur. This was his mentor, his friend, his kin. This was the only family he'd ever known. This satyr had been father, brother, and tribe to him since he was too young to remember. He had hardly even known him, he was coming to find in recent days. Only at this desperate gathering had Dragyr begun to realize the extent to which the elder had been venerated by all of his kind.

Rage welled up inside him, but not the raw anger he had felt many times throughout his life. This was a purely savage rage, refined and honed with the sorrow of loss. He lowered his mentor's form back to the ground with exaggerated tenderness and care. He brushed his hand along one of his great spiraling horns before striding away to retrieve the heavy axe that lay discarded nearby. The loss burning through his soul, he stalked toward the nearest cluster of struggling forms and cleaved the elder's blade through an orc skull, and then another, and then another.

The battle would rage here, the orcs throwing themselves at the beastmen until their wrath was spent. If the warlord lived, and it seemed like not even an arrow embedded in his skull would see him dead, he would probably rally his remaining forces and do precisely as Malgar predicted. Dragyr could already see it; over the next few months, the greenskin horde would stream from the mountains and plains. The herd would fight a long and brutal campaign to protect their home alongside all the forces of nature the Green Lady could muster.

It was the way of things. The cycle did not limit itself to wolves and rabbits and deer going about their days. The cycle was here too, in this fight between the natural and wholly unnatural. They were but pieces of a greater whole. War was terrible, but perhaps it wasn't so different from the daily hunt. The stakes were just larger. Though he hated to admit, this was a hunt he loved, one he reveled in. The words of his elder a distant echo, for this enemy, there would be no mercy.

INTO THE STRAITS OF MADNESS

By Robert E Waters

Lukhantl stared at a large ship through Captain Poraqa's spyglass. At their distance, he could only make out vague shapes on the deck. Thin, dark shapes. The details of the ship, however, were clearer, though not conclusive.

"Is it our ship?" Poraqa asked, leaning on the railing beside Lukhantl.

Lukhantl shrugged off the anxious heat emanating from the captain's smaller, though powerful, salamander frame. "It fits our informant's description. It's a Twilight vessel for sure. It's square-rigged fore and main; lateen-rigged on the mizzen. My eyes could be deceiving me, though, at this distance. It may not be an elven vessel at all; it may just be an old carrack merchantman out of Geneza."

"Alone, and this far south? That's doubtful." Poraqa took the spyglass and had a look herself. She adjusted the focus, walking it up and down the railing, changing her angle. "It's a slaver, and in good shape. Can't see much of the crew, though."

"That is worrisome, but not unprecedented when it comes to Kin buccaneers. They hide their numbers well."

They had been shadowing the ship for a full three days, up from Hokh-Man, the Serpent's Mouth, and the massive battle that had taken place there near the port city. Lukhantl had only seen a handful of Kin on deck at any given time. That meant one of two things: either the ship had a small crew, or they were hiding their true strength below-decks.

The Kin were a collection of elven cabals that had succumbed to evil and wickedness, their skin growing so pale as to be almost nickel-blue. Those who had no experience with their relentless savagery on the battlefield might consider their dark simplicity beautiful. Lukhantl did not. He hated them all.

"We may have an opportunity here." Lukhantl flashed his thick, red tongue in excitement, letting it rippled along the line of teeth in his long red snout. "If we act swiftly and before it leaves the straits and enters the Infant Sea."

"They have a full gun deck," Poraqa said, changing focus again. "And I see two swiveled ballistae stem and stern, with oiled chains attached, and a fixed forward-firing falconet. Pretty fearful armament."

"Yes, but if they are under-strength..."

The captain nodded. Lukhantl could see foamy drool at the corner of her broad, toothy mouth. The green scales along her spine rose up like small daggers. "I wouldn't mind getting my hands on whatever cargo they are hauling, besides our captured brethren," Poraqa said. "But we can't know for sure about the crew. If we go in under the assumption that they are short-handed, we may be in for a deadly fight. I've never shrunk from a brawl, mind you, but I prefer having a better handle on the odds before I show my fire. If we fail, we will join our dead brothers and sisters on that bloody field of Hokh-Man."

Lukhantl had not been at the battle of Hokh-Man, but stragglers huddling on the beaches, awaiting rescue, had told of a total salamander rout as monstrous, eight-legged Abyssal fiends—with Twilight blade-dancers astride—carved huge swaths through terrified, fleeing Prime columns. Lukhantl's brother, Battle-Captain Lorquan, had been among those fleeing.

Lukhantl tried keeping angry heat welling up inside him under control as he clicked his sharp teeth and looked out over the chop toward the Twilight ship. Praise Kthorlaq the Deliverer, but his brother had survived the rout. Now he lay somewhere on that slaver ship with his personal guard, en route to another, more dangerous, mouth.

The Mouth of Leith.

It would have been better for Lorquan to die with honor on the field.

Salamanders did not possess the same kind of familial structures that other races of Mantica possessed, so there was no concern about Lorquan's capture shaming the family. Salamander mothers laid their eggs and kept their young safe for a short time afterward. Then they were gone. But strong bonds sometimes formed among the clutches as they struggled to survive in a dangerous world, and Lukhantl owed his life many times over to Lorquan for his protection in those early days.

"This ship can do circles around that big box of lumber," Lukhantl said, refocusing his mind on the discussion with the captain.

"Yes, but one mighty broadside, and we're matchsticks. Or if one of those ballistae penetrate our hull, she'll be ripped to shreds." Poraqa grunted and spit fire over the side. The boiling phlegm sizzled in the waves. "I wish Kantolq and Burlinq were here. Three corsair captains against one Twilight slaver... we'd make short work of it."

Lukhantl sighed and spit into the chop as well. "We're wasting time talking. Let's go get it."

Poraqa lowered her spyglass and looked at Lukhantl. She cracked a smile, and Lukhantl could see the fire, the lava, coursing through her face, her eyes, her body. "Under better circumstances, you'd make a fine sea captain. But you're angry,

Lukhantl. I've seen angry brethren such as you throw themselves against wall after wall, and get pounded to dust. Anger got you that nasty wound in your shoulder near Cacryn Golloch—don't look at me like that; I've heard the stories—and anger will get you killed, my friend. We'll follow it for a little while longer, see if we can better ascertain numbers for their crew. Then we'll rake their sails from the rear with fire eggs. That'll get the bees buzzing, and then we'll know for sure. All right?"

Poraqa was correct. Going in without better intelligence would be foolhardy, but it was difficult for Lukhantl to stow his anger, to be patient under these circumstances, when just over that short distance between ships, his only surviving family was in chains and probably suffering immeasurable privations. Time seemed more important than patience at this moment, but he nodded and tried to return Poraqa's smile. "You're right, my friend. We'll do as you say, but when the time comes to engage, I will lead the boarding party."

*****

Another few hours of watching and shadowing the Twilight ship from a safe distance, then Poraqa finally gave the order once her ship, Devourer's Fire, had moved within a hundred meters of the enemy's port side.

"Fire!"

Fire eggs roared out of cannon on the starboard side at the top of the roll. Poraqa preferred to fire at the top of the roll, as it more readily guaranteed some strikes on the initial volley from rigging to hull. Unfortunately, the shot was at an oblique angle, the Twilight slaver moving fast to evade, and thus about two-thirds of the eggs missed. The rest of the volley, however, struck the ship and showered the gunwale on the port side with gouts of small, but lethal, magma. From this distance, Lukhantl could not see if any shot found flesh. He certainly could not hear the terrifying screams that inevitably followed being hit by a fire egg. But all in all, a decent first volley.

The gunners loaded quickly and fired another round, still at an oblique angle, but they had correctly anticipated the pitch of the enemy ship. More fire eggs tore through the slaver's aft-castle and further down into the rear gun ports. Lukhantl waited to hear any explosions that the shot might have caused further into the hull, but none came. The Twilight ship was still standing, still sailing, and still looking very formidable. An explosion would have been good for them tactically, Lukhantl knew, but he was glad one did not occur. Chained salamanders were in that hull somewhere.

That last volley got the bees buzzing on its deck, as Poraqa had predicted. Kin crewmen scrambled about as their ship tried to turn into the shot and bring its port side gun deck to bear.

"She's going to stand and fight," Lukhantl said, adjusting the focus on the spyglass.

Poraqa nodded. "Yes, but look: still very few crewmen. I figure they have half their complement at best. Perhaps there'd been a revolt onboard that shaved their numbers, but whatever the reason, they've decided that they can't outrun us; might as well stand and make a good show of it." She leaned back, cupped her mouth, and shouted. "Turn starboard. Quickly now. Stow the eggs, and ready chain-shot!"

By turning sharply to the right, they allowed the Twilight ship freedom to turn fully to its portside and open its undamaged gun ports. As ordered, Poraqa's crew tucked away their fire eggs and readied half-ball split-shot; Lukhantl could hear their muffled voices through the planks but kept his eye on the Twilight ship and watched as one after another, doors were opened along the gun deck and barrels revealed. Too few. He shook his head. "That's only half. Something must have happened."

"Mhmm," Poraqa grunted, spitting into the waves once more. "Steady now! Bring us about!"

The Twilight ship opened fire. Lukhantl observed the expulsion of smoke from each barrel and then heard the roar. His instinct was to duck. Captain Poraqa stood there like a rock, arms folded over her chest, a tiny little smile on her long, angular face.

The Twilight ship, in its desperation, fired at the top of the roll, but in this instance, it would have been better to fire low, as well over half its round shot flew harmlessly through and over the ship. The Devourer's Fire had too low a profile and was moving too fast to be a firm target, at least at this angle. One lucky ball struck the crow's nest and shattered it to a pulp. The unlucky salamander in the nest screamed and fell to his death. Another round bounced across the deck, smashing everything and everyone in its path. Three more crewmembers were killed, but Poraqa didn't blink an eye.

"Damn the gods!" Lukhantl said, collecting himself. "She may be short-handed, but she's got some powerful guns."

"Aye!" Poraqa said, shifting her stance a little to get a better view of the situation. "We got lucky, though. We won't be next time if she's got another volley in her. We have to bring this matter to a close soon. Fire the chain!"

They fired a full load of split-shot. They hadn't reached the ideal rake position of fifty meters or so, but it didn't matter. The guns sounded, and the lateen sail on the mizzenmast of the Twilight ship dissolved before their eyes. Collateral damage from its destruction poured over into the main-mast, ripping deep gashes into the sail and bringing roughly a third of it down. Lukhantl could even see some of the crew being ripped apart by shot that flew head-height across the deck.

Everything grew quiet, save for Poraqa's crew who scrambled to reload another volley of chain-shot, and the wounded on the Twilight ship screaming their last. Lukhantl waited as Devourer's Fire completed its reposition to the starboard side of the Twilight ship and then moved into firing range.

"Will she try another broadside?" he asked.

Poraqa shrugged. "I'd wager that, due to limited crew, they have to shift gunners from port to starboard to reload. They could if time were convenient, but we're not going to give them that time."

She barked orders to her crew. "Bring her about, and turn her into the prize!"

"Get your boarders ready," she said to Lukhantl.

Lukhantl nodded and handed over the spyglass, his face reddening with deep fire.

His borders were assembled near the main-mast, with make-shift clubs sharp with lekelidon teeth, boarding axes, cutlasses, and rusty broadswords at the ready. A corsair crew rarely had the finest weaponry, but they made up for it in tenacity. Grapplers with hooks, rope, and modified ladders waited near the port railing. Lukhantl made sure everyone was in place, then he said, "All right, brothers, sisters, steady your courage. They have a weakened crew, and the raking has weakened them even further. But a wounded snake will fight to the death; you know this. Stay together and attack en masse. They have our brothers in the hold.

"I understand that our nature is to battle with fury; trust me, I do. I know that sometimes, the fire, the rage, can overwhelm you in your desire for blood. But in your rage, take caution and do not kill any of our own. If you do, I will kill you. Understand?"

They gave a collective "aye," and Lukhantl led them to the railing.

Despite their skill and care, Poraqa's sailors purposely slammed Devourer's Fire into the Twilight ship. Not strong enough to be considered a ram, true, but one of Lukhantl's crew fell overboard. There was no time to try to save him, as the hull ran him over, and he was lost forever.

"Fire!"

This time it was Lukhantl who gave the order. Chain-shot roared out of the ship's port guns and hit the Twilight ship at point-blank range. The slaver had a higher deck than the salamander corsair, and thus the shot was angled upward for maximum effect. Wood splintered. Kin inside the Twilight ship screamed as shot found its way through gun ports and slaughtered cannon crews. The enemy gunwale shattered up and down the hull, and the few men who had been defending it, trying to ready their serrated short-swords and small hand crossbows for the assault, either died in place, or fell back from the concussive rush of so much hot, whistling iron.

One culverin from the Twilight ship fired a half-load of razor-sharp iron needles known as 'The Teeth of Leith,' cutting a swath through Lukhantl's assembled boarders, killing three and knocking many others down.

Then the Twilight crew fired the ballistae from the stern swivel. The iron chain attached to the massive bolt sounded like a lightning strike as it pulled taut flying over the Devourer's deck. Lukhantl ducked to avoid being struck as it smashed into the main mast and hooked itself on the starboard side. Splintered wood, sail, and rigging fell everywhere; and for a moment, it seemed as if the crew might lose its heart. Then the ships struck each other again due to the pull of the ballistae chain, and Lukhantl wasted no time barking his order.

"Attack!"

The distance was short, but the angle gave the defenders the advantage. Grapples were set, and salamander crew began to climb up the hull of the slaver, rough and scaly hand over hand. Each grapple team had a stout brother assigned for spitting duty. Whenever some Twilight sailor was brave enough to return to the gunwale and try a crossbow shot down at the climbers, the spitter was required to put him down with a nasty gout of poisonous fire in his face. Lukhantl watched the action for a time, but he could not resist joining his brothers in the fight.

He took to a rope and began to climb, his boarding axe tucked in at his belt. Despite the grapple hooks set all along the slaver hull, the movement of the waves made climbing difficult. His hands, his shoulders, ached at the effort. But he kept climbing, kept pulling his weight up from one knot to the next, until he was at the top.

There, he pulled his axe and punched it into the face of a waiting Kin crewman who took an errant sword swing at Lukhantl's head. The wretched and twisted elf, whose dark armor glistened with salamander blood, whose pale skin shined with sweat, dropped the sword and fell into a bloody lump.

Other Kin defenders had tried to hastily assemble a battle line along the port gunwale. They fired their crossbows as Lukhantl's boarders rushed them, and a few went down in the powerful volley of bolts, but Lukhantl kept pressing the attack. With his axe swinging, he hacked and hammered his way through the defenders like raw meat.

An explosion rocked the assault. Lukhantl fell to the ground, kept himself from being crushed by the weight of the attack, and noticed that one of the Kin had a bag of small handheld bombs. The Kin pulled another bomb out and tried to light the fuse, but in the chaos of the fight, he was finding it hard to keep steady.

Lukhantl sprang to his feet, muscled his way through the press of fighters, and reached the elf before he had a chance to light another bomb. He knocked the bag from the Kin's grasp and struggled with him to pull the bomb from his other hand. He hammered at the Kin's thin, sallow face with the spike of his axe, and finally, as the spike pierced his eye, the Kin screamed and his hand unclasped. The unlit bomb rolled free into the center of the clash, and it was kicked repeatedly as the assault wavered back and forth.

The Kin were putting up a good fight, and it seemed to Lukhantl that his boarding attempt would be in vain. Then he saw salamander crew fighting for control of the ballistae swivel gun at the stem of the ship. Its base was damaged, it teetered on the swivel, but the bolt and firing mechanisms were in good order.

Lukhantl fought his way through the mass once again, taking one Kin sailor down with a crack across his sweaty, bald pate with the boarding axe. In turn, Lukhantl took a cut across his right arm. He fell to his knees in pain, feeling raw heat emanating from the wound. He staggered forward the last few remaining meters and found salamander crew there, holding the ballistae and fighting off three Kin sailors. But his allies were a mess. Lacerations everywhere; hot, fiery blood seeping out of every deep cut. Their energy was waning, but they were holding firm.

Take a rest, my brothers, Lukhantl said to himself as he pushed them all out of the way and took their place.

He killed the first Kin assailant outright with a spike stab from his axe through the throat. The others hesitated, then tried to reengage. Lukhantl saw the closest holding a long knife dripping with some form of oily yellow poison. He twisted the ballistae swivel and knocked the creature aside. Lukhantl hugged the bolt in place, knowing how foolish it had been to use it as a club. One more harsh push or yank, and the swivel would crack and be useless. But wasn't that the point: allow it to be damaged, destroyed, so that it could not be used again? Under normal circumstances, yes, Lukantl knew that. But this was not a normal circumstance. The Kin had bombs, and used improperly, or fumbled in battle, they could knock a ho—

The Kin came at him again. Lukhantl ducked, letting the ballistae take the sword slash. The blade skidded off with a spark. The Kin struck again. The ballistae sparked even greater.

A boot struck him in the side of the head. Dizzy, Lukhantl rolled away, using his tail for balance and dodging another boot strike, and another. Another Kin buccaneer was coming on strong, and Lukhantl found it difficult to recover. To his surprise, however, the boarding axe was still in his hand. He gripped it tightly, held it up, and blocked another sword strike with its haft. He turned the Kin's ankle and hooked his pant cuff with the axe spike. Lukhantl kicked up and struck the buccaneer's groin. The Kin groaned, grabbed his crotch, and stumbled to the left.

He pushed the screaming Kin away. He tried getting up, but a large explosion below-decks rocked the entire ship. Another explosion and the center of the ship buckled upward.

The main mast toppled like a tree, its crumpled and shattered rigging and canvas falling like lava ash everywhere, indiscriminately covering and striking both salamander and Kin. Sea water began to rise up through the cracked hull, and the ship listed to the left.

Lorquan!

He suddenly remembered why he was here, risking his life and the corsair crew. Poraqa's warning about his anger and about how it could get in the way of his mission was ringing loud and clear in his mind. But what did her words matter anymore, for the explosion in the center had pitched her body up and then down into the salty waves. Perhaps she and the others around her thrown into the sea as well had survived the explosion and were clutching wooden planks to keep from drowning. It did not matter. His captain was out of the fight, the Kin ship was sinking, and he was in charge now.

He staggered to his feet, using the ballistae like a crutch. Ignoring the chaos around him, he turned the weapon toward Devourer's Fire. The Twilight ship was still listing left, taking on water, and pulling the smaller salamander corsair ship with it. Lukhantl aimed carefully, pitching down so that the ballistae was pointed right at the center of his ship, toward the galley and captain's quarters, and pulled the trigger.

The large bolt whistled as it flew through the smoke-filled air, pulling the oiled chain with it. Lukhantl stepped away to ensure that he did not get caught up in the pull. He could feel the wind off of it as it unraveled beside him.

The ballistae struck Devourer's Fire and punched a hole in the captain's quarters, finding purchase below. Probably on the barrels of their guns, Lukhantl figured, but that too didn't matter. Shooting at one's own ship was grounds for execution, even between pirate crews, but it was necessary under the circumstances. For now, the ballistae's chain mechanism was pulling the chain back, strong and taut, and keeping its sinking ship into contact with the corsair's. Lukhantl steadied himself as the ships struck one another again, the smaller hull now holding the larger in place. Good, he thought, that'll keep us afloat long enough for me to find my brother.

He moved to the center of the ship, through the continued chaos of hand-to-hand. The deck was slick with salt water, blood and gore, and it was difficult to walk without slipping. He used his tail again for balance, a nice advantage that all salamanders had over their non-prehensile foe, though it could get in the way as well. This time, it did not, and served to knock a few Kin aside as he moved.

Beneath a mixed pile of bodies, he found a companionway down into the hold. There was a commotion down there, he could hear, and a large one. But he could also hear water pour through the crack in the hull. Lukhantl's heart grew hot with fear, but he breathed deep, girded his courage, held his boarding axe at the ready, and descended.

It was dark, the air filled with smoke. It was hot, but that did not bother him, for his own rough hide was giving off even more heat. It was obvious that salamanders were near, for as he moved further into the hold, the heat climbed higher and steam replaced smoke.

Water now was knee deep, but Lukhantl moved with conviction toward the most horrible sounds that he had ever heard, echoing off the insides of this doomed ship. The piercing screams of dying Kin, and guttural barks of dying salamanders. Chains striking chains. Swords cutting through leather and bone. Other, though smaller, explosions, and the flashes of light from erupting bombs. That's what must have caused the explosions, Lukhantl thought as he struggled to find his brother. A bomb must have ignited the powder used to fire the cannons.

He entered a room, and there, three salamanders were beating a downed Kin with belaying pins. One of them Lukhantl recognized.

"Lorquan!" he shouted, though his clutch brother did not respond, so enraptured he was in the fight. His enslavement shackles still hung from his pink, swollen wrists, though their chains had been cut. Under the thrill of battle, his body was near twice its size and blood red, his back muscles rippling with each strike against the Kin. He was intimidating to look at, even here, in this small space. Perhaps even more so in such cramped quarters, Lukhantl thought, and that was why Lorquan had risen in the ranks above all others in their clutch… including Lukhantl.

But now was not the time to revel in the lust of battle. The ship was sinking and all their lives were at risk.

Lukhantl moved forward swiftly and grabbed Lorquan's arm in mid-swing. It took all his strength to stop the blow.

"Lorquan!" He shouted, and this time, he was heard.

In his rage, Lorquan rounded on him, his breath the stench of sulfur. Then he stilled as he seemed to recognize who held his arm.

Lukhantl finally let go. "It's me, brother. Me! Lukhantl. I am here to save you. Come, let us get out of here, before—"

Lorquan looked down at the Kin corpse, nodded, and moved to the door, toward the fight still roiling near the gun bays.

"No," Lukhantl said, trying to reach out and grab his brother. "You come with me. The ship is doomed. We have little time. Let us gather who we can and go!"

Lukhantl tried pulling his brother in the other direction, toward the companionway he had descended, but Lorquan was too strong, too angry, too filled with rage and battle lust to listen. He pushed Lukhantl aside. "No! I am going to kill them all for what they have done, to me and to my men."

"And then what?" Lukhantl asked. "They will be dead, and we will be too. The ship is sinking, Lorquan. Look to your feet, your legs, and tell me I am wrong. I have delayed the inevitable for a time, but it's sinking. We have to leave… now!"

Lorquan paused as if he were considering Lukhantl's words, then his face grew red and stern, his teeth clicked, his black-red tongue darted. "No! We have to finish this, so that they do not rise again and take more slaves. We finish them now."

He pushed Lukhantl away and raced out of the room with the other two salamanders. Lukhantl followed, calling his clutch brother's name, but Lorquan did not listen, did not respond.

Everywhere Lukhantl turned, there was fighting. Close in, desperate hand-to-hand action. One such engagement had a salamander wrestling the Kin's first mate to the floor and biting its neck like a beast. Blood flowed out from around his teeth as the Kin tried pushing his assailant away. Another Kin was trying to take a belaying pin away from a salamander in shackles, but the place where they struggled was narrow, and the elf didn't have the proper angle and leverage. The salamander prevailed, keeping his hold on the pin and smacking it across the Kin's mouth in a shower of blood and teeth. The knocked-out enemy fell atop Lukhantl, and he lay still, protected by the elf's weight, waiting for the maddened, out of control salamander to move on to the next fight. When it was gone, Lukhantl pushed the dead Kin away and kept going.

He followed Lorquan into another room where a row of lockers lined the far wall. Chains ran through the handles from locker to locker, and each had a strong cast-iron lock.

A mass of salamander slaves pressed into the room, as if they were trying to crush the Kin therein, who were lined up in front of the lockers, desperately trying not to get crushed. The Kin tried firing crossbows into the mass. One shot hit the salamander next to Lukhantl. He convulsed and fell dead. Then Lukhantl saw Lorquan, in the middle of the press, swinging a belaying pin at a buccaneer.

"Lorquan!" he screamed, but his brother couldn't hear him.

A little further into the room, the right side of the mass lurched forward, and the Kin on that side in front of his locker went down. A breach was secured. The salamanders rushed the locker, grabbed the chain, and started pulling. Lorquan tried moving to help, but Lukhantl had had enough.

With all his strength, Lukcantl reached into the mass and grabbed his brother's tail and yanked back so hard, Lorquan fell to the floor. Lukhantl did not let go. He pulled and pulled, heedless of Lorquan's struggle against him. His brother screamed, and Lukhantl screamed back. He pulled Lorquan free, and then grabbed him in a hug, wrapping his body around his brother. Lorquan struggled. He punched, pulled, pushed, bit. He was strong, and it hurt, but Lukhantl did not let go.

Then an explosion hit the locker room. The mass of bodies above them shielded them from the brunt of the concussion. Kin and salamander alike were tossed into the air, their torn, mangled bodies falling in heaps upon them. Another explosion, this time from the other side. The wail of the wounded was deafening, as more bodies were tossed about the room. Lukhantl tried seeing what was going on, but they were buried beneath the heap. It was hard to breathe, but he found a hole in the wounded mass and pulled himself and Lorquan to it so that they could find air. There was smoke, thick choking smoke that filled the locker room. They could not get a fresh breath.

And then the hull wrenched, turned, twisted, and finally gave way.

The entire mass of bodies was flushed into the sea, below the wreckage of the Twilight ship. Lukhantl held his breath; he hoped Lorquan was smart enough to do as well. His brother struggled in his grip, but he did not let go. He held on tight with one arm and swam with the other.

It took time and effort to pull his massive, wailing brother out of the mangle of bodies and battered ship debris, but they crested the surf and took deep breaths.

"You damned fool!" Lukhantl said, trying his best to grab a plank nearby. "I told you the ship was gone, but you didn't listen. Why do you never listen?"

Lorquan spit steaming salt water from his mouth, cleared his throat, and breathed deeply. He took hold of the plank as well and hooked his other arm on a passing barrel. He shook excess water from his face and eyes, blinking several times. "There are—there are some things more important than survival, my brother."

"Well, you survived all right," Lukhantl said, "but how many of your guard are now dead because of those last two explosions? And how many will drown and become food for sharks due to your stubbornness?" He pointed to the ships. "And look there. The Twilight ship is now dragging our ship to its death."

And indeed it was. The larger Twilight ship, heavy with water, began to slip below the waves, and the two ballistae chains were holding tight and pulling Devourer's Fire down with it, despite the desperate attempt of a few of its remaining crew to cut tethers and run. Lukhantl shook his head. Both ships were out, both crews down. Was it worth it?

He was about to scold his brother again, then thought better of it. Lorquan's tortured expression gave his true feelings away: he was aggrieved and sorrowful for his dead men. In the cool water, his face grew pale, sallow, and though salamanders could not cry like other races of Mantica, they felt the pain of loss all the same.

"Well," Lukhantl said, "I'm glad you survived."

"Thank you, brother," Lorquan said. "I will tell you someday about my trials at the hands of these infernal slavers, but not now. Now, we must make for that clump of rocks yonder, climb them, dry, and receive the gift of the sun."

Lukhantl nodded and began waving his tail back and forth. Lorquan did the same, and they swam quickly through the wreckage toward the small rock island on the horizon.

"Don't worry," Lorquan said as they swam, as if he could read Lukhantl's thoughts. "Your blood is too hot and bitter for shark bait. We'll make it, though I can't say the same for the Kin."

All around them, the tainted elves struggled to survive the attacks of sharks. It was another horrific and bloody symbol of this terrible action that he, Lukhantl, had put in motion to save his brother. And despite the madness of it, he was happy. He was alive. His brother was alive, and perhaps that was all that mattered. For they would survive and rise again to bring war to the Twilight Kin, and that always made salamanders happy.

Lukhantl beamed with pride and joy, and together, he and his brother swam toward the sun.

THE EMERALD EYES

By Michael McCann

"These are the new supply lines here? South of the steppes?" Commander Agrias said as she tapped the map laid out in front of her. The makeshift war table that she had erected in her pavilion was covered in various figurines, maps, and scrolls. Several days of combat had begun to take its toll on her, and one would know this simply by looking at what her current living conditions were. The cot that served as her bed, where restless sleep would only serve to distract her, was home to various tunics and surcoats; the chest that kept her things was wide open with even more items spilling out of its insides. She was not the woman who would tidy things up just to make herself more comfortable. Not with her men risking their lives against the Abyssal creatures edging ever closer to the encampment.

"Aye, ma'm. The runners returned a short while ago. Missives have already been sent to the Kingdoms." The scout stood ever at the ready for Agrias's next command, but it was clear he was tired.

"Thank you. Find a meal in one of the tents and get some rest, soldier. Dismissed." Agrias peered at the map once more. No matter how many times she'd find herself staring at the thing, she had always hoped something would jump out at her. Some hidden path that she hadn't noticed before or some long-forgotten trail that the Primovantians may have used when treating with the elves. No matter how long she stood there, the breastplate of her armor growing heavier and the weight of the longsword at her side feeling like twice its size, nothing ever came.

She let out a sigh between her teeth and let her head hang loosely, several spots popping as she rotated it. The temporary relief soothed her. She closed her eyes and could remember the sounds of spells colliding with the stonework, the screams her men made as an efreet got lucky and met its mark. The sound of warfare kept her awake most nights and little rest was in her future. Especially if she failed her duty and lost the battle.

While they had been able to turn back any Abyssal forces, the efreets that had burned alive any militia she had sent past the no-man's-land of the battle had proven to be the biggest thorn in her side. She had ordered her finest archers to scale the precarious, unfinished ledges of the wall to try and pick them off; but after one of them, Darren Longstrider, had taken a bolt to the chest and landed just outside the camp, she called them back. By the second day, morale was beginning to wane, and seeing the half-charred corpse of one their comrades did little to bolster her troops' confidence. The only hope she had remaining was the envoy she had sent requesting aid… and the reply was not what she had wanted to hear. One of her runners had gotten lost and had been sent back mutilated beyond recognition. Not by the Abyssal fiends that she had beaten back, but by a previously unknown horde of orcs. Thank the gods that the other runner had made it to the Kingdoms, but the word she received from home was almost just as concerning.

She had asked for reinforcements. No care was given as to how many or what they specialized in. She didn't care if the additional warriors were archers she could line the wall with, or swordsmen to meet the orcs head on. If the rumors were true, then a horde of orcs would be a flood in which she could not stop with the options left now. She had eaten her meals over conversation and contemplation about when exactly the barbaric orcs would lay siege upon her camp, but so far no sign of their arrival was given. Agrias's stomach churned when she received word the Kingdoms weren't sending her any reinforcements... at least not human reinforcements. The letter addressing the issue simply said one thing, or it might as well have, Agrias thought.

We've hired a mercenary band of ogres to bolsters your forces, Commander.

"Any day now they'll be here. And I have not the supplies to handle them." Agrias leaned back, not knowing if she meant the orcs or her ogre support, the faulds on her armor clinking against the cuisse upon her thighs. The plate armor she wore was not pretty, nor was it home to any decorative etchings or metalwork. It was exactly as she wanted it, the armor of a soldier, a warrior. The blood she had spilled in the years gone by proved her prowess, but she had requested nothing of her newfound rank save for the ceremonial sash that hung off her right shoulder. It was once a stunning ocean blue that looked like a wave itself when she rode into battle, but not after the trying fight her and her soldiers had put up securing the building site. Now it looked like a tattered cloth, stained with mud, singed at the edges where she was nearly engulfed by an efreet's blast, and spotted with blood that she knew was not hers.

As she tucked a loose strand of her blonde hair behind her ear, the bun she wore had long since began falling out before midday, she heard shuffling just outside the pavilion. Someone had barked an order to several soldiers, but not with the voice of a hardened general who shouted obscenities at his troops to light fires under their asses; it was the smooth almost liquid-like words of her lieutenant, Sir Ewan Alistair.

She did not raise her head from the map as the lieutenant stopped just five feet from her; she could almost feel his eyes squinting and his head cocking to one side as it was apt to do. She tapped the metal banded finger of her gauntlet against the war table and cleared her throat. Without addressing his presence, she made for the small bedside table where a bottle of wine, a plain looking goblet, and her waterskin lay.

"If I'm bothering you, I can go write my name in the ash upon the wall?" Sir Ewan asked with a bite of his all-too predictable sarcasm. She slowly turned her head, her cheek pressed against the raised collar of her cuirass. Out of the corner of her eye, she could see the smug expression on the man's face. She was a soldier willing to unsheathe her sword alongside her men, and Sir Ewan would do the same, but he would be critiquing their form and position of their shields while doing it.

"Your jokes never seize, Lieutenant." She took a deep drink from the waterskin and winced as some forgotten bruise reminded her of itself as she sat down on her cot.

"No, I suppose not. But neither does your sulking. It's a healthy balance, I'd say." He crossed his arms and stood looking over the war table. His dark, charcoal eyes darted back and forth as he took in the latest addition, a hand running through the equally as dark mop of hair on his head. Agrias looked the man up and down and saw a splotch of blood that had stained the pauldron upon his shoulder.

While she was covered head to toe in plate mail, Sir Ewan was more haphazardly armored. His arms were uncovered, save for the chainmail hauberk hidden beneath a cuirass and a sleeveless gambeson. No armor covered his legs, save mismatched poleyns to protect errant blows to the knees. If it weren't for the greatsword strapped to his back, one would wonder why someone with his rank would risk injury over being so unarmored. But the movement that Sir Ewan was known for, despite the size of his sword, had earned him many nicknames and sobriquets among the troops. Agrias's favorite was Sir Ewan the Streak. It only filled her head with images of the man happily wandering into battle stark-naked.

"We've managed to set up supply lines. That's good news. After seeing that boy come back after the orcs had gotten done with him, I didn't know if it was possible." Sir Ewan picked up a small scroll and began reading it; finding it uninteresting, he tossed it to the side and picked up another. "How did you manage it?"

The commander rose, once more feeling the pain in her hip, and pointed to a small circle she had made over a noticeably bland piece of land on the map.

"There's a few miles of unmarked forest there. I told the messengers to take the long way south, to duck into the foliage as to avoid any enemy scouts from spotting them."

"Orcs have goblins, Commander. Unlike their large and sloppy masters, goblins are skirmishers. You could have sent them into a death trap."

"I know this, sir. But I didn't. And now we have our supply lines. Need we discuss it further?" Agrias took the tone of voice she had when she needed to pull rank. With his quick tongue, Sir Ewan was just as swift to not press any issue when that voice came out of her.

"Of course not. But, I should update you on our red, hellish friends from the Abyss."

"Hopefully, this is good news."

"Come see for yourself, Commander." With a forced and over exaggerated bow, Sir Ewan parted the flap leading out of her tent. With a disgruntled snarl and a look that could kill, she ducked out of the pavilion.

The scene was not pretty, but she had seen worse. Men and women were all scattered around going about their duties. Some were chopping wood for fires, some were eating bread while rolling dice. Smaller tents dotted the landscape, a relatively flat ground with only slight elevations here and there. The commander's tent lay at the very top of the highest hill, which Sir Ewan thought a poor choice as it made her an easy target should the errant Abyssal gargoyle get courageous and attack the camp, but she swore that she needed a view of the wall more than anything.

And it was what her eyes went to immediately. The half constructed wall was of a pale stone, it was sturdy and inexpensive; but not unlike her armor, it didn't have to look pretty, it just needed to be stable. Most of the scaffolding had been torn down to prevent fires when the efreets showed up. The top of the wall was nearly three stories high and would serve as an ample defensive position once it was complete. The ramparts were dotted every six feet with arrow windows as to provide full cover for any long-ranged assault, and the areas in between were smooth and beveled to allow boiling oil to be spilled onto anyone, or anything, from scaling its surfaces. If it weren't for the alarming, jagged v-shaped hole of incomplete stonework, one would think it'd be complete. The Abyssal horde had saw fit to halt the progress.

Agrias stopped midstride and focused all her attention on the wall. She examined every little crevice, every imperfection of the stonework. In her head, she looked upon it as if it were another enemy, one she needed to outthink, outmaneuver, and finally put down. Out of the corner of her eye, she could see Sir Ewan with his hands on his hips, judging her for analyzing the stone enemy.

There was more to it than that though. As the clouded sky gave way to some sunlight, she could see that look in his eyes; the one where he tried to see through the guise of a commander and toward the woman underneath. She was sure that he, like most others, found her beautiful, but Agrias knew that Sir Ewan did not focus on such things on the battlefield. He took her word to heart, and though her sharp jawline, petite nose, and thin lips offered much in the way of attraction, she often found him giving that look into her eyes. Her green, vibrant eyes that attracted many long looks of men through her life.

But, to almost define the dynamic between the two leaders as Ewan was busy mulling over whatever thoughts in his head, Agrias had already restarted her stride and nearly passed him before he shook himself and fell in behind her. Unnoticed by Sir Ewan, she let the faintest hint of a smirk appear on her face.

They walked the camp for nearly an hour. Agrias stopped to check in with her spymaster, the medical tent, the blacksmiths; each reporting the usual and nothing of interest. Finally, she came to Darius, her taskmaster. He was an aged man, Darius, but he was kind and had survived countless years of being on the field of battle. While he was no war hero with tales of valor and bravery like Sir Ewan, Agrias had always thought the man deserved a song or two about him.

"Commander! I can only hope you found some rest?" he greeted with a bow and a caring gaze.

"Yes, she did actually. Though the muttering of battle plans in her sleep was a bit disconcerting," the knight piped up from behind her. Darius gave a quick, confused glance behind Agrias's shoulder, as though he wasn't sure if he should believe Sir Ewan.

"I did, Darius. The constant bombardment from those fiends however…"

"Ah, yes! The efreet. Fascinating though they are, I am glad to see them finally put down. The man who put a bolt through the last one has named his crossbow Fiend Killer." Darius smiled warmly, almost father-like.

"He named his crossbow!? Hah!" the lieutenant laughed, and while it wasn't unusual coming from the knight, Agrias enjoyed the brief moment of levity and the comforting thought of one less enemy to contend with.

"That is terrific news. It was well-timed too. The men are recovering nicely in the medical tent as well. Minor burns for most, though I am retiring the soldiers who took more damage. I need not go down in records as a woman who forced her men to fight on after such a thing."

"We are going to need all the sword-arms we can get, Commander." Sir Ewan chimed in, the humor had left him just as swiftly as it had come.

"I'm not throwing already injured people against this horde, Ewan. The orcs are merciless. They'd cut them in two before they could take a swing." Once more, the voice of someone in position took over. Agrias noticed Darius shuffle uncomfortably at the disagreement. It wasn't often she was openly defied, but

Sir Ewan had also earned some 'titles' for his quick tongue as well as his quick feet.

"Which brings me to my next point, Darius," the taskmaster regrouped his stance and once more looked like a man ready to take an order. "We're expecting... guests."

Sir Ewan clicked his tongue and scoffed. If she were in private, Agrias thought she may have done the same.

"Ogres. They're sending us fu-"

"Enough, Lieutenant!" It was barely a yell, but the bite behind her order was enough to catch the attention of a few passing soldiers. Sir Ewan sighed and crossed his arms, shaking his head.

"Y-yes, Commander. There have already been tents made up for them, and we've rationed what we can manage for their meals. I am afraid, however, that unless we send out a hunting party or two, we're going to be in short supply of food. Unfortunately, we do not have enough supplies to see to the treatment of any of their wounded or-"

"Ogres don't have wounded, Darius. They either live or they die on the battlefield. I saw one of them fight off a werewolf with its arm hanging on by a sliver of flesh. And despite the fact that it died, it managed to take the werewolf with him. You need not worry about the medical tents." Sir Ewan chimed in once more. The disdain in his voice for the ogres wasn't hidden, and if he could wear a sigil showcasing his displeasure of the mercenaries, he would.

"Very good, Darius. If you could give me written reports of our coffers and food stuffs by nightfall?" Agrias asked.

"Of course, Commander." With one final glance, Darius nodded to Sir Ewan and returned to his duties. Darius was quickly met by a cloaked man who was carrying a crate of poultices, rags, and other medicinal agents. The two quickly began to make their way across the camp. Agrias was not envious of Darius. She only had to send the men out into the field, she didn't have to listen to their longings for home and their cries for help as they lie dying in a tent. Darius seemingly did it all, always quick to jump in with whatever task needed doing while at camp.

"He's not going to be able to do this much longer." Agrias said aloud to no one in particular.

"Who? The old man? Well, you'd be better off fighting a horde of orc by yourself then to try and get him to stop." Sir Ewan added.

"Do you intend to fight until you're gray in the hair, Ewan?" the commander asked as she watched Darius walk away.

"I don't think we get to live that long, Commander. We'll die on the field with our swords in hand as the battle continues on around us." Sir Ewan's voice grew grim, an oddity in and of itself. "Its what warriors do. We die bloody, but we get the songs and the tales over campfires. Men like Darius get a warm bed and hopefully their children's children watching over them in their final moments. But no one will remember them. It's the way it has always worked."

Without a word, Agrias turned on her heel once more and made her way down the main stretch of the camp that led to the wall. She wanted to see what kind of state it was in after being buffeted during the last skirmish. Behind her, the knight followed with his clean-shaven cheeks taught as he clenched his teeth. She had caught him doing this in the past, and she knew the warrior well enough that she needn't even look at him. The cloak he wore around his neck billowed in the wind like the legends that they would one day depict him as.

The two of them walked the length of the wall, talking strategy and tactics. Commander Agrias pointed out areas where the wall was damaged and pieces of it had been blasted off. The ground had been stained a dark shade of red from the bloodshed; areas where injured men bled out leaving their echo on the area. The v-shaped hole was littered with axes and swords that had been discarded in favor of a hasty retreat. Bolts from her soldiers' crossbows glistened as the afternoon lit up the battlefield, and every so often, a fleeting ray of sunlight would reflect off of a dead man's shield out in no-man's-land.

Agrias and Ewan scaled the ramparts and peered out into the distance. As they stood in silence looking out into the north, the knight took out a small wineskin from his pouch and took a heavy swig; after he was finished, he silently offered some to the commander, who turned it to down with a stern, admonishing look. She could sense that he was concentrating on her eyes, perhaps trying to see something in them that she dared not reveal with words.

Agrias leaned on the merlons, her gauntlets clicking as she put her hands down. Ewan followed her lead, with his bare forearms supporting his weight.

"You know if it weren't for the carnage that occurred below, this would be quite a sight." As he finished speaking, the wineskin found its way to his lips once more.

"The world is a beautiful place, Ewan. You just have to look past all the creatures and people populating it," the commander said without even taking a second glance at her subordinate.

"That's just the most uplifting thing I heard all day, Agrias. 'Look at the world and behold! But look at its people and tremble!'" he said in a mocking, almost preachy, tone.

"Your words don't cut me, Lieutenant," she said, fighting the smile she felt slowly coming across her face.

"Never said I was trying to, Agrias." She watched as he switched his position so his back was to the northern wilds, watching as the camp began to light their evening fires and the men who had been resting all day came out of their tents. "But don't think I didn't notice you smirk. You should try it more often, you'll find it is much easier to kill things knowing you had a hearty laugh about it first."

"Is that all this life is to you, Sir Ewan Alistair? Laughing and fighting? Are those the only things you consider yourself? A jester and a killer?" Agrias asked, finally taking a good look at the man next to her. It was in the glowing light of dusk that the man's glossy scars, running from all different directions upon his arms, finally became apparent to her.

"You ask so many questions, Agrias, but never answer the ones people have of you," he said, slyly dodging the inquiries himself.

"I lack answers that I am unwillingly to give." An edge of self-defense made its way into her words; she saw him twitch as Ewan registered the tone that was not terribly unlike the one she reserved for commands.

"Oh, yes. I know that. You'd spend an entire evening answering questions about battle, tactics, how best to use a kite shield, or how to properly cut into a Gore Rider's haunch to spill its rider out onto the ground. Those are answers you'll go into full detail about."

"What are you-"

"And don't deny it, Commander! I've seen it myself. This is our... what, sixth assignment with one another? These aren't questions that people want to hear unless you're standing over that accursed war table of yours. What about the real ones?"

"And what real ones would those be, Ewan?" She stood with her arms crossed, a look of determination on her face. It didn't help matters that Ewan took one look at her and laughed.

"Never mind. You'd send me to the stocks, even if a Krudger stood over me with its warhammer, for asking you."

"No, Sir Ewan. I command you to tell me." She could feel her cheeks becoming flushed as she sought to keep her cool.

"Questions about real life, Agrias! What's your favorite flower? What kind of wine do you like after a proper meal? Do you prefer cotton or wool? Who was the first boy to ever have your heart?"

"We are not talking about this," she declared as she began marching off toward the ladder leading back into the camp.

"Oh, now you're just doing this on purpose!" Sir Ewan said, tucking his now wineskin back into its home on his belt. She stopped and shot him a look that caused him to tense. Wordlessly, she continued to make her way down.

"Agrias, stop."

"What do you want, Lieutenant?" she asked, the agitation barely being hidden.

"I'll give you one of my answers. You asked me if I only thought of myself as a killer?" She only gave him silence as he stood with his mouth half-opened. She gestured for him to continue, despite wanting to keep him standing there looking like a fool for a few more seconds.

"Daisies, a deep red wine, wool in the winter but cotton in the summer, and Gretchen, she was a lord's daughter I met shortly before my knighthood. Those are what make me much more than a killer."

Commander Agrias remained there with one foot on the rungs. She went to answer, but a commotion just below them, back at camp, caught her attention first. Peering behind her to the best of her ability, she could see men stop and all stare in one direction. Sir Ewan also stood straight and his eyes narrowed as he watched the camp below.

"They're here."

*****

The two of them finished their quick descent, Commander Agrias leaping off as soon as she was a safe distance down. It wasn't until she stood straight that the bruising on her hip made itself known once more. Behind her, she could hear the loud crashing of armor as Sir Ewan slid down the ladder behind her. The two of them firmly in stride, side-by-side, made their way into the eastern end of the camp, the soldiers nervously parting for them to make their way through. Some of them were too busy trying to steal a look at what the rising noise was about and were nearly pushed out of the way by Sir Ewan. She had been trying to make her way through the growing crowds, and just behind her she could hear the knight starting to bark at the soldiers to return to their duties or meals, albeit with expletives thrown in for good measure.

As she passed her troops, she caught fragments of the men's gasps and their almost fascinated conversations about their visitors. Agrias had only fought with ogres once before, and though she was merely a foot soldier at that time, she remembered the brutality and the unending stamina that they brought to war. If the Abyssal forces, or even the orcs for that matter, tried a full-scale assault on the camp, they would be met with a relentless wave of muscle, gunpowder, and violence. A small part of her was happy that her men would perhaps now feel more comfortable, but the other was worried that she'd be viewed as weak for having to rely on the infamous mercenaries. She didn't blame her forces for not understanding why they'd been employed for the upcoming fight, nor did she want them to. If they knew that without the ogres they would all die horrible deaths, she would be commanding ghosts and scarecrows with bucket helms and short swords strapped to them.

When she and Sir Ewan finally made it to the edge of the camp where the ogres had arrived, the breath was nearly taken from her. The gores that pulled their chariots were all squealing mercilessly and were two seconds away from trying to impale one another. The infamous smell of an ogre mercenary company eked its way into her nostrils, and she had to fight to exclaim its awful potency. But just as she finally found herself choking back the bile, she saw one of the ogres, with its orange, reddish skin covering rippling muscle, pick up two barrels from the back of a chariot like they were nothing. He cried out with a guttural tone and laughed loud enough to wake the entire camp as he watched another one growl at a passing human, causing the man to yelp and scurry along.

She breathed in quickly, kicking herself after she nearly tasted the smell on her tongue, and made her way to one of the heavily armored warriors who was busy pointing and growling at the others. He was bald on top, leaving only the heavy, grime-filled beard coming to a point just below his clavicle. The signature under-bite of their skulls was particularly pronounced on this one, and she couldn't help but notice the cruel blades that were strapped to his back, large enough that a human would have to two-hand them like one of Sir Ewan's greatswords.

"I am Commander Agrias, I'm in charge of this unit. Are you the leader of this band?" The duel-wielding ogre quickly turned around, and whether his face contorted into a deep, hate filled scowl or if it was merely always like that, the commander did not know. He snorted deeply and walked away from her without a word.

"Sir!" Agrias called out. She closed her eyes and kicked herself realizing how stupid it sounded referring to an ogre the same way she would a knight. Now she could only hope that the entire camp wasn't watching her fail miserably at her diplomacy.

"He ain't gonna answer you, Commander." The deep, booming voice nearly shook her out of her boots, and she quickly turned around to see two ogres quickly making their way over to her. Much to her embarrassment, she caught a glimpse of her soldiers all huddled up in a crowd, stopped just thirty feet of the gores that were now being fed what looked like slop. At the very edge of the group, she saw Darius and Sir Ewan staring, the latter with his arms crossed and all but radiating his hatred as if it was some spell.

The two ogres stomped their way over to her, and for the first time since she was a little girl, she felt small, almost powerless to do anything. A quick wave of sadness and frustration rippled through her, and she wanted to be anywhere but there.

But, she was a commander – a commander that was assigned a duty – and even though she wanted nothing to do with the mercenary band in front of her, it was what her lords had given her, and she was honor-bound to fulfill her duty to them.

"Are you the leader of this band?" She asked, knowing that ogres were not one for pomp and circumstance, nor have any desire for the pageantry that some knights and lord's bannermen oft were prone to.

The one who had spoken was massive, even among his kin. Two well-built soldiers could fit in the dented and stained plate that he wore across his chest, and the pauldrons that sat atop his colossal shoulders could be used as helmets for the average infantrymen. They weren't decorated, save for the twin spikes that jutted out at the bottom in a way that threatened to pierce his own arms with the slightest bit of ill-timed movement. He lacked faulds to protect his thighs, but instead there was matted animal fur that was decoratively braided and hung to his knees stopping just short of the armored ankle-boots that were also tipped with a spike. The jutting jaw of the ogre was covered in a fierce beard that started at the mop of hair that was slicked back with oil of some kind, and if he was a human, he'd have been told by his commanding officer to trim it in danger of looking like a vagrant. To finish the image, the ogre leader had blue war paint covering one side of his face that was starting to flake in various spots. If it was some ogrish design that had since come off, or it was designed to look that way, Agrias did not know.

"I am," he responded. It wasn't until he cracked his neck that Agrias took notice of the long handle that peered out from behind his back. The weapon it belonged to, however, she couldn't see past the ogre's massive chest.

"I am Commander Ag-"

"We heard you the first time, girl," the other ogre who had followed their leader piped up from behind him. Instantly, Agrias was reminded of Sir Ewan. And as if to read her thoughts, she saw the knight leave the gathering crowd and march his way over to her. Unfortunately, this did little to comfort her.

"She's the leader of this operation, Ogre, and we don't handle disrespect lightly in this camp." Sir Ewan scolded. She was surprised to hear the venom behind those words. It wasn't often Sir Ewan's tone lacked some kind of sarcasm or ill-timed joke. The knight stood more rigid and straightened than she had ever seen him. He quickly took his place beside her, still staring daggers at the one who had called her girl.

"And who is this ponce? The pretty one with the black hair. Your bed warmer?" the second ogre shot back with a hearty chuckle. His voice wasn't as deep as his leader's, but that meant little for this race of humanoids. While not as large as most of his brethren, this one looked no less intimidating. He lacked any beard, and he had his hair done in a tight top-knot. The warpaint on his face was much more intricate, and it seemed to loosely resemble a skull. Agrias did not allow herself to stare, as her gaze was too focused on what the man had in his arm. Slung over one shoulder and lazily keeping his wrist to balance, it was the weapon in an ogre's arsenal that would send their enemies cowering.

The blunderbuss. To call it a firearm was to do it a disservice even among human armies. While they were of dwarven craftsmanship, a blunderbuss was most deadly in the hands of an ogre. The kickback alone would be enough to knock anyone prone, save for the mercenary bands. While their crossbows were as deadly, these guns would render their target unrecognizable if they struck true.

"I am Sir Ewan, savage. And I find your sense of ineptitude when talking to superiors to be... inauspicious," the knight said, clearly enjoying his noble schooling perhaps for the first time.

"I don't know what you just said, man-girl, but I sure can tear you from limb to-" the smart-mouthed ogre was quickly stopped by a swift punch to the gut by his leader. Agrias stood there wondering when the monstrously sized one had spun around and struck him; she felt as though she merely blinked. Sir Ewan was perhaps no longer the quickest warrior in the camp.

As for the punch, Agrias thought, that was well needed.

"As I was saying," Commander Agrias continued.

"Yes, you're Captain Aggrass. I got that," the leader boomed once more. The commander did little to correct both of his inaccuracies when addressing her, fearing a punch that would send her lungs into the tent behind her.

"And you are?" she asked, trying not to stare, as she realized the ogre with the two blades on his back was now taking his place on the leader's other flank.

"I am Gresh. They call me Boss Gresh. The one who can't keep his bloody mouth shut is Ogrin. And the one you attempted to talk to is No-Tongue." Agrias was going to press for more information, but she suppressed that thought after realizing that it was probably all she was going to get from this Boss Gresh.

"No-Tongue? However did he get that name, I wonder?" While she had hoped it would comfort her, Sir Ewan's ill-timed sarcasm decided to come back at the worst time.

"He challenged me for leadership of the boys. He lost." Gresh said, as if the answer should have been obvious.

"And you didn't kill him? I daresay, maybe we could learn a thing or two from you ogres should there ever be a civil war," Sir Ewan jested, his signature smirk returning once more.

She felt lost within this group, a fact that she was not comfortable with. She was the leader of the operation, and if she had an inkling that was easy enough to dismiss before, now the feeling that she was losing grip of the situation was becoming all too overwhelming.

"Now that we've all become... acquainted. Would you care to join me in my tent and I can show you what our scouts have found out about the position of the orcish horde? There are strategies I think we'd be able to quickly defeat them with."

"Food and drink," was all Gresh answered with.

"Excuse me?" she asked.

"My men and I have been on the road for several days now. Had to put down some of those devils from the Abyss on the way. We're hungry and in the need of some strong drink. After that, we discuss your strategies," Gresh said, before he yelled orders at the rest of the band. When he turned his back and spoke the harsh language of his people, Agrias's eyes went wide as she finally saw the weapon that Boss Gresh had equipped.

"What, dare I ask, is that?" she said, weakly pointing to the weapon.

"It's a greataxe. You never seen one before?" Ogrin answered for him. To that, Sir Ewan could no longer hold back his laughter. Ogrin shot him a menacing look.

It resembled no greatsword that she had ever seen. Its blade was a dark brown, almost black in color. It was slightly curved, and instead of a clean, sharp edge, it had jagged teeth. The crude design of the blade was rivaled only by what passed as its hilt. What looked like animal bone, bent like a longbow, was wrapped in boiled leather and was peeling off in random places. The length of the 'axe' was far too long for even the most mountainous of men to wield.

But the most notable feature of it was the goblin skulls that were crudely roped around the pommel and left dangling behind Gresh's back. One was cracked down the middle, another was missing the bottom jaw, and the third and final one was larger than the others that Agrias speculated may have actually been a human's in life. She shuttered at the thought.

"With all due respect, Boss Gresh," she knew that under any other circumstance, Sir Ewan would find it hilarious to hear her say such a thing. "I beg you reconsider. Take your meal into my pavilion at least."

"Hah!" Ogrin cried out, startling several onlookers. "A human, beggin'? Usually you lot die screamin'!"

Sir Ewan flexed his fist next to her, and as subtly as she could muster, she put her hand on his forearm, attempting to calm him down.

"Look, Commander," Boss Gresh said. "We ogres don't take to fancy plans and your stratagems." With that, he shot Sir Ewan a defiant look. "We fight whatever we're paid to fight, and we don't stop until it's dead or bleeding out. So when this horde of orcs show up, we'll do just that. Point us in the direction you want us to go, and make sure the money finds its way into our hands. Is that enough talk of tactics for the night?"

Commander Agrias did little to answer the question. For once, Sir Ewan's words haunted her ever so briefly. No answer came even for a question of military topics. She watched as Boss Gresh turned his back on her and walked toward his men, No-Tongue expressionlessly following behind him. Ogrin turned as well but not without looking her up and down, snickering to himself.

"Well, that went well." Sir Ewan added right on cue.

"I don't understand why the Kingdoms wouldn't send us more soldiers. Why they hired... them, is beyond me." Agrias admitted. She ran her hand through her hair and sighed. While she too could use some food in her belly, the thought of eating only made her queasy.

The two of them turned back around and left the ogres to whatever they did when setting up a camp. It wasn't long before more Red Goblins appeared, and as the commander and her lieutenant broke up the still bunched up soldiers, they gave orders and told them to go about their business like the ogres weren't even there. Agrias feared that one of them would grow too curious or they'd start asking the wrong questions and end up on the receiving end of one Boss Gresh's blows.

Before long, Agrias and Ewan sat in her pavilion, and one of Darius's assistants brought them meals. She stood once more, staring at the war table, again hoping that the map would have changed to allow an easy answer. But the sheer embarrassment she had suffered when trying to communicate with Gresh weighed too heavily on her, and the knight's hurried eating failed to help her concentration.

"And a greataxshe!?" Ewan exclaimed with a mouth full of pheasant. "It looked like nothing more than a shaw blade shtrapped to a big shtick!"

"Why do you taunt them, Ewan?" she asked, finally unstrapping her gauntlets to put them down on the table. She sipped from the waterskin that she unbuckled from her belt and was torn between touching her food. The sheer army of flies and gnats the ogres had brought with them was something that was not lost on her. The desire to eat had left as quickly as it came with that realization.

He took a chug from his goblet and let the wine take the mouthful of food down his throat. "Because I studied for years honing my skill with all manner of weapons. The sword, the pike, I even used a lance once. Yet ogres walk around like they're the best warriors just because they can swing big clubs and hold oversized crossbows. And Whatever-He-Is Gresh's axe? I bet its name is Skull Crusher or Back Breaker!" The knight scoffed as he tossed the bones of his meal back onto the dish, the rest of the scraps discarded.

"Well, we did have one of ours name a crossbow Fiend Killer." She let a smirk actually appear on her lips for once. Ewan took notice immediately.

He laughed warmly himself instead of in the mocking manner he usually did. "So is that the secret for you finally dropping the title of commander for a night? Bring ogres into the mix and we'll see that the renowned Commander Agrias is still Cassandra Agrias after all? Though I bet even a dead man would seem funnier with ogres around."

"I haven't heard anyone use my first name in quite awhile, Ewan," she admitted.

"Well, that's what happens when you become important. The only reason people stopped referring to me as Captain Alistair is because I got a sir put in front of it all." He once more took out the wineskin and held it up for Agrias to have a sip. "Besides, you weren't always Commander Agrias, were you?" he said, quickly realizing that she once again refused the offer of the drink.

"Don't," the weight of command came through in her voice once more.

"Oh, please. No one even remembers that nickname," he said, smiling as he drank.

"I said don't, Sir." For once, she mocked him back. It was a return to the dynamic that had existed before she was elevated to command. The two of them were put in charge of smaller units and would often pair together on the battlefield. The results that usually came from their combined strategies were enough for the military leaders of the Kingdoms to keep them together even after all this time.

"Emerald Eyes Agrias," he blurted out. "I remember it was one of the most beautiful names to ever have weight to it, as far as soldiers go."

"I'll force you to choke on that wineskin of yours if you don't stop talking, Lieutenant." She hated the name. Always had. While the men under her command wouldn't dare use it with her in earshot, she knew that when she wasn't around, that was still what they called her. It had been some time since she'd heard it though. Once she received the title of commander, she thought it was all but forgotten. Some embarrassing story from her younger days, the kind of fact that Sir Ewan claimed was what one needed not to become like an ogre and just get told to kill things. It made Agrias think if maybe the same could be said for Gresh's band. Did they have favorite flowers or a preference for their meals?

"Yes, well. As far as I'm concerned, you, yourself, are quite-" Agrias watched as Sir Ewan's nerves started to get the best of him for what he was about to say, but it quickly became unimportant when the last thing any of them wanted to hear filled their ears.

The war horn blasted again.

"What the hells?" Sir Ewan said, quickly getting up from his seat. "The orcs? Already? Our spies said they hadn't moved from the last reports!"

Agrias barely heard the knight's words as she, without hesitation, grabbed her heater shield and slid her hands through the straps. Luckily, she had never undid her scabbard, her hand reflexively going to its grip as she flung the flap of her pavilion to the side.

Outside, men were readying themselves for the worst. Shouting overtook everything, accompanied by the clanging of swords and armor being put on in haste. The soldiers that were already prepared for combat were busily helping those that weren't or running toward the sound of the eastern war horn. Commander Agrias swiftly accompanied them, nearly in full sprint.

Sir Ewan followed just as quickly and answered the soldiers that were battering Agrias with questions as she sought answers for them in haste. All he told them was to just follow, shut up, and prepare for battle.

Her mind reeled at the possibility of the orcs finding a way around their scouting parties, or even worse, discovering them and butchering them. But they were smart – at least she thought they were. They wouldn't have been so sloppy to get themselves found. Whether or not they had gotten restless and started marching, or had just given up and went out for a full-scale attack, she would have received word, wouldn't she?

These questions filled her now pounding head as she darted through the camp, weaving in and out of the panicked civilians who had been told to gather in the center of the encampment, should they be attacked. She called out for Sir Ewan, but between the now rabid blasts of the war horn and the chaos happening all throughout, he did not hear her.

When they finally arrived at the edge, she was greeted with Boss Gresh shouting his own words of command to his band. Ogrin was busy having his fellow shooters load their guns and prepare their hand-axes, should the orcs get in so close as to make their blunderbusses useless. Gresh barely acknowledged her when she finally came to his side.

"What happened!? The orcs haven't been-"

"It wasn't the shaaving orcs, Commander!" Gresh shouted, nearly knocking her backward. She hadn't known what the word was exactly, but she took it as an ogre obscenity.

"Then what is it? More Abyssals?" Ewan demanded, finally catching up to Agrias, his hand staying steady on his greatsword's handle. The humans received no answers from the ogres.

"Gresh!" Agrias shouted in a tone that even Sir Ewan had never heard come out of her. It was one of pure frustration and perhaps even hostility.

The hulking mass of armor and muscle turned toward her and peered downward, standing nearly twice her height. She felt her hair now completely loose from its bun as it fluttered around her shoulders; and yet she stood unwavering against Boss Gresh, who with a single bat could knock her several feet backward.

"Goblins. The damned goblins." Gresh said as he shrugged his axe off of his back and planted it into the dirt underfoot. "I think we were followed."

"You what?! You didn't cover your tracks or send a host of scouts to trail behind you?" Sir Ewan screamed. His own anger was beginning to surface, and Agrias could see him let go of his sword, his hands balling into fists.

"You really think ogres are that stupid do ya, man-girl?" The cutting words of Ogrin suddenly joined in on the argument.

"Need I have a better example than this? Your own strategy of swing until it's dead might get us all killed, you idiot!" Ewan shot back.

"Enough of this!" Agrias cut the air with a hand. "The time for talk is over. We're faced with a threat we weren't prepared for. I will not let that mean we're already defeated! Lieutenant, gather all the men you can-"

The deafening blast of a blunderbuss caused everyone to stop and turn in the direction. The war cries of ogres suddenly overtook everything, and the sounds of battle quickly followed.

A fair-sized group of armed and armored men had gathered behind Commander Agrias and Sir Ewan. She scanned the line of her troops. Even though she couldn't see their faces, their lack of fear was shown by the way they banged their swords upon their shields in well-honed unity. They were ready to fight, and for the first time in her entire military career, Agrias felt that they were ready to die.

She had been bested, she admitted. No time spent staring at her maps could have prepared her for the obvious. The orcs had maybe sent their goblin skirmishers to hide out into the woods, secretly tailing the ogres who probably were loud enough that they needn't come out of hiding to track down their location. Or maybe they sent their best fighters to crash on the camp, thinning the herd for their eventual approach.

"We need to secure positions, Lieutenant. Boss Gresh, can your men handle their eastern approach?" But as she asked the question, she saw that Gresh wasn't looking at her as he slowly picked up his axe; as a matter of fact, neither was Ewan.

She turned to share the direction of their gaze, and her mouth fell open.

Past the wall, descending from the hill in which they had previously taken down the efreet, countless number of torches were lit and cascading downward like a wave on the ocean. Two columns of goblin forces were rapidly approaching up and over the hill. The tactics weren't their own, Agrias thought, no goblins were that organized. This was an orcish strategy. One that they had fought before.

"Look at all the fodder!" Ogrin broke the silence as the loud thump of the barrel of his blunderbuss landed in his mitt of a palm.

"Men!" she shouted, her gaze still not leaving the hastily approaching goblins. "To the wall!"

She unsheathed her longsword and charged. The soldiers behind her gave their best rallying cry but were quickly drowned out by a similar one from Boss Gresh's men. The two forces of human and ogre quickly ran toward the scene of slaughter; her archers had already begun picking targets, and the pikemen guarding the v-shaped hole still stood vigilantly.

When her army linked up with the guardians of the gap, Agrias began to make out individual, horribly fanged faces from the light of their torches.

"Take up positions!" she shouted.

"TAKE UP POSITIONS!" Sir Ewan answered even louder.

Soon, they were as neatly assembled as they could be while shoved behind the wall. It was a sound strategy, Agrias thought. Limit the movement of her soldiers until one army would be able to break through and invade the other side of the wall where the real fighting would begin. What made her nervous now was that her archers were not met with answered volleys. The spitters, or so the goblin-kin called them, were highly valued, and their location during a battlefield was not quickly revealed.

"Gresh!" Agrias shouted among the clamor.

The ogre turned his head toward her and raised a single eyebrow.

"Get your shooters to the top of the wall! Start thinning their numbers!"

"You ain't fought goblins much, eh? My shooters are staying right here." Agrias took note that Ogrin and his compatriots had lined up several heads behind her pikemen. She cursed the ogre under her breath and shoved her way toward the front of her men.

As she moved through the line, she could see Sir Ewan's black hair whip back and forth as he was hurriedly giving orders. Always the first in the vanguard, that fool.

"Oh, I'm so thrilled you could make it here, Commander! The view is glorious!" he said with a face that purposely betrayed his sarcasm. "We're crammed in here! Our formation is too tight. We're going to be swinging at ourselves soon enough!"

"If they breach this side of the wall, we can't let them get into the camp, Lieutenant. We have to fall on them as hard as we can, should the pikemen go down."

"I don't think that's the best course of act-" Just as his protest was once again going to be voiced, the slow yet guttural growling of the ogres caught her attention.

"Mawbeasts!" one of the mercenaries shouted.

Before she could even collect her thoughts, the sound of rapidly fired ranged weaponry sounded. Heavy footfalls of something much larger than the average goblin was charging toward the wall. She turned her head quickly enough to see her pikemen uneasily backstep and the tips of their spears reluctantly descending.

"Hold steady!" Sir Ewan shouted. He shot Agrias a look and winced. Before the words could even travel to the pikemen, the mawbeasts crashed into them. In a flash, the tanned hides of the bear-like monsters tore a hole into the frontline, the gnashing teeth bit clean through the chainmail, and first blood was spilled. The creatures whipped their heads back and forth, separating bone from bone.

Commander Agrias went to order her men to start attacking, but a different voice beat her to it.

"Fire, you bloody twits!" Ogrin gave his command, and suddenly the firing line of ogre shooters all lurched forward, their blunderbusses fell into firing position nearly in unison.

The flash of their guns and the thunderous sound of all of them going off together was enough to nearly halt all of Agrias's men. The mawbeasts exploded into gouts of blood, gore, and viscera.

Agrias and Ewan watched as two, three, even four of the creatures were reduced to mangled heaps. The one mawbeast that remained was quickly put to rest by one of her soldiers, who in a rage, seeing his own men get mauled, plunged his sword into the injured beast's neck and kicked it off his blade.

"What the hell was he waiting for!?" the knight shouted. "We wouldn't have lost those men if-"

"Now is not the time for this, Ewan. Tell the men to patch the hole, drag the fallen behind the wall, and regroup," Agrias ordered.

"And where are you going?" he asked incredulously.

"To have a word with Gresh." She quickly pushed and shoved her way out of the block and walked around, peering over her shoulder, anxiously awaiting the spitters to finally be unleashed. As she walked up the small incline where Gresh stood with No-Tongue at his side, she was lost with the thought of seeing more of those mawbeasts be let loose into her ranks.

"Now you see why I kept my shooters back here, Commander?" Boss Gresh asked, one hand was on the pommel of his axe, the skulls clinking against one another like a visceral wind chime.

"You are being paid by the Kingdoms are you not?" she asked, already knowing the answer, and in turn ignoring the boast he had given her.

"Quite handsomely, too," Ogrin added as he reloaded his weapon.

"You need to keep your mouth shut or I'll cut your tongue out like this one!" Agrias threatened Ogrin while pointing at No-Tongue, who stood like a stone sentinel.

Boss Gresh laughed at her remark and smiled. "Now you're talking our language, Commander. But, yes. We are being paid by the humans. What of it?" he asked, squinting his eyes at the enemy forces who still remained in their separate columns. She realized now that they were amassed beyond the top of the hill, the columns ready to pounce on any soldiers she sent through the hole in the wall.

"Next time you have something in mind like that? Tell me about it! I could have sent men who would have been decimated by your shooters while fighting those creatures!"

"Mawbeasts, Commander. They're called mawbeasts, and your men will get their chance to whet their blades on them soon enough. Far more of them beyond that hill there, I assure you." Agrias bared her teeth and cursed. While it was growing easier to communicate with him, she had started to notice that this Gresh was far more well-spoken than his brethren.

"How many more?" As she asked the question, Gresh stood straight and quickly wrapped his arms around and spun her. Before she could even conceive what he was doing, she heard the thwack of arrows crash into his armor and the sound of them ricocheting off of his shooters. She heard the hard impact of one of them hit the ground and the gasping breath as the arrow pierced his throat.

"There they are," Agrias said as Gresh let her go. She looked toward the base of the hill and saw that Sir Ewan had already ordered more archers to the wall. The commander watched as ladders went up and men scurried up them with quivers slung over both shoulders.

"Aye, damn spitters. They got Gort!" Ogrin spat as he looked at the corpse of his fellow shooter.

"Thank you for that, Boss." She said, still looking up at him.

"Live long enough to hand us your Kingdoms' gold, Commander. That's all I care about." He scratched his beard, and Agrias could have sworn she saw a bug fall from it as he surveyed the area. "Tell your men to fan out, give me and my warriors a lane. We're going in." Without addressing her further, Boss Gresh walked past Ogrin and No-Tongue, who had since unsheathed his swords.

If it weren't for the sounds of war behind her, Commander Agrias would have all but said the ground shook as the ogre warriors marched to war.

Led by Boss Gresh himself, his 'greataxe' in both hands, she quickly darted back to the wall. She hadn't had time to seek out her runners who would be doing this themselves, but there was nothing about this fight that she was accustomed to. Her eyes were drawn to the bloody mess that used to be one of her pikemen; Darius's men had him on a wagon and were wheeling him out of the field.

She nearly collided with the wall itself as she picked up speed in her descent. When she made her way to Sir Ewan's side once more, she saw blood on his hands.

"Yours?" she asked without hesitation. Wordlessly, he nodded behind him, and she sighed when she saw the corpse of one of her soldiers, the arrow from the spitters had found its mark in between the man's armor.

"We need to give the ogres a lane," she repeated the command that Gresh had given her. "He and his warriors are forming the vanguard. I agree we can't just sit here and wait to be picked off." Her glance went from Sir Ewan to the archers above her firing their bows in quick waves, as to not allow the goblins any break from the volley.

"Fine, let them get overrun by these things. We'll pick off whatever is left. Easy victory for us, right?" Sir Ewan smiled at her ever so slightly. He walked past her and began to order the men to move into nearly identical columns as the goblins on the other side, with the remaining pikemen forming the outside lane.

She turned back, hearing a loud commotion that she assumed was the ogres preparing to march. Her eyes went wide and she felt a sense of awe as she watched their discipline. From atop the hill, the heavily armored ogres stood, some with swords, some with axes and mauls; they were silent as they cracked their necks and spat on the ground. It wasn't until Gresh himself took steps forward, turned his back to their enemy, and began to give them harsh words that only the fellow ogres began to cheer and holler with ferocity. With a growl that was almost beast-like, Boss Gresh turned around once more and charged down the line her men had given them, and one by one, they disappeared past the wall. The hard foot stomps against the dirt rumbled the ground beneath her.

She realized now that despite it being an entirely different language that she did not know, nor ever cared to, she too felt the strength through their war cry, to take the battle to its end. Just like she had heard them do before, and she herself had done when she was still 'Emerald Eyes', she began to bang her sword against her shield.

And soon, the entirety of her troops did the same.

As he stood with his greatsword poised to strike, leading the men to form up once again, Sir Ewan met her gaze. Without words needed, Sir Ewan Alistair nodded in confirmation.

He made his way to the front of the army, a mere fifty feet from the hole in the wall, and raised his greatsword with one hand, high above his head.

"Soldiers of the Kingdoms!" he shouted, his voice so loud, that it drowned out the chaos ensuing on the other side. The men answered with a cry in unison. "We fight!"

Sir Ewan turned toward the fray, his greatsword held with both hands at chest level as he brought it down. There was an answering roar from the behind him, and they charged past Commander Agrias, past the wall, and into the fray. As they did so, Agrias no longer found any humor in the sobriquet of Sir Ewan the Streak.

His host of the vanguard disappeared into the battle and the tremors of fighting grew louder just before her. She peered out into the soldiers left under her command.

"Stay steady, men! Those are our brave brothers out there! While your blood screams to join them, know that behind you lie your homes! Your families! We cannot fall and let those who seek to destroy them get past us!" She felt the conviction of her words take over as she paced the frontlines of her soldiers, meeting as many in turn as she could.

Her unit raised their swords and once again cried out in unison.

"Oh, piss off, lady-knight!" Ogrin shouted from behind them. She could see the smile on his face, and despite the stoicism she tried to maintain before her soldiers, she smiled right back.

"And should any of your blows take that damned ogre's head off... know that a knighthood shall be rewarded!" She looked back at Ogrin, who was nearly doubled over with laughter. Now she could see what fighting was for them.

"Any of you piss-pots comes near me with a swo-" As volley of jests seized, Agrias saw that something had caught Ogrin's eye. And before she could even turn to see what could have stopped the fierce shooter in his tracks, she gasped as nearly a half-dozen of her archers were sent careening overhead, some not even in one piece. She cried out as her units put their shields up to protect themselves from arrows and... the bodies of their brothers.

"They got throwers, lady-knight!" Commander Agrias saw as Ogrin led his shooters down the hill. With a tenacity that shook the ground they treaded, they slung their blunderbusses onto their backs and climbed the ladders so quickly, Agrias was afraid they'd buckle and snap.

The deafening sound of their guns drowned all other noise as ogres and humans stood side-by-side defending the wall in perfect cohesion. When a shooter ducked to reload, a human archer would stand to cover them. Once their rhythm was achieved, they worked without words, in perfect harmony.

The time was now. She no longer could keep her remaining soldiers huddled together, watching as the men and women who they just shared meals with died. Commander Cassandra Agrias needed to march.

She fell into position and once more unsheathed her sword. No words of encouragement came to her, no rousing speeches were left in her bosom. It had been replaced with the fury of battle once more. She had let too many die against the Abyssals, she hadn't had them prepared for this, and she had wasted too much time trying to find a way to win and not enough actually doing it. Reminded of how easily Boss Gresh roused his men, Agrias let out a battle cry and slammed her sword into her shield.

With her men crying out behind her in anger and fury, she led them past the hole in the wall and into the fight.

She saw ogres and men fighting alongside one another. All evidence of either side's formations was lost, and now it had broken down into sheer battle. As she focused her attention on the bulbous nosed goblin that dug an axe into one of her soldier's sides, she brought her sword up and quickly brought it down, cutting the creature's chest wide-open. It fell in a heap next to its latest and final kill.

Behind, her unit fell upon a particular group of goblins who were outnumbering one of Gresh's warriors six-to-one, and they quickly saved the ogre's life by tearing away at the enemy.

She put her shield up just in time to block the heavy swing of a crude, sharpened bone that she assumed served as a sword of some kind. Her arm and body went with the force of the blow, allowing her to quickly turn around, thus not letting her target get to her back. Without any caution, the goblin sneered; it wiped away slobber that dripped down its open mouth, and then it charged. She gave a simple horizontal slash and cut the goblin down, using its own momentum against it.

The next goblin was upon her in seconds as a morning star came flailing wildly at her. She was successful in keeping a tight circle around the goblin, who couldn't quite keep up with her speed. But the quick motions it made with its weapon cut off every path, every opening she saw.

It jerked the weapon backward and snapped it forward, sending the spiked ball over Agrias's head. With a quick motion and a cry of hope, she side-stepped the head and put her shield up, letting the spikes catch in the wood; she prayed they didn't pierce it and stick into her bare arms. She cursed to herself, remember that the gauntlets she should have been wearing were left on the war table.

But her plan worked, and as she let her right arm fall with the weight of the morning star, she moved and hacked downward. The goblin's arm fell to the ground with a sickening thud, and as it cried in pain, she brought her sword across its face and put it down. She quickly undid the straps of her shield with the fingers she could manage, while still gripping her sword, and let it fall to the ground, the head of the morning star still stuck in it. The bruising would surely be felt should she survive this, she thought. Looking around, she noticed a kite shield lying on the corpse of one of her fellow humans. She said a solemn prayer to him before taking it and storming off into the battle once more.

*****

Sir Ewan was fighting side-by-side with Boss Gresh, the two of them cutting goblins in two with their great weapons. Ewan charged one, seemingly larger than the rest, and swung straight for the beast's head, cleaving it off; but with the spinning motion, he turned on his heel, the blood and mud-soaked ground beneath him giving him added speed, and was poised to strike again. However, this time, he pierced straight through a goblin's chest, lifting it up and then slamming it into the ground. He removed the blade from the corpse and made for his next kill.

Gresh was less graceful in his approach to the fight. Remaining completely unaware of the various slashes and cuts the goblins had managed to land, he kept swinging the crude yet highly effective greataxe. With massive, weight filled swings, the ogre cut a bloody swathe through the battle; being covered in his enemies' own innards and perhaps even his own blood did nothing but fuel the Boss.

Charging at Sir Ewan was a mounted goblin, holding the reins of the fleabag it sat atop in one hand and a twin-forked spear in the other. He knew that his sword was too heavy to get off a swing without catching that spear in the neck, and as it made pass after pass at him, all he managed to do was deflect the thrust to one side. He winced in pain; it had come too close and caught him slightly in the cheek. It was naught but a scratch, but it burned. With a battle cry that eerily reminded him of a cackle, it charged once more.

"Oh, come on. Come on. Come on." He repeated to himself. All the air left his lungs as it grew closer and closer. With a sharp exhale, he hopped on one foot and brought his greatsword up. He could feel it bite into something, but his eyes went to the splash of red that burst from his shoulder. It had went wide this time, perhaps reading his footwork or giving him a wider berth accounting for his greatsword.

He spun, clutching the pectoral muscle on his chest, unsure of where it had connected due to the armor, just in time to see the fleabag collapse and fall on top of its rider. Letting out a relieved laugh, he turned his attention back to Boss Gresh... but to his horror, he saw only the ogre desperately fighting back.

Goblins had wizened up and attacked the leader of the mercenary band en masse. Two of them hung off of the ogre's hulking shoulders, others had dug their daggers into his legs. There was at least six of them all sticking him with their blades. The Boss had dropped his axe and was hurriedly using both of his hands to try and throw the goblins off, but every time he did, they would come right back to it.

Sir Ewan tried to hack and slash his way to Gresh, but the goblins were determined to bring him down and let no one get to him. Across the way, past where the Boss was slowly being stabbed to death, the knight saw No-Tongue crying out and slashing at nearly everything that got in his way; but he too was being overrun. Ewan grit his teeth and nearly swore when he came to the realization that they were thinning out their enemies' numbers, and in desperation, the goblins sought to take down as many as they could before their loss.

But when Ewan finally cut his way to the circle in which the goblins let their kin tackle Boss Gresh to his knees, he heard a thunderous sound. He turned his head just in time to see the last reserve the goblins had on their side.

A giant.

The creature was massive, standing nearly half the height of the wall itself. Sir Ewan's eyes went wide as he saw the creature barrel through the forces under its feet. Whether it was human, goblin, or ogre, the monstrosity cared not what it crushed nor what it swiped at with its spiked club. Sir Ewan assumed that the goblins must have stuck spears in a tree that they cut down and given it to the giant as a weapon.

It was dressed in crude furs, and a small mantle of auroch fur fell to just above its shoulder blades. A makeshift loin cloth sat loosely around its thin hips, and bands of pure iron were fastened to its wrists and ankles. The face was a horrid form of twisted teeth and uneven eyes. Every breath sent hot air into the now cooling night sky.

Sir Ewan turned his attention back to Boss Gresh, to go and defend the ogre, but he was too late. The goblins finally managed to bring him to the ground, still stabbing at the ogre relentlessly. In a heap that saw goblins fall off of him and tumble to the ground, all life had left him; Gresh had fallen.

Seeing his Boss being brutally taken down, No-Tongue went wild – a fury that even Sir Ewan had never seen on the battlefield. The silent warrior cried out to the best of his ability and began taking slashes at every goblin that stood in his way. Digging his swords through their flesh and kicking and shoving to get to his fallen leader, No-Tongue failed to realize that he too was being taken over by the goblins. One finally managed to get its spindly arms around his neck, trying to balance its knife enough to cut to his throat.

Sir Ewan was on the move once again. Trying his best to ignore the giant and the now screaming pain that was in his shoulder, the knight charged forth.

He passed Boss Gresh's corpse and took swings at the foes that tried to get in his way in a fashion that would have made the bearded ogre proud.

When he finally reached No-Tongue, he threw down his greatsword and tried to tackle the goblin off of the ogre's back. It hung on just long enough that Sir Ewan tumbled to the ground, landing harshly on his injured shoulder. Crying out in pain, Sir Ewan flipped onto his back and sat up, just in time to see the goblin lose its grip on No-Tongue's collar and slip off. With a quick motion, the ogre spun around and dug both swords into the creature's back.

If it had been any other day, any other fight, Sir Ewan would have swore the duel-wielding ogre was walking over to him to put him down. But he simply put both of his swords in his massive hand and shot the other out, helping Sir Ewan up.

Without questioning the gesture, Sir Ewan cried out in pain at the weight he was forced to put on his arm. No-Tongue smacked one of his swords into Ewan's chest. Wordlessly, Ewan took it in his left hand.

"That giant is heading for the wall. We have to stop it!" Ewan went to move, but the pain was too much.

He looked at No-Tongue, forgetting that he wouldn't get a response, at least not with words. All he got was a dismissive head shaking from the ogre.

There wasn't anything they could do. The giant had already blown past the vanguard, who were turning their attention back to the now thinning horde of goblins.

As the day had completely turned to night, Ewan knew that the only hope of keeping the wall secured was Commander Agrias.

*****

Many goblins had attempted to make it past her and her unit, to try and sneak in past the wall and between the archers and the shooters, but none had made it so far.

As Agrias took out the legs of another goblin and plunged her blade into its heart, she saw it. A hulking giant had made its way over the hill and she was horrified to see that it was hurling men and ogre alike into the air, sending them crashing down to their deaths.

She had never known the kind of terror that worked its way into her stomach, tightening every nerve in her body, as she watched the massive creature striding toward the wall.

"Form up!" she shouted. Agrias sheathed her sword and took out her war horn. Letting out two quick blasts, the men in her unit quickly dispatched the goblins that they had become entangled with in order to regroup. "Take that giant down! We cannot let it breach the wall!"

The command had nearly fallen on deaf ears when the men saw the thing march toward them, taking swings with its club that sounded like thunder echoing across the valley.

There wasn't anything she could do now. Some of her soldiers began to retreat and make their way back to the hole, but just as quickly, a shot from one of the blunderbusses stopped them in their tracks.

"Oi! You sorry lots really gonna run now!?" Ogrin was perched atop one of the merlons, his blunderbuss was still smoking. "Listen to her, you pissants!" For the first time, Agrias felt grateful for Ogrin's vulgarity.

"Men, that thing is fast approaching, but it won't matter how far you go. That thing will make short work of the wall and everyone behind it. I can't speak for the vanguard, but we aren't dead yet!" She turned her attention to Ogrin, who was watching the chaos the giant was causing. "Ogrin! Can your shooters take that thing down?"

"Aye, if you get 'em close enough. These things aren't the best at a distance. You'll have to get him to us first."

She wasn't sure how she was going to do that. She turned once more, the blonde hair sticking to her face with blood or mud, she hadn't been able to tell the difference yet.

"We have to do this." she said to herself but then turned back to her men, her voice barking once more. "Get into formation! Loose ranks, men! Don't let that thing take out so many of us with one swing. Archers! Let your arrows fly true! Keep its attention on us and not the wall! Ogrin!"

"I know what to do, lady-knight," he responded in typical fashion.

She let out a shaky sigh and took a stance.

The giant came to a stop as it witnessed the soldiers forming up before it. As if sending a warning to them, it smashed the club on the ground, in the middle of an entanglement between goblin and human forces, sending them into the air with dust and rock alike. The ground shook from the crater the creature created, but Agrias's forces did not budge. Ogres and humans who had been around the impact took the initiative to charge at the giant and slice at its foot. It took a few moments, but the giant finally realized what was going on and picked up a human soldier and crushed it in its grasp.

"Move back! Move back!" she commanded, and while they kept their eyes on the hulking beast, they shuffled backward just out of the creature's reach. It stepped closer, but this time its attention turned toward her archers. To Agrias's horror, it wound up a strike from its club once again.

"Get down!" one of the soldiers next to her cried out, just before the massive weapon came crashing down on the wall and sent the rock work careening downward onto them. Those who had shields managed to get them up and winced as the rocks crashed and broke apart before them; while others fell to the ground, either concussed or dead.

"Just a little further!" she shouted, not even knowing if anyone was listening now. Dust kicked up and destroyed any visibility she once had. She coughed as she desperately kept her eyes open, but it was too much. Tears filled her vision, and she felt suddenly blinded.

When some of it cleared from wiping her face with a bare hand, she saw the club of the giant heading straight for her. Commander Agrias's eyes went wide and she tried to get her shield up, but she was unaccustomed to the weight. Just as the club crashed into the shield, shattering it into splinters, Agrias felt her feet leave the ground, and all the air left her lungs when she crashed onto the ground below. She heard a crack at some point, but she wasn't sure when. Her view started to dim and all she could see was the silhouette of the giant behind the smoke and dust it had kicked up.

Agrias couldn't keep her vision steady, and things began to dim as she fought the urge to finally sleep. It had been days since she had. Too worried about her maps and strategies.

Agrias's eyes finally shut as she heard the muffled sounds of Ogrin's shooters.

*****

The pain brought her back as she shuffled in her sleep. She nearly screamed when she felt a resistance against moving her arm. Light poured into the darkness, and she struggled with opening her eyes to it. The flap of the tent was open, letting the sunlight in almost as if it was right outside.

She put her hand up to prevent it from blinding her, but it was quickly eclipsed by a vaguely human shape.

"My god, she's awake!" the familiar voice of Darius said as she quickly felt him put his hand on her forehead. "The fever broke. Good, good, good, good." He was shuffling at a table nearby Her vision was beginning to solidify as she watched him shuffle to a nearby table. She was relieved she was in a private tent. She tried to speak, but her voice barely came out; instead there was only coughing.

"Water, water! I'm so sorry, Commander! Here! Help me, please?" She was too dazed to realize that someone else stood behind her, and next thing she knew, firm hands gently lifted her head up. Just as Darius went to help her drink from the mug of water he had, she quickly snatched it out of his hands and drank it herself. If she wasn't a smarter woman, she would have been convinced she'd been giving a magical potion for how much better she felt after nearly drowning herself in the water. She began coughing after drinking too much, and despite her desires, forced herself to stop.

"Wh-what happened?" she finally mustered. She went to move but realized quickly that she was naked from the waist up. A large bandage had been placed over her chest, covering her breasts and the majority of her left arm; a sling had been fashioned to hold it in place. Looking down at herself, she realized she was covered in new scars that accompanied the old ones. Most alarming was the one that nearly extended to her neck, shooting out from beneath the bandages.

"We won." She was shocked to hear the voice of none other than the ogre, Ogrin. The hands she had felt holding her head up were his.

"The g-giant," she stammered trying to remember all that had happened.

"Eh, a few blasts from my shooters put it down. The wall might need some work though." The hoarse laughter, that only a few days ago had brought her so much anger and frustration, now brought a smile to her face.

"I'm surprised you're still-" before she could finish her statement, the pain in her head caused her to nearly chip her teeth with how hard she bit down.

"I'm afraid to say that our victory against the goblins did not come without costs, Commander." Darius said, handing her another cup of water. "I'm sure you've noticed that the creature broke your arm."

"Still though. I've never seen a human get hit by a giant and live, lady-knight," Ogrin added. But what concerned her was the grave look Darius still had on his face.

"And...?" She asked, but she was afraid she already knew the answer. Her good hand went to the bandage on her face.

"When it shattered your shield... a bit of the fragments slashed your eye. I'm afraid... you won't be able to see out of it ever again, Commander. I'm so terribly sorry." Darius said, taking her hand in his. "I'll give you a few moments to absorb this." He bowed low as he left the tent, slowly.

"I'll be with the boys. We're scouting the field trying to find the Boss. No-Tongue and your man-girl knight, Ewan, think they know where he fell," Ogrin said as he ducked out of the tent.

"Ewan... is alive?" she said aloud, feeling more alone then she had during the entire campaign. She lay there half-asleep, half-awake trying to accept her injuries as best she could. Nearly an hour went by when a familiar shape appeared in the entrance of the tent.

"AndIthoughtIlookedbad."Sheknewthevoicefromanywhere.Agriascried outinpainasshetriedtositup,butSirEwanplacedhishandonhershoulder,calmingher down.

"You lived... how? The giant..." Her mind raced as she struggled to put all of the pieces together.

"Is dead. That's the important part. Don't worry. Once you're up and moving around, I'll have the reports ready for you to read. As for now?" She hadn't noticed that in his other hand was the bottle of wine from her pavilion. He had sat two cups on Darius's table. "You never accept my offer of a drink. So for right now, while you don't have any battles to win or soldiers to command... we drink."

She smiled at the knight and noticed that he had taken off his armor. He was wearing a loose fitting shirt with bandages covering his own chest, but he had not nearly as many as she had. If she weren't a soldier, first and foremost, she would have gotten self-conscious of being without a shirt herself.

He sat down in a chair at her bedside and gave her the cup of wine. She slowly sipped and her taste buds went wild over the strong taste of it. She couldn't fight the smile that forced its way forward.

"I'd like to answer your questions now, Ewan." She said while staring into the deep red swirling around in her cup.

"And what questions are those? You've been unconscious for two days now."

"Sunflowers, this kind of wine which I brought from home, and like you, wool in the winter and cotton in the summer."

She looked up at him with a sly smile. Ewan laughed, which quickly brought her to laugh herself for the first time since they had arrived at the wall. Both of them winced in pain, but this only made them laugh harder.

"There was one more you know."

"One more what?" she asked.

"Question. Who was the boy who first stole the young lady's heart?" His sarcasm was all too welcomed, Agrias thought.

"You'll never know that one, Lieutenant," she said into her cup.

"Fine. But, I'll have you know that you aren't called Emerald Eyes by the men anymore." She shot him a look that seemed to contain a glimmer of the commander in it. She raised a single eyebrow at him. "Now it's just Agrias, the Emerald Eye," he said, pointing to her face.

"That's cruel." She responded, but the humor was still there.

"I'd say not. It's a beautiful eye," he said, his all-too familiar grin coming upon his face.

"You're dismissed, Lieutenant. But, you're to leave the wine."

"Not a chance in hell I'm missing this chance to share a drink with you, Cassandra."

She scoffed at him as she finished off her first cup.

RAT-CATCHER

By Scott Washburn

The humans rode into the halfling village of Meadowbrook on a beautiful spring day. There was nothing unusual about this; the League of Rhordia was an alliance which held a number of different races. But these humans were not simple travelers or merchants; one was clearly a knight, and he was accompanied by a banner-bearer, carrying the emblem of the city of Norwood, a human city fifty leagues to the west. Official business of some sort?

So it seemed; an inquiry at the Heady Brew Inn directed the pair to an open field just outside the village. The halfling they were looking for was there—with several hundred others. A bit of shouting brought halfling and humans together.

"Rat-catching?" Dunstan Rootwell asked, his eyebrows arching up in surprise. "With all respect to the duke, Sir Hedrick, my rat-catching days are behind me, thank the gods." He turned and gestured to his militia company of halfling archers practicing on the village green. "I've come up a bit in the world since those times."

"Aye, he knows that, Master Dunstan," said the tall human, nodding, "and he means no disrespect—quite the contrary! But he feels that your reputation, in both your past and current activities, makes you the ideal person to deal with this. The situation in Norwood is most serious, I do assure you."

Talking with humans was often quite literally a pain in the neck for halflings, and Dunstan took a step back to reduce the angle at which he had to tilt his head. "Surely, a city the size of Norwood has its own supply of rat-catchers. Why would the duke want to bring me from fifty leagues away to deal with an outbreak of rats?"

Sir Hedrick, a thick-set and ruddy-faced man with a bushy mustache, looked from side to side as if afraid of being overheard, and his voice sank to a near-whisper. "If it was just rats, you'd be right. But the duke suspects—and I do, too—that it's far more than just rats, Master Dunstan."

Dunstan twitched as the man's meaning got through to him. "Are you saying that…?"

"Aye, the signs are all there: people disappearing off the streets at night, granaries broken into, strange outbreaks of ghastly diseases all over the city, men sent to search the sewers not returning. The people are frightened."

"Damnation," growled Dunstan. "Ratkin."

"So it would seem."

"I thought we'd dealt with those vermin years ago."

"We did," said the knight. "I was there when we did, although I was just a squire. So were you and your people."

"Just as an ordinary archer," said Dunstan, shaking his head. "I was only learning the trade then—the usual rat-catching trade, I mean. Master Hadrin is who you really need for something like this."

"Unless I'm sorely mistaken, Master Hadrin has been in his grave these ten years passed. Right now, the one we need is you—and as many of your troops as you can bring. You've proven your worth in… in this sort of thing."

"You mean that we're not afraid to go crawling through sewers, and short enough to walk upright in the ratkin tunnels."

Sir Hedrick shrugged and looked sheepish. "A man is at a terrible disadvantage in those situations, and… well, as you say."

Dunstan frowned and turned away. Ratkin! Of all the horrors spawned from the Abyss, there were few as hateful or horrifying as the ratkin. True, individually, they really weren't much to fear. While full-grown adults could be nearly man-sized, most were smaller, and with their hunched-over stature, that put them almost eye-to-eye with a halfling. From what Dunstan heard of them, they were cowardly, awkward above ground in the sunlight, and not terribly skilled with weapons. The problem was that you didn't have to deal with individuals, you had to deal with swarms. They bred at a furious rate, and their offspring could fight almost as soon as they were weaned. Most had little more intelligence than their normal-sized kin, but some had a cunning which could match that of a man—or even a halfling. They could make and use weapons and other fiendish devices, they carried and spread disease, and they were as cruel as anything that walked the earth. They took delight in capturing people alive and then working them to death as slaves, or just torturing them for amusement—and then eating them.

"Master Dunstan, the duke knows that he cannot command you or your people to come, but he hopes that you will remember the friendship and tradition of cooperation which our people share. I realize this is a difficult thing he is asking, but you know as well as I do that every hour is critical."

Yes, time was surely against them here. If a band of ratkin could establish themselves under a city, with a rich supply of food just overhead, they could grow their numbers with terrifying speed. They would burrow out a vast network of tunnels from the city's sewers until there was nowhere they could not strike. Deep caverns would hold their workshops, armories, and slave pens.

With time, they could take a whole city—and then send out parties to infest the next one. Given enough time, they could form armies which no longer needed to hide in the shadows. Clearly, things had not reached so dire a state in Norwood, but if measures were not taken swiftly, they soon could. Years ago the whole eastern part of the Rhordian League was threatened by such an invasion. It had been defeated, and after a bitter struggle, the ratkin exterminated. Dunstan had been there.

But you could never get every last one…

He turned back to face the human. "You're right. We're wasting time."

*****

"There it is!"

The shout came from the head of the column and every weary halfling jerked upright at the sound. Dunstan stood in the stirrups of his pony and saw what had prompted the shout: the city of Norwood. A ragged cheer came from the halflings who still had the breath for it. A fifty league journey wasn't all that much for a human on horseback, but the short stride of a halfling made it seem twice as far. And the pace had been grueling. Everyone knew that haste was needed, and they'd covered the distance in just twelve days. Dunstan was proud of his troops, proud of his people.

He'd feared that he would have trouble convincing the mayors of the halfling shires to send troops, but his fears had proved groundless. Everyone saw the need immediately. Humans tended to ridicule the ratkin threat—until they came to their city—but halflings knew just how dangerous the things were. Mothers still used the threat of ratkin to scare unruly children into being good, and the old gaffers would thrill youngsters with tales of the old battles against them. The people understood, and even Dunstan's wife understood. She wasn't happy about him leaving, and his children had cried a little, but they knew he had to go. The militia companies had been mustered in short order, and Dunstan was now leading over a thousand troops down the long sloping road into Norwood. Five hundred more—people who could not leave immediately—were following three days behind.

Most were spearmen and bowmen, but Dunstan had made a special effort to bring along some engineers. Halflings in general didn't like machines, but a few did, and those who did, really liked machines. Halfling engineers and builders were rare, but highly prized, not only in their own communities, but by other races as well. Dunstan suspected he would need their skills in the coming campaign.

"It's bigger than I expected. But then everything about these bloody humans is bigger than you'd expect, eh?"

Dunstan looked to his side and saw one of those very engineers walking next to him. Paddy Bobart was a bit… odd, even for an engineer, but Dunstan had known him for years and could forgive him his eccentricities because of his obvious talents. He was a builder, tinkerer, and inventor who was almost legendary among the people. He was always creating new devices, and some of them were even useful.

But it was Paddy's less obvious talents which might prove of the most use here. For Paddy was among the even rarer group of halflings who could channel magic. He couldn't throw fireballs or call down lightning bolts, but what he could do, might be just what was needed. Dunstan had been doubtful he could convince the elderly halfling to make the journey, but to his surprise, he'd been strangely eager to come.

"They do seem to like their big, stone cities, don't they?" said Dunstan, turning his gaze back to the road ahead.

"Silly sods. If they didn't live all clumped together like this, they wouldn't need t' build sewers t'carry away their crap, and there wouldn't be any easy place for the ratkin t'form a nest, and there wouldn't be any need for me t'wear out me tired old feet marchin' fifty leagues t'get here."

Dunstan's lips curled up in a smile. As a youth, Paddy had spent years among the dwarves, learning their arts. He'd also learned their language, and even though he'd come back to the shires years ago, he still had a noticeable accent. "I offered you a pony, Paddy," said Dunstan. "Or you could ride in one of those wagons you insisted on bringing along." He gestured to where a half-dozen large wains rumbled along, pulled by oxen.

"Ach!" said Paddy, spitting in the dust, as if that was an answer. "Like me feet better, tired as they are."

Dunstan continued to look at the wagons. "What all are you bringing there, anyway? I saw that two of the wagons were full of your tools, but the others are all packed with barrels. What's in 'em?"

"Powder."

"Gunpowder?!"

"Right enough."

"Gods, Paddy! That could blow us all to bits! Why didn't you warn me?"

"Safe enough. I put an enchantment on 'em. Can't go off by accident."

Dunstan relaxed slightly. "Still, you should have told me." Paddy just shrugged. "And why haul it all this way? The people in Norwood surely have a supply they could lend you."

Paddy shrugged again. "Couldn't be certain o' that. I got me a plan for that stuff."

"What plan?"

"I'll let you know when I'm certain it'll work."

Dunstan frowned, but he knew he wouldn't get anything more out of him. He nudged his pony into a faster pace and rode to the head of the column. Norwood was fully in view now. It stood astride the muddy waters of the Allsop River. Even from this distance, he could see the ships and barges on the water. The city was a trading center, and there was a lot of traffic on the river, even now in the dry season. Most of the city was clustered inside the high stone walls, dotted with towers, which stretched in a ring on both sides of the river. There were some newer buildings outside the walls, but only a few hundred. Most people preferred to live inside the protective defenses. *Not that they can protect them from this threat!* Further from the city lay small villages and isolated farmhouses, not too different from what could be found in the halfling lands. Fields full of crops and orchards filled the whole river valley. It was a prosperous land—which could quickly turn to a desert if the ratkin had their way.

As he watched, Dunstan noticed a pair of horsemen galloping along the road in his direction. When they got closer, he recognized Sir Hedrick and his squire. The knight had ridden off to Norwood as soon as Dunstan had agreed to come to tell the duke; now here he was.

"Ho! Master Dunstan!" he shouted, raising a hand. "You made good time!"

"Aye, we did, even on our short legs."

"We're setting up a camp for you outside the walls. We know your folk don't much care for our big stone houses. We'll have food and drink waiting."

"That will be good. We didn't burden ourselves with any excess that would slow us down."

"You'll lack for nothing, I promise. The people are very grateful to have you here." He paused and his expression darkened. "And it's none too soon. Things are getting worse day by day."

"More disappearances?"

"That, and a few outright attacks. The scum are getting bolder and bolder. The duke would like to talk with you as soon as you're settled."

*****

Duke Albustus Alberson occupied a sturdy keep on an island in the center of the river, connected by bridges to each shore. Sir Hedrick escorted Dunstan through the main gate a few hours later. Paddy Bobart insisted on coming, too, complaining the whole way. There were armed men everywhere along the route from their camp. They looked edgy and the common folk looked scared. But all of them seemed glad to see the halflings. *They expect us to solve their problem.* The thought disturbed Dunstan. *What if they couldn't?* He looked at the children—many about the same height as him—and thought about what would happen to them if he failed. The ratkin had no mercy for anyone, young or old, big or small. Norwood held almost fifty thousand people, a nearly unimaginable number to Dunstan, and they could all become ratkin fodder.

The duke met them in a comfortable chamber overlooking the keep's great hall. A half-dozen men were there with him, counselors and commanders, Dunstan guessed. The introductions were so hasty he could not match the names and the titles with the faces, but the only one who really mattered was the duke.

"Thank you for coming, Master Dunstan," said Albustus. "There were some who didn't think you would, but I never doubted." He was short for a human, but still more than a head taller than Dunstan. A bit stout, but much of that muscle. He leaned over and offered his hand. Dunstan took it and squeezed.

"We take our membership in the League seriously, my lord. If we don't stand by each other, we'll all fall separately like ripe peaches."

"Surely! Surely! But now that you are here, we need to decide what to do."

"Tis not the what," growled Paddy. "That's plain as a pikestaff: root the bastards out and kill 'em. It's the how that needs to be decided."

Dunstan hadn't had the chance to introduce Paddy, and the duke—and the other humans—frowned at his plain speech. "Uh, yes," said the duke. "And you are...?"

"This is Learned Paddy Bobart, Articifer, Master Engineer, and Channeller," said Dunstan hastily. "He's agreed to use his arts to help us, my lord."

"Ah, yes, of course! I have heard of you, Learned," said the duke, nodding at Paddy. "We are honored to have you..."

"Ach!" Paddy hocked, looked around for a place to spit, found none, and glared at the assembly as he swallowed. "Drop the blasted learned! Never wanted the damn title. And blast you, Dunstan Rootwell for even usin' it! I've told ye that before!"

"Sorry, Paddy," smirked Dunstan. "But on the way here, you said you had an idea. Can you tell us about it?"

"I can tell you what I need to know if it has a chance of workin'." He looked around the room. "Have ye got records... drawings of yer sewers under the city?"

The duke looked to one of the men. "Kelson, find the master archivist. Tell him what we need and tell him we need it now!"

"Yes, m'lord!" The man scurried off.

"It might take a while, I'm afraid," said Albustus, turning back to Dunstan. "While we're waiting, can I offer you some refreshments?"

"Aye! That'd be most welcome!" Paddy said as he pushed forward. "Ale if you've got any worth drinkin'! Got fifty league o' road dust to wash out of me gullet!"

The duke chuckled and sent a servant to bring food and drink. A low table had been placed in the middle of the room and Dunstan realized it had been brought special because of the halflings. Chairs had also been provided; small but conventional ones for them and large, but rather low-sling ones, for the humans.

Soon, they were all sitting around the table with cups of wine or beer and plates with simple, but good food at hand. The humans were extending them every courtesy, and even Paddy seemed to appreciate it. *It is a true alliance. We need each other and everyone knows it.*

"So, Sir Hedrick tells me you've brought a thousand of your people, Master Dunstan," said the duke.

"Five hundred bow, four hundred spear and sword, and the rest odds and ends—like Paddy here. Another five hundred are three days behind us. What sort of forces do you have to hand, my lord?"

"Well, unfortunately, the bulk of the duchy's troops are off at Eowolf for the annual muster. Nearly all the mercenaries, too. All I have on hand are five hundred of my household troops. Half of them mounted knights and men at arms; I'm afraid, probably not much use for this sort of work."

"Ah, don't count 'em out," said Paddy. "There might be work for 'em before this is through. Can use 'em to plug up rat holes if nothin' else."

"Ah… yes, well, there are also about fifteen hundred of the city guard. Mostly spears and crossbows, but a company of musketeers, too. I can also call on about a thousand of my local liegemen from the countryside, but I haven't done so yet. Not until I have something definite for them to fight."

"Sir Hedrick mentioned that there have been some open attacks?"

"Yes," the duke frowned. "At night we had been setting guard posts all over the city with three men in each. Larger groups, ten or twelve, patrolled the streets. Four nights ago, one of the guard posts was openly attacked by thirty or forty of the ratkin. One of the men was killed and another wounded before a patrol arrived and drove the vermin off. We did manage to kill a half-dozen of the ratkin, though. It's the first time we've managed to secure any of the bodies. At least we know for sure what we're dealing with."

"Couldn't have been much doubt," muttered Paddy.

"No, but it's good to be certain," continued Albustus. "But then two nights later, another post was attacked. And when the nearest patrol arrived, they were ambushed by at least a hundred of the beasts. Only two men got away."

"They're testing your defenses," said Dunstan.

"Yes, and wearing us down. The men won't stand for being put out in such small groups now. The guard posts have to have at least twenty men and the patrols thirty or more. I don't have enough men to cover the whole city with groups so large. That's why we're so happy to have you and your people here, Master Dunstan. Can you help out?"

"Aye, we can, but my whole force would only break down into thirty or forty patrols. Not enough—even with your troops—to secure the whole city. And in any case, just guarding areas isn't going to solve the problem. We need to get rid of the ratkin, not just keep 'em contained."

"We are hoping that your halflings will be willing to go down into the tunnels and see to that, Master Dunstan," said another man, a priest of the Church of the Children, Dunstan thought, from the look of his robes, but he couldn't remember his name. "Our men can fit into the city sewers, but the ratkin tunnels are usually much lower."

"We shall. But we need to plan out a strategy for this, not just go blundering around down there in hopes of finding and killing 'em."

At that moment, two men came bustling into the chamber. One was elderly and the other quite young. Their arms were filled with rolls of parchment. "My-my lord," gasped the older one. "I-I've brought what you asked for. Or at least I hope I have. There is so much in the archives, and it's never been properly cataloged. My predecessor left things in such a mess, and I don't have the staff to properly…" The old man seemed agitated.

"Yes, yes, Master Paley," soothed the duke. "Once all this is settled, I'll see that you have all the help you need. Now, what have you brought us?"

"Well, my lord, fortunately, drawings such as you are seeking are stored in their own section. If they were all mixed in with everything else, then, by the gods, I'd have been a week just finding these! Really, my lord, you should come down there and I can show you just what a task I face every day and…"

"Yes, Master Paley, I'll have to do that someday. Here, let's clear off the table and lay these out."

The parchments were very old, dust-covered, and cracked and splintered all too easily. But with care, they were finally unrolled and laid out on the table. Some were faded almost to illegibility, but Paddy fell on them the way he would a mug of really good ale and was soon almost oblivious to everything—and everyone—else in the room. He looked at one after the other, muttering to himself the whole time.

"I don't know how much use these will be," ventured the duke after quite a time had gone by. "They are very old and I'm sure there have been changes made over the years that never got recorded."

"And surely the ratkin have been carving out their own tunnels since they got here," said Sir Hedrick. "Those are the ones we need to know about."

That seemed to get through to Paddy. He looked up and squinted at the knight. "Aye, we do. But the ratkin didn't just walk into the city one day and start diggin'! Even you might have noticed that. So they surely started in the sewers and then dug their own tunnels from there. I don't suppose you noticed where they might have been throwin' the dirt and rocks from their diggin'?"

"Uh… there have been some unusual sand bars and rocks in the river the last few months," said one of the counselors. "Some ships have gone aground in channels which are normally clear."

"Yes, the beasties were tossing the spoil in the river," said Paddy, nodding. "Makes sense. So, by starting with what we know of the sewers before they got here, we can…"

"I don't see what that matters," said the priest, his chubby face turning red. "We know they are down there. They are killing our people! My healers are busy day and night dealing with the diseases that are breaking out! You need to go down and get them!"

"They will, Your Grace," said the duke, "they will. But you have to give them a little time to prepare."

"Aye," said Paddy, frowning at the priest. "I'll just take these back to our camp and study them tonight and…"

"My lord!" exclaimed the archivist. "You can't let this… this… person walk off with my documents!"

"Now, now, Master Paley, I'm sure Learned Bobart will take good care of them. But I think this is a good time to close the meeting. Our guests need to rest, and we all need to prepare for what lies ahead. Thank you all."

The archivist and the priest went away grumbling, but the rest appeared in better spirits than they'd been at the start of the meeting. Duke Albustus escorted the halflings out. He waved his guards back so that they could have a moment of private speech. "Don't mind Prelate Lesnak. He's very worried about the people here, and I can't blame him. But he's never been a patient man."

"Seems like half your job here is soothin' ruffled feathers," growled Paddy.

Albustus snorted a laugh. "Yes, it does seem like that sometimes! But without ruffling yours, Lear… ah, if you don't like that title, what should I call you, sir?"

"Just call me Paddy. 'Tis me name after all."

"Very well, uh, Paddy, how long do you think it will take to devise your plan?"

"Depends on what I find in these drawings," he replied lifting the rolls of parchment. "But I think I'll have somethin' to talk about by this time tomorrow. Mayhaps we can talk again—without the priest fella."

Dunstan glanced at the duke. The Church of the Children wasn't the only religion in the League, which was quite tolerant about people's beliefs, but it was the largest denomination by far and held considerable influence on secular affairs. Its leaders could not be dismissed easily. But to his relief, the duke made no objections.

"Very well," said Albustus. "Master Dunstan, I won't ask your men to stand a watch tonight after your long march, but could you do so tomorrow night? It would help a lot and raise the spirits of the people."

"Yes, certainly, my lord," said Dunstan.

They left the city and walked back to their camp. The boys had already settled in, erecting tents and making themselves at home. A sizeable crowd of the locals were there. Some were trying to sell the halflings food and drink, but there were so many others there just giving it for free, business was poor. Before he went off to his own tent, Dunstan turned to the engineer.

"Paddy, you were right about the humans doing things big. It's been a long while since I visited one of their cities and I'd forgotten just how big. Can you really come up with something? Because if you can't, and we have to go down into those tunnels and dig those bastards out, it is gonna cost us more of our people than I want to think about."

"Aye, that's for sure," replied Paddy, nodding grimly. "Miles o' tunnels, all black as pitch, and them vermin reoccupying them as fast as we clean 'em out. We need a better way. I'm hoping that these plans will let me find it."

*****

The night passed uneventfully, the boys too tired for more than a song or two. Dunstan got up once during the night to attend to necessities and noticed a light burning in Paddy's tent. He knew better than to disturb him.

The next morning, he drilled the troops for a while, but then just waited for the meeting with the duke. Paddy stayed in his tent. As the time for the meeting drew near, Dunstan went over to remind the engineer. Standing outside the tent, he could hear Paddy mumbling something in a sing-song manner. But then it stopped, and after a moment, the mumbles became clearer. "No, no it's rubbish.... I canna do it from here... All rubbish..."

"Paddy?" Dunstan pulled the tent flaps open a few inches to peer in.

"Rubbish, I say!"

The sudden shout made Dunstan flinch back, but then he pushed his way into the tent. Paddy was crouched over a small camp table covered with new parchment, the human's drawings in a pile on the ground next to him. The parchments were covered with a scrawl of ink. Paddy sat with a quill in his hand and an inkpot nearby, but his hand was shaking and spatters of ink were all over the parchment and the table—and Paddy.

"Paddy, are you all right?"

"What? What? Oh, 'tis you, Dunstan. Aye, aye, I'm all right. What time is it?"

"Time to see the duke."

"Ach, so it is. Well, let's be about it. Here, I'll need these." He took a few of the old drawings and rolled them up. "Let's go."

"Do you want something to eat? You missed breakfast—and elevenses."

"No, me stomach's in knots right now. I'll eat later." He pushed past him into the sunlight.

As they walked toward the city, Dunstan dared to ask: "Didn't go well, I take it?"

"What? No, no, it's all right. I was just hopin' I could take a shortcut, but it didn't work. We'll have t'do it the hard way. But I think we can do it."

"Do what?"

"Win."

They met in the same chamber as before, but aside from the duke, only Sir Hedrick and two other men were in attendance; Lord Barton, Albustus's chief advisor, and Sir Giles, commander of the city guard.

"Were there any attacks last night?" Dunstan asked.

"No, all was quiet, thank the gods."

"I'm sure they have spies planted in secret spots all over the city by now. They're sure to have seen our arrival, and they are probably lying low to see what we do next."

"I think you are right," said the duke. Then he turned to the engineer. "So, uh, Paddy, do you have anything for us?"

"Maybe, maybe," replied the engineer. "But I don't want to raise any false hopes until I'm sure."

"And what do you need to be sure?" Lord Barton asked. "We can't wait forever, you know."

"Oh, I know that! As for what I need, I'll show ye." He unrolled one of the plans on the table. It had a layout of the whole city, although from the date written in the corner, it was the city as it was over a hundred years earlier. The parchment kept trying to roll up again, so they pinned down the corners with cups and mugs.

"Now then," said Paddy, pulling out a bit of charcoal from a pouch on his belt. "From what I could learn from all those other plans you gave me, there are main sewer lines runnin' here… here… over here… and here. There are more, but these are all we need for now." There were now thick black lines on the parchment.

The duke cringed and muttered. "Master Paley isn't going to like this…"

Paddy took no notice. "Now, what I need is a rock sample, not just a loose stone, mind you, but a bit o' bedrock chipped from the main stone. I'll need six of 'em. From these locations, or as near as you can get to 'em." He started marking spots on the map with his charcoal.

"And just what do you need them for?" Barton asked.

"T'do me work! I don't ask you why y'need swords and spears for yer men, do I?" Barton snorted, but didn't say anything more.

Dunstan leaned closer and stared at the map. "So you're saying we need to go down in the sewers and then find a way further down until we can find bedrock and then hack off a piece of it for you? How big a piece?"

"Oh, big as yer fist, say. And I'm hopin' you can find what you need right in the sewers. Pry a few of the building stones loose and see if there's solid rock behind it."

"That might be true in these four spots you have near the city walls, Paddy," said the duke, "but I know that near the river, where you want the other two, they have to drive piles into the ground pretty deep before they find anything solid to build on."

"Aye, I was afraid of that. Well, we could just start digging down until we find what we need, but that could take weeks. We don't want to give the beasties that much warning of what we're up to. I'm sure they've dug down far enough, so you'll just have to find one o' their tunnels and go as far down as you have to."

"What do you need these rocks for?" demanded Barton. "If we are going to ask our men to go down in those holes, we want to be able to tell them why!"

Paddy looked annoyed. "I canna explain it to a… a…"

"A what? A human?" Barton was getting angry.

"That's not what I meant!" snapped Paddy.

"It's to work your magic, isn't it?" asked Dunstan, hoping to calm things down.

Paddy glared at him. "Well, yes, I suppose ye could call it that if ye want.

But it's a lot more than that."

Barton leaned back in his chair, looking thoughtful. "Well, why didn't you say so before? Magic, is it? What sort? What do you hope to accomplish?"

Paddy snorted in exasperation. "I dinna have the time to explain me art to ye! Now do ye want me help or not?!"

"Of course we do, Paddy," said the duke, who made a tiny gesture toward Barton with his hand. "We shall get you what you need."

"My lord," said Dunstan, "I would be willing to get the two samples near the river using my people. If Sir Giles and his men could manage the other four near the walls, I think we could get this done quickly."

"That is an excellent idea, Master Dunstan. How quickly can you move?"

"We could go this afternoon, before it gets dark," said Dunstan.

Sir Giles looked uncomfortable. "I… I'd prefer to wait until tomorrow, my lord. My men are edgy. I'd like to pick the men for the four parties myself. The best ones, you understand."

"Very well, but no later than that. Is that acceptable, masters?" He looked from Dunstan to Paddy.

"It's best that all six groups go at once to divide any reaction they might have," said Dunstan. "We can wait a day. You all right with that, Paddy?"

"Yes, better for certain to get all six at once."

"Very well then," said Albustus. "We'll move tomorrow at noon."

*****

The sun wasn't quite at its peak when Dunstan led a company of his troops into the city. There was no telling how numerous the ratkin spies were or how good a system they had for passing messages, so all six parties were doing their best to look like ordinary patrols until they were ready to strike. They had put the delay yesterday to good use by unobtrusively walking around the city to locate the sewer entrances closest to where they wanted to go.

He had brought fifteen swordsmen, ten archers, and five with cut-down spears which he hoped wouldn't get hung up in the close quarters they were likely to encounter. Plus four men with picks, pry bars, hammers, and chisels to get the rock Paddy wanted. They all wore stout leather jerkins and caps, but all their shields had been left back in camp. They would be too clumsy down in the tunnels.

Once the assault went ahead, another fifty halflings would converge on their entry site to cover their retreat if necessary. A second group under the command of Lurry Bevrige, his most experienced lieutenant, was doing the same thing across the river at the second location. Sir Giles's men should be moving into position about this time too, at the other four locations. They had torches, ropes, and lanterns hidden among their gear. He hoped that he'd planned for everything.

The one thing he hadn't planned for were the twenty or thirty children who had started following them.

Apparently, the sight of a group of armed soldiers just their size was irresistible to the little imps. More and more of them were tagging along, trying to mimic the movements of the halflings, laughing and shouting. He was a bit appalled that their parents were letting them wander loose in these dangerous times; but from their ragged appearance, maybe they didn't have any parents. There were still a lot of things he didn't understand about humans. Dunstan dropped back to the rear of his company.

"Toma," he said, addressing one of his troops, "when we go in, you hold back and make sure none of these pups try to follow us."

"Aw, but Dunstan…"

"No back talk! I mean it. In any case, I want someone minding the rope we'll let down to get back out again. Don't want that comin' loose! When Lubbin and his boys show up, they can take over and you can follow us down if you want. All right?"

Toma didn't look happy, but he nodded. "All right."

"Good. Now on your toes, we're nearly there." Dunstan hurried back to the front.

Their entry point into the sewers was a metal grate he'd found yesterday. It was set into the street in a little square where two streets intersected. They approached it just as one of the city clocks struck twelve.

"All right! Go!" he shouted.

Four halflings with metal hooks ran to the grate and pulled it loose in one smooth motion. Others took out torches and lit them from the lanterns carried by their fellows. Dunstan peered into the opening and saw that the drop was only about eight feet. He grabbed the frame which had held the grate, swung his legs down, and jumped, short sword at the ready. "Follow me!"

He splashed into… water that was about ankle deep. With his eyes still adjusted to the noon sun, he couldn't see a thing for a moment, but then others with torches joined him and he could see a few dozen feet in either direction. Paddy had no suggestion on which way would be best to go, but to follow the flow of the water would only take him to the river a few hundred feet away, so he chose the opposite direction.

"Gods! Human crap sure does stink!" someone hissed behind him.

"Quiet," he hissed back. "Noise carries down here!" His people shut up, but there was a steady series of splashes as more joined them in the sewer.

Dunstan moved forward, scanning the walls for openings.

He didn't look down, he looked up. If the ratkin had dug a connecting tunnel into the sewer (or more likely out of the sewer) they would have made it as high as possible so that water flowing through the sewer didn't end up in their tunnel. They moved several hundred feet through the stinking passage, now silent as only halflings could be, but found nothing. Dunstan was growing edgy; they needed to do this quickly, before the ratkin could respond.

He nearly missed it. An irregular patch in the stonework only caught his eye when he was almost past it. He stopped and looked closer. Yes, there was something here. He reached up and ran his fingers along the edges, wiping away the sludge and ooze. "There's a hidden hatch here. Give me that pry-bar," he whispered. It was handed to him and he stuck the point of it in a gap between the stones. He gave a pull and there was crunching sound, and then a whole piece of wall popped loose and splashed into the water. A black hole, about two feet square, gaped behind where the piece had been.

One of the boys gave him a boost, and Dunstan held a torch up to the hole and looked in. A narrow tunnel, little bigger than the hatch, led away into the dark. It was empty, but he could see the paw prints of ratkin in the dirt. He took a deep breath. There was nothing for it but to go on. He scrambled up into the hole. It was just high enough that he could go on hands and knees.

Sword in one hand and the torch in the other, he shuffled forward slowly, to allow his boys time to follow. If he met a ratkin in such close quarters, he'd be at a disadvantage; the miserable creatures went on all fours as often as they ran upright. But he met no one, and after about fifty feet, he came to what he first thought was a dead end. Then he saw that the tunnel went straight up for about three feet before continuing on in the original direction. A water-stop. They'd built it this way in case the sewer ever became completely filled and the water seeped through their hatch. This would keep the water from getting down into their tunnels.

He crawled up into the higher passage, but it only went on a few feet before dropping down again, and now the roof was actually high enough for him to stand upright. He advanced a few yards and then paused, listening for any sound other than his own people following along, but there was nothing except for the trickle of water. He was already dripping with sweat beneath his leather jerkin and cap.

Unless there were hidden side-tunnels, there was no obvious place from which an ambush could come except straight ahead. Would there be traps? Hidden pits with poisoned stakes? He found himself quivering.

This was no good, they had to keep moving. Every moment of delay put them in greater peril. The ratkin would soon know they were here—if they didn't already—and would not take long to attack. He moved forward again, the tunnel sloping gently downward now. He searched the walls for any hint of solid rock, but while there was stonework and rubble as well as plain dirt, it was all loose and clearly not part of the bedrock.

Then they reached an intersection. A new tunnel crossed the path of the one they were in, and just ahead, there was a shaft leading down with a wooden ladder in it. All right, this seemed promising. "Caldin," Dunstan said, turning to one of his older troops, "take five of the boys and hold here. The rest of us are going down. Hope we won't be long."

"Right," said the halfling, pulling five others aside.

Dunstan started down the ladder. He could not tell how far down it went or what might be waiting below. After about thirty rungs, he reached the bottom. It was in a larger chamber, maybe ten paces square. There were boxes and bags and piles of refuse scattered about, but no ratkin. Two tunnels led off in opposite directions.

Holding up the torch, he quickly examined the walls. Was there any solid rock here? No… no… there! A slight discoloration in the surface of the dirt led him to a spot on the far wall. He brushed at it with his hand and then dug out dirt from around it with his fingers. It was rock, but was it bedrock?

"Help me dig," he whispered. "See how far this piece extends."

Several others came up beside him and clawed away the dirt and loose gravel, and bit by bit, the rock was exposed. Soon they had an expanse four or five feet wide and extending down below the level of the floor. "Can't tell if it's bedrock," breathed someone, "but it's one big chunk of stone." Would this do? Dunstan did not want to have to come down here again!

"Dunstan! I hear something!" one of the others hissed. He looked and saw one of the boys guarding a passageway gesturing toward it. "Something's coming!"

"All right, this will have to do! Knock a piece off and we'll get out of here. The rest of you, stand ready!" The ones with the tools came forward; the others took up defensive positions near the passageways. The spearmen were in front with archers ready to fire past them, swordsmen in reserve to plug any holes.

One fellow held the chisel up against the rock and two with hammers stood on either side and swung them. The noise they made was shockingly loud in the enclosed space. Well, that's torn it! Every ratkin within a half mile will hear that! The chisel slowly penetrated into the rock, but no conveniently large pieces broke off.

A shout from his right drew Dunstan's attention away from the work.

The spearmen were poised and ready. An archer loosed off an arrow into the dark and an instant later was rewarded by a snarling shriek. He'd hit something.

"Hurry up!" He snapped over his shoulder as he moved to bolster the fighting line. Shielding his eyes from the glare of the torches, he peered down the tunnel. He couldn't see anything distinct, but there was movement. "Keep shooting, even if you can't see anything."

The archers obliged and a steady stream of arrows shot away. There were a few answering grunts and groans, but no more screams. Had they driven them off?

He looked back at the hammer and chisel men, but another commotion at the line spun him around again. The spearmen were fighting; thrusting spears at enemies Dunstan couldn't see. The archers were firing and everyone seemed to be shouting at the top of their lungs. Dunstan started forward, but just then a dark gray shape flew over the heads of the spearmen and landed on an archer, knocking him to the ground. The ratkin had a club in one claw, but it was using its teeth against the hapless archer.

Dunstan sprang forward and slashed the awful beast across the back of its neck. It stiffened for a moment and then collapsed. He dragged the carcass off the archer and winced when he saw the halfling's face covered in blood. "Tend to him!" he shouted, turning back to the fight. But the attack seemed to have been driven off. Dark shapes were piled at the feet of the spearmen, and the archers had their bows knocked but weren't firing.

"Dunstan!" cried one of the ones helping the wounded archer. "He's hurt pretty bad, but he'll live if we get him to a healer!"

"Then get him out of here!" He motioned back the way they had come.

"Dunstan! I think there are more coming from this way!" shouted a boy at the other passageway.

"How many do you…"

"Dunstan!"

"What?!"

One of the hammer men stood there with two large rocks in his hands. He flinched back at Dunstan's shout. "Uh, will these do?"

"Yes!" he cried in joy. "You take one and let me have the other. All right! Let's get out of here!" He stuffed the rock into a bag hanging from his belt. As he did so, his hand brushed against the little 'toy' Paddy had given him. He might need that soon.

The wounded halfling was being hauled up the shaft with a rope. Dunstan pulled everyone else back to form a ring around the base of the ladder. They stood there, breathing heavily and listening to the growing noise down both passageways.

"We're clear," came a shout from above. "You can come up!"

"Toolmen first," commanded Dunstan. "Archers next, swordsmen next, and spearmen last. Go." He could hear his people scrambling up the ladder, but he didn't look back. His eyes were locked on the passageways.

The swordsmen were just starting up when the attack came.

A grey-black wave erupted from both passageways at once, moving with that terrible quickness the ratkin possessed. In an eyeblink, they were on them, hideous shapes in the torchlight. Not quite rats, not quite people, they were an obscene mix of oily fur, red eyes, grasping claws, and snapping fangs. The spearmen skewered several, but they would have been overwhelmed in moments if the sword-carrying halflings hadn't immediately come to their aid. Dunstan was in the middle of it, hacking and slashing and parrying the blows of the enemy. Most of the ratkin appeared to be carrying weapons—clubs, knives, spears—but there were also some of the smaller ones with nothing but claws and teeth. One of them, darting between the legs of their larger kin, tried to sink its fangs into Dunstan's foot, but he managed to kick it away.

They beat off the first attack and the enemy retreated, leaving a dozen dead and wounded.

"Half of you get up the ladder! The rest of us will hold them!"

They crowded into a dense clump around the ladder, some going up, others facing outward. The ratkin began edging out of the two passageways, and realizing that all the archers had gone up, became bolder. Some began throwing things, rocks, mostly, a few of which found their targets.

A spearman stumbled back, clutching his head. Dunstan shoved him toward the ladder and took his place in the line. He had his sword in one hand and a torch in the other. The ratkin got up the nerve to make another rush, and there was a moment of savage fighting around the base of the ladder before they drew off again.

He kept sending his boys up, but every one that went up was one less to hold the line. The last one up was going to have a hell of a time making it…

Another rush and another repulse, and two more wounded halflings. Both could still climb on their own, fortunately, but there were only four of them left at the bottom now. The ratkin were massing in the room, watching for their chance.

"Last one up use the rope," came a call from above. Dunstan dared to glance behind him and he saw a rope had been thrown down with a loop in the end of it.

"All right," he said, "the rest of you get going."

"But, Dunstan," protested one.

"Go!" He stuck his sword under his left arm and dug into his bag with his right hand, being careful not to grab the precious rock. He pulled out Paddy's 'toy'. It was a clay pot with a wick-like fuse sticking out of it. He stuck the wick into the flame of his torch and it sputtered to life.

The ratkin were coming forward again, and he tossed the pot to the ground right in front of them. They flinched back and he turned away as a dazzlingly bright light filled the chamber, accompanied by a loud hissing.

"Go! Go on!" He pushed the others up the ladder and then turned. The light was obscured a bit by the cloud of smoke quickly filling the chamber, but it was still lit up like day. The ratkin were squeaking and snarling. A shape emerged from the cloud right in front of him, and Dunstan slashed at it and it fell back squalling. One with a spear appeared and its thrust was turned by Dunstan's leather jerkin. He shoved the torch into its face and its fur caught fire.

"Dunstan! Come on!"

The others were gone. He threw the torch into the smoke, grabbed the rope with his free hand, stuck his foot into the loop, and shouted: "Pull!"

There must have been a dozen boys on the other end of the rope, because he shot up the shaft so fast, he actually flew in the air at the top for a moment before landing on the floor. He scrambled to his feet and saw that most of his troops had already retreated back along the tunnel. He got the rest moving and brought up the rear, patting the bag to make sure the rock was still there.

Back along the tunnel, up over the water-stop, and then crawling through the low tunnel back to the sewer. Every moment he expected to hear the sounds of pursuit—or the grip of a clawed hand on his legs—but there was nothing. He half-fell out of the hole, but even the stench of the sewer was a welcome thing.

He organized a rear-guard and then they fell back to where they had started. A shaft of light came down through the opening, beckoning to them. Moments later, they were all back up on the street, and the iron grate was shoved back in place. Barri Lubbin was there with his troops, keeping back a small crowd of curious humans.

"Get what you wanted?" Lubbin asked.

"Yeah, I hope so," replied Dunstan. "But what I want right now is a bath!"

*****

"Will they do?" asked Dunstan.

"Oh, aye, aye, these are splendid," said Paddy, fingering the rocks. He clutched one in both hands and closed his eyes. "Yes, yes, it remembers."

Dunstan sighed and leaned against the tent post, the afternoon light streaming past him. He was freshly bathed but tired and sore in a dozen places.

All six forays had been successful. The four by the townsmen had been as easy as they'd hoped. They found some bedrock right there in the sewers, gotten their rocks, and gotten away with nothing worse than frayed nerves. Lurry Bevrige and his boys had to go deep, but they had been lucky and only encountered a small group of ratkin before finding their rock. Only Dunstan's group had met real trouble.

But they'd gotten off lightly; none killed and the wounded would survive to fight another day. He was grateful for the human healers. Ratkin often poisoned their weapons, and they were such filthy things; even unpoisoned wounds could fester.

"So you can work your magic? When?"

"Oh, right now, Dunstan, right now. There's not a moment to lose."

"All right, I'll leave you to it." He was looking forward to an early night.

"No, you can stay. I'll need your help with this."

Dunstan straightened up in surprise. Paddy rarely let anyone see him work and had no patience with people looking over his shoulder. "What… what do you want me to do?"

"Oh, it's nothin' hard, and nothin' uncanny, so don't worry." Paddy was spreading out a blanket on the ground inside the tent. He had the plan of Norwood, and he put it in the center. Then he set the six stones he had chosen near the edges of the blanket. Dunstan realized that they were arranged in the same pattern as the locations they'd come from on the map. Finally, he put a stack of large, blank sheets of parchment to the side with his ink pots and quills and then sat down on the blanket.

"Sit across from me. I'm gonna do a bit o' drawin' here. When I fill up a sheet, take it away and give me a fresh one. If I run low on ink, refill the pot. If I break a quill give me a new one. I… I won't be able to talk to you while I'm doin' this, but I think you'll know what t'do." He took a blank sheet of parchment and laid it on top of the map right in front of him.

"Drawing?" Dunstan asked, sitting down as directed. "But what do the rocks have to do with that?"

"Oh, but the rocks remember, you see. They remember where they were, what was near 'em. Right, left, above, below, they remember. At least for a while. Once they're broken loose from the whole, they start to forget. That's why loose stones won't do. But they remember for a while."

"And they talk to you?"

Paddy laughed. "In a manner o' speakin' they do. If y'know the language. If y'know how to tickle 'em into talkin'. Some rocks can be mighty close-mouthed, but I think these here are just dyin' to tell their tale!" The engineer was grinning.

"How long will it take?"

"Won't know until I see how much they have to tell. I hope not too long. Just a couple o' hours if we're lucky. All right, get ready, I'm gonna start."

Paddy took one last look around and then closed his eyes. He began to hum and then to softly sing, and Dunstan realized it was the same song he'd heard from outside the tent the other day. He could make out words but did not recognize what language they were. This went on for quite a while. From time to time, Paddy reached out his hands to touch the stones, his movements unerring despite having his eyes closed. He would touch one and then another in no pattern Dunstan could see.

Perhaps half an hour went by like this until Paddy became completely still. Then he picked up a quill and dipped it in the ink. With his eyes still closed, he began to draw on the parchment. Somehow the engineer could 'see' what he was doing. The lines were precise and he knew when to dip the quill again. The drawing that took shape was as clean and clear as if it had been drawn by a master scribe at his workbench! Dunstan looked on in fascination as Paddy worked.

When the sheet was nearly filled, Paddy froze in place, and Dunstan realized that he wanted a new sheet. Carefully sliding the full sheet out, he put a new one in its place, trying to get it in exactly the same spot. Paddy immediately went back to work. Dunstan leaned forward to make sure there was still ink in the pot.

The second sheet was filled and then the third. It was starting to get dark inside the tent. He put the fourth sheet in place and then dared to slowly light some candles. Maybe Paddy could work in the dark, but he couldn't. The 'couple of hours' were long past, and Paddy kept working. Dunstan's stomach was growling, but when one of his boys pulled the tent flap open a bit and held up a plate, he waved him away. Five sheets, six. He refilled the inkpot. Twice. It was fully dark outside and the stack of filled parchments was now higher than the pile of blank ones. How long was this going to go on? His earlier fascination was fading and his fatigue was growing. He could barely keep his eyes open now.

There was only one blank sheet left when Paddy suddenly stopped. "More?" he whispered. "There's more, you say? No, no, that's enough. More than enough." The quill fell out of his hand. "Enough!" he shouted, and Dunstan nearly fell over.

Paddy opened his eyes and blinked in confusion for a few moments. Then he closed them again and sighed a long, long, sigh.

"We done?" asked Dunstan.

"Aye, aye, we're done." Paddy opened his eyes again and stared right into Dunstan's. "And if I can't get me plan to work, we may all be done for good!"

*****

"Forgive me, Paddy, but are you absolutely sure about this?" asked Duke Albustus. "How could they possibly have dug something so extensive without us knowing?"

They were back in the duke's meeting room and the table was strewn with Paddy's drawings. Somehow his magic and the rocks' 'memories' had allowed him to draw a detailed plan of all the tunnels and chambers under the city. There were far more of them than anyone could have guessed—even in their worst nightmares. Mile after mile of tunnels; dozens, hundreds, of caves and chambers, leading down and down and down.

"This can't possibly be right!" sputtered Lord Barton. "It would take thousands of ratkin, years to have done this!"

"Well, if y'don't believe me, yer welcome to take me plans down there and check 'em for yerself!" Paddy said.

"Calm down, Paddy," said Dunstan. "They aren't trying to insult you or your work, and I can hardly blaming them for being doubtful. This is…" he waved his hand at the drawings. "…pretty hard to believe."

"We've only had the disappearances and attacks in the last few months," continued Barton. "If there were thousands of them down there, as these plans would indicate, how have they been feeding themselves? And there would have been thousands of tons of dirt and rock from the digging. Where have they been hiding that, Learned?"

Despite Barton's rudeness, it was a good question. Paddy looked sullen but kept his mouth shut.

"There… there's another possibility," said Dunstan.

"Really?" asked Barton skeptically. "Such as?"

"As you say, if there had been thousands of them down there digging all this recently, you would have had far more disappearances. But what if it wasn't all dug recently?"

"What do you mean?"

"Perhaps there weren't thousands working for a few months, perhaps there were just a few hundred, few enough that they could have fed themselves by stealing food or raising regular rats and eating them and no one up here would notice. For years, I mean. They could have been slowly digging the tunnels and the caves for years and years. In small amounts, the dirt and stone dumped in the river wouldn't be noticed."

"Aye, aye!" Paddy clamored excitedly. "Some of the memories… some of them were old… very old."

"But why would only a few hundred dig out such an enormous complex of tunnels and caves?" asked the duke.

"To be ready when more of them arrive," Dunstan said, grimly. "And it looks like they have."

Albustus frowned deeply, his bushy eyebrows drawing close together. "You're talking about an invasion. Not an infestation, an actual invasion. From outside."

"It could be, my lord," said Sir Giles. "There are tales that the ratkin were created by the dwarfs of the Abyss, but they've spread all through the lands since then. There could be dens of them anywhere, there's no one to dig them out. The gods only know how many of them there could be out there beyond the borders of the League."

"They could have sent an advanced party here years ago to make ready for this," suggested Dunstan. "They slipped into the sewers unseen, and they've been at work ever since, getting ready for their fellows to arrive. The ratkin we normally see are little better than beasts, but they do have leaders, and some of them are very clever."

The duke paged through the parchment sheets again. "If this is true, there is no way we can send our men down into this maze. We'd lose every one of them and the city would be left defenseless."

"I think you are right, my lord," said Dunstan. From the little he'd seen yesterday, there was no doubt in his mind that the ratkin lair would become a death trap.

The duke rubbed at his nose. "I can send word to the Council asking them for help. Have them send all the troops that are gathered at the muster here…"

"But that could take a month or more, my lord! We can't sit back here and do nothing!" Lord Barton exclaimed. "The ratkin aren't going to just hide there anymore! If we don't go down after them, they will come up after us!"

"Aye, that's true enough," said Paddy, breaking his silence. "But there may be another way than goin' down to them."

"What do you mean?"

"Dunstan," said Paddy turning to him. "In yer job, yer old job, I mean, when you found a nest o' moles or field mice under a garden, would you dig the whole place up, tryin' to get 'em out?"

"Not if I could help it."

"What would ye do?"

"Well, sometimes I'd use poisoned bait, but if there was water close by I'd… Flood them out!" He looked at the engineer, hope filling him. He was grinning.

"Aye, that y'would. And that's exactly what we are gonna do!"

The duke leaned forward eagerly. "Can it be done?"

"After studyin' the drawings I made, I think it can. T'won't be easy, but

I think it can be done. I'm gonna need a quite a bit o' stuff from you though."

"You'll get it. What do you need?"

"I've made a list. But you should also call in all those liegemen you were talkin' about before. If this works as I hope, there will be plenty for them to do!"

*****

"What do you need the barges for?" Dunstan asked as he followed Paddy down to the city docks along the river. He had a copy of Paddy's list, and while most of it made sense to him, he couldn't see the need for fifteen river barges. Barges loaded with rocks!

"Water's too low this time o' year," he replied. "And even in the rainy season, it wouldn't be high enough. We can't just trickle the water into their tunnels, y'know. With all the natural seepage they would have down there, they must have a right clever way of getting water out again, or they woulda been flooded out long ago. Pumps maybe. But whatever it is, it can probably handle any slow increase. No, we gotta dump it all in at once, surprise 'em, or it won't work."

"Makes sense, but I ask again: what are the barges for? You can't be thinking of using them like some giant set of buckets. How'd we pull 'em up and empty 'em into the holes? And why all the rocks?"

"No, yer right, Dunstan. I had a different idea. See that bridge down there?"

He looked down the river and near the edge of the city there was a stone bridge with five arches spanning the Allsop River. "I see it."

"Lovely thing, ain't it? I checked it out the other day and it's really well built. Not like some of the things you see humans make. Almost as good as dwarf work. Heh, maybe the dwarfs built it for 'em."

"Paddy…"

"Anyway, all the water flows through those five arches. If we were to block 'em up…"

"With the barges?"

"Right enough. Block up those archways and the water will back up right through the city. I've got six of the sewer outlets in mind, and once they're good and covered with water, we can do the other things I've got planned and… well, then we'll see what we'll see."

"Huh. But with only five arches, why do you need fifteen barges?"

"Well, I'll sink the first five and…"

"Sink?"

"Of course. Just floatin' 'em up against the arches won't do anything. So we get 'em in position, knock holes in the bottom, and let 'em sink. Once they're settled, we do the same with the next five and then the next five. All goes well, and we'll have all five archways nearly stoppered. That will back the water up along the river like we want. Then… well then the real fun begins."

"But the ratkin have measures to keep the sewer water out of their tunnels," protested Dunstan. "I told you about that water-stop we had to crawl over. Just backing the water up into the sewers won't do it!"

"Right you are! That was the real reason I needed the rocks to make those plans. I needed to know the layout of their tunnels and all. The beasties will have made provisions to handle any sort of natural influx of water. So we need to give them something they haven't planned for. I'll show you what we're doin' as soon as I finish up with these barges."

Dunstan looked at his old friend. "You had this all planned out, didn't you? Right from the start."

Paddy shrugged. "I had the idea from the start. Wasn't sure we could make it work. Looks like we might."

They reached a dock where a number of barges were tied up and several of the duke's men were waiting.

"Did you tell the duke you planned to sink those barges?" Dunstan asked.

"Ah… it might have slipped me mind."

*****

Three days later, they were ready. The duke's vassal troops had arrived, the city guards were mustered, the second group of halflings were there, the barges were loaded and in position, and the women and children and old people were barricaded in houses, taverns, and temples, guarded by anyone else who could wield a weapon.

And the holes were dug.

Along with the barges, the holes were the key part of Paddy's plan. In a dozen locations around the city, large excavations were underway. Half of them were decoys to prevent the ratkin from realizing what was really going on. Hopefully the vermin would think that the townspeople were making some foolish attempt to literally dig out the ratkin. They'd laugh and pull their forces away from the digging areas and wait for the humans to wear themselves out or make an even more foolish move to send their troops down into the ratkin tunnels. By the time they realized the truth, it would be too late.

The six excavations which were not decoys had been precisely located by Paddy using the drawings he'd made. Once the water started to back up, the existing sewers would bring the water right to where the digging was going on and then… then, as Paddy, put it, the fun would begin.

Dunstan, Paddy, and the duke met near the bridge to watch things get started. It was just before dawn and the river men were moving the barges into place. To Dunstan, who had no experience with boats at all, it looked like a tricky operation, but the men knew what they were doing. Using poles and long oars, they got the first five barges lined up with the bridge's arches and let the current carry them up to the massive stone supports. Even from two hundred yards away, he could hear the wooden ends of the barges grinding against the stone as the river pinned them in place.

Shouts from the barge crews and from men on the bridge carried across the water. Ropes were let down and most of the men scrambled up them to safety. Two men remained behind in each vessel. Dunstan couldn't see, but they were hacking holes in the bottom of the barges with axes. Then they too climbed the ropes up the bridge.

The barges, already lying very low in the water due to their load of rocks, quickly settled deeper. Once the water started to spill over their sides, they disappeared with amazing swiftness, leaving just some momentary swirls on the surface, which quickly vanished.

He couldn't notice any immediate change in the flow of the river, but the second set of barges were already being moved into position. Things didn't go quite so smoothly this time. Four of the barges reached their positions with no trouble, but the fifth did not and was nearly swept under the arch and on downstream. A great deal of shouting and activity followed with ropes being tossed to men on the shore, and after almost a half hour, the barge was finally pulled into the proper spot and sunk. All the watchers were chafing at the delay. The sun was fully up now and they wanted this to go quickly, so things could be settled before nightfall.

As the final set of barges were moved up, Dunstan thought he could see some change in the river's flow. There were swirls and eddies around the bridge that he didn't think had been there before. He focused on one section of the stone on the bridge, and as he watched, it looked as though the water was slowly creeping higher.

Then the last five barges sank from sight and things began to happen. There was a very distinct turbulence in the flow of the river through the arches, almost like the rapids in a river. The water was backing up! Just like Paddy had promised. Dunstan could clearly see the water climbing up sides of the stone supports.

"It's working!" he cried.

"Course it is," said Paddy. "The big question now is how fast it will work."

"Looks like it's working pretty fast."

"It will, at first. But the flow is constant and the volume it needs to fill keeps gettin' bigger as it backs up farther and farther upstream. Didn't have good figures on the amount of flow or the width o' the river, so I couldn't calculate it exactly, but it will probably be noon or later before we can do the next step. But come on, let's get some breakfast."

Dunstan wanted to stay and watch the water climb. But he realized that he needed to eat, and anyway, a commander had to look calm and controlled. The duke invited them to eat with him, but he insisted on going back to camp and eating with his troops. Most of those troops had questions about how things were going, so he spent more time talking than eating, but eventually the meal was over and he and Paddy could go back and have a look at the progress of the river.

By midmorning, the water was up six or eight feet and getting close to the mouth of the sewer outlets closest to their improvised dam. "The locals tell me that durin' the spring melt, the water gets higher than this, and they often have a back-flow in the sewers," said Paddy.

"How high d'you think it will get?"

"Hard t'say. The barges are about five feet tall from bottom to top. Three of 'em sittin' on top of each other ought to raise the river twelve or fifteen feet, allowin' for leakage. We might even get more than that 'cause the support arches narrow down at the top, naturally, which might restrict the flow even more."

"Fifteen feet will put it up over the banks in some spots," said Dunstan, eyeing the water cautiously.

"Aye, it will. I warned 'em about that, and they said they'd get the folks out of the buildings close to the river. Hope they did."

By noon, the water was starting to move into the sewers, and Paddy decided they needed to proceed with the plan. He led Dunstan to one of the excavations which cut through the sewer line that would soon be flooded. The work crews were swinging barrels of the gunpowder Paddy had brought down into their hole. Water was already rising against a temporary dam built across the sewer line.

"Once the powder is in place and the fuse set, they'll back-fill as much as they can," said Paddy. "That'll send the blast down more than up. Ought t'punch a hole right into their tunnels. I'd rather set off all six at once, but we can't wait. This hole an' the one on the opposite side o' the river will be flooded long before the four farther upstream. Can't risk having the water douse it all before we can blow it."

Soon, the powder was all set, and fifty men were madly shoveling dirt and rock back into the hole. A messenger came saying that progress at the other holes was coming along at the same rate. Dunstan looked around at the surrounding buildings. "How much damage will the explosion do to these?"

"A fair amount, I'm afraid. We got all the people out o'course, but they'll have some re-buildin' t'do once this is all over."

"It's a shame," said Dunstan, "but not near as much as they'd have if the ratkin have their way."

"Now that's the truth," nodded Paddy. "All right, looks like we're about ready." He walked over to the foreman and soon all the men were moving away to a safe distance. Dunstan joined him where the fuse came up out of the hole. Paddy pointed to it. "You want t'do the honors, Commander?"

Dunstan shook his head. "This is all yours, Paddy. You do it."

"All right, get ready to run." He had procured a small lantern and used it to light the fuse. It sparked and sputtered and burned off toward the hole. "Let's go!"

Paddy trotted rather than ran, and Dunstan kept pace with him. They stopped where most of the men were waiting about a hundred yards down the street. The burning fuse was lost to sight and they waited. And waited. "Did the fuse go out?"

Boooom!

A massive explosion erupted from the hole and the ground shook. A geyser of smoke, dust, dirt, and rocks flew skyward. The cloud swirled down the street toward them, and pebbles and a few larger rocks rained down all around. One man yelled when a rocked bounced off his shoulder.

"In answer to your question," said Paddy. "No."

Dunstan grinned. "So did it work?"

"Let's go see." Paddy led the way back to the hole, as the breeze carried off the last of the dust and smoke. The opening was considerably larger now, and several of the nearby houses had some impressive rents knocked in them, too. Even before he got close enough to see down into it, Dunstan could hear water rushing.

The bottom of the hole was now a whirlpool.

Water flowed steadily into it from the direction of the river. Round and round it went and then down. Bits of wood and debris were sucked down along with the water. From time to time, huge bubbles would erupt, disrupting the flow for a moment. Paddy looked down and nodded. "Just like I was hopin'. The explosion blew through into a main ratkin tunnel that was below the sewer and now the river will fill it up—and all the connectin' tunnels."

"Surely the ratkin will have ways to seal off something like this," said Dunstan.

"Of course they will. That's why we're doin' this in five other places."

As Paddy spoke, there was another explosion from across the river. He nodded. "I studied the plans until me head was ready to burst. By getting water in all six locations, we ought to flood almost the whole system."

"Paddy, you're a marvel!"

"Th' river's doin' all the hard work."

They went across to the site of the second explosion and the situation there was about the same, although one of the nearby houses had collapsed completely after the blast. Then they went back to the river and saw that it had risen even more and was indeed spilling over its banks in some areas. The next two sewer outlets would soon be covered, and Paddy hurried off to supervise the next explosions. Dunstan stayed and watched the river for a while. Duke Albustus found him there.

"So it's working?"

"Seems to be. Accordin' to Paddy, once all six explosions have gone off, we ought to flood nearly the entire tunnel system."

"Oh, that's wonderful!" Albustus cried. "I had been steeling myself for some awful battle down in those tunnels, and now there won't need to be a fight at all. Those awful creatures will be drowned instead!"

A chill went through Dunstan. "Uh, my lord, I've dealt with rats and similar vermin, one way or another, for much of my life. And I've learned a few things. One of those things is that rats don't drown easily. They can hold their breaths for an unbelievably long time. I wouldn't be counting on this lot of rat-men to drown. At least not all of 'em."

Albustus looked startled. "But… but if they don't drown…"

Dunstan nodded. "They'll have to come up."

*****

By mid-afternoon, all six bombs had gone off, and the Allsop River was pouring into the ratkin tunnels. Dunstan didn't doubt that quite a few of the ratkin would drown in the flood, trapped in deep chambers cut off by the rushing water. But the water would naturally make its way to the lowest levels by the most direct route. Many tunnels and chambers wouldn't be flooded immediately, but as the waters rose, the ratkin would be forced up and up. They'd lose a lot of their weapons and their fiendish devices, and hopefully, much of their organization. But they'd come up, desperate and angry and ready for a fight.

The big question was where?

Paddy's maps suggested a few likely locations; but while the engineer could determine with a certain amount of confidence the routes the water would take down, he couldn't predict at all how the enemy might come up. So the defenders had to try and protect everywhere, and it wasn't possible with the troops they had on hand. They established outposts with good views, sent out patrols, and kept striking forces in central locations to respond when they were needed. Dunstan and his troops were stationed on the eastern side of the river, close to their camps. Everyone was nervous, but most seemed confident.

The sun was well in the west when the first reports of fighting came from across the river. Small groups of ratkin were emerging from sewer openings. Most were exhausted and disoriented and easily dispatched by the duke's soldiers, but some fought back savagely. Worse, others escaped into the streets of the city and would have to be tracked down.

Shortly after, similar reports started arriving from the east side of the city. Dunstan had a dozen patrols of about fifty troops each moving from place to place in tandem with the city guards. He kept the bulk of his halflings in the market district, ready to dispatch reinforcements wherever they were needed. For a while, the patrols seemed able to deal with the situation, but as it started to get dark, the ratkin appeared more frequently and in larger numbers. Dunstan had to send out party after party, and his reserves dwindled. Still, the fighting was going well and human and halfling casualties had been light.

"If we can keep wiping them out as they come up in small groups, we ought to be able to deal with this," said Lurry Bevrige, munching on a piece of bread.

Dunstan shook his head. "We haven't dealt with a tithe of 'em yet, Lurry. There have got to be a lot more coming. Paddy, will there be areas down there that the water never reaches? How many could stay hidden below?"

The engineer shrugged. "Hard t'say. If they had time, they might be able to seal off the tunnels leading to some areas. They have to have dug a lot o' air shafts to keep from suffocatin' down there, so there could be places where they could survive for a while."

"How long can we keep the place flooded?"

Another shrug. "That depends on how long our hosts are willin' t'have their sewers backed up and their waterfront under water. As long as we keep the river blocked, it will keep the tunnels flooded."

Dunstan nodded. "Can't say I look forward to a fight, but I'd rather have it done with now."

It was fully dark when a message from the duke reported serious fighting in a section near the western walls. It seemed that the ratkin had secret tunnels which emerged into the basements of some of the larger buildings. They had emerged, slaughtered the people in the buildings, and when they felt strong enough, came out to fight. The duke wasn't sure how many, but there seemed to be several hundred, at least. His troops were trying to keep them contained to that one area.

"Damnation," said Dunstan. "They could be doin' that over here, too. We're gonna have to start sending patrols house to house to check on things and warn the people to look in their cellars!" He dispatched messengers to give instructions to his existing patrols and then sent out more patrols. He only had about five hundred left in his reserve now.

The night wore on and the fighting seemed to be dying down in the west. The patrols were still finding and dispatching small groups that were coming up, but everyone was getting tired. Dunstan started rotating his patrols, bringing some back to the marketplace to rest and eat, and replacing them with halflings who had not been out yet. And this could go on all night and into the next day…

He had just sat down and leaned against a sack of turnips to try and catch a short nap when Paddy was suddenly shaking him awake. "Dunstan! Wake up!"

"Wha…? What is it?"

"Trouble! The temple district! Ratkin! A whole swarm of 'em! The humans are beggin' for our help."

He sprang to his feet and shouted for all his troops to get ready to move. In moments, they were trotting down the street toward the great square where all the main temples were located. "Did the messenger say how many?" he asked Paddy as they moved.

"No, just that there were a whole lot of 'em comin' outta the temples. The bastards musta gathered in the catacombs underneath."

"Didn't the bloody priests post guards?!"

"Guess not."

"Gods!"

"Yeah, them, too, from the sound o' things!"

As they got closer, the sounds of fighting were growing. Clashing weapons, men's shouts, the higher-pitched voices of halflings, and the teeth-gritting squeals of the ratkin echoed down the street. Several great bells were ringing wildly. There was a strong smell of smoke in the air. Dunstan stopped his troops for a few moments to get organized. Spearmen in front, backed by swordsmen, archers behind. When all was ready, they started forward at a quick march.

The street they were on emptied into the square on its eastern side.

The great temples to the gods reared up on all four sides. They were huge stone structures many stories high with imposing facades and tall polished columns. The biggest was the temple for the Church of the Children, but there were others for different gods and beliefs. Dunstan was unsettled by this sort of architecture, but he supposed the gods liked it.

At the moment, though, some of the gods' houses were on fire. Flames poured out of the high windows, lighting up the square. Bands of soldiers, some human, some halfling, were battling the ratkin in half a dozen places. It was a swirling melee with little order that Dunstan could see. More troops were spilling into the square as the city's reinforcements were arriving. But more ratkin were pouring out of the huge doors of the temples, too. There didn't seem to be any real order on either side.

"We need to form a battle line!" Dunstan shouted. "This sort of fighting favors the ratkin!" There weren't any enemies close by, so he used the opportunity to deploy his column into a fighting line about a hundred yards long. He had a few halflings with horns, and he had them blow for all they were worth. "Rally on us!" He waved to the friendly troops nearby and some fell back to join him, extending the line.

As soon as they were in position, the halfling archers opened fire on any ratkin not closely engaged. This got their attention, and soon a mob of the vile creatures was forming, trying to work up the nerve to attack. They hesitated for a few moments, clearly not liking the solid line they faced, and that allowed the archers to hit more of them. But then a ratkin, much larger than the rest, came to the front and led them forward in a charge.

The archers brought down a dozen more, but then the ratkin smashed into the line. The halfling spearmen impaled many, but once they were close in, all they could do was use their shields to try and keep them at bay. The second rank of swordsmen pushed in and slashed at anything they could reach. Archers stood on tip-toe and fired over the heads of their fellows.

The fight only lasted a few moments. When their charge failed to break the halfling line, the ratkin fell back across the square. They left at least two score of their dead behind. A dozen halflings were down, too, although only four of them were dead. The dead and wounded were pulled to the rear and the line reformed.

All the while, the other fights going on had petered out. The humans fell back to join up with the halflings, and the scattered bands of ratkin merged with the larger band which had made the charge. Dunstan didn't have any authority over the human soldiers, but he took charge of them anyway. Well, most of them. There was a group of temple guards in gilded armor surrounding Prelate Lesnak who ignored him when he directed them to a section of the line. The priest looked dazed, but Dunstan noted that he carried an ornate mace and it was not unbloodied.

Once he had everything in order, his battle line stretched almost the whole way across the square. Still, he didn't have more than half his halflings and no more than five or six hundred humans. Where was everyone else? He rounded up a dozen runners and sent them out with orders to send anyone they could find to the great square.

His archers and some human crossbowmen were firing at the ratkin, but the enemy was massing at the far end of the huge space and was barely in range. But more of them were still coming out of the temples to join the others.

The ratkin he had seen so far had carried little in the way of armor, nor weapons larger than a dagger, club, or crude spear. But now twenty or thirty individuals came toward them and began to use slings to hurl stones. A stone the size of a fist flung by a sling could shatter an arm or a skull, and people began to get hit. Some had shields to cover behind, but others did not. The fast-moving ratkin made poor targets, and the archers had little luck in bringing any of them down. And unlike the archers, the ratkin slingers were never going to run out of ammunition.

"We're gettin' the worst o' this exchange," said Paddy, dodging a rock. "We may have to go and drive those critters off, Dunstan."

"I know, but damn it, they outnumber us. Where the blazes is the duke and his men?"

"Might be tied up fightin' across the river. Have ye sent for help?"

"I have! But you're right, we can't just stand here gettin' hit. Let's push and see what happens."

He sent the word up and down the line that they were going to attack. It took a while to get everyone ready, and they lost more people to stones in the meanwhile, but at last he sounded the horns and the line lurched into motion. Another one of his patrols showed up just as they began, and he formed them up with him as a reserve.

They advanced across the square and the ratkin skirmishers fell back in front of them. But the rest of the enemy horde stood their ground on the far side of the square. That was odd; ratkin usually met an attack with a countercharge of their own. Had they been demoralized? Were all their leaders dead? *I don't like this…*

He glanced to either side, but there was nothing there except abandoned temples.

Are they abandoned?

"Halt! Halt!" he screamed.

As he shouted, ratkin erupted from the doors of the flanking temples. Not a huge number, a hundred, perhaps, but they were flanking his line. If they got around into the rear…

"Dunstan!" Paddy was there at his side. "You take care o' the ones on the right! I'll handle the ones on the left!"

"How are you…?"

"Just go!"

He went. Crying to his reserve to follow, he ran toward the right end of the line. All the troops had halted at this unexpected attack, and the two ends of the line were curling back to try and face the ratklin on their flank. But now the main force of ratkin was surging forward again, too. If the formation came apart, they would be finished.

Dunstan and his fifty halflings threw themselves at the ratkin on the right. The vile creatures seemed surprised by this sudden counterattack and flinched backwards, toward the temple they'd been hiding in. Dunstan pressed after them, cutting down several; his halflings killed more. The survivors scampered back through the huge temple doors. Dunstan halted his troops on the steps and looked back.

On the opposite side of the square, there was a sudden burst of light, followed by crackling booms that echoed off the temple walls. More of Paddy's toys? It seemed likely. The other ratkin flanking force fell back in disarray at this sudden shock.

But the whole line was engaged now, and the ratkin had the momentum. Yard by yard, the humans and halflings were pushed back by a tide of black and gray-furred vermin. People were falling, and there weren't many reserves left to fill the gaps. Dunstan brought his group back to the main line and tried to plug holes. The line contracted as the flanks pulled in toward the center and the ratkin threatened to lap around the ends, flanking them again. The ones in the temples, seeing their fellows winning, came out again and added their weight to the attack.

Somehow, he managed to keep things from falling apart, and finally they were back on the east side of the square, the line was now a crescent with each end anchored on a temple. There was a single street to their rear which would be the only way out if they had to retreat again. He couldn't tell how many they had lost, but it was far too many—and any wounded left behind wouldn't survive long out there.

Paddy came up to him and shrugged. "I'm all out o' tricks, lad." He looked around. "This could o' gone better."

That was the truth, but they were still holding. A few score of men and halflings came up along the street behind them and he threw them into the line. Then the roof of one of the burning temples collapsed with a roar, and the commotion to their rear seemed to startle the ratkin. They drew off to regroup, giving the defenders a chance to catch their breaths.

Dunstan did what he could to shore up the line, sure the enemy would be back. But his troops were exhausted, the archers nearly out of arrows, and many on the verge of panic. In the middle of the square, the ratkin were reorganizing, too; and to his dismay, another large group was emerging from one of the temples, and these were the largest ones he'd seen yet. Easily man-sized, some were wearing armor and carrying deadly-looking weapons. The lesser ratkin were driven into a frenzy by these reinforcements and leaped in the air and howled spine-chilling battle cries. They can smell victory.

"Steady lads!" he cried, but his words rang hollow. They couldn't hold, and they all knew it.

But they didn't run. They held their ground and gripped their weapons. The men knew that if they lost, then their families would be killed or worse. Their homes would be burned and the city of Norwood would become a ratkin colony, a foothold for an invasion of the League. The halflings didn't run, either. They'd pledged to help their friends, and they would hold to their word—to the last.

The ratkin started forward, the newcomers leading the way. The archers let loose their last arrows and brought a few down, but it wasn't enough.

"Well, it's been an honor, Dunstan Rootwell," said Paddy, holding out his hand.

"For me, too, Paddy," said Dunstan, taking it. "I just wish that…"

He was interrupted by a horn call. No, by a dozen horn calls. Their music rang off the sides of the buildings and filled the square. There was a roar in the distance, and the ratkin host came to a halt, the creatures looking around and sniffing the air.

"Look!" someone cried.

At the far end of the square, behind the ratkin, a column of armored cavalry burst into the open. A banner bearing the duke's emblem was at the front. Hundreds and hundreds of horsemen emerged from the street, and without pausing, formed a line and charged into the enemy rear. Hundreds more men on foot emerged from other streets to join the attack.

The ratkin were thrown into a panic and could organize no defense before it was too late. The horsemen slammed into them, skewering them with lances, or simply crushing them under the hooves of their warhorses. The infantry followed along, and in a twinkling, the enemy was hemmed in, trapped between Dunstan's line and the duke's men.

Dunstan's troops held firm and became the anvil for the duke's hammer. Some of the ratkin fought fiercely, but many simply tried to get away. Few succeeded. There were a lot of them, and the slaughter lasted until dawn.

As the ray of the rising sun peeked through the clouds of smoke and revealed the scene of carnage, Duke Albustus rode up to Dunstan and dismounted. "Hail, Master Dunstan!" he cried. "Victory, my friend!"

Dunstan just stared at him, too tired to speak. Victory? Yes, it was, he supposed. But at what cost? How many of his people were dead? Hundreds, he was sure. Many more were wounded. It would not be a joyous homecoming. But it was a victory. They had done their job and could go home proud of what they had done.

The duke was still waiting for him to say something. But the only thing that came out of his mouth was: "What kept you?"

*****

"A safe journey, Master Dunstan," said the duke. "Words cannot express the gratitude of my people or the debt we owe you. Without your help, we would have been lost."

Three weeks had passed since the battle, and the halflings were preparing to go home. There had been a lot additional work and a little fighting to do, but the Battle of Temple Square, as it was now being called, had broken the backs of the ratkin, and their resistance had been minimal. They had kept the river dammed up for a week, and Paddy had talked to some more rocks to divine where any ratkin might still be lurking underground. A bit of digging and a bit of fighting, and one more rather large explosion had done the job.

The cost had been shocking. A hundred and ninety-two halflings were dead and nearly that many more wounded. Twice that many humans had died, many of them civilians, and the damage to the city would take a year to repair. But compared with what might have happened, Dunstan supposed it was a bargain.

There had been some grumbling among his people about pulling human chestnuts out of the fire, but he'd reminded them that they'd found the human's cavalry useful in driving off mounted raiders often enough in the past—something the halflings were ill-equipped to handle—and the grumbles had subsided.

Even so, the force that was marching home was a lot smaller than the one which had come to Norwood. Well, not exactly smaller, they were all still there, except a quarter of them were not marching. Paddy's wagons were now carrying bodies instead of gunpowder, and the duke had lent them enough wagons and teams to allow the wounded to ride.

The good-byes were all said and they started out. As they crested the rise and looked back at Norwood, Dunstan said to Paddy, "I hope they keep a watchful eye and make sure those vermin don't come back. I had thought that my rat-catching days were behind me. I surely don't want to have to do this again!"

"Well, with the flooding and the lack of anyone to maintain 'em, most of those tunnels and caves ought to collapse very quickly. I suppose I ought to offer the League my services as a rock tickler and check out all o' their cities from time t'time."

"That might be a good idea. And it certainly is a good thing you knew how to do that! Where did you learn it?"

"It's dwarf magic. Learned it from one o' them years ago in exchange for some favors I did 'em. They use it for mining."

"I guess it would be very useful for them."

"Oh, it is, it is!" Paddy fell silent and then looked thoughtful. "D'you suppose I should tell the duke about that big silver vein I saw under their north wall?"

THE LAST STAND

By William Donohue

The horses pawed the ground nervously when the dragons were near. No matter how long they spent around the scaled beasts, there was a healthy fear in the hearts of the steeds. Sindfar Greenspar whispered to his horse to calm her. She bowed her head several times in acknowledgement, but he could still sense her unease. The morning was colder than usual for this time of year; a slight trail of steam rose from the horse's nostrils, but it was nothing compared to that which he had seen coming from the dragon's. What was even most disconcerting was the smell of decay that came on the crisp wind.

"Commander Sindfar." Sindfar turned to look at the elf that approached and put his hand to his breast in salute. "Lord Greybar wishes you to approach."

Sindfar returned the salute and followed the dragonrider's aide. They passed by many of the dragons that his clan was known to ride into battle, and Sindfar could not help but stare at them in awe. For the most part, the dragons rested calmly with their eyes shut. One in particular shook its head and raised its long neck, towering high. Sindfar watched as its trainer stroked its paw gently, causing the beast to lie back down and rest its eyes once more. There was nothing more sacred within their clan than the bond shared between dragon and elf; they were not master and pet, but instead kindred spirits.

Lord Greybar's command tent was next to his dragon, pens of sheep on either side to feed both mount and rider.

"Commander," Greybar opened his tent flap and motioned the cavalryman in. "Please, come in. Drink?"

Sindfar nodded and went to pour the ewer, but the dragonrider waved him off and poured the nectar in two silver goblets himself.

"I am sorry to be brusque, Commander, but we need to move fast on this." Sindfar followed Greybar over to a map hanging on the side of his tent. The latter moved his hands over several areas as he spoke. "We've located several large formations of the undead host moving toward our borders. They seem to be led by both a necromancer and a vampire lord, and their army will most likely go to old battle sites in the hopes of raising more troops. In the old days, the humans especially did not burn the dead, and there is still a potential for them to raise more skeleton troops. One in particular, here," he jabbed a spot on the map, "we believe is a potential site of a great battle. If they get there before we can clean the area, they can produce a dangerous force."

Greybar paused and circled several plains on the map past some of the large woods. "We have several mages trying to scourge the main areas, but these areas," he pointed again with a stabbing motion, "need to be held to delay the enemy. Although our dragons are powerful, the necromancers have some formidable spells to use against them. By dividing their attention, we can pierce their defenses."

Sindfar nodded again. "You can count on my troops to do what is necessary, Lord. But… there is always something else unspoken."

Greybar turned from the map and waved his hand in a circular motion. "On top of that, our mages feel something else is happening."

"Something else?" the junior officer put his goblet down before he had even taken a sip, raising an eyebrow inquisitively.

"Yes," replied Greybar. He stopped and turned to Sindfar looking deep into his eyes, concern and anger waging with one another. "I have to believe that there are Nightstalkers within the undead ranks."

"Sir." Sindfar felt his eyes narrow as a chill ran down his spine. Their forsaken brethren, trapped forever between worlds, had started appearing more frequently in the past few years, especially with the agitation of the demons from the Abyss. They all knew that the time would come to face them, but Sindfar always hoped that he would be lucky enough to never encounter them. "Are you sure?"

Greybar sighed as he looked away from Sindfar. "Yes. I can feel it and so can the dragons. We've only just recently calmed them down, but while you and your troops have been scouting, the dragons have been restless; their eyes are constantly searching the woods, their tails ever wagging, and their flames ever in their throats. In all of the years I have ridden Esukha, she has never behaved this way. Beyond the trace of death and decay, there is something... darker. Something more sinister."

"Lord Greybar, you have my utmost respect and confidence," Sindfar narrowed his eyes, carefully choosing his words. "But, we have fought the undead before. Surely, whatever forces they have, should they even be the Nightstalkers, we will overcome and triumph, as we have in the past."

"You suppose much, Commander." Greybar tore his gaze away from Sindfar, seemingly lost in his own thoughts. "I fear they will pose a much greater threat than shambling skeletons. I worry about what horrors await us."

Sindfar did not know what to say. Weren't the undead bad enough? Necromancers, vampire lords – and now the potential threat of the Nightstalkers? His brain and his mouth worked several times as he thought through the questions that raced to his mind, but every time, he decided to remain silent, afraid of seeming ignorant. What he really wanted to ask was what sort of suicide mission was he being sent on?

Greybar must have noticed Sindfar's expression and gently led him by the elbow back to the table. He picked up the forgotten goblet and sipped his drink, and then he paused and looked Sindfar in the eyes. "You, Commander, have to delay the necromancer and his minions as best you can while we deal with his forces and secure our rear. We shall bring the bulk of our army to bear on them, but we can't let these flanking forces loose in our rear. They would devastate the countryside and that would only bolster their forces in the process. Get what supplies you can from the depot, as well as the maps that our flyers have been able to make about the terrain. We will give you some additional troops to help, but you are the far-left flank of our troops. No one can get around you; no one can get past you."

Sindfar held the stare back, nodded, and then brought his hand to his chest. "Yes sir, my men will do their duty."

Sindfar took the other goblet, downed the contents, and bowed. Turning on his heel, he exited the tent and headed back down the path to the camp area that his Silverbreeze cavalry was located. His assistant command, Lemar, was waiting with their horses where he had left them. Taking the reins of his steed, they started back to their post. Lemar looked at him with raised eyebrows and held a palm up.

"Well? What is it?" His female assistant chortled. "You look like they have consigned us to death."

"Lemar, you might not be far from the truth." Sindfar swallowed hard and turned to look at her. The slight humor that had been there was now gone, and she looked back at him, hardened. "We will need strategy and finesse to survive this task. I will need your council if we are to come out of this venture alive."

"I stand by your side, no matter what, Commander." There was no hesitation in her voice; only determination. "Speak of what we must do, and I shall do my all for our survival."

*****

The dead walked in silence. Spread out for a hundred yards or more, the warriors moved as a collective guided by the wraith lord and the necromancer. Occasionally, the sound of old armor rang against bones with loosely rotting flesh.

"You will keep leading your forces toward the ford at Echo Springs. I will keep raising troops for you." As if on key, the lesser necromancers hummed their incantations, and the dead warriors of the past started to emerge from their ancient plots like newborns to join the ranks of the undead herd. "Our new allies will be a great aid, but I do not trust them. Be ready for my signal should it become necessary." The wraith lord gave a slight bow to the necromancer and moved along. Mounting his ethereal mount, he led his reverent cavalry forward.

The necromancer heard a commotion and turned to see the approaching vampire lord. He growled and looked skyward, knowing well that the vampire would have his list of grievances.

"Zar! Zar, you scoundrel! Where is this army going? I need to feed – all my kind need to feed – and all we have are these dusty bones and a few muskrats. Muskrats! Even the forest creatures run away." He bared his fangs and threw his arm out to the side. "Zar! Are you listening to me?"

The necromancer pinched the bridge of his nose and looked at the lord. He could feel the bile rising in his throat. He could feel the anger welling up inside of him ready to unleash dark magic on this creature, but just as quickly it subsided. Even drained of energy, the vampire lord's supernatural voice irritated the dark mage. "I hear you, Yarik. The whole valley hears you. Lower your tone – you'd wake the dead if they weren't already rising." Realizing that humor was not the vampire's suit, he tried to calm him down. "We can't make blood from stones. Surely you and your brethren can find some stray humans or elves to prey on?" Zar smoothed out his robes, his long nails catching on loose threads and forcing him to shake them free. He adjusted his gold headpiece and looked at the vampire lord.

Yarik made a grumbling noise that sounded something like a hiss. "I do not like these new abominations. They make me nervous and they claw at the inside of my head. You say they will help us to exterminate the elves and their winged beasts, but I don't see how."

"Yes, these creatures, these... Nightstalkers... will either be a blessing or a curse. They are the remains of elves and dwarves trapped in the path between worlds at the sundering. Many of them are mad – figuratively and literally. They want revenge on their brethren. We will soon see just what they are capable of."

"What about the captives you have penned up?" Yarik pointed back to a pitiful group corralled near Zar's tent.

"You know I need them to sustain these spells. If I can spare one in a day or two, I will give you what I can."

"Well, we must do something soon, or my kin may just take them."

The necromancer did not acknowledge Yarik's last comment and headed back to his tent to rest; magic of this intensity took its toll heavily on his body. There were not the normal logistics when leading an undead army. There was no need for large amounts of supplies that a normal army would use, just fresh blood. The captives in his corral – both humans and elves – no longer put up much resistance. They seemed resigned to their fate, or perhaps the Nightstalkers had gotten to them. The look on the faces of some of the prisoners suggested at something going through their minds even greater, more primal, than the fear of the dead coming back to life – their eyes reflected something closer to hysteria.

*****

Commander Ulle stalked forward, leading his troops under the pitch of night. Their blackened armor did not reflect the slightest hint of the moonlight as they hurried under the hush of branches. Commander Sindfar had sent them forth to scout the territory ahead; his plan was simple – try to find where the enemy was going and stop them if they reached the Mogarth Valley. There was no time for elaborate camps – no fires or noise allowed until they knew where the enemy was located. Water, waybread, and short rest were part of the routine for the troops before they were back on the go; and they continued this way for three days before they came to the Mogarth Valley. There was a small fort at the entrance to the valley that the kings of old had kept as a border station to control the flow of goods and people. Sindfar felt if they could at least get there, it could be a base of operations, and Ulle was determined to make sure he carried out the will of his superior.

The old fort had seen better days. Large patches of stone were missing from the wall, and even at the base level, the fixtures and pillars were crumbling. The earth itself seemed to be clawing to reclaim the land at which the building sat on, as moss and vines ran up the side to the roof. As they grew closer, Ulle was surprised at the first sign of life; there were children and scrawny young adults, disheveled, dressed in rags, with a burning hunger in their eyes, hanging around the outside and doorway to the fort. As they grew closer to the plumes of smoke from scattered fires, older figures appeared from inside, wielding rusty blades they pointed aggressively at the elven troops. They ushered the younger ones inside as the elves halted, weapons raised defensively, before the group.

"Ho there, gentlefolk." The voice was human in tone, booming and clear, and caused the scavengers in front to turn toward the fort. A rotund old man with a staff, much cleaner and better fed than the lot in front of him, shuffled his way forward. He pushed the weapons down of the vagabonds as he passed. "No need for trouble. We are of no bother to you folk, no bother at all. No one has been here for years, except our people. Come, let me offer some ale."

Ulle's face tightened in disgust and he shook his head. "What in blazes is going on here? Whoever you folk are, you must leave. This fort is being commandeered by the elven army of Commander Sindfar Greenspar!"

Blades went up on both sides as Ulle's elves were ready to back his words with steel and the vagabonds before them readied to defend themselves.

"Please sir, it is not safe out there." Again, the big man spoke in assuring tones. "There are foul things on the move. Some of my charges have made their way here through great peril. Don't throw them back to the wolves."

Ulle felt some of the rage fade away and he lowered his sword slightly. "What sort of peril?"

"They have spoken of the dead pulling themselves from the earth, ghastly remains reincarnated for nefarious purposes. They have seen former friends come back and draw steel against them."

"The undead." This caused Ulle to put his hand up to steady his soldiers. "Tell me, what do you know of necromancers?"

"I know they are capable of bringing worse things than the undead." The man smiled and gestured to the fort behind him. "I am Brother Anselmo. I have created a refuge of sorts in this fort."

"I'm sorry, Brother, but your refuge here is over. My commander will arrive shortly, and this will soon be a base of military operation – not a place for civilians." Ulle looked uneasily at the younger members of the group. "Where did all of these children come from?"

"They seem to be from all over, like a moving herd of birds. Dawes, there," he pointed to one small lad, "came from way up the plains. It was a small settlement. They attacked in the dark – overwhelmed the settlers. He escaped through the forest while his parents were being torn apart. They all have a similar story, they are all traumatized. If you just leave us here in peace, we'll be alright."

"I'm sorry, Brother, but this area is not safe." Ulle's voice was stern; he felt sympathy for these humans, but there was naught he could do. Sympathy would only get them killed. "You must take your people and get far away from here. This area will be our last line of defense against the enemy. We must make sure they do not get past here. If you stay, they will slaughter you without hesitation."

Anselmo frowned, studying Ulle's armor. "You are of the Dragon Kin, are you not? Surely your people have dragons that can swoop in and stop the enemy before they ever reach this point."

"It's not as easy as that. Dragons can be outnumbered, overwhelmed, and destroyed like anything else of this world. It is our job to weaken the undead horde here."

"Ah, but you see, it is not the necromancer you should be worried about." The brother turned to stare at the ground before looking solemnly back at the elf. "It is the Nightstalkers that you should concern yourself with."

Ulle stared at the brother. Was he speaking honestly? Commander Sindfar had warned them all about the potential presence of Nightstalkers, but what did a human know of them? His kind thought them nothing more than tales to scare their young. Could this Anselmo know the truth of what they were?

"What do you know of the Nightstalkers?"

"The Nightstalkers can attack through dreams; they can enter a person's mind and tear away at the consciousness that links a person to this world. You must shield yourself against them – both your kin and dragon alike."

Ulle looked the man in the eyes, staring at him for a few seconds before speaking. "Just what sort of man are you?"

"Just a simple cleric, but I have studied the ways of the undead and the old legends."

It was against Ulle's better judgment, but after a few moments he sighed, running a hand through his long blond hair. It was tangled up from too much time in the field – matted in several areas, which made him realize he had not seen a hot bath in many weeks; not much better off than the urchins. "Very well, stay here until the commander arrives. I will let him speak to you about what you know of the dangers at hand." He turned to look at one of his troopers. "Thorn, take a few men forward and see if you can find anything."

Thorn nodded and took six men with him into the fort. Ulle kept his distance from Anselmo and his vagabonds. He was cautious to keep them in his sights from the back of his band; he made sure to put his best men at the front of the group between himself and the strange monk. It was rare for a human to understand the truths about the Nightstalkers. For this man to speak about them in such plain words…

Thorn returned an hour later, about the same time as Commander Sindfar came striding up with the rest of his guard.

"Commander!" Ulle saluted as Sindfar approached and dismounted, confusion evident on the latter's face.

"Ulle, what is this, a town meeting? Who are these people? We have a battle coming and these are mouths to feed and no arms to fight."

"Apologies, Commander, but this is something that I had to bring to your attention. This man's name," he indicated to the priest as he came limping up through the elven soldiers, "is Brother Anselmo, and he has information that I think you will find important."

*****

The priest, Anselmo, as Ulle had called him, led Sindfar and his retinue into a large room with a table and chairs. At one point in the fort's history, this area was probably used for planning and strategizing. Sindfar stationed his men outside the room as he and Anselmo sat down.

"So, my commander says that you have information that would be vital to us?" Sindfar gestured with one hand for Anselmo to speak.

"Yes, Commander Sindfar, was it?" When the elf nodded, Anselmo continued. "My refugees have come from across the area, each speaking of various horrors that you would call the undead. Many of them have spoken about a vampire lord that rides a nightmarish beast into battle. He attacks with reckless abandon, his thirst unquenchable, but he does not seem to be the one in command of the forces. Some have spoken about a withered man, robed in black. I believe this to be the necromancer that you are concerned with. As you have predicted, they seem to be heading this way. While I have not seen any of them face to face, with each new person I take in here, they seem to have come from closer a location than the last."

"Hmm," Sindfar tapped the fingers of his other hand on the table. "That is disconcerting. I would hardly believe the word of vagabonds and children, but for their stories to coincide, that is something indeed dreadful, but not unexpected. Where do you think they are most likely to come from?"

"These are the best approaches to this area." Anselmo had sketched a small map in the dirt and pointed to some poorly-sketched locations. "I would suspect they might camp in this hollow up above the ridgeline. We wouldn't see them easily and it allows access to the valley."

Sindfar tapped his fingers on the table once more. His eyes narrowed as he looked at the brother, thinking back on what he had said.

"I find this all very coincidental, sir. A man that knows so much about our enemy just so happens to be at a fort that has long since thought abandoned. How do you know so much? Why should I believe what you have told me?"

"That is not important. Every moment we spend talking brings the enemy that much closer." When the elf continued to stare at him and not speak, Anselmo sighed. "Very well. I have lived here for the past few years. I am a simple man of the woods. I keep an eye on the valley. I help those who flee the darkness. If you do not believe me about those who have escaped the undead, ask them yourself. They will tell you exactly the same as I have done. I have told you all I know, and what I know is that there is danger coming."

Sindfar stood and looked at the depictions of the area that Anselmo had drawn in the dirt of the table for some time. If he trusted this man and it turned out that it was a ruse, then the elves would be doomed. But if this priest was indeed just a normal man, and the heavens had taken this opportunity to smile on Sindfar and forge fate to work positively, then perhaps they could actively prepare for the enemy. He turned to look at Anselmo and inclined his head toward the soldiers waiting in the hallway. "Kew!"

An elven cavalryman hurried into the room and saluted. "Sir!"

"Kew, you and Dingle carry this message back to Commander Greybar as quickly as possible." Sindfar grabbed an archaic stone tablet on the table. He looked around for a writing utensil, but Anselmo was quick to hand him one. The priest smiled, and Sindfar nodded his thanks as he took the tool and began scratching a message onto the tablet. When finished, he handed it to the soldier. "Go, and don't stop. One of you must get through to him and bring some help here."

The soldier took the message and saluted as he left. Sindfar led Anselmo back outside, and they walked around the courtyard as the elven commander collected his thoughts. He knew Lemar stalked several paces behind him, so as not to make him feel she was on top of him, but also to make him aware that she was keeping him guarded. He was thankful for her vigilance, especially when he did not fully trust this Anselmo; who knew what he had set up around the fortress?

Sindfar stopped and turned to the priest. "What is the state of this place? How are the walls? Has anyone kept it up? This used to be a garrison station; are there any supplies left?

"You can see, Commander," Anselmo said, motioning to the walls, "I have made some effort to prop it up, but it will not withstand a prolonged siege."

Sindfar looked around the fort. There was a small gateway and tower facing the ridge that seemed to be the main gate. A curtain wall surrounded the exterior with towers in the middle of the side walls, and the keep they emerged from was in the rear of the fortress. For the length of time this place had been abandoned, most of it seemed in good shape, except for various parts of the walls that were in various states of disrepair, as if locals pulled out some stones for other buildings. Some gaps were plugged with wooden stockade fencing and were not in terrible shape – the cleric knew a bit about engineering.

"What about supplies or armory? The lords used to keep this place stocked in case of an emergency."

"There are some foodstuff and ale. Much of it I stockpiled." The priest shrugged. "There is some armor and arrows but not much in the blades. There are three disassembled onagers as well."

The sound of galloping hooves made Sindfar turn. The horse skidded to a stop, whinnying loudly, as the scout all but fell off the saddle. "C-Commander...! We were scouting about ten miles on the other side of the pass. We stumbled across a pack of ghouls in the forest. They... they killed Sinqua, one of our lead scouts! We found them eating him and made sure we killed the bastards, but there are surely more on the way! We left a string of outriders to keep an eye on them." The scout's face hardened as he took a deep breath and looked at his commander. "They are coming!"

Sindfar nodded, placing his hand on the elf's shoulder. "Thank you. Go, and rest. We will take it from here. We will need your strength."

When the scout left, Sindfar turned back and sketched out a map of the post in the dirt. He turned to Lemar and pointed to the map as she approached. "Start shoring up the walls here. The keep gives us a wide view, so let's get someone up there to make use of it. Brother, you and your ward have just been conscripted. You know where the weak spots are, help us get this in order. It's too late now to flee, but I have a feeling you were all too aware of that."

*****

The army of the dead did not care about stealth; they shambled on toward their commanded destination with deadly purpose. Troops of skeleton warriors marched on behind eyeless faces, but the remnants of their armor clanged on the bony frames, and their feet pounded earth in which the vegetation died as they passed over. They surely did not notice the trail of bare trees and dusty soil that marked their passage, but Yarik, the vampire lord, was not as oblivious as the mindless minions.

The ghouls and zombies snarled and moaned around him, creating a cacophony of noise like an undead choir when joined with the howls of the werewolves and vampires. Yarik, instead, chose to remain silent on the back of his proud horse of the damned. He was hungry and only becoming more infuriated and annoyed with every passing moment he did not feed. He stared at the 'human' element to the army with disdain; the coaches that carried the necromancers, their minions, and their thralls. How easy it would be, as he told Zar, to snatch one of them and suck the blood dry from the bones before it was even noticed.

The ghouls would stop for short periods, then speed on ahead along with bats and other malevolent spirits. As such, the columns of the dead moved in irregular patterns back and forth across the land. At any moment, sections of the army or the whole force itself might veer off in the direction of fresh souls.

The vampire lord was trying to keep his group moving – the lack of fresh kills combined with the meager rations the necromancer allowed them kept the vampires weak but able to move. Yarik had his suspicions that Zar was doing this on purpose. He must have been giving the vampires just enough to fend off the blood lust, but this made it so they would fight that much harder when the battle came.

One of the vampires had begun to wander off on its own, and

just as Yarik was about to bare his fangs and give the offender a warning bite to drain some of its energy, his nostrils caught the scent of meat – fresh meat. There was a kill! Looking around, he noticed a small group of ghouls tearing at a carcass on the ground. He got off his nightmare steed and bounded over to them with determination. The ghouls turned, and he only had to hiss with bared fangs once before they parted for him. All but one.

He could make out an arm behind the crouched ghoul, and the scent of blood flooded his nostrils, his eyes enlarging.

"Move, peon," Yarik hissed, trying to shove the ghoul aside. It turned to him, seeming to acknowledge he was a vampire lord, but it went back to gnawing flesh from bone.

Realizing that he did not have the physical strength to push the minion away, nor would his compulsion work on the undead being, Yarik drew his sword. With one quick slice, the ghoul's head rolled to the ground and then it fell limp. The vampire lord kicked the body aside and glared at the rest of the ghouls, who groaned and then shambled away. His vampires fell on the mortal corpse and Yarik was pleased to watch blood spurt into the air from the vampires' incisors.

"Yes. Drink, my children. We feed, and we shall grow stronger." He picked up the limb he had seen before and began to drain the precious liquid from the veins. The arm withered and grew limp quicker than he expected. He made his way up the shoulder to the neck, the spot his kin reserved for their lord. "Feast and grow stronger. For the next time we sup, it shall be upon the sweet blood of the elves."

*****

"They are not the most articulate of creatures," Zar remarked, staring at the ghoul staked out on the ground. "But Cilo can get what we need out of him."

The ghoul continued to howl in pain and whimper while the cloaked figure circled it. Yarik tried to watch what was going on, but every time he stared at the figure that Zar referred to as 'Cilo', flashes of pure white light and divine winged entities bathed in that same aura entered his mind. He knew this Cilo was the furthest thing away from being of a holy nature; it was the nightmarish power that it was capable of, to conjure the mind's greatest fear. Eventually the wailing from the ghoul stopped altogether, and the visions faded in intensity in Yarik's mind's eye.

"I do not like these emissaries of the Nightstalkers," Yarik stated with his arms crossed. He noticed Zar looking funny at his mouth, so the vampire brought a hand up to wipe the remnants of his meal away. "The more I am around them, the weaker I feel. And I say that even after feeding. I should not feel as drained as I do."

"You are a vampire lord," the necromancer shook his head. "You must fight them, as we all do, from entering your mind. Their whispers might be tempting, and they might drain our energy in doing so, but steel your mind, Yarik. They have wandered between worlds so long that most of them appear only in dreams – that is how they enter this world. Those people most affected by magic are most susceptible to them. That is why elves, dwarves, and beings such as ourselves are affected. Keep your mind closed to them and you will be fine. "

The vampire lord watched the necromancer approach and stop in front of the emissary. The creature seemed to float just above the ground, and as it stood before Zar, Yarik thought he could see numerous skulls within the hood, all slick with some supernatural fluid, as well as a long tongue behind jagged teeth. But there seemed no eyes.

Even though it did not seem as if words were spoken, the necromancer nodded and backed away before turning and approaching Yarik once more. It had been no more than a few moments.

"Well, Cilo has done the trick, assuming the ghoul's mind did not mistake the surrounding land, we have an idea where these elves are. Maybe not their numbers, but I suspect they have sent a sizable force to try and stop us. Let's start to move this juggernaut of a force in that direction."

Yarik stared at Zar with narrowed eyes, one arm across his chest and the other cupping his chin. "How do you communicate with them?"

"You need not concern yourself with that." The necromancer stared expressionlessly at Yarik, as if in that moment he was devoid of whatever humanity he had left, a husk without a soul. From what Yarik had witnessed and known, humans were controlled by their emotions and based everything off of them. In that moment, there was no emotion on Zar's face or in his words. It unnerved the vampire ever so slightly. Finally, the necromancer turned and walked away, some of his usual voice returning. "Come, we must plan our attack."

As the necromancer walked before him, the robe he wore caught Yarik's eyes. He had always thought it to be some exquisitely made, lavish human garment, trimmed in gold with detailed designs. But as he walked behind Zar, the closest he could remember being, he looked altogether different. The fine-looking silk was tattered and seemed to have been eaten by moths. The gold was faded and tarnished. The shadows at his feet looked stretched and unnatural.

Yarik had never trusted Zar – or any mortals for that matter – but he was beginning to question just what had been real and what illusion this trickster had pulled over his eyes. And then the question loomed of what was being controlled by the Nightstalkers, what aspects the necromancer had lost all control of.

*****

With the exception of some Gladestalker troops and some archers, there was nothing but cavalry in the encampment; however they were trained for fast action and movement – not for sieges. Yet, a siege was what they were facing. Meanwhile, Brother Anselmo directed his charges like a veteran tactician. Sindfar believed that this was not the cleric's first time in a fight, but then, very few in this world could have lived as long as he appeared without some combat experience. The garrison of elves worked alongside the humans through the day to patch the holes in the defenses.

When they were done, Anselmo approached Sindfar and wiped a bead of sweat from his brow.

"It would never pass elven muster, but it will give the illusion of strength." The old priest bent down by a large rock that bordered on being a bolder. When he went to pick it up, Sindfar nearly leapt to stop the man, but he moved it with ease and placed it in part of a breach. "Of course, that only applies to the living creatures. The dead ones have no fear."

"You are a book of surprises, brother," Sindfar said, eyeing the man cautiously. "I hope you can fight as well as you can lift."

Brother Anselmo smiled and nodded, leaving the thought in the air. The serenity of the night was broken as a Gladestalker detachment came in through the gate. A winded Captain Frebar came up to the commander and saluted despite the evident exhaustion.

"We've made contact, sir. I think we've identified the main body. My troops have eyes on them to track their movement."

"Thank you, Captain Frebar." Sindfar saluted the captain, and then he turned toward Anselmo and nodded. He stormed off toward the rest of his troops, Frebar close behind. It was time to prepare for the coming battle.

*****

Quequa could not hear his own footfalls as he hurried through the forest; the shadows that danced by his sides and in front of him were his fellow Gladestalkers, just as silent. He looked up and down the landscape, always prepared that an enemy was around any turn in the trees. Hikow, his leader, held his hand up, and the warriors came to a stop. There was movement. As a group, they all stooped down. If this was the bulk of the enemy forces they had been tracking, there would be too many of them to take them on directly. Their main task was to scout, locate, and report.

They fought, but only when they needed to, and that didn't need to be now.

Hikow leaned over to his file leader, Tareal, and whispered. "Leave two men and move on. Send a runner back to report what to expect."

Tareal nodded to Quequa and another elf by the name of Rafe, and he motioned for them to stay. Quequa nodded back and remained crouched low as he watched the others disappear into darkness.

The minutes began to blend together, and Quequa started feeling this strange sensation in his brain. He thought he had only been on guard for a few minutes, but something nagged in the back of his mind to make him believe he had been here much longer. He was trained to go long distances, without food or sleep, but for some inexplicable reason, he struggled to stay awake. It was as if a heavy weight was on his mind that he could not shake. He crouched ten yards from Rafe; still in visible sight.

"Did you see something?" he whispered to Rafe in a rumble no louder than the breeze.

"No. I didn't see anything," the other shot back, barely audible. "Quiet."

Quequa kept an eye on where the enemy was camped, but he kept feeling himself nodding. He was starting to feel his eyes closing but then startled himself awake. Again, time seemed to blur; he was not sure if he had dozed off for a second or a few minutes. He looked over to the other position but didn't see his comrade.

"Rafe. Rafe?" It was a low whisper, but he received no answer.

"Rafe!" He cried out, and immediately after he realized how stupid it was to do. The tiredness was addling his brain, clouding his judgment. Quequa felt something looming behind his shoulder. Turning slowly, he saw what looked like a scarecrow in the woods. It was not there before. Where did it come from? He turned back momentarily to look again for Rafe, but he was still not there. He turned back when he heard the rustling of branches, and the scarecrow was just about on him.

Panic rippled through him; this was no ordinary scarecrow. It seemed ethereal, as if it had some sort of cloudy aura around its body; and where the head should have been, there was nothing but a gaping mouth with rows of jagged teeth. He tried to move, but he couldn't. His arms and legs didn't work the way they should. He couldn't get up and crawl; it was on him, grabbing his legs. Its overgrown talons cut into his flesh as it wrapped one long, pointed hand around him.

The Gladestalker tried to reach for his knife, but it wouldn't come out of its scabbard. He started to scream for help as the terror gripped him. He saw the hand of bark reach up, moving toward his neck. The knife came free and he slashed at the creature until it finally let go. Finally, he stabbed away at the being, screaming in his head, making sure it was not moving.

All of a sudden it was as if a fog was lifted from his sight and his head cleared. It was deadly quiet, but there he was with blood up to his elbows. He started to hyperventilate and collapsed in a heap, cross-legged, dropping his knife. Rafe was next to him, dead. There was a noise ahead of him – he could see the enemy coming his way. He sat there for a second, broken in spirit, when he reached for his knife.

He saw the scarecrow of his nightmare standing there. He opened his mouth to scream again, but the scarecrow plunged its pointed arms into him. In his last moments of life, he finally found the eyes of the beast, and he stared into its blank sockets. They seemed to light up – as if his soul was passing into it.

*****

The Gladestalkers arrived back into the camp in small groups as they collapsed their screen of scouts around the fortified position. Frebar approached Sindfar for his report.

"Commander, we have confirmed our previous suspicions. The creatures that walk among the undead ranks are as you feared. Their army is much larger than anything we have seen before, as well. We can fight a hit-and-run battle to delay them, but I'm not sure we can stave them off if we stay here. To remain is suicide." He paused, straightening. "Of course, that is only my opinion, sir."

"We do not have the option of choosing our orders, like a roll of the dice, Frebar." Sindfar rubbed his chin as he looked at Frebar. "We have orders. If these bones get on the plains, it will be harder to contain them. We must stall them here and give our allies time to arrive."

"What sort of abominations did you see, Captain?" Anselmo, nearly forgotten, spoke up from where he stood.

"I have seen skeletons and vampires before, sir, but these were like walking nightmares – specters that seemed to float and scarecrows that walked. Their numbers kept ever-growing; I couldn't keep track of them after some time. Many of the creatures had no eyes, but rows upon rows of fanged teeth. Beyond that, there are hundreds of the undead, more than I had ever seen before."

"It sounds indeed as if the forces of the Abyss have called forth the Nightstalkers," Anselmo nodded and then looked off into the distance, as if in thought.

Sindfar closed his eyes for a moment, sighed, and opened them once more. "Indeed it does. This is most unfortunate, but not unexpected. We must carry on our duty."

"Commander, pardon me, but are you sure this is wise?" Sindfar looked back at Anselmo, a look of real concern on his face. "I have heard stories in the past of their link to the elves. It seems your race is especially susceptible to them. I have been worried that their arrival on this earth would be nigh once more, and because of that, we have been working on a few contraptions for our defense before you came."

Sindfar nodded. There was no hiding anything from this human anymore. "What sort of defenses do you speak of?"

The brother smiled and pointed toward the towers of the fort. "We have a few onagers scattered for launching stones. When I arrived, they were hardly in working condition, but I've been overseeing their repair, and they are ready. I have some small jars filled with combustibles and holy oil, as well staff slings and rocks. They might not seem like much, but these tools will be of great aid in the coming battle from keeping these creatures from the walls. I worry that the stones might be loose enough that they could tear through them. If they get in among us, they will overwhelm us."

Sindfar turned when he heard one of the lookouts call out from the tower at the central gate. One of the children pointed toward the hills to the northeast. Finally, he saw two shapes that seemed like giant birds – no, they were bats – flying toward them. The bowmen were taking aim when Anselmo called them off.

"Don't waste the arrows, fools!"

The bats circled the outpost twice before they dropped something from their claws and fluttered back to the hills. The objects hit the ground with a thud, bounced, and then rolled slightly. Hikow, back from the patrol, went over to them. He brought his torch over the objects and then visibly let his body sag. Sindfar already knew what it was, but he approached to look nonetheless.

"These... are the heads of my two scouts that went missing," Hikow said to Sindfar, a mix of rage and disgust taking over his face.

"Brother Anselmo!" another one of the children lookouts called. "There… is something on the hills. Someone is there!"

Sindfar cursed under his breath and followed Anselmo as the priest ran to the courtyard. There, where the boy said, on the hills, were two necromancers conjuring up magic – there was a sulfuric smell that made their dark presence unmistakable. The sky seemed to light up with static electricity as they worked whatever devious arcane spells.

"There!" Anselmo yelled as he pointed at countless shapes moving down the hill. "They are here!"

*****

"We haven't a minute to waste!" Ulle shouted as he pointed to the curtain walls. Soldiers hurried to their posts, bows at the ready. "Let your arrows fly true! Do not let any approach!"

The elven commander readied his own bow as he joined the other archers. A mass of ghouls was fast approaching with lines of skeleton warriors behind them. The archers set up on the wall with drawn bows aimed at the galloping ghouls that charged down at them. Ulle waited until they were within forty yards before he gave the signal, and the archers let loose a volley that shuddered the enemy line as the arrows found their mark. Another barrage of arrows flew true, striking down the line of ghouls. Those remaining milled around slightly and then retreated, howling in frustration, as they continued to take casualties from the bowmen. They fell in behind the skeletons, using them for cover.

While the skeletons knew no fear, they could be more easily disrupted, as the magic that held the bones together and animated the creations was not as strong the further they grew from their masters. Their approach was slow, but it was unrelenting. A wraith lord was at their head, leading the army in a mix of robes and armor. Ulle heard a noise and then turned to see the first of the onagers let loose; a large rock smashed through a line of skeletons and the ghouls behind them. The bouncing rocks took out large blocks of the tightly-packed bone units, and he noticed that the lord was amongst the ranks taken out by a lucky shot. The magic which held the skeletons together, likewise, began to slacken.

The skeletons were thinned out, but they did not stop in their march. Despite his men's best efforts, they had made it to the wall. Ulle cursed as he aimed down. If the wall seemed breakable from the outside, the skeletons did not notice it. In place of ladders, they climbed one another. It didn't last long, as the arrows rained down and demolished the boney enemies. The last of the skeleton units were reduced to dust and the remaining ghouls returned back to the undead lines.

Ulle sighed, but the respite was short lived, and he straightened. The cacophony of the damned swelled to a frightening pitch and was all that he could hear. They were just being tested. This battle had only just begun.

*****

"What is wrong with you? We should have just overwhelmed them!" Yarik seethed, cutting the air with his arm. "Why didn't you just let me lead this?

You may be a good magician, but your wraith lord is a lousy general."

Zar contained his rage, smoothing out his robes before making a quick move with his hands and throwing the vampire lord back against the tent wall and out through the opening. There was smoke rising off his fingers, blackening his nails a little more.

"Don't ever question me like that again. You are lucky I am drained from controlling these blocks of undead."

The vampire lord came up in a roll with his sword drawn, and he growled. The necromancer pointed a long bony finger at Yarik. "None of that. This is a waste of resources." He exhaled from his nostrils and rubbed his gaunt cheeks with one hand. "Fine, Yarik. You feel you can lead us to victory? What would you have us do?"

* * * * *

"They will probably come at us at once with a big force," explained Sindfar, standing over a crudely drawn map, "and with that, the worst of the beasts will be there. They were just testing us with the skeletons and ghouls, but what they send next… they will not be so tame. Do we have any idea what we are dealing with?"

Ulle stepped forward. "We know they have giant bats, a troop or two of vampires, we've heard the howl of werewolves, and there are countless wights, revenants, and skeletons. We have yet to see any of the Nightstalkers that were reported, which is most worrisome. Leading the enemy are at least two necromancers, a vampire lord, and the wraith lord has been seen resurrected."

"Get fires going and brands made if we can," Sindfar nodded to his assembled soldiers. "Fire arrows may help with some of the undead, but the vampires will be the most difficult."

"If I may," Anselmo broke in, to which all eyes turned. "We have some oils for cooking and a little pitch left over from repairs. I would suggest setting up barrels for chokepoints to deal with them. I can also weave some wards to help."

"Wards?" Sindfar's eyebrows shot up. "I… didn't realize that was part of your skillset, Brother. Just how powerful are you?

"I never said I was powerful," the brother smiled calmly. "I just said I could weave some wards."

Sindfar threw his hands up in exasperation. "Whatever the case, do what you can to arrange some sort of defense. Are there any other secrets we should know about?"

"No, Commander Sindfar," the brother smiled calmly once more. There was something in that calm that the elf found almost eerie. Holy man or not, this

Anselmo seemed to keep pulling ace cards out of his sleeve. He only hoped that luck would continue when they needed it most. "Oh, and the children will help me, of course."

"The children?" Sindfar scoffed. "Whatever it is you think best. Just keep them out of the way when the fighting starts!" He turned back to his assembled men. "You have your orders. If there are no questions, get to them at once."

After his soldiers dispersed, the elf commander walked out into the yard and surveyed what was left of his command. He placed his people where he could, where they would do the most good, with a small reserve to throw at any potential problem spots. A fear niggled in the back of his mind. He hoped those wards would prevent the fallen from rising back up and turning their blades against him.

*****

Yarik was a sight to behold at the head of the undead troops. Poised upon his hellsteed that screeched into the dead of night, he led the army of the undead down toward the fort that the elves had holed up in, his blade held high. What fools; there would be no more time for the ghouls to plod a slow course into the tips of arrows. Now was the time for his people to feast.

He gave off a ferocious howl, and the army of darkness behind him roared in response. It was time for them all to feast.

*****

Sindfar saw the undead charging down the hills. This time, there were no necromancers summoning ozone discharge. It was a brute force, dead and deadly. The onagers were ready when the first of the giant bats came roaring in and fired trying to hit the monsters. The archers, quicker than the archaic hurlers, managed to force one to the ground. It was wounded with a broken wing, and despite its dangerous claws and fangs, the foot soldiers were able to overwhelm and kill it. There were still two more circling the fort.

One dove down in a shriek, aiming straight for one of the catapults. The men manning the machine stood no chance. The monster tore them apart in the blink of an eye and broke the machine – two more soldiers were killed before the beast was stabbed between the shoulders by a lance. The second bat attacked another machine and broke it before a crack of fire engulfed the monster. Sindfar turned to see smoke coming from the cleric's hands.

That spell – that magic. Had it really come from Anselmo…?

The commander was now down two machines and there was very little to stop the horde from reaching the walls. The archers had taken aim as the ghouls ran full-steam down toward the walls of the enclosure. Twenty yards away, they let loose a volley that annihilated the first rank. They were again so tightly packed that the ones that fell in the front tripped the ones in the back.

Sindfar gave a signal, the gates opened, and a section of riders streamed out to meet the ghouls. They rode down as many as they could, stabbing with lances and swords. The ghouls panicked at the death raining down on them and ran back from where they came again. This time, undead spearmen came forth and began thrusting toward the elves. Fearing they would be overwhelmed, the cavalry retreated back to the fort and prepared for the main assault. The vampire lord galloped into view and the earth seemed to shake with each step.

"Now my fellows, forward and feast!" His sword was pointed at the fort as he thundered onward. The dread in the voice sent shivers down Sindfar's spine, and he gripped the handle of his sheathed blade tightly.

They came onward at the gallop as if they were going to run down the walls. It wasn't until they stood within ten yards of the walls that the nightmares came to a halt. The lord tried to urge the creatures forward, but they would not budge. Sindfar turned toward Anselmo on the tower; the man was moving his arms in erratic circles, his eyes shut. One of the other vampires cried out as it was struck by an arrow – a holly shaft – then a fire brand, each hit the mark leaving an undead in pain or dead. The vampire lord rode his horse back and forth around the walls as the defenders shot at him. He used his shield to protect himself, but he was clearly looking for a breach in the ward.

The skeleton warriors continued to march on amidst all this confusion. As they got closer to the walls, the defenders let loose a barrage of rock and projectiles in the hopes of knocking the skeletons down. If they could hold them here, they might be able to decimate them before the old man's strength wore out.

Sindfar took in what was going on around the walls to see where the weak points were. The old man was shaking as he concentrated. He could see that trying to maintain the wards around the encampment was taking its toll on Anselmo. The old man did not seem to exude a great deal of power, and the fact that he was able to do what he was impressed the elf commander.

"Hold fast, Anselmo, and yet we might win this battle," Sindfar muttered under his breath.

The dead warriors congregated at the edge of the ward field, unable to move forward anymore, and they began to pile into one another. It was as if they couldn't notice that they were unable to proceed; they kept pushing forward, as if driven on by some sheer will to kill. Some of the front rank began to disintegrate into dust under the pressure against the ward, but cracks began to appear like sparks of light.

The pressure built until Anselmo could take it no more and he fell in a heap. With that, a burst of energy pushed out from the cleric. The first ranks of the skeleton warriors fell forward as they were released from their hold, and the back ranks marched over them. They approached the wall and again, without ladders, began to climb on each other to get to the defenders.

Sindfar began to grow anxious. His hand flexed on the handle of the sword as he watched the undead pile toward his men. What made it worse was noticing the bloodlust on the face of the vampire, realizing the ward was gone. The horse reared again and tore across the battlefield, faster than any mortal steed could. With a single leap, the nightmarish steed bounded the wall, and the vampire lord leapt off, onto the neck of one of the elven defenders. The horse bucked and kicked at the elves as its lord drank its meal.

"Stop that beast! It will run amok if not defeated!" Sindfar barked orders and the men around the stallion began to encircle it.

The encircled men began to dig spears into the creature when it was not looking at them. It bucked and dragged a few of them, but after twelve spears had found their mark, the beast slowed. Frebar was down amongst them, and he severed the creature's head with one swift stroke.

While one beast was put down, another still roamed. It took Sindfar a moment before he was able to find the vampire lord once more. One by one, every defender that stood to challenge the undead monster was slain in quick strokes. One by one, elves died before Sindfar's eyes, and he had had enough.

He tore through the keep, into the makeshift armory Anselmo had made up. They had only fashioned a few of the weapons he was looking for, but he only needed one to make the kill. He grabbed the long piece of wood and made his way as quickly as he could down into the scene of chaos. It took him a moment to reach the last area he had seen the vampire, but there he was. Sindfar watched as the vampire lord had busied himself with one of the children defenders. The vile creature threw the young man's sword away and stalked upon him.

"Brave boy, but foolish." The vampire lord licked the side of his blade, seemingly in preparation to feed. "I'll savor your blood!"

Before the vampire could make his move, Sindfar rushed behind him and stabbed a stake through his back. He pushed until he heard the point emerge from the front, showering the face of the young man with gore. The vampire was rapidly losing blood when he fell to the ground on his side. He kept clawing at the wood with his claws, breaking off pieces at a time. Sindfar came to the front of the beast, the child standing at his side, determined despite the blood splattered on his face.

There seemed to be something of recognition in the vampire's eyes as he stared at the young man. A smile finally crept onto his face, showing the hideous fangs that were covered with blood. He laughed.

"I... I recognize you," he raised a shaking finger, pointing at the boy. "We... came to your settlement. Your mother... She tasted the best. Her blood, so sweet, it—"

Sindfar kicked the vampire in the side of the head, and then he impaled the sword into the back of the creature's neck. It stopped moving and then burst into flames as it died. Sindfar recovered his weapon before any harm could come to it, turning to take stock of the situation.

The skeletons were now continuously climbing over the walls, and the elf warriors valiantly tried to keep them at bay. The reserves that were left helped to beat back the skeletons that made it over. Eventually, the skeletons pulled back, returned under the control of a necromancer. There was a cry that rang up through the defenders, even though they all knew this was far from over.

A couple of the soldiers fell where they stood, dead tired. Sindfar watched as officers tried to get the men ready for the next attack, but some refused to stand. He walked over to the closest sleeping man and placed a hand on his shoulder. His head lolled and an expression of terror was etched forever in his face.

The soldier was dead.

*****

Thorn was walking through the fog. Where it came from, he did not know. He was no longer in the fort with the rest of his troop. Where was he? Where were the others? It felt cold suddenly – there was a chill that was not there before. He felt fear rising in himself. He didn't know why, but the hairs on his neck were stood on their ends. He found himself walking down a deserted street when he suddenly heard a shuffling. It was muffled like cloth on a floor. First, he thought it was to his left, then his right. He was twisting and turning as bile rose in his throat, and he kept feeling that there was a thing behind him. He kept trying to move, but his legs felt like they had cement in his shoes. Thorn kept trying to go onward, but he could not move fast enough.

Then he felt something on his neck. It was like a stick, but he knew it wasn't. He turned slowly, but not of his own will. He couldn't help himself, as if something was willing him to do so. This thing was in a tattered robe, there were tentacles billowing out of the hood and arm slots, and they reached out for him. There were purple eyes that penetrated his soul. He tried to scream, but he couldn't. It kept surrounding him, enveloping him, and he couldn't breathe. He tried to yell, but he was muffled.

Then he heard the voice say, "Welcome home, brother."

*****

As Sindfar was making the rounds, he lost count of how many dead he had found. There was no mark on them, just a look of sheer terror. He went down the line and three or four men were in the same state. He shook his head as he passed Thorn's corpse. He knew who the killers were despite not physically being seen on the battlefield. They had let their guard down, and the Nightstalkers claimed the lives of too many of his warriors.

"A-Anselmo!" The voice that came out of Sindfar was more panicked than he wanted. The old man came haltingly, leaning heavily on his staff, until he reached the dead soldiers. He examined them but did not seem surprised by what he saw.

"They have been here all along!" Sindfar slammed his fist against the nearest wall, trying his best to compose himself. When he looked back at Anselmo, he knew he could not hide the defeat from his eyes that he felt in his heart. "The Nightstalkers have been amongst our ranks all along and there was naught we could do to stop them."

"Commander Sindfar, you must remember that you and your people are most susceptible to their touch. The closer you are to them, the more susceptible you are. I have been trying to keep a ward up to protect you, but the strain of trying to keep the undead out besides keeping them out is too much. You need to train your mind to resist them. They are your people – or what is left of your people. I have been drained to the point that I need to rest."

There was a ragged tiredness in Anselmo's features that Sindfar had not seen before. He now looked the age he was supposed to be.

"I've seen your magic, I know you are no ordinary holy man. Just… who or what are you, Anselmo? Come, we are too tired to keep up charades."

The old man sat down on a stone block. "I can hold my own with other mages. I was from Basilea originally, but I clashed with the ruling powers and was banished. I roamed the land in search of knowledge and made my way to the young kingdoms. I found the darkness of vampire lords taking hold to some places and escaped. I have studied the Magi and Djin and have lived several lifetimes more than I should have. I found peace in this valley until now, as war and evil will always try to stretch their fingers." Anselmo leaned on his staff and tried to rise, but he was unable. He tilted his head and looked at the elf commander. "You know what you must do."

"Yes," Sindfar nodded. "The men must stay occupied; they cannot doze, or else the Nightstalkers will attempt to infiltrate their minds."

The old man nodded. "I can't help you if they attack again soon. I've done all I can for now."

Sindfar tried to help the man up, but the children appeared and took him back to the main building. He turned to Lemar; one of the few of his trusted left. "Get the troops ready for review."

Although they were exhausted, Sindfar pushed the men as far as he could. They did their best to shore up the defenses, trying to fix the stone throwers and getting the last onager almost serviceable. They extended a ditch in front of the walls to break up any possible attack. If the elf soldiers looked like they were getting ready to doze, Sindfar or Lemar made sure that the file leaders woke them up. Anselmo instructed the children to brew a concoction that would give the elves more energy to stay awake.

At dawn, with the sun coming up over the hills, the dead started to march again. The elves looked them down from their prepared positions. Realizing that they were making a last stand, Sindfar blocked the gate so no one or thing could get in or out. This is where they would fight, and if fate decreed it, this is where they would die.

The dead came on again. It looked like the final push to overwhelm the defenders. Lemar came up beside Sindfar and saluted.

"Status report?"

"Sir… Things are grim," Lemar swallowed hard. "The onager is no longer serviceable. We tried, but we can't get off any shots. We have staff slings at the ready, but they are barely affecting the skeletons. Even now… the enemy threatens to overwhelm our defenses."

Sindfar stared at the battlefield for a few more minutes before he turned to Lemar. "Pull them back. Pull them all back."

Lemar passed the word around and elves ran back toward the main building. Some few brave souls still attempted to snipe their enemy off as they fled, but soon, the whole courtyard was overwhelmed. Sindfar stood at the doorway, waiting as his troops piled in, and watching as the skeletons marched ever closer. A few bolts of fire singed down on the bones and shattered them; he looked up to the tower and saw Anselmo leaning against the wall. Even at the brink of exhaustion, the old man was willing to help them – even if it meant his own death.

Sindfar stood at the head of the defenders, Lemar by his side, and readied to meet the skeletons with one final stand.

"Commander," Sindfar turned to stare into Lemar's eyes. She smiled grimly and gave a solemn nod. "It's been a pleasure serving under you."

He chortled and nodded in return, readying his blade. "The pleasure has been all mine, Lemar. You and I will become dragon riders yet. We'll ride the backs of our ancestor's companions in the afterlife, my friend."

They both turned, together, as the first wave of skeletons approached with weapons raised high. Rallying his own blade, Sindfar felt a feral growl erupt from the depths of his core.

But before any of them could bring their blades to bear, a wave of fire struck the courtyard. Sindfar shielded his eyes from the intensity of the light. It took a few minutes, time he was sure they would be killed, so when he opened his eyes and they began to focus again, he was surprised when the skeletons were dust. It was then he heard the cries of the dragons.

"The relief force!" someone shouted from behind him. "We're saved!"

A cheer went up through the haggard remaining elves as they watched the dragons fly through the air, hurling balls of flame at their opponents beyond sight. Sindfar nearly collapsed from overwhelming thankfulness. They had done it. They had staved them off, bless the fallen.

As Sindfar hurried to the ramparts once more, he watched as the dragons breathed destruction on the remaining undead and the necromancer on the hill. The sound of hooves beat out, and a column of riders barreled in to support their dragon allies. The skeletons slowly began to fall as the magic which held them dissipated.

"I can't believe it," Lemar breathed next to him. She laughed as she leaned over the wall and placed her head in her hands. "We really did it, Commander."

The elves in the fort began to dismantle the barricade to open the gates. As Lord Greybar's dragon prepared to land inside the fort, Sindfar hurried to greet him with Lemar close behind.

"Thank the Green Lady, you are a sight for sore eyes!" Sindfar nearly hugged the dragon rider that stood before him, tears beginning to form in the corner of his eyes.

"I'm sorry it took us so long to get here, Sindfar. You fought well, but I think it is still too late."

Sindfar composed himself, standing stiff. "You are right, Lord Greybar. Your suspicions were correct. The Nightstalkers have made their way here to support the forces of the undead."

Greybar looked grim as he turned to look out across the valley. "The enemy here shall be destroyed, but from what we can see, this was only a small part of the undead army – a decoy to fix our eyes here. The main body is still out there, and with them..."

Sindfar looked up to the tower, but Brother Anselmo was no longer there. He forced himself to bring his eyes back to Lord Greybar. "The Nightstalkers grow more powerful than ever before."

EYES UNBLINKING

By Marc DeSantis

With eyes unblinking, a pitiless enemy kept watch over the host of Basilea. With eyes unblinking, she plotted its destruction.

*****

Dillen Genemer watched the dictator with nervous anticipation. Ever eager to please, the young horse messenger waited impatiently for any chance to ingratiate himself with Trence Andorset, hero of Basilea and the commanding general of the expedition to Galahir. The general appeared to be absentmindedly stroking the gray whiskers of his luxurious mustache, lost in annoyed thought. Dillen wondered what bothered him so. He lifted his eyes briefly, taking in the claustrophobic denseness of the Forest of Galahir in one, uncomfortable glance. It was scarcely possible to see the sky from within the woods, so thickly did the ancient trees of the primeval forest cluster together. Their great boughs intertwined, like the limbs of dancers engaged in some unholy, carnal ritual. It was not an agreeable place for one of Basilea's faithful to be, Dillen knew.

Now Andorset grimaced. Dillen knew that the general had not wished to come here, having listened to the dictator speak acidly about the Galahirians on more than one occasion. But for the direct command of his liege, Andorset would never have agreed to lead his soldiers to the aid of the fey creatures of the Green Lady's wood. It was well-nigh impossible, the dictator had opined on several occasions, to distinguish the wild inhabitants of her realm from the savage races that constantly troubled Basilea. He allowed that while they might not be as outright wicked as the denizens of the Abyss that even now were pouring forth to trouble the lands of Men, the Galahirians were hardly civilized. Their armies, if one could dignify such mobs with the name, Andorset had sniffed, displayed the merest semblance of direction, surging across battlefields obedient only to the commands of their druids, a bizarre sect of nature-worshiping devotees of the Lady. They could be maddeningly treacherous too, Andorset had insisted to Dillen, divulging that in bygone days, the Lady's warriors had fought both alongside, and against, Basilea, switching sides seemingly on a whim.

Visibly irritated, the dictator snorted. In his war councils, he had stated that he would much rather have allowed the demons vomiting forth from the

Abyss to depart the forest before he fell upon them with his army of mailclad cavalry and stout spearmen. This foray into the woods was unpleasant in the extreme for both man and beast of his legion, but time was pressing, and they needed to move fast. Andorset stroked the tightly-braided mane of his warhorse. "There, there," he cooed to the animal. "I know you don't like the dark of the woods. We won't be in here for long."

Dillen saw a golden opportunity to deliver useful and relevant information to Andorset and impress him with his knowledge at the same time. "I think that we still have quite a way to go, General," advised Dillen. "The forest here is so dense that we are barely averaging a league per day. It's a hard thing to move an army through an almost trackless wilderness. It will surely be a lot longer."

Dillen smiled, but that smile faded instantly when he saw Andorset's lips curl in a sneer. "Is that so, Genemer? I suppose that you have acquired so much experience in war that you see fit to lecture me and correct me."

"I'm sorry, General. I. . . I only meant to be of service."

"And your service is to be a messenger, a great honor that I bestowed upon you. However, I will not abide being contradicted by a novice with unmarked armor." The aged dictator spurred his horse forward so that Genemer's unwelcome shadow would no longer fall upon him. "Spare me your insights."

Coming up beside Dillen, another horseman laughed lightly. "I don't think the general appreciates your comments, Brother Dillen," observed Brother Tebald Priscon.

"I was just trying to be helpful," Dillen protested to Tebald, a Hearth Knight of the Unquenchable Flame. "I've ridden ahead, and we've got at least a day or more left before we will make contact with the Green Lady's forces. There's no road in here. We're really just following a dirt footpath. Our army is moving much more slowly than if we were marching through open country, or on a proper Basilean road."

"All true," the older knight agreed, "but you must learn your place in this army. You are a simple messenger, no matter your pedigree." Tebald pointed to Andorset, who was now riding several horse-lengths ahead of them. "Your job is to carry missives to their recipients on behalf of your commanding general. Otherwise, you keep your opinions to yourself."

"That doesn't sound intelligent," Dillen complained. "What if the general were about to make a terrible blunder and I had information that would help him avoid it? Am I even then to remain silent?"

"You're a young man," Tebald said while smiling with no little sympathy. "I remember being young. So enthusiastic!" The paladin chuckled, and then grew serious. "Not a bad question. No, you are not to be silent. In such a case, speak up! But try to refrain from contradicting the dictator when you don't have to. Think about it, Dillen! You told the general he was wrong, before two of his senior officers, about something he had said to his horse. Was that truly necessary?"

"At least he is trying," offered Brother Bartolomo Hullus coming up beside them, before Dillen could respond. "He is motivated. Have you seen this youngster ride? Like the wind!" Bartolomo clapped Dillen on the back. "If only all of us tried so hard to be useful." The knight paladin of the Chapter of the Blades of Onzyan thrust out his chin, indicating Andorset. "The dictator is an old man," he whispered, "very set in his ways, and mindful of the prerogatives of rank. You should be a little more mindful of them too."

"But what if it's something important?"

"If it's something of real import, tell me or Brother Tebald. We'll handle it from there."

Dillen nodded. "Thank you, Brother."

The two paladins were a stark contrast. Brother Tebald was tall and thin to the point of gauntness. He wore almost always a serious mien, though he was not without a sense of humor. Brother Bartolomo, was much shorter, and stocky of build, with a florid face and eyes full of mirth. Both men were of roughly the same age, though Bartolomo enjoyed referring to Tebald as 'Elder Brother Tebald' every now and again. Dillen guessed that Tebald was the older of the two by a negligible margin and that Bartolomo took some pleasure in pestering the other knight about his greater age. Their relationship was at times warm, and at times cool. It was, in short, much like that of any pair of brothers born of the same mother.

Dillen had known them for just a few months. He had been an initiate of the Blades of Onzyan for only a short time when he was summoned to serve as a messenger in the headquarters of Dictator Andorset. It was a high honor, and Andorset had never tired of pointing that out to Dillen or the magnitude of the favor that he had done him by bringing him aboard.

It was a great distinction, Dillen admitted. Yet he suspected that it had not been pure altruism that had caused the dictator to offer him a place at his side. The Genemers were an ancient family of Solios, possessing a lineage that could be traced to the foundation of the Basilean state and beyond. Many had been the Genemer that had held exalted positions in the church or in the uppermost ranks of the army. General Andorset himself was a man of gentle birth, but he had come only from the lower gentry. "A mere country squire in origin," Brother Bartolomo had snarked on one occasion. The dictator was therefore very sensitive to rank and was assiduous in cultivating young nobles of more lofty status than his own. Two other young paladins were currently serving as horse messengers for the general. Both Stevven Orroy, a daredevil of a horseman from Cortia, and Arkbald Nell, a Sparthan youngster who hardly needed to shave, were scions of families as old and distinguished as Dillen's own. It could not have been pure accident that had caused Andorset to offer all three of them - each a thirdborn son of a Great House - positions on his staff. The dictator was employing those young men whom he expected would one day wield great influence within their respective houses. Basilean society, like all others, was based on a web of patronage and reciprocal loyalties. Andorset, a canny politician if there ever was one, was ingratiating himself with men who might in time come to hold enormous power.

If Andorset had hoped to establish a solid relationship with him, then Dillen thought that the general must now be very disappointed. His recent misstep was just the latest in a string of gaffes that had seen the dictator sour on the third son of House Genemer. People were often difficult for Dillen to fathom, and he had been unable to help but step on the general's toes. He had hoped to make a good impression, but adjusting to military life had been a trying experience. Dillen had never truly felt that he had been called to serve as a paladin. He preferred his books and would rather have devoted his life to scholarship and indulge as much as possible his love of languages. He thought perhaps to become a churchman, like so many of his ancestors had, but his father, a bluff and hearty man with a passion for battle and the tournament, would not countenance such a pacific career for his son. He'd sent the youngster for training in the arts of war as soon as he was of an age so that Dillen might take his place in the Holy Army of the Golden Horn without delay.

Dillen had proven to be a good warrior, with reflexes that made him one of the better swordsmen among his peers. His riding skills were top-notch too, a legacy of the lifetime of riding that he'd done on the several country estates owned by his family. They had served him well in his role as a courier delivering messages on behalf of the general. In time, he might rise higher in the ranks of the Blades of Onzyan, but only if he could break his habit of annoying his commanding officer, whose word would carry no little weight among Dillen's superiors in his chapter. Dejected, Dillen removed a tiny book from his saddle bag, a bestiary of creatures mundane and extraordinary that he expected to find within the Green Lady's strange wood.

*****

The Basilean army soon reached a spacious clearing. Tall maples and lofty oaks rose all about the edge of the space, their leaves turning rich browns and yellows in the lowering autumn sun. It was not large enough to accommodate the whole of the army, but it sufficed for Andorset. He called a halt, and the order to stop marching filtered slowly backward through the army, which was stretched out for a mile behind the vanguard in the trackless forest. He next ordered that his tent be set up in its exact center of the clearing. A crew of ten men deftly erected the general's gargantuan tent and had it pegged in place with ropes within minutes. They'd had much prior practice in putting up this movable palace of canvas and wood.

With late afternoon turning into night, Andorset held a meeting of his senior officers, as was his customary practice. Dillen was invited to attend, as apart from ferrying missives for his commanding officer, the primary purpose of his service with the general's headquarters was to learn how a general thought, acted, and commanded his subordinates. He stood at the rear of the tent, silent. The deliberations of the small band of counselors ordinarily went very smoothly, with the staff delivering crisp, to-the-point reports to the general. On this evening, however, there was dissension. Brother Tebald, commander of the army's cavalry contingent of paladin knights, spoke out first.

"We must push on, my general, and find the Green Lady as soon as possible," he pleaded. "This host is but a weak legion in strength, and is in a bad way here, vulnerable to sudden attack. The ground is uneven and the way narrower than a keyhole. We are slowed, and most of our army is still strung out far along the line of march."

Brother Bartolomo, master of the men-at-arms and paladin infantry, echoed the sentiment more bluntly. "This is a terrible place to stop for the night. We are nearly blind too. In our sudden haste to leave the Golden Horn, we were unable to include a wizard in our ranks who might scry the enemy's presence with his magecraft. Our own scouts have found nothing, but the enemy is about, believe you me. We also lack the aid of even a single Elohi. Let us begone, and either force march our way to the folk of Galahir, or else fall back a league or so. We passed a much larger and more defensible open space not too far back in which we could erect a proper, fortified camp."

Andorset laughed harshly. "Alas, that both of my lieutenants should lose their courage on the same day! You take too much counsel of your fears, which are unreasonable. If we go forward, then we shall march all night and simply arrive exhausted and incapable of action. If we go back, we will waste time on the morrow retracing steps we have already taken. Our scouts have found no sign of the enemy because they are not here, but engaged elsewhere. No! We stay here. Tomorrow, at dawn, we shall set out once more, and make contact with the Galahirians."

There would be no arguing with Andorset's decision. It was standard procedure for a marching Basilean army, when it made camp for the night, to surround it with a ditch and an earthen rampart surmounted by a staked palisade.

It was often the case that the soldiers of Basilea would find themselves deep inside hostile territory, far from the support of friendly forces. A strong camp might not be as impregnable as a high-walled castle, but it would be stout enough to fend off all but the most determined attack. More importantly, the ramparts, guarded at all times of the unlit hours by watchful sentries, were sufficient to prevent an assault by surprise. Basilea's armies must never be taken unawares, all agreed. Within the camp, the good soldiers of the Golden Horn could sleep soundly under the guard of their brothers who stood sentinel upon its earthen walls.

So important was this cautious practice, Dillen had been taught, that often an army might halt its progress with much of the light of the day still left when a good location for the camp had been found. Better to be safe and secure in the howling wilderness than to take a risk all for the sake of a few more miles of distance. Unhappily, Dillen noted, the present spot was neither safe nor secure. Less than half the army might be accommodated in this glade, and it would be not till after nightfall that the last soldiers of the straggling column reached it and learned that they would have to pitch their tents between the thick trunks of the trees. The men, especially the common footsoldiers, thought the wood bewitched. Asking them to sleep outside the confines of a regular camp would do nothing to lessen their fears.

"I beg you, Dictator Andorset, to reconsider your decision," Tebald urged, "and allow the army to press on. If we march through the night we will surely make it to the rendezvous with the Lady's people."

Andorset's eyes narrowed with irritation. "When did my fine warriors become such fainthearts? Was it not you, Brother Tebald, who single-handedly held the Gate of the Elohi at Plenoria? Have the Hearth Knights now lost their mettle?" Andorset tapped his chest. "Not this one." He turned his head slightly to fix his gaze upon Brother Bartolomo. "And was it not you who led the charge of the Blades of Onzyan that broke the back of the orc horde at Stemkor? The orcs were routed that day as a result of that very charge. Please tell me that you are the same men, or have I chosen my subcommanders unwisely?"

Both paladins were silent for a time. Dillen prayed to every Shining One he could name to open the dictator's mind to the good counsel of his lieutenants, but Andorset remained adamant. Tebald relented first, undone by the general's questioning of his courage. "No, my general," a chastened Brother Tebald answered. "I am one and the same." Bartolomo said nothing, nodding his assent to Andorset's order, but his eyes were full of his misgivings. The army would stay where it was.

*****

"Not surprised am I," Bartolomo declared as he placed the reins of his warhorse into those of his squire, a zealous youth named Jedd. "Once Andorset has made a decision, he is as stubborn as a mule. Virtually immovable. Very certain in his judgment, no matter how many may question it."

"He was not always thus," added Tebald, who was busy removing his coat of mail before retiring to his tent. "It was Amola. That is what changed him."

"What happened at Amola?" Dillen asked while sharpening his sword in the ruddy glow of the firelight,. "That was a great victory."

"Aye, it was," Bartolomo agreed, "but the dictator lost his only son there. He's grown rigid since."

"He blames himself?"

"Yes," replied Tebald, "but it was not merely his son's death that has changed him so. I was there with him. We were attacked by orcs. His senior officers convinced him to withdraw our forces beyond the Irasus River. A good portion of our army was holed up in a redoubt. The enemy was bound to overwhelm them. But Andorset thought they would be better off staying where they were and weathering the storm in place."

"Their insistent pleas managed to change his mind, at last," continued Bartolomo, "but events did not go as well as hoped. Though most of our army made it across, the forces ordered to abandon the redoubt were run down by the orcs and cut up badly. Some survived, but many more fell. One of the slain was Andorset's son, Alexan."

"The dictator thinks that it was his vacillation, that he listened to the counsels of others, that caused Alexan's death," said Tebald. "Not so, I say, as do most others too, but Andorset, ever since, has reproached himself for going against his own judgment. Now, when he makes a decision, it is final."

"Such inflexibility is hardly a good quality in a general," Dillen said. "Was it not Ebar Teft who wrote that 'a willingness to adapt is the one constant quality that a good general must possess' in his Treatise on War?"

"Indeed, it was," smiled Tebald. "I did not expect a Blade of Onzyan to be so well-read in the classics. I had thought you all to be merely rich horsemen with no time for intellectual pursuits."

Dillen grinned, and Bartolomo let out a hearty laugh. "Every now and again we are blessed to find a thinker in our midst. The Hearth Knights of the Unquenchable Flame are not the only ones in this army with a bit of learning."

*****

"The sky is gray and threatening," Dillen said. "We'll have rain soon."

"Then we'd best be on our way," Tebald yawned, emerging from his own tent. "We have tarried here too long, and the folk of Galahir are in need of our aid."

Morning could not have come fast enough for Dillen. There was something unnerving about being in Galahir. It was not merely that it was a forest. All forests made him uneasy, being dark and filled with wild animals. No, Galahir felt alien in a manner that defied ready explanation. This forest seemed alive and hostile in ways that went far beyond what he had experienced elsewhere. He felt as if eyes were always upon him, as if the denizens in this forest were inimical to Men to a degree far greater than the beasts of the woods in the world outside.

The host of Basilea had been dispatched to bring succor to the beleaguered peoples of the wood. Even now, the Green Lady and her warriors were defying the onslaught of the denizens of the Abyss. Though the blackhearted fiends were hurling themselves against their defenses, the brave inhabitants of the forest had held the line against repeated assaults.

But only just. An urgent plea had come from Galahir, in the Lady's name, written in black ink upon a broad golden leaf. It had begged Basilea to send help to stem the dark tide that threatened to overwhelm her wood. There were those in Basilea who were skeptical of the Lady and her people. Wiser, and more generous counsels, though, had prevailed. Time was short. An expeditionary army of scarcely a half-legion in size was hastily assembled from amongst the city's militia, and the several hundred paladins, mostly Hearth Knights of the Unquenchable Flame and Blades of Onzyan, still resident within. Inside two days, the Basilean host was marching north to Galahir. Andorset, an experienced general, had been appointed commander of the force, and within a fortnight, the army had reached the eaves of the wood. The dictator had been an odd choice as general. Dillen had listened closely to the impassioned debates of Basilea's foremost nobles before the Hegemon concerning whether the Holy Host should be dispatched in response to the request for aid. Andorset himself had been one of the voices that had argued most loudly against sending an army to the wood and he had also expressed a deep distrust of for the Lady and her people.

Nevertheless, and much to Dillen's surprise, Andorset had been chosen to lead the host to war on account of his excellent battle record. A solid, if unimaginative, commander, the dictator, a Hearth Knight of the Unquenchable Flame, was the highest-ranking lord paladin left resident in the Golden Horn. In addition to the tragic, but ultimately successful defense of Amola, Andorset had won victories at Plenoria, Coponia, Neora, and Yast-Edeless. In the eyes of the Hegemon and the great lords of Basilea, Andorset was a man to whom they could safely entrust an army. Dillen had heard that said many times of the dictator by his father and his fellow aristocrats. Caution and calculation, not daring brilliance, were the hallmarks of his generalship.

The young paladin wondered what they might say of him now, if they could see how deaf he had become to the counsel of others. A collegial style of generalship had long been the norm in Basilea. No one man, no matter how elevated his rank, could ignore the advice and entreaties of his fellows without repercussions of some kind. The warriors of Basilea, whether grand paladins or common footsoldiers, were all subjects of the same kingdom and had to live together when campaigns ended, helm and armor were removed, and weapons were set down at fireside. A commander who was so close-minded as to discount the reasoned proposals of his officers would eventually hear about their displeasure, and possibly suffer a rebuke from his king and comrades after he had laid down his command.

Dillen saddled his own horse, as he did not yet have the right to engage a squire, and whispered softly in the animal's ear. He lifted himself up easily into the saddle, casually grasping the reins with one hand. Bartolomo frowned unhappily. "You are much too spry for so early in the morning, Brother Dillen. Some of the rest of us old men have not quite awoken from our slumber yet. Have a care not to show off so in before the elderly men of this good host."

"I grieve that I have distressed you so, Brother Bartolomo. Forgive me my eagerness and youthful energy."

Bartolomo eyed Dillen closely. "You know, Tebald, he says that with such sincerity I almost believe him. Almost, but not quite."

Tebald was busy buckling his sword belt about his waist. He did not look up. "I believe him entirely. Even now I can hear his tears splashing to earth. He is clearly deeply distraught at having caused you pain by his display of a vigor that has long since deserted you. Thus he weeps."

"Yes, of course, that must be it," Bartolomo rumbled. The older paladin sat down heavily on his pack and began eating the small breakfast that Jedd had prepared for him. "I will ignore you both now."

*****

"Report, Damathana."

The succubus folded her ebon bat wings smartly behind her and stood to attention. "I have observed the Basileans since they entered the wood, Lord Zelgarag. They wander about it like lost children, fumbling in the darkness, trying to find their way to the Lady." Damathana did not blink as she spoke.

"They are vulnerable?"

A thin smile, cruel and alluring, curled Damathana's full ruby lips. "Yes, Lord. Just as you predicted. They are many, but the narrowness of the path through the forest has forced them to thin their line. Only two or three men may walk abreast along the winding way through the trees. They are further slowed by the need to throw planks over rents in the earth to let their animals pass. They have broken camp and are now corralled like cattle, ready for the slaughter."

"Fools," Zelgarag growled. He brushed aside a gaggle of imps that cavorted around the crude throne that had been carved for him out of a sorcery-withered tree stump. "They think that they are safe. They believe that we are far from them, and that they have merely to march and arrive like heroes to bolster the defense of Galahir." Zelgarag stood. Damathana caught her breath as he rose to his full height. The champion of the Abyss was a paragon of all that the warriors of the hordes of Hell might hope to be. Great wings, leathery and blood red, spread out behind him, casting ominous shadows in the morning twilight of the forest. Zelgarag's dark star was on the rise, and Damathana intended to ascend along with it.

He strode forward on cloven hooves, muscles rippling beneath skin the hue of glowing embers. A pair of lengthy sable horns emerged from his head, soaring upward like tongues of dark flame. He reached out a massive hand and cupped the succubus's delicate chin in it. With a finger that ended in a wicked black claw, he gently caressed her porcelain cheek, leaving behind a rosy, blushing line where he traced.

"Well done, Damathana. Well done. When you presented this plan to me, I was unsure of its wisdom. Now I see that everything you promised was correct. The Basileans, cursed be they for all time, are haughty and blind to the dangers into which they are marching. We shall make them pay for their arrogance. Let this day go well for us, and you will have pride of place at my side. No one will be above you, save me."

"My lord, my love," she whispered. Damathana did her best to hide the full extent of the joy his words had kindled in her heart. It would not do to allow him to see how much he had thrilled her. Yet it was a grand honor indeed! She would be the consort of a great champion! At his side, she too would be exalted in ranks of the hordes of the Abyss.

Together, they left the small clearing that Zelgarag had turned into an impromptu court. They found the lesser Abyssal troops waiting for them in the tight spaces between the ancient trees. Damathana sneered inwardly but kept her face an impassive mask that hid her disgust. These things were an unlovely bunch, no more than dregs spewed from the Abyss. She saw towering amongst them a handful of guards. These were the hard core of Zelgarag's army and would fight beside him in the coming battle. All others were contemptible and would have been beneath her notice had she not needed to hurl them at the Basileans within the coming hour. Most were common Abyssal footsoldiers, vicious and bloodthirsty. She also glimpsed gargoyles, gray of skin and yellow-fanged. There were mortals too, wretched men who had pledged their souls to darkness in exchange for a glimpse of the truth and glory of the Abyss. They were little more than parasites now, hungering ravenously for the soulfire of the living. Beside them huddled herds of even worse degenerates; the larvae, mind-addled mortals whose only role would be to assault the Basileans in wave after expendable wave. They would make up in numbers what they lacked in skill. Around them stood glowering torturers, cruel pitchforks in hand, ready to drive the damned men to their doom.

Damathana wished that Zelgarag had been granted better troops, but his superiors had looked askance at the plan, especially because it had come from her, a mere succubus. The Abyssal swarms were engaged up and down the line at the edge of Galahir, locked in combat with the denizens of the wood. Only when Zelgarag had pledged his unholy soul to them as a guarantee that he would annihilate the Basilean army did they relent, and then only grudgingly. To Zelgarag, they had given the equivalent of a full regiment comprised of their lesser troops to do with what he might, or forfeit his soul to their tender mercies.

Her plan had to work! The Basileans were blundering about in the deep woods with scarcely a care for their security. It had been easy to hide from their scouts, few in number that they were. None amongst the people of the Golden Horn seemed to worry in the slightest that an army of the Abyss was forming amongst the trees just out of their sight.

Perhaps it would be for the best that they had come with such a small force. To evade the watchful eyes of the Lady's subjects, Zelgarag's host had set out only when a major assault by the rest of the Abyssals was underway. They had used the distraction to race into the forest, unpursued by the wretched beings of Galahir, while their attention was riveted on the monstrosities that threatened to overwhelm the borders of their home.

"Arise, loyal army of the Dark Masters!" Zelgarag cried, his ink-black eyes blazing with unholy fury. "It is time that the people of the Abyss take what is rightfully theirs! It is time that we take our place in the World Above, and right the wrongs done to us in bygone ages." Zelgarag paused and cast his eyes toward the scum that fawned around him, feigning sympathy. "Many are those here who have been driven out unjustly from their homes in the sunlit lands."

Zelgarag was enough of a diplomat, Damathana noted, fighting back an urge to smirk, that he left out that they had all richly deserved their ostracism for whatever myriad crimes they had committed as they pledged their souls to darkness. Some were cannibals, some violators of the dead, almost all were criminals of one abhorrent sort or another.

"You have been outcast from your birthlands," the demonic champion continued, "unwanted by the societies into which you were born and set adrift. But now you have found a new people, and together, we will take back your homes, repaying in blood tenfold, a hundredfold, no, a thousandfold, all of the hurts that were done to you!"

The repulsive idiots were cheering, or what passed for cheering among their decayed kind. Their roars sounded like the snorts of pigs crossed with screams issuing from the throats of brutes.

"Even now does an army of the hateful Basileans march through this wood, careless of their flanks. They have no idea, none at all, that we are waiting for them in these trees, ready to pounce on them when they are least ready. Now that time has come my friends. This is why you have been driven so hard, that we might reach this spot, unseen by the mewling forest folk, so that we might fall upon the slaves of the Elohi without anyone seeing us as we made our way here. We have found them. They trudge unsuspectingly through a tree-choked gorge, slow and ripe for the slaughter. We have them just where we want them."

There came another guttural cheer from the throng, and Zelgarag exulted in their approval, though they were hardly more than enthusiastic animal grunts and squeals. His eyes had grown bright, as if lit by the inner forge fire of a smithy in Hell. "They have become like a snake, stretched and thin, and like a snake they are all but blind. Let us, together, cut the snake into pieces!"

More roars now, and the Abyssal host seemed to pulse and quiver with anxious anticipation. Zelgarag raised his clawed hands higher and higher, encouraging their cheers, until they reached a frenzied crescendo. All at once, he let his hands fall, and the throng of the damned ceased its cheering.

"See now how it begins to rain? The Masters smile upon us! The rain will muffle the sound of our approach and hide us from the eyes of our enemies. Bring me the heads of the men of the Golden Horn! A bright gold coin for every one taken! Go now! Go now! Spill the blood of the enemies of your kindly Masters! Rip their hearts from their breasts and feast upon their eyes! Go now!"

Zelgarag signaled, and the officers of the Abyssal rabble goaded their charges away toward the Basilean army that they knew lay in the distance. Thousands of hate-filled hearts were filled with a hideous glee as they marched, scampered, ambled, waddled, or ran ahead, in search of a reckoning with the humans who represented all that they most loathed. Blood they smelled, blood they would soon taste.

With eyes that did not blink, Damathana watched them go. Many, most, perhaps even all, would fall. They would not be missed.

*****

"Did you hear that?" Dillen asked. "It sounded like. . . I don't know what. Roars? Cheers?"

"You are just hearing things," Stevven Orroy said. "These woods are getting to you. Playing with your mind."

"Yes," agreed young Arkbald Nell. "Just some forest creatures doing forest creature things. Pay them no heed."

Dillen was quiet for a time, but he was not mollified. He had heard something, hadn't he? Perhaps his mind was playing tricks on him. He'd never liked the woods, and he had been uneasy ever since he had entered Galahir. He wondered if he was susceptible to some disquiet of the mind, in which trauma reaching back into his childhood might have made him inordinately uneasy in the tree-shrouded darkness. A gray gloom had settled upon the twilit wood of the early morning. It was no wonder, Dillen struggled to convince himself, that he was uneasy. He felt a slight chill in the air and shivered. Then it started to rain.

"We are too sure of ourselves," Dillen said after a time. "We don't know these woods, and we failed to obtain a guide through them as we should have."

"Not needed," Stevven countered. "Or else the dictator would have requested one from the Lady."

"I would not be surprised if he did not bother to ask," Dillen said. The two younger men had been off delivering messages, and thus not present, when Andorset had browbeat Brothers Tebald and Bartolomo into accepting his decision to bivouac where they had last night. It had not resulted in disaster, as Dillen had feared, but today was a new day. He explained his misgivings to his fellow messengers.

"Come now," Stevven said. "The dictator has more experience of war that almost any other man in Basilea. He knows what he is about. If he did not, then he would not have been appointed to lead this host. Such decisions are not made lightly. All three of our fathers cast their votes in his favor, did they not? Knowing that their own sons would be marching with this army, they would never have voted to place Andorset in command of it unless they had the utmost confidence in him."

Arkbald grinned. "We are just thirdborn sons. Not so special."

Dillen ignored Arkbald. He was forced to admit that Stevven's argument was sound, insofar as it was based upon the limited information that the older messenger possessed. Dillen had not revealed what Brothers Tebald and Bartolomo had told him about the dictator the day before. For a short while, he tried to relieve his anxieties by telling himself that scions of Houses Genemer, Orroy, and Nell, would not have been entrusted to any but the finest and most careful of generals. Then the rain came down harder and his worries returned. The steady downpour began to soak through his cloak and clothing. His skin became cold, and he began to shiver, though the early autumn day was otherwise warm.

The three messengers were walking their horses alongside a deep ravine in the forest with sheer sides that rose high above their heads. To their right and below, in the middle of the cleft ran a trickling stream. Teams of engineers labored to place planks across the narrowest breaks in the ground, so that men and animals, of which the army had many, could cross. It was not hard to traverse them, once the bridges had been thrown over, but it was time-consuming, with just two or three men able to march abreast. Rather than going the long way round the forest, Andorset had thought that he might shave a day or two from his march by cutting across a portion of the wood. This had proven a vain hope. Instead, the Basileans had been slowed by at least as much time because of the density of the trees and the ruggedness of the terrain. They were late in coming to the aid of the Green Lady and they would be lucky to reach the frontline by the next morning.

Arkbald led his horse across first, followed by Stevven, with Dillen going last. Their animals were sleek and fast, as befitted the mounts of messengers. Dillen's own steed was a chestnut stallion with a white blaze on his forehead. His father had purchased the horse for him when he had been selected to take part in the expedition. A bellicose, harsh, but unstintingly generous man, the Lord Genemer had always seen to it that Dillen wanted for nothing where war was concerned. He had been trained by the finest of Basilea's weapon masters and riding instructors. Nor had his father neglected his equipment. The mail coat he wore was composed of a triple thickness of case-hardened, riveted links. It was proof against sword strokes and all but the most determined spear thrusts. The bright helm dangling from his saddle was a work of art, beaten into shape out of a single piece of sheet steel, and topped with a horsehair crest, dyed red and yellow, the colors of his house. The sword at his side, a blade of Solisian steel crafted by the leading weaponsmith in the Golden Horn, had cost a small fortune. If there was a better outfitted man in the whole of the army, Dillen had not encountered him.

If only such external trappings could change him inwardly. Dillen felt as if he were an actor hired to play the role of a warrior, and that the arms he bore and armor he wore were nothing more than props given to him to allow him to look the part. His father had seemed to think that once his son had gotten his first experience of battle that he would develop a taste for it. Not so. Dillen had fought goblins in a handful of skirmishes the year before, and though he had fought well on each occasion, he knew that soldiering was not the life for him.

"Ow!" Dillen scratched his forehead on a low-hanging branch and scolded himself for not paying better attention. If he had not been so occupied with pity for his own predicament, he would have noticed the branch jutting into his path.

"You okay?" Stevven inquired.

"I'm alright," Dillen said. "A bothersome branch. Just another reason for me not to like the woods."

"You're bleeding a bit," Arkbald noted, pointing to Dillen's forehead. "You never wear your helmet. That would have prevented it."

"Arkbald's right," Stevven added. "You should put it on."

Embarrassed to have become injured by foliage - there were no medals to be earned, he was certain, for wounds obtained in such cases - Dillen unhooked his helmet from his saddlebag and undid the chinstrap. He struggled with the thing, it having become slick in the rain, and it fell from his hands, tumbling down the ravine, splashing through the stream, and then coming to rest amidst the gnarled roots of a massive oak.

"I think you're going to need that helmet before this campaign is over," Stevven observed. "Here, I'll take your reins."

Dillen carefully picked his way down the steep slope to where his helmet had rolled. He bent over and lifted it from the mud, brushing off dirt from the brow and neckguard. He dried the inside of the bowl as best he could and lowered it onto his head. It was cold and damp.

There was an odd noise, something like a cross between a bark and a snarl. Dillen looked up to the other side of the ravine where the ground stood a little higher than the path on which the Basileans trod. He thought it might be a forest animal looking for shelter in the rain, which had grown fiercer. He climbed to the top, grabbing handholds of exposed roots to pull himself upward. As he peered over the top of the rise, his heart sank. He realized that the sounds he had heard earlier were not those of nature.

It was singing.

*****

It was Dillen's shout that alerted the Basilean column to the destruction that rushed toward them. A horde of monsters crested the ridge, just as confused men-at-arms readied their spears and drew their swords. The guttural roar of the surging Abyssals was like a peal of thunder unexpected, and thereby all the more disconcerting. Their yell was answered by the sounding of a horn, deep and clear. It could only have come from the dictator's own herald to signal that the general still stood, and that his men were to hold firm against the onslaught. Up and down the line of march, the Basilean soldiers formed serried ranks, as best they could manage in the broken ground, their iron discipline edging out the mordant fear that welled up inside every one of them. The first volley of missiles flung by their attackers clattered on the stones at their feet, or embedded themselves in the stout plywood shields they held. They stood like a wall, the pride of Basilea, but their numbers were few compared to the demonic tide that assailed them. Then a few javelins found their marks, where a shield had not been held high enough, or a black-fletched arrow with accursed aim found the narrow gap between helm and mail.

Dillen scrambled up the slope to where Stevven and Arkbald stood with their mounts, swords drawn and resolute gleams in their eyes. He turned and faced the oncoming creatures, wishing he had just half the courage of his companions. Then their attackers were upon them. He slashed with his sword and took off the head of a shambolic, man-shaped thing. It fountained red blood from its headless trunk, until it fell over and rolled back down the slope. Another misshapen, soul-damned man reached for his throat, a maniac grin on his face as he cackled a litany of the dark crimes he had committed. Dillen held his shield out, keeping his attacker's gorestained hand away from him, and then stabbed with his sword. The point pierced the enemy's ribcage, emerging from his back. Disconcertingly, the lunatic cultist did not seem to care, but he gripped the sword with bloodied fingers, pulling himself closer to Dillen. With mouth wide, he made to bite the young paladin, who shoved him backward with his shield. The cultist was too strong, and they wrestled now for the shield and sword, until Stevven clove the man's head open with a swift cut of his sword.

"This isn't much like arms drill," Stevven deadpanned.

"We'd have been overrun already were it not for the charge uphill these things have to make!" Dillen shouted as he lopped an arm, and then a head, off of another frothing cultist. "But what's happening elsewhere? The army is trapped in this gorge. There's scant protection to be had, and little room in which to form a true shieldwall."

Stevven stepped forward and landed a heavy blow, bursting the skull of a drooling spearman. "This army is doomed if we don't summon help!"

Arkbald stood beside Dillen. "And where are we supposed to get help here in the forest? There's no one but the birds and the beasts all around!"

Another surge of warriors of the Abyss came at them, impelled by some hideous urge to spill the blood of the struggling Basileans. With Stevven to his left, and Arkbald to his right, Dillen fought for what seemed an eternity against the black tide of hate that washed up against them. The Abyssals' numbers seemed inexhaustible, with wave after wave running forward to claw and scrape at them. The Basileans, trained soldiers all, gave better than they got, but their number was slowly being whittled down by the inexhaustible enemy. Had this been a battle fought out in the open, where drill and discipline would have counted for more, the small Basilean host would have prevailed eventually, if not without difficulty. But in the close press of the ancient wood, there was no room in which to form into squares, nor any space in which to maneuver. There were just little knots of desperate men struggling to survive in a terrifying battle. The dictator's horn sounded again. The general still lived.

*****

There was a short lull as the demonic army regrouped. "We can't go on like this," Dillen said, panting to catch his breath. "We've been at this for an hour. Someone needs to do something."

"What do you propose?" Stevven asked. He was tending to Arkbald, who sat upon the sodden ground. The Sparthan had been struck by a javelin in his right thigh and a crimson stain ran down his leg to the top of his riding boot. Once Stevven had finished binding the youngster's wound, he turned to Dillen and leaned on his shield, which had been scored by a dozen blows. Stevven seemed dispirited, something Dillen had never seen in him before.

"There's nowhere to run," Stevven said. He gestured further up and then back down the line of march. "We're too deep in the woods to make an escape back the way we have come. We must presume that we are being assailed everywhere up and down our column. "It is only a matter of time." Stevven stamped his foot, spraying rainwater and mud. "This will be where we stand our last."

"We must not give up!" Dillen objected. "We can't allow such a fine army to be destroyed by the spawn of the Abyss."

"What do you propose?"

"One of us must ride to get help from the Green Lady. She can't be too far off, maybe a day or so for a swift rider."

A weary Stevven shook his head. "That is suicide. No one will break through the lines of this foe. Look at their multitude on the other side," he said, pointing with his sword at a milling mass of foul men and even fouler demonic creatures.

"I will chance it, nonetheless," Dillen said. "My horse is fast, and I will not die today."

Stevven wore a grim smile and cocked his head to the side. "I am not sure if you are the bravest man in this army or the craziest."

Dillen sheathed his sword. "Maybe both. We don't have much time to discuss this. The dictator and Brothers Tebald and Bartolomo are up ahead. They are either dead or so beset by the enemy that they can't get word to us. We have to act on our initiative."

Stevven nodded. "Go then. I must stay with Arkbald." He pointed to the assemblage on the far side of the ravine. The Abyssals' numbers had swelled to the point where it seemed that they were ready to launch another assault on the Basileans. "Be ready to make your break when I give you the signal."

"What are you going to do?"

Stevven chuckled. "I will cause a distraction that men of this corrupted sort will be unable to resist."

"What kind of distraction? There isn't much that these soul-damned knaves haven't seen already. Not much will impress them."

"Of that, I am well aware." Stevven grew suddenly serious. "Ready now! They come again!"

Dillen mounted his stallion and spurred the animal forward, carefully picking his way down the ravine. The beast was surefooted and descended the slope without incident. He hid himself and his mount in the dense undergrowth at the bottom and looked back to Stevven, who stood at the front of a knot of spearmen, his face an unreadable mask. Then he smiled, and in a friendly voice, called out to the Abyssal warriors who were advancing once more, gaining their attention. When they had closed, Stevven held up his pouch, a bag of brown leather tied with a yellow cord. He undid the closure and removed a handful of silver and gold coins from within. He showed them to the soul-damned men, who looked upon the money with a startling mixture of avarice and lust. Stevven delivered a mocking salute to them and hurled the coins to the bottom of the ravine. "This is what you really want," he shouted, his voice carrying easily to them amidst the clamor of battle. "Come and get it!"

The mob of the Abyssals wavered, as their overseers struggled to maintain their hold over their charges. Whips cracked and flails struck the backs of the miserable once-men. Then the power of their greed overcame their fear of the lash, and they lunged forward to grab the coins that Stevven had cast before them. They rushed down the slope, falling over one another to be the first to claim their prizes. Stevven tossed another handful of coins to their side, and this riveted their attention away from where Dillen and his horse hid. A clever ruse, Dillen admired, but there was no time to lose while the enemy was momentarily distracted. He spurred his horse up the slope, and the animal drew him upward, its hooves slipping now and again in the mud, until it reached the crest.

*****

Dillen rode forward, winding his way as fast as his horse could gallop within the confines of the trees. Soon he was far enough from the battle that the sounds of screaming men were muffled. He turned to the southeast, thinking that he would take a parallel course to the one that the army had traveled and make his way to the folk of the wood. Then his horse bucked and collapsed, a javelin protruding from the beast's neck. Dillen sprawled across the damp forest floor, rolling upright as he fell.

He stood and caught a blur passing in through his field of vision, a black shadow streaking from left to right. A scarlet blade slashed at his face, and he dove, the weapon passing above his head so close that it sheared the horsehair crest from his helm. His attacker cursed, and he saw now that it was a woman, tall and lithe, but unlike any he'd ever seen before. Spreading behind her were two leathery wings. Her legs ended in delicately cloven hooves. Two small horns emerged from her forehead, which was high and broad. Intelligent eyes, large, blue, and unutterably cruel, stared at him angrily. They never blinked. Most disconcerting of all was the sheer beauty of the creature before him. She possessed a loveliness that would have melted his heart had she not been so intent on killing him. Her face was a soft oval, framed by coal-black hair; her skin was the purest ivory. She was scarcely clad, too, and a proper Basilean woman would have been ashamed to be seen in public wearing nothing but two skimpy pieces of fabric about her breast and hips. He could not help letting his eyes linger on her a bit too long.

"Well, boy, haven't you ever seen a woman before?" she mocked.

"None such as yourself. I count myself blessed."

She broke into a run, holding her saber high, and slashed in a descending arc at his head. He blocked the blow with his sword and kicked outward, slamming his boot into her calf. She cried out, and stumbled off, hobbled by the intense pain.

Regaining his footing, Dillen circled, still unsure of what manner of the Abyss's residents was before him. He looked at her closely. He had never given the rumors of what roamed the Underworld much credence, thinking them tales stitched together either to frighten children or to fill idle and too-welcoming minds with the salacious. Yet here she was, a woman of frightful aspect and yet still grandly beautiful, more akin to one of the Elohi than to the fiends that he associated with the Abyss.

Her lips twisted in an evil smile. She charged at him once more, feinting from the right before pulling back and then thrusting forward with the wickedly sharp point of her blade. He dodged the saber well enough so that the edge of it caught him only slightly, grazing the mail covering his left shoulder. He winced and then responded with a flurry of blows that pushed her onto the defensive.

She was a competent swordswoman, Dillen saw, but there was no brilliance in her bladework. His instructors had taught him well, enabling him to quickly analyze the fighting technique of any opponent upon seeing him, or in this case, her, in action. She was used to winning quickly, Dillen surmised, and had thus never had to develop a full suite of attacks, parries, and ripostes to do battle against an accomplished foe.

Her face, lovely but suffused with frustration, betrayed her emotions. Dillen rammed into her with his shield, knocking her backward. She unfolded her wings instinctively to prevent herself from falling over, and Dillen slashed, cutting a bloody tear in the skin of her left wing. She cried out and then tumbled over, rolling down a low slope. She ended in an angry heap, her right wing broken and hanging limply by her side. Her unblinking eyes blazed up at him with impotent fury.

"What are you?" Dillen asked. She was nothing he had ever seen before, or hoped to see again.

"Nothing that you need to know," the woman sneered. "Ha! Go on! Run away! You'll be dead soon enough!"

"Perhaps, but I have a job to do before that happens."

"I know what your mission is, mortal, where you are headed, and you will never succeed. There are things in this wood that owe no fealty to the Green Lady, though she may extravagantly claim all of it as her realm. You will be dead before sunrise."

"That may be so," Dillen answered. "I will at least be rid of you in my final hours. Enjoy your walk back to your own people. It will be a rather long one, I think." Dillen ran off as fast he could through the trees. The afternoon sun was setting, and there was an army that needed rescuing. In the distance, he heard the peal of a horn, dim and faltering.

*****

Wiping the mud from her wings and knees, Damathana watched as the young paladin ran off. She consoled herself with the certainty that, by this time tomorrow, the knight would be a moldering corpse, and the trapped host of Basilea would have been exterminated.

*****

Dillen ran on, sucking breaths as he wound his way through the close-packed forest. He leapt over protruding roots of trees of such girth that he guessed that they were as old as the world itself. It was well past midnight, and yet the darkened wood was curiously alive, filled with the hoots of owls and other animals he could not identify. Now and again he caught glimpses of creatures looking back at him, the light of his small lantern illuminating their eyes in unearthly hues of amber.

Within Galahir, Dillen felt as if he had stepped back in time to the dawning age of the world; when the sun was young and all beneath it was covered, so the wise said, in a primeval forest that stretched from sea to sea. It had been a forest untouched by the rude hands of Men, filled with trees that had not known the bite of an axe, with roots buried in soil that had never known the cut of a plow.

He began to despair as he realized that he had lost his way. He turned about, trying to seek out the sun, but it had not yet risen, and the moon was not visible from within the deep darkness of the wood. He had been hoping to follow as straight a course as he might from where he had fled the demon assassin, but the denseness of the vegetation and the roughness of the ground had left his sense of direction hopelessly muddled.

In an incipient panic, he began to hurry up whatever high ground was in reach, hoping to find the moon and gain some idea of his correct course. He trotted up a slope and found himself enmeshed in a thick bundle of sticky fibers invisible in the darkness. He pulled, but the glue that covered the cable-thick strands refused to release him. Soon, both his arms were stuck fast. He dropped his lantern, which fell to the soft wet earth, flickering. Dillen looked up, and in the dim lamplight he saw that he stood at the base of a vast web, all but impossible to see except within an arm's length of the thing. He yanked again, but the strands, though pliant, yielded only a little, and he could not free himself. Above his head he saw that a large bird, perhaps an owl, was suspended, upside down. Another victim of the great spider that had woven this iron-like web between the trees. At his feet were also stuck a rat and what looked to have once been a rabbit.

There came a slight tremor, transmitted fitfully along the fibers of the web. Dillen looked above him and saw a tight grouping of multiple eyes examining him. Eight of these there were, some smaller, some larger. None betrayed any human feeling such as pity or forgiveness. Coming downward along the web, which did not hinder its movement in any way, Dillen saw that the spider's body was an elongated tube, with long legs thrust out before it and behind. It opened its jaws, displaying dagger-sized fangs. A bird, a man, a rat, a rabbit. Such things would all be part of the meal for this creature. Was he the main course, Dillen wondered, or a mere appetizer for this horrid beast?

He pulled once more with all his might, straining to free himself from the strands that held him fast. They were unyielding; strong, sticky, and as massive as the ropes used to haul river barges. Dillen's swelling panic threatened to overcome him altogether. His heart raced. He struggled to order his thoughts. He tried again, in vain, to free himself, twisting uselessly in the web. Still the spider closed on him, unhurried, its alien and emotionless eyes staring blankly at him. Its mouthparts clicked several times. Dillen imagined them snapping through his bones and flesh.

He struggled to remember his training. So much of it had been pressed into his head, but he could recall little of it now that death approached him on eight spindly legs. He attempted to clear his mind, uttering a wordless prayer to the Shining Ones for the grant of courage. His quivering muscles tensed as he pulled again. His teeth chattered, loud and fast. Perspiration poured from his face, stinging his eyes. It was almost upon him. A calmness came over him. Perhaps it was a blessing of the gods. He felt a clarity that had been missing only moments before. He would meet his death with his eyes open. He was young, and even though he had not been a man for long, he would die as one this day.

The vast thing stopped a few feet from his head, busying itself with consuming the owl. A patient predator, Dillen thought with detached admiration. The creature was utterly confident that nothing caught in its web would escape.

Dillen gave a thought to his comrades, fighting for their lives in the outer reaches of the wood. He had failed them, miserably. Soon he would be a feast for a beast of the forest, his remains never to be found, his story never to be told. The Blades of Onzyan, or what few of them would be left after the debacle in Galahir, would strike his name from their rolls, and perhaps inscribe his name on a temple wall to honor the fallen. Better that his end be never known, Dillen mused unhappily, and that story of how he failed his fellow soldiers never be told among Men.

A pair of small hummingbirds came and hovered about his face as he stood trapped in the web. Brightly colored, they seemed to eye him, examining him in some way, as if trying to see into his soul. Dillen laughed without mirth. "Come to get a little taste of my tears before the big fellow has his fill?" In a conspiratorial whisper, he added, "Just don't tell your fellows how I died, will you?" The little birds hovered, and cocked their heads, as if they somehow understood what he was saying to them. "You would not consider drawing my dagger from its sheath and finish me off yourselves, would you?"

Ignoring his plea, each bird flitted to his arms and wrists, which were bound tightly in the webs. With their beaks they snipped and cut away at the strands until his arms were free. The mysterious birds then descended and did the same for his legs. He stumbled backward, grateful to be loosed from his bonds. He looked about for his tiny saviors. They hung in the air, still studying him, and then disappeared into the gloom of the night.

The great spider had noticed that its prey had been freed and stared at Dillen, perhaps wondering how any creature had escaped from its web. It came at him in a rush, faster than Dillen would have thought possible for a beast so large. It charged down the web and leapt. He jumped aside and the thing missed, but only just. It snapped its jaws, seeking to cut off an arm or envenom him. Either would prove fatal. Dillen raised his sword above his head and chopped down on one of the spider's long and exposed legs. He severed it, and the animal flinched and scurried off, the agony causing it to retreat from its tormentor. It soon found safety in the darkness, and Dillen watched it run away until he could see it no more.

*****

Dillen continued his journey, climbing over fallen tree trunks and wading through brooks swollen with rainwater. He sank to his knees several times, exhausted. Dawn was now not long in coming, but it was still dark, and he was hopelessly lost. He scooped water from a small stream with his helmet and drank greedily. It tasted better than any he ever before imbibed, but the pleasure of it faded to nothingness as he contemplated his mission. By the time he found the Green Lady's folk, his own people would have been slaughtered by the Abyssal horde. He must go on and try to save them, or die doing so. He despaired knowing that he would fail.

"The Lady shows you her favor, young one," came a soft voice out of the darkness.

Dillen scrambled to his feet and drew his sword. He could see nothing. "Show yourself! Who are you? Where are you?"

"Such a typical human you are," said the voice. A winged woman appeared in the inky blackness, seemingly lit by her own internal light. "Your kind is always waving iron swords about, this way and that, making yourselves appear dangerous and mighty." She giggled softly. "Like little boys, playing with sticks, fancying themselves knights."

She was a wispy thing, sweetly pretty, and full of mirth. It must have been a sylph, one of the creatures of the air that owed allegiance to the Lady of the Wood. Dillen had seen a portrait of one such as her in his bestiary. "She does not show me enough favor, or she would have lit the way for me to her by now."

"Things are not all going your way?" The sylph asked with not a trace of sympathy. "And you blame someone else? Perhaps you would prefer that the Lady herself come here to hold your hand?"

"I am not complaining," Dillen protested. "I am cold, wet, and tired. I apologize if my manners are deficient. I have an army to save and time grows short. Please help me."

"The Lady already has helped you," the sylph corrected. "The birds that rescued you answered her summons, as have I now. She is otherwise occupied fighting the same enemies you are, and her attention is elsewhere, but she has seen you. I am called Shaarlyot. Come, follow me. I will lead you to her."

Dillen stood and his spirit lifted. "Is it far? Can she not send us help right now?"

"I have told you that she has already sent me, as well as the birds that freed you."

"If she has known of me all this while, why not send more. . ."

Shaarlyot ignored him and flitted off, staying just within his sight. "Hush now! Enough of your questions! We must hurry!"

Dillen trotted behind her, falling behind as she skimmed over the broken earth that hindered his passage. He rolled himself over a large trunk and fell heavily into the mud on the other side.

"You are clumsy," she teased.

"I have no wings, but I am glad that I amuse you so."

"Alas, truly, you are not blessed as I am," she said with a look of real pity in her large blue eyes. She fluttered her gossamer wings. "It must be a sorrow for you to look upon the birds of the air and the butterflies of the wood and feel your imprisonment upon the ground so keenly."

"We make do."

Shaarlyot nodded, a pensive look settling upon her doll-like face. "As you must."

Dillen followed her for the better part of an hour. He was forced to stop several times to catch his breath. He scolded himself inwardly again and again that he had allowed himself to become so used to riding a horse that his stamina had declined so dramatically. He was grateful to the fairy woman who had become his guide. He had been traversing the forest in almost entirely wrong direction for much of the night and would never have discovered his error before morning.

They came to the mouth of a cave, hidden behind a large boulder and a drapery of vines.

"The Green Lady is within this cave?" Dillen asked, incredulous.

Shaarlyot laughed and her wings rippled along with the peals of her laughter. "No, don't be silly! This is the way to her. Faster when one of us needs to go afoot. We take the Root Road now."

"The Root Road?"

"The road beneath the roots of the trees, of course."

The sylph disappeared through the mouth. Dillen stood, wary of entering the black portal, and then, berating himself for his faintness of heart, strode in, unwilling to be left behind by a mere slip of an airborne girl.

He followed her, along a winding pathway that led ever downward, until he came upon what seemed to be an amphitheater hewn inside the rock. He stood on a ledge; below him was a slender river of swift-flowing water. The walls of the cavern glittered with embedded gems. A faint glow emanated from lamps ensconced along the sides.

"There must be a king's ransom of gems in here," Dillen marveled.

"This is wealth of a kind I've never seen." He turned to his companion. "And you just leave them all in place?"

"Where else should they be kept?" the sylph countered. "Locked up in a vault where none but their owner can view them?"

"That would make sense. What if someone should try to steal them. . ." but Dillen's voice faltered as he saw her face cloud with disapproval.

"You think according the rules of your own society, where money buys things, and things are worth more than the wonders of the natural world which birthed us all." She shook her head and smiled sadly. "You humans understand nothing."

Chagrined, Dillen kept quiet for a while before he finally spoke. "Do we follow the river?"

Shaarlyot nodded. "Yes. We will take a boat and let the current carry us downriver. Follow me."

The sylph led him down a narrow staircase cut into the rock of the cavern wall. At the river's edge, she found a little wickerwork coracle. Inside was a short oar.

"Get in," she ordered.

Dillen looked uncertainly at the coracle. "Will it hold me? Is it watertight? In my country such things are made of leather."

Shaarlyot shot him an angry look and snapped her wings imperiously behind her. "Of course they are made of leather in your country! You use the tanned hides of beasts, just like the ones that inhabit the Lady's Realm. And you have the nerve to call yourself one of the 'Noble Peoples'! Ha!" The anger soon drained from her face, and she sighed. "It was Keris's idea to call for your aid. Not mine." She shrugged her small shoulders. "Come!"

*****

The coracle moved downstream on its own, the force of the current pushing them along through a high and broad tunnel water-cut from the surrounding granite. Dillen paddled a little, hoping to steer the tiny craft, but it seemed to be determined to follow its own course. For an hour, it seemed, they rode the sunless river, their way lit by gemstones seemingly illuminated by their own internal light. Ahead, Dillen spied a sheet of falling water, rippling in the sunshine outside. The coracle plunged through, and he was drenched. Shaarlyot had escaped the boat just beforehand, and she hovered above him, completely dry, her trilling laughter filling his ears.

"You might have warned me," he said.

This only made her laughter more intense. "Oh, silly fool of a man! Do you think I expected that? I fly around such things. I forgot for a moment that you are not so blessed as am I." She fluttered her wings for emphasis. "Follow. The Lady is not far."

Dillen stepped heavily onto the bank and trudged through the mud until he reached level ground. Soon he came upon what he took to be the war camp of the folk of the wood. They stood in an open glade. Morning had come and the sun was out. He recognized, from his study of his bestiary, many of the creatures that were about him. There were centaurs, grim and hostile, standing side-by-side with naiads of lake and stream; as well as what could only be described as sentient, mobile trees. Sprites and sylphs like Shaarlyot flitted above them all. There was a scattering of elves, haughty in demeanor. A few Men there were also. They were attired unlike those of the world outside the wood, but they had in them the manner and bearing of priests. Dillen took them to be druids, overseers of the Green Lady's cult.

With them were stranger things still to Dillen, if anything could best the former in oddity. A mound of earth, solid and squat with stubby arms and legs, plodded up to the circle that had formed around Dillen. Beside it writhed a pillar of living flame. Over both circled a gale that had taken on a life of its own.

None but Shaarlyot seemed friendly.

"This is what you summoned to help us in our war, Keris?" The voice came from a wizened centaur. "He looks as if he can barely stand."

Dillen felt as if a thousand eyes were upon him, studying him, and judging him.

The man called Keris, a druid by the look of him, gestured, pleading for forbearance. "There are more of them on the way, but now they need us to help them before they can help us. We have a common enemy. Don't forget that! To preserve the balance, we must be ready to fight beside others as required."

Another creature, of man-shape, but diminutive, came forward, and was more pointed in his questioning than the centaur. "These are the people that hunt my kind for sport. But for the Lady's favor, we gnomes might all be gone. On behalf of the Lady, you and you alone asked them to come here, Keris." The gnome gestured to the other nonhumans around him. "We, however, did not. I see no reason to risk ourselves for them."

Keris's shoulders slumped. "I know what travails you have suffered in the World Without. I am from that world too, and you must trust me when I tell that not all Men are wicked. We can work with some of them against our mutual foe, who even now stands at our border, plotting another assault on our lines. This human's people have already engaged the enemy and drawn off a portion of their strength. That is why we have felt a slackening of pressure along the front."

A naiad, looking like nothing so much as the tiny image of her kind in his bestiary come to life, tilted her head disdainfully as she gazed, narrow-eyed, at him. "Perhaps he is not wicked, as you say, Keris. Perhaps too his folk fight the same enemy we do. Yet he wears upon his feet boots made of the skin of once-living creatures. His sword, too, is sheathed in the same. Would you be so forgiving if he came clothed in the skin of one your own kind?"

Keris turned to look at Dillen, who knew that he must cut a pathetic figure. His helmet was dented, his surcoat was filthy, and his armor was encrusted with drying mud. "He does not know," Keris offered. "He does not know our ways."

"Then he must be instructed," said a clear voice, deep and commanding. Emerging from behind the centaurs was a woman, regal in bearing and taller than any other person Dillen had ever seen before. The folk of Galahir either knelt or paid homage as they could to their queen. The Green Lady, ethereal and beautiful, came and stood before Dillen. Her pallor was ghostly, and yet she seemed vibrantly alive all the same. The woman, magnificently crowned with long, lustrous hair the color of ripened wheat, towered above the young paladin, who felt like a mere child in her presence. In her face, he saw revealed all of that was uncanny and wondrous in the natural world. The Lady's face was kind, and then stern and forbidding; it was a visage of a woman in her prime with flashes beneath of a young girl, and then of an old woman. Very soon it had reverted to its former sweetness, and then changed once more. Her's was the hand that gave freely and the hand that took away. She was the sower of life and the reaper of death. She was abundance and dearth. The glorious bounty of summer and the grim scarcity of winter. She was all these things at once. The Lady personified the endless dance of life and death, that Man, in his naive simplicity, called 'Nature.'

"This is one of the Men you called to come to our aid, Keris?" She asked, never removing her eyes from Dillen. "This one does not look like much."

"He has seen better days, Lady," Keris said. The druid seemed embarrassed by Dillen's tattered appearance. He must have hoped for the grand paladins of the Golden Horn to stand beside his people against the Abyssal demons. Instead, Keris could only present a bedraggled young knight to his queen.

"I know. I have watched him for some time." The Lady's eyes bored into Dillen, as if she was seeing inside him and through him. Dillen, for all of his callow youth, saw now that she was far beyond his own estimation. Why, he had recently puzzled, if she had known of his plight and that of his comrades, had she not send aid to him or them sooner? It was a naive question formed from thin tissue of his own limited understanding. He perceived at once that within her was a primordial essence that defied mortal comprehension. She was a being of the Time Before Time, a Celestian; not merely old, but ageless in a manner that even the elves and the other ancient peoples of the world were not.

There was a hint of a smile at the edges of her perfect mouth. "You are now in need of our help?"

"Yes, Lady. The host I come from has been set upon by the forces of the enemy of both our peoples. We came to help you, but we find ourselves in need of your succor. The creatures of the Abyss threaten to overwhelm us. I have come here to beg your aid."

She seemed to consider his plea for what seemed an hour. Or perhaps it all happened in an instant. Looking into her face, Dillen felt as if he were gazing into eternity.

She smiled, and her face was radiant with kindness and understanding. "You shall have it," she said. Dillen felt as if a great weight had been lifted from him.

The Lady smiled again and was silent for a moment, submerged in unfathomable thought. Then she spoke. "There is one price that I ask in return for saving your comrades."

"Name your price," Dillen said, without hesitation.

* * * * *

The remnant of the legion of Basilea stood in the center of a clearing, atop a low, treeless hill. They were surrounded by the warriors of the Abyss who outnumbered them many times over. In the dark of the night, the scattered bands of the Basilean army had united to make a final stand. They would stand back to back until the last man fell. The banners of the Shining Ones were still held aloft in proud defiance of the enemy, but these had become torn beneath the barrage of missiles that assailed the Basilean soldiery.

Stevven wondered what was left of the legion. Less than half, that was certain. Among the dead was the dictator, his decapitated corpse respectfully laid in repose in the center of the dwindling host. "Still with me, Arkbald?"

"Still here. No better place to be." How the boy remained on his feet despite all the blood he had lost amazed Stevven. It seemed that Arkbald must have stood upright out of sheer Sparthan stubbornness.

Brother Bartolomo had been grievously wounded in his left eye. A bloody bandage covered it, but a trickle of blood nevertheless escaped and fell down his cheek. "Missing an eye will make archery a bit more difficult for me," he groused to Tebald.

"You were never much of an archer anyway. You can always hurl rocks instead," Tebald consoled. The Hearth Knight pointed with his sword, notched and dulled in the constant fighting, at the foe that hung about the edge of the woods to reform their ranks. "In any event, I don't think you're going to have much time to miss your skills. They form for another charge. We can't take much more. Alas, Dillen has been long gone, nigh a full day. If he had found the Galahirians, they would have come by now. I think instead that he is dead."

"Have faith please, my good brothers," Stevven said to them. The Cortrian had been wounded in several places, and blood drenched his surcoat, but he was animated with fiery determination. "Dillen will get through with our plea. We will be saved. We have but to wait."

"You have much faith in your friend," Tebald said, unconvinced.

Arkbald limped up to stand beside Stevven. "He'll be back."

"Then he'd better return to us soon," Bartolomo said. "Here they come again, and the one that took the dictator's head is with them."

*****

"Onward my comrades!" cried Zelgarag. "Feast upon the flesh and bones of the hateful foe! Avenge yourselves for all of the hurts they have done you! Let them know that we of the Abyss are the true children of the gods! Soon, we will be the lords of this world!" He held the gory head of the enemy general whom he had slain earlier in the day aloft at the end of a cruelly-barbed spear, and showed the sightless eyes of the dead Basilean what was left of his army.

There came a throaty cheer from the assembled warriors around the Abyssal champion. Zelgarag exulted in the triumph that he knew would soon be his. Damathana, by his side, beamed in joyful anticipation of the annihilation of the Basileans. About them stood the surviving wretches of the ferocious battle. They'd lost far more than had the warriors of the Golden Horn, but that was only to be expected. These degenerates were no match, one for one, with the paladins and men-at-arms of Basilea. That had not mattered. In the ambush, with weight of numbers on their side, they had pulverized the enemy army, and herded them into an ever-shrinking ball. The march route, along which Zelgarag's minions had harried the embattled enemy, was littered with many more bodies of the Abyssal fallen than those of the insufferable Basileans; but that was of no consequence to Damathana. What mattered was that her plan would succeed, and that she would rise with Zelgarag, as his consort, in the ranks of the Hell's Army.

She watched in awe as Zelgarag raced forward, long muscular legs carrying him crashing into the diminished Basilean ranks. Beside him came his guard, and Damathana herself, who was as eager to spill the last drop of Basilean blood as any other. His sword, black as the darkest pit in the Abyss, struck out in a dark blur, leaving two unlucky Basilean footsoldiers headless. On the return stroke, he severed the arm of a third and then beheaded the same man before his spear had time to fall to the blood-soaked earth.

Damathana's heart raced. With eyes that did not blink, she watched his masterful performance on the field of battle. Zelgarag was like a god striding amidst mortals, delivering death to all around him. Within a minute of attacking the Basileans, their shieldwall began to falter, and he and his guard stood amongst them, a salient of gory-red death in the wavering white and gold ranks of the host of the Golden Horn. Was there anything that Zelgarag might not accomplish with her at his side?

More Basileans fell, their bodies ripped apart by the crushing blows of his midnight blade. Damathana gave them the credit they were due. They did not cower as this dark angel of death came upon them, and if they felt fear, they did not show it on their faces, which remained fixed with expressions stoic and resolute.

Of the offal that composed the bulk of her own army, she saw only the demented grins and maniac smiles of men warped and twisted almost beyond recognition as human. Their loathsomeness offended her, and she felt no regret as they were cut down in droves by the stabbing spears and swinging swords of the enemy. Once this was all over, and Zelgarag and she were elevated in rank, she would never need to engage so closely with such things again, except to order them to their deaths in the Abyss's interest. They were serving their purpose, nothing more.

*****

Bartolomo had never been given to worry or foreboding, but now, he was overcome with dread. The general of the Abyssal army, a champion of its kind and the same bestial demon who'd slain Andorset earlier in the day, snarled a challenge to the dwindling band of paladins. Brother Tebald, stalwart and valiant, had proudly accepted. Bartolomo's admiration for his brother's courage warred fitfully with fear for his life.

He looked on as Tebald stood toe-to-toe with the terrifying creature. Their blades met in a shower of sparks, as each strove to get past the other's defense. Tebald aimed a cut at the champion's neck. It parried easily and knocked Tebald's sword back, following up with a flurry of blows. Tebald stopped the last slash with his sword just inches from his head and stared into the glowing red eyes of the Abyssal general. They were alive with hate and rage, but also a fierce intelligence. It kicked him in the knee and his leg buckled. Tebald sprawled on the ground, face down in the mud. The champion raised his blood-slick sword high above his head to deliver a blow that would sever Tebald's head.

Challenge or no, Bartolomo could not fail to intervene. Inches from its target, the black blade's descent stopped, halted by Bartolomo's intruding sword. "No you don't!" the paladin knight bellowed as he knocked back the giant creature's weapon.

The champion snorted in surprise and stepped back a pace, allowing Tebald time to regain his feet. Bartolomo helped him stand, and together they counterattacked with all the furious skill befitting lord knights of their chapters.

It was not enough. The champion was pushed back several steps by his tormentors, but then his hulking guards came up beside him, and the paladins were again on the defensive. All around them, the lines of the Basileans shrank as men fell to enemy sword cuts and axe blows. Though three and four of the slaves of the Abyss might fall for every one of the Holy Host, the weight of numbers was still much in the enemy's favor.

Brother Tebald fell, his chest pierced by a hurled spear. Brother Bartolomo stood over Tebald as the Hearth Knight's lifeblood flowed from his wound. Tebald's face had already turned deathly pale. Bartolomo's only desire now was to prevent the defilement of his friend's corpse before he too perished in his turn.

"There is nowhere for you to run, puny man," the demon jeered. "You have fought well. I will honor you by placing your head atop a spear and set it beside ones bearing those of your brother paladin and your general." It roared with laughter, as if it had been told an uproariously amusing jest.

"Don't waste your time!" Bartolomo shot back, aiming a cut at the champion's grinning visage. "You'll be too busy looking for the heart I've ripped from your chest!"

Bartolomo struck again and again at the hateful thing, with skill enough to cleave its shield in two and draw blood from the enemy general's wrist.

The demon made no sound as Bartolomo's sword cut open the red flesh of its arm. Its eyes became suffused with anger, and it responded to the strike with a flurry of mighty blows. Bartolomo was driven back and then stumbled over Tebald's corpse. He awaited the end as the champion raised his sword once more.

Then he heard the blowing of horns.

*****

Along with the sounding of horns there came shouts and songs and the myriad noises of a forest that had come alive. Hundreds, and then thousands, of the People of the Forest emerged from the eaves of the trees that encircled the clearing to take vengeance against the invaders of the Lady's wood. They came in swarms, they came in small bands and packs, and as lone warriors too, tackling the stunned Abyssals who too late saw them attacking from behind.

A tremor of panic rippled through the horde as the warriors struggled to adjust to the new enemy that had struck them from behind. So intent on their imminent victory had they become, that they had imprudently abandoned all thought of flank and rear security. They had stood, just moments before, on the verge of a great victory. Now, they were on the precipice of defeat. The horde of the Abyss seemed to waver as if pressed by a mighty wave that it feebly attempted to resist. Panic became terror. The urge to flee seized the Abyssals, their miserable hearts filled with fright, but the enemy came at them from every direction, and they had no idea which way to run.

Hundreds of the Abyssals were felled within moments as centaurs and elves emerged from the treeline, their bows flinging inerrant arrows against the stunned enemy. Great rents in the ground opened wide, cracked apart by elementals of the earth. Into them fell hundreds of shocked demons and their thralls. Their cries of dismay were silenced just as quickly as the torn fabric of the soil was closed over them by the elementals, who knitted the tear they had created with the skill of a surgeon stitching shut a wound.

From their air too, the Galahirians attacked, sylphs and sprites filled with rage at the desecrators of their fair forest. Eagles struck from above, talons tearing at the eyes of the cowering mortals and demons beneath them. The darts of the Abyssals could find no mark among the onrushing warriors of Galahir. Elemental spirits of the air blew mightily, driving their missiles back into their own ranks.

Naiads of the waters, armed with tridents, came upon the foul demons in a rush and struck heads from shoulders. Others of their kind felled soul-damned mortals four and five at a time with harpoons sharper than razors. Elsewhere, horned things were crushed beneath the trunk-like legs of a sentient oak, one of the mystical herdsman of the trees of this ancient land.

The demons were pressed ever more tightly together, until they stood shoulder to shoulder, with not even room enough to raise their crude shields or swing their rusting swords. Then spirits of caged fire were among them. These descended like meteors, bursting among the dense-packed islands of the enemy. The Abyssals were seared in the elementals' flames, shrieking in pain and fear as they sought any means of escape. The horde had never been much of an army. It had been kept together more by easy victory and lust for the flesh of the Basilean foe than by discipline. With hope of victory gone and death by fire imminent, the Abyssals abandoned all thought of mutual protection in favor of personal survival. Like a tall tower that had been shaken to its foundations by a quake, and reduced to a tottering collection of stone blocks, the army of the Abyss split apart into an atomized mob of directionless individuals.

Without a word, the folk of the wood parted in several places so that the Abyssals could find avenues out of the trap. This was not done out of a sense mercy. A cornered animal will fight to the last when all hope of escape is lost, and this the Galahirians understood better than anyone else. No, the panic-stricken were purposely allowed to flee into the woods where they would be hunted to extinction, with much less danger and cost to their pursuers. The Abyssals began to flee as soon as they found these paths, little suspecting that they were being directed to their slaughter beneath the Lady's trees.

All around the Basileans, it seemed as if legends had come to life and walked now beneath the blue sky. They recovered from their shock quickly, glad beyond words that this new force was not some reinforcement for the enemy, but the very people whom they had come to fight beside. They redressed their ranks, and made ready to launch their own counterattack.

*****

Zelgarag turned from the prostrate form of the paladin to face the new threat. With the Galahirians was a hydra, a creature made much in the form of a drake, but possessing five heads attached to its body by long, sinuous necks. These heads rose and fell, dragging demons and degenerates alike from their hiding places on the corpse-strewn field and swallowing them whole. Zelgarag prepared to engage this beast and pointed his blade at it, marking it as his chosen foe. Then another thing interposed itself between Zelgarag and the hydra, which briskly stomped off to find other enemies to devour.

Zelgarag looked at the man - for it was a man, and a Basilean paladin at that - with wonder. "Who are you?" Then Zelgarag laughed, and there was no joy in it, but only the cruel humor of one who finds comedy in the pain of others. He gestured to his guards, indicating that they should stand aside and let him deal with this new foe. "No matter, you will be dead soon enough, unremembered, with nothing to mark your passing. Come closer."

"I want you to know my name, demon," said the paladin. "I am Dillen Genemer, sworn champion of the Lady whose realm you defile." Eyes filled with terrible purpose, Dillen raised his sword in challenge. "I know your name as well, demon. You are Zelgarag, a champion amongst the hordes of the Abyss and the master of this army of the damned."

Dillen strode forward. "Not today will I die. My destiny is other. You, however, have come to the end of the thread woven by Fate. She has decided that yours will be cut today, and I have come to enact her judgment."

Black blade and silver sword met in a shower of orange and yellow sparks. The paladin swung his sword once more, aiming his cut at the demon's neck. The fiend parried deftly and sidestepped so that he stood closer and to Dillen's left, shielded side. He next unleashed an avalanche of blows against Dillen, battering his shield until it fell from his arm in a shower of splinters.

With both hands on his sword, Dillen countered the assault, neutralizing each new attack made by the Abyssal lord. His skill with the blade seemed to bloom, with every lesson he'd ever been taught by his instructors coming together in him in this moment. He cut and thrust efficiently, and very soon, he had forced his foe onto his back foot. With a snap of his sword, he grazed the nose of the enemy general. Black blood dribbled from the scratch.

Zelgarag stepped back from the combat, touching his nose. Blood covered his fingers. Clearly, no previous opponent had ever landed a blow to his face.

"A bloody nose suits you well," Dillen said as he circled his opponent, careful to keep the demon champion in front of him at all times. "Perhaps, if you had taken such a wound beforehand, you'd have learned caution, and been more reluctant to invade my Queen's sacred woods."

Zelgarag growled. "I will drink your blood from your skull before this day is done!"

"You talk too much. I prefer to fight."

"I have been merely toying with you, but now, you will die."

"Your army of fainthearts has fled, creature of Hell. Look around. They have abandoned you. Your plan was clever, but it has failed."

Zelgarag glanced about and saw that the paladin had spoken truthfully. The vermin that he had led into battle were deserting the field, leaving him alone but for his loyal guard, who were now surrounded and being cut down by the resurgent Basileans.

"I have no idea what trickery you have worked," Zelgarag hissed, "but I will take your head before I depart!"

"It is your head that will be mine," Dillen promised. He raised his sword, saluted the champion, and assumed a defensive posture. "Are you scared? I hope that you are."

Zelgarag bellowed with rage and strode toward Dillen. He lifted his sword above his head and broke into a run. He did not get far. A spearhead of Basilean steel protruded from his chest, blood gushing from the wound. Behind him stood Bartolomo on unsteady feet. The knight paladin sank to his knees, drained of what little energy he had left to him. Dillen rushed forward and struck Zelgarag's head from his torso. It plopped to the ground, a look of fury mixed with shock frozen forever onto his dead visage.

Bartolomo wheezed. "So good of you to show up, Dillen. I was afraid you'd miss this party entirely." He chuckled a little. "Don't look so worried. I'll live, minus an eye." Then he grew serious. "I had feared the worst for you. But you have saved us."

Dillen knelt beside the older knight and sat him up. "I found the People of the Green Lady." He nodded to the folk of the forest, who were chasing the remaining Abyssals from the field to meet their doom in the depths of the woods. "I am one of them now. I must leave."

Bartolomo coughed. A small rivulet of blood fell down his cheek from beneath the bandage over his left eye. "What do you mean?"

Dillen stood. "I am the Lady's knight now. I am no longer a Blade of Onzyan. I must go, and join my people."

"What are you saying? We are to fight beside the Galahirians too."

"And you will, but without me. I belong to her now, not Basilea." What else could he say that Bartolomo would understand? That the Lady's price for saving the Basileans was his sworn service to her unto death? The Green Lady had showed him many things, of the past, the present, and perhaps even the future. She had shown him what lurked in the deepest parts of the earth, horrifying and unfathomably wicked things inimical to all life. She had allowed him a glimpse of the very fracture in her own soul, in which light and darkness vied unceasingly for supremacy. She had granted him comprehension of the grand stakes for which she played. She competed for not just cities or border fortresses, as did the lords of Men, but for the survival of all living things. There had been so many other revelations in the transcendent vision which the Lady had gifted to him, inexpressible in speech, but much of which he had nonetheless understood with his heart. Not all of it had been clear, but after seeing it, he had not hesitated to pledge himself to Her. He was needed to be a defender of Nature in the World Without the Lady's realm. He would go where the Lady's other folk could not; into the cities of Men and their castles too; he would sail aboard their ships to the far lands where his knowledge of Mannish ways and his sharp sword would be invaluable. He would venture into the dark places where the Lady's light too often failed to penetrate. The weak and defenseless he would uplift; the wicked he would humble. Just as an earthquake might change the age-old course of a river in an instant, the trajectory of his own future had been forever altered by this fleeting moment in time. He knew that he had made the right choice.

Bartolomo's face was creased briefly with confusion. Then he smiled. "Whatever has happened, I know that I can do naught to stop you. Go."

"Thank you, Brother."

Dillen waited until Stevven, Arkbald, and Bartolomo's squire, Jedd, came up and took charge of the wounded man. "It is good to see you both alive."

"I knew you would make it back to us," Stevven said. "There's no braver man in this army than you."

Dillen nodded his thanks. He stood and turned to leave.

"What shall I tell your father?" Bartolomo asked before Dillen had gone far. "He will want to know what has become of you."

"Tell him. . . tell him that I have found myself."

*****

Night had come and a stillness covered the field. There were no survivors from the Abyssal army. The Basileans and their forest allies had been thorough in dispatching the enemy wounded before they had marched off.

A solitary figure picked her way across the sea of bodies. Damathana had waited until after midnight to be sure that she would not be seen. She stood in the center of the field, standing before the pile formed from the cold corpses of Zelgarag's guards. In their midst was an upright spear, a black spear, that had once belonged to Zelgarag. Now it was his head that adorned it, and not that of the Basilean general whom he had slain. She looked at her dead lover in his eyes. They were blank, staring mindlessly into the distance. Her own eyes did not blink as she studied his. No tears either escaped them to moisten her cheeks. She turned on her heel and strode off.

She did not look back.

CRIMSON WINTER

By Brandon Rospond

Despite the burning passion and adrenaline of combat, the northern winds bit thoroughly through Gavin Stalspar's armor. Even though the colors of the banner he fought under were different, he was ever accustomed to the heavy armor and the two-handed greatsword that he used to cut down another infernal creature of the Abyss. Immediately, his eyes shifted to the next demon that furiously charged at him. Gavin brought his sword up on the defense, parrying and blocking where he could, but this inferno-fueled beast with skin reddened by hellfire was stronger than the last of its kin; he felt himself retreating slightly from the press of steel. Utilizing years of knowledge of knighthood, Gavin found his footing and pushed back with both hands to gain ground. Finding an opening in the demon's haphazard defense, he sliced diagonally, cleaving the lower Abyssal's chest in two and leaving the beast bleeding out in the snow.

"Ho there, Sir Brooding!" a voice called out from behind Gavin. He pulled off his winged helmet, exposing his shaven head to the bitter winds, as his green eyes looked behind him. "Save some of the beasties for the rest of the Alliance!"

An elf, probably in his late twenties, only a few years younger than himself, came sauntering over with his bow held low in one hand and an arrow twirled between the fingers of the other. A sly smile was curled inside of his dark goatee as he eyed over the fallen Abyssals surrounding Gavin.

"I know you're no novice to this sort of thing, but I think some of the others would like the chance to send these bastards back to the Abyss!"

"Darriel," the grizzled man nodded toward his ally. "So is that it? Have they stopped their assault?"

"For now."

Gavin turned when he heard a snarl behind him. One of the demons that he had struck down had not been killed. It dragged itself onto its knees, the snow stained red as it pulled itself forward, its hell-forged blade still held in an offensive gesture. Gavin turned back to Darriel, who casually held up his bow with his one arm, eyeing the Abyssal with one eye closed, scrunching up his facial features in mock analysis. Eventually, he made a clicking of his tongue and shook his head, dropping the bow and shrugging with a smug grin at Gavin. The former knight sighed before taking a few steps forward and driving his blade through the creature.

Retrieving his greatsword, he turned to face the unit of leather and fur clad northmen he had been assigned, each person with long, thick beards and hair, which were in stark contrast to Gavin's light scruff. "We're done here. Fall back to the city."

His men obliged without hesitation, slinging their heavy weapons over shoulders or back in sheaths, and Gavin turned once more to Darriel. The two led their respective units through the battlefield, along icy paths that led to the fortress of the Northern Alliance, the citadel in the Winterlands known as Chill.

"What is the status of our forces?" Gavin's gravelly voice spoke just above the bite of the winds as he replaced his helmet.

"Eh, nothing exciting," Darriel shrugged, still twirling his arrow. "Casualties minimal on our side, seems the enemy just threw together another force to keep us on our toes."

"Or to probe us," Gavin added, grimly.

"Yes, or to probe us. Whatever bizarre and amazing secrets our visionary leader, the great Prince Talannar Icekin has hidden in this icy tundra!"

Darriel waited several long seconds before Gavin finally turned to look at him, wiggling his eyebrows as if to accent his words. The older man did not share in the elf's humor and looked away.

"Ah, Sir Brooding, I expected as much stoicism from you. But alas," the elf pointed ahead to where another group of warriors gathered under a gold, blue, and silver banner, "there are some friendly faces that still live!"

The elf finally put the arrow in the quiver slung to his back and raised his hand to wave at their allies. As they continued walking, two more unit leaders joined them, their troops following several paces back. One man was formerly of the clans known as the Varangur; Gorram Shurad, while wearing color ribbons identifying himself as part of the Alliance, wore armor even heavier than Gavin's, sporting a helmet with horns spiked into the air. His neckline and where each piece of armor ended was lined with a mixture of different furs, all wolves that he had fought alongside that had fallen in battle, each a piece now forever remaining with him. The other was a woman, Hilde Taneber formerly of the Hegemony of Basilea, whose intimidating presence in her own heavy armor was only further accentuated by the three dark scar lines that ran diagonally down her left cheek.

"That is the fifth assault against us in the past week," Hilde remarked as she sheathed her blade. "Prince Talannar would be wise to press the attack on them."

"We would need a lull first," Gorram's deep, almost monotone, voice drummed on. "We must wait for their advances to weaken before we push back. We have the fortress and all of its defenses at our disposal here."

"Yes, but every loss that we take is more detrimental to our cause than all of the Abyssals that we slay," Hilde shook her head, her blonde curls bouncing on her neck under her helmet. "Who knows how these vile creatures keep spawning from the pit of hellfire that they emerge from? For all we know, there is never to be an end to these demons, as long as the pit to the Abyss remains agape in our world. And there are only so many willing to traverse these frozen lands to defend Prince Talannar, his cause, and his secrets."

Gavin agreed, but he did not say as much. As he trudged on the snowy path, his greaves kicking up tufts of white, he sorely missed the warmer climates. Where he was from, he had experienced a diversity of temperatures throughout a year, but it was always moderate; never extreme hot or cold. It was times like this that he considered growing his hair back out to at least help provide some form of warmth.

"Elf, how is it that you stay so warm?" Hilde glanced at Darriel out of the corner of her eye, measuring up the leather breastplate, furred cloak, and otherwise bare arms.

"Well, woman, my elven heritage makes me part of the Ice Kin clan, so while you're all freezing," Darriel held his arms out from within his cloak, "I've actually worked up quite a sweat from that battle."

Despite the clouds that seemed to continuously dump snow and never leave their grasp on the sky, Chill was located high in the mountains, dominating the landscape where no others dared; and occasionally, on the rare occasion when the sun would sneak through the blankets in the sky, it would reflect gloriously on the wall of ice that surrounded the city. Enhanced by Prince Talannar's magic, the ice that acted as a fortification for the town's borders would not melt by even the strongest of Abyssal flames – at least, not that Gavin had witnessed in his short time in the Alliance. But the sight, as very rare as it was, really made him appreciate the beauty that the prince put in to creating the town.

Today was not one such of those days, he noted with some chagrin, as they approached. Every time he returned, he hoped he would be able to marvel in awe; to be welcomed home from the tiring battle with such pure beauty of nature and magic coming together. It heartened him – it heartened all of them – just to see it. The men in his unit, in particular a man by the name of Tomas, had started calling the phenomenon the 'aurora', but Gavin had never heard such a name before.

Once they passed through the imposing gates and arrived in the heart of Chill, the four warriors dismissed their men; many of which were eager to find the warmth of a hearth and a constant drip of ale. Gavin followed the trio of his allies through the walkways that were surprisingly devoid of ice and snow.

"Magic truly is an amazing thing, is it not?" Darriel held a palm out, and a single flake of snow danced down to melt in the center of his hand. "Here we are, on the highest peak of the Ice Mountains, surrounded by the elements on every wall, and yet the snow melts before it can even reach the ground."

Gavin nodded. He too was amazed; whenever they passed the walls to Chill, there was indeed a slight shift in the temperature. Whatever magic that had blessed the frozen walls rose the internal temperature for those from the southern climates, while still making it perfectly hospitable for those from the north.

"Yes, it would be amazing, were Mantica not at war on every front, and every nation of people were not at each other's throats," Hilde added grimly.

"Ah, it doesn't seem so bad," Darriel shrugged, inclining his head to Gorram. "Your people seem to get along well with everything going on, eh?"

Gorram regarded Darriel with an indifferent look. "They thrive in combat and bloodshed, eager at any opportunity to sacrifice their opponents to appease Korgaan. They revel in the current state of the land. But that is a life I have left behind. A life I wish no part of anymore."

Gavin looked briefly at Gorram, searching for any more hint of emotion in the man's words, but there was none to be found. Darriel smiled broadly as he patted the former Varangur on the back.

"Well, we're glad to have you fighting with us and not against us! I wouldn't want to be standing across the field of battle from you! Eh, Gavin? Am I right?"

"I agree. While you no longer follow the Varangur way of life, the skills you have learned under their tutelage are impressive," Gavin eyed the long shaft that ended in an axe head that was equipped to the man's back. "Your tenacity and ferociousness in combat is indeed inspiring."

Gorram met Gavin's look and nodded at the man of approximate equal age, holding his gaze all the while.

Darriel and Hilde continued to talk as they walked, most of which, Gavin was not paying attention to. Every night, the soldiers of the Alliance were always welcome to eat in the dining hall of Prince Talannar's palace. And no matter how many times he came to the castle, the shimmering crystal was always an immaculate sight. The beautiful, high-rising spire glistened like a jewel in the sea of snow. Men and women of varying nations and races patrolled around the grounds and parapets across the outside of the castle, just above intermittently spaced stained glass windows. Gavin and his allies approached the portcullis, guarded by two heavily armored figures; Darriel gave a two finger wave, Hilde saluted casually, but the guards raised their hands to halt them.

"Soldiers. Where are you coming from?"

"The battle, you know, just over yonder?" Darriel jerked his chin back the way they had come.

"There was a small skirmish with Abyssal demons just outside the entrance to Chill," Hilde stepped in to cut off the elf's sarcasm. "We have just returned to deliver our report to the prince."

The guard on the right exchanged a look with his comrade before looking the warriors over. "Which one of you is Stalspar?"

Gavin inclined his head back, crossing his arms over his chest. "I am."

"The prince wishes to hear the report from you," the left guard said sternly before both of them took their blades down. "The rest of you are to carry on."

Gavin narrowed his eyes and let an exasperated breath out from his nostrils. He usually left that part of it to one of the other three, filling in details only when asked. He especially did not want to be shown any special favor. The less attention, the better.

Gavin felt a rush of warmth come over him as he entered the main hall behind the other three, but it did not do much to improve his soured mood. His eyes did not have much to adjust to, as torches and tall candelabras lit the way forward, as well as to the turn-off paths left and right. The constant whipping of the wind in his ears was replaced with the sound of music; lutes, flutes, percussion, and other instruments Gavin couldn't name, came together to produce a welcoming melody that fluttered along the corridors from somewhere deeper within.

"Well, Stalspar, I suppose this is where we part," Darriel indicated the large main staircase ahead of them with his chin. "What in the Abyss did you do to get singled out? What member of the prince's family did you sleep with? How much gold did you take?"

Gavin clenched his teeth together hard, trying to remind himself that Darriel was his ally, and that slamming him against the wall and berating him to silence his incessant chatter would do no good.

"Darriel, enough already," Hilde barked as she placed a hand on her temple. "We get it, you're hilarious, but come off it already."

"Oh, alright, alright. I just find it odd that Sir Brooding here gets a special audience with the prince is all."

"I don't know what the prince wants either," Gavin said, his tone a bit more biting than he wanted. "You needn't worry. I will make sure that the prince knows we all did our parts. I did nothing more than any of you three."

"Right, then," Hilde let her gaze wander on Gavin, as if almost leery of exactly what he was worried about – being shown special treatment. She quickly shifted her gaze to her other two comrades. "Off to eat we go."

"Save you a plate of whatever we can scrounge up," Darriel winked and pat him on the shoulder as he walked by. Gorram followed the first two, but there was no mirth in his expression. He gave Gavin a glancing nod before trudging away with the others.

Gavin sighed, trying to collect himself and rouse out of the dour mood, as he took two of the giant steps up at a time. The armored guards at the top of the ascension crossed their blades over the door as Gavin approached, their faces stoic as they eyed him.

"Gavin Stalspar," the scruffy warrior saluted, bringing his closed fist diagonally across his chest to his opposite shoulder. "Reporting the results of the latest Abyssal attack."

"Proceed," he heard a voice call from behind a pair of closed dark blue doors with silver adornments run from top to bottom. The blades recoiled, and the guards used their free hands to push open the entrance.

Gavin proceeded slowly and respectfully into the throne room. He had been in here on numerous occasions, but he could not help but take note of the adornments on the walls; exquisite and strangely colored furs were stretched farther than the width of the largest wolf Gavin had seen, spoils of war that ranged from gilded trinkets to heavy suits of armor were arranged neatly, and a banner with the emblem of the Northern Alliance hung from ceiling to floor behind a giant throne that seemed it was carved out of ice itself. An elf sat slightly slouched back, his elbows resting on both arms of the chair, his fingers steepled together before his mismatched colored ice blue and silvery purple eyes. His long blonde hair with a single streak of silver was regally pulled back from his pale face, while still having locks hanging down on both sides of his cheeks. His sharp features, combined with his elegant armor dyed the colors of the Northern Alliance, marked him out as Prince Talannar Icekin.

Gavin stopped and kneeled a respectable distance away. He took his helmet off, holding it in the crux of his arm, and dropped his head low.

"Please, Gavin, stand."

The knight raised his head, meeting the prince's icy gaze as he stood respectfully. Gavin waited a few moments in awkward silence before he finally spoke.

"Your Majesty, you have summoned me?"

"Yes. Thank you for coming with such great haste, Gavin. I assume that the Abyssals have been successfully pushed back once more?"

"Yes, Your Majesty. I have just come from the skirmish. Our forces have succeeded in slaying all that would try and assault Chill with minimal casualties. Huscarls Tanebar, Shurad, and Lores led their men admirably in the fight. They would have come themselves, but they were dismissed by your guards."

The prince nodded pensively. "That is indeed good to hear, but it is regrettable that we lose any men – as minimal as the casualties might have been. Soldiers are not lining up by the millions to join our cause, and every loss we suffer is unfortunate."

"Yes, Your Majesty. Those that did sacrifice their lives made sure that the enemy did not get anywhere near Chill. We met them out in the snowdrifts, along the side of the mountain, and halted their advance upon first engagement. It was the usual sort of rabble; lesser Abyssals, mostly. Nothing of greater threat, nor any surprises we have not seen before."

"That is most fortuitous," Prince Talannar inclined his head back slightly. "How is the morale of the men under your command?"

"High, for the most part, Your Majesty. Unlike myself, they are born and raised in the cold of the mountains, so the frosty winds do not bother them. They fight emboldened that you have given them a place to call their home. The deaths of any of our comrades always weigh heavily, but it also invigorates the men and women to keep their fighting spirit alight, to avenge their brethren."

Prince Talannar narrowed his eyes as his head bobbed ever so slightly. "I see. And you, Gavin? How do you fair?"

Gavin paused, trying to find the right words. "I... feel no different than the others, Your Majesty. I appreciate it more than words can convey that you have given me a place to fight in your army, as a sergeant, no less. I do not take my position lightly, Your Majesty. While I'm still not used to the cold winds of this eternal winter, I am happy to pledge my blade under the colors of your banner."

"That is good to hear. I have noticed that when your comrades report in, it seems you are loath to say anything, unless directly spoken to. I was beginning to wonder if you resented being made a huscarl."

Gavin bowed his head, fighting the color that began to rush to his face; the prince was no fool. "I apologize, Your Majesty. I-..."

"There is no need to apologize." Gavin raised his head to witness the prince wave his hand dismissively, the smile a bit wider on his face. "We all have our secrets and our reasons for being who we are. I do not question that. I am concerned though, if the duties I have placed upon you are too much."

"No. Your Majesty." Gavin clenched his jaw tightly as he spoke. It was as the prince said, they all had their secrets. "I apologize for my lack of enthusiasm. I would just rather let my blade be my voice upon the battlefield, to speak for my loyalty and devotion."

"Very well," the prince nodded. "I thank you for the service you do the Northern Alliance on the battlefield, and I ask that you continue that dedication."

"Thank you, Your Majesty." Gavin bowed low before standing back up once more.

*****

Gavin thoroughly chided himself during the walk to the dining hall. He had been given a chance to start over. He had been given a chance to command men once more, without having to claw and fight his way up the ladder, as he had once done. Now, here he was; almost about to squander his new life, all because he was too wary to trust the prince that had given him a position of rank, when other men of the north, men that would fight and die without hesitation for Prince Talannar, deserved it more. That wasn't to say that he was not loyal to the Northern Alliance, but Gavin still was not sure that this was a cause worth giving his life over.

He entered the dining hall and saw his allies sitting at the same table as they always had, a seat at one of the ends reserved for him, as he liked it. He plopped onto the bench next to Darriel and slammed his helmet down with him. There was a dwarf that sat across from him with a long orange beard, wearing goggles with zoomed lenses, as he tinkered away with some device, his food and ale forgotten at his side. The dwarf looked up at Gavin and blinked, his eyes appearing three times the size as normal.

"Benthur," Gavin nodded to the familiar face.

The dwarf's face twitched in a smile, but he turned his face back to his gadget, mumbling something under his breath rather quickly.

"Benthur, for the millionth time," Darriel slammed his hands on the table. "We. Can't. Understand. Your. Mumblings!"

"I said hello, Gavin, was wondering if you'd be coming." Benthur still spoke rather quickly, but Gavin knew that was his version of slowing things down. His voice was still just barely above a mumble, but Gavin heard him and smiled politely.

Darriel threw his hands up and shook his head. "Unbelievable."

"What'd the prince want?" Hilde asked, staring daggers across the table at Gavin.

Before he answered, Darriel passed him over a haunch of meat and a stout mug of ale. Gavin downed half of the contents of the drink in one go, noting that the elf was occasionally good for something.

"He just wanted my report, same as always."

"He wanted to see just you for the battle report?" Hilde seemed to lean in a bit closer as she asked.

Gavin thought about chomping into his food, but noticing that now Darriel and Gorram were staring at him too, he exhaled deeply through his nose. "The prince was concerned about my loyalties because of how little I speak during our reports."

"Hmph," Gorram shook his head as he stared down into the flagon he was nursing. "If he's looking to question loyalties, you're hardly the one to look to."

"Are you saying that there're people we should be questioning?" Hilde turned in her seat to stare at the former Varangur next to her as he swirled his ale.

"In an army full of those who seek their purpose, with no place to call home, why would there not be those with ulterior motives? Surely not all that come to call the Northern Alliance their 'home' are here out of the goodness of their hearts, to serve a master in the northern wastes of the world, for a mysterious purpose none known of. Why have you come here, Basilean?"

"Much like yourself, my former life is a title I wish not to be called," Hilde said bitterly as she took a swig from her own ale.

"Ooh, is it story time?" Darriel clapped his hands in mock excitement. "Oh, I do love story time! Hilde, my dear, there is so little we know about you. Why have you come to serve the Alliance?"

A scowl crossed her face for a few moments, but she sighed and drank deep, looking at each of them with a look of exasperation.

"I was once a paladin of renown. I fought in many campaigns to beat back all forces that would dare oppose the Hegemony; when those of Neretica would get ornery and come up on land to raise trouble, when the orcs and their pet goblins would come to assail our lands, and even those men and elves whose hearts were as black as night would let their avarice get the better of them, I was always on the field of battle to defend Basilea. I trained the heartiest of soldiers, watching many of them expire to the forces of darkness over the years. When this all started, when the Abyss opened up – what, almost two years ago? – I was wounded in the first battle. Before we truly understood the might of the Abyssals, we engaged them in battle. Because we underestimated their might, many good men and women died that day. Somehow, gods only know, I lived. I watched as almost my whole army was slaughtered, and my recompense was that I was branded by a gargoyle."

Hilde reached up to touch the scar down her cheek, but she quickly brought her hand back down when she realized what she was doing.

"It's a wonder I did not lose my life that day. It was decided that I was to relinquish my sword and title. That the horror I had seen, witnessing my entire army get massacred, was too much for any one paladin. The Hegemony would not hear my plea otherwise. They wanted me to retire my blade and work in Basilea instead as a… a… civilian." The word exploded out of her mouth like some insult she was appalled to utter. "I gave most of my adult life to the Hegemony, and they wanted to dismiss me! It was then that I remembered hearing tales about the Northern Alliance and, since I had no better options, decided to see for myself what it was about."

Gavin found himself nodding at the end of her tale as he was halfway through the haunch of meat. He had often wondered how she got her wound, and her story was similar to the one Gavin had devised in his head.

"Bravo! Encore!" Darriel clapped his hands as he wiped away an imaginary tear. "What a heartfelt story. And so here you are, well-fitted to join the band of merry misfits, indeed!"

Hilde swore some sort of racial slur under her breath before emptying the contents of her mug. Darriel stared at her expectantly.

"What, you don't want to hear my tale?"

"No, not really," she leaned back on the bench, crossing her arms.

"Not much to tell," Benthur mumbled, his eyes still glued to his project. "You lived 'round here. You were bored. You saw the Alliance banners. You signed up in search of some fun. You've found it in annoyin' the piss outta others."

Darriel held out a finger pointed at Benthur, his mouth held agape for several moments. "You… couldn't be further from the truth! You see, I… Well, my sister's lover, he…" Darriel dropped his hands down, slamming them open palmed on the table once more. "Damn you, dwarf! Yes, you're right. I was bored. The army was here. And I find most of you entertaining. You being the very exception to that!"

If Benthur heard him, he didn't pay his words any heed. He just kept playing with some small mechanical device, spinning things here, wrenching things there, inspecting the finer parts of it. Gavin chuckled slightly into his drink. He was always keen on the dwarf, even if he never joined them on the battlefield, due to his jobs within the castle.

"Alright, fine," Darriel held his hands up, running one of them through his slicked back, shoulder-length black hair as he composed himself. "Fine. Gorram?"

"I already told you. It was a life I chose to leave behind. Other than that, I'll pass on the details."

Darriel drummed his fingers on the table, as if trying to muster the courage to challenge the former Varangur to regale more of his tale, but he decided against it.

"Okay, how about you, Sir Brooding?"

"I'll follow suit with Gorram," Gavin said as he drained the last of his ale. He stood and grabbed his helmet. "I'll pass. Good night to you all."

Gorram looked up and locked eyes with Gavin, sending a strange chill down his spine, but the bigger man eventually nodded before returning to his drink. Darriel sat defeated, and Benthur and Hilde said their good nights to Gavin.

*****

Gavin awoke with a strange feeling. His eyes opened from the blackness, and the short rectangular room in which he came to looked nothing like he remembered. The walls looked to match the architectural style of Chill and not the barracks he resided in. There were no windows and very few things of actual interest. It was cold and empty.

He tried to stand and faltered, realizing he was already on his feet when he awoke. He had a vague recognition of the room, but he wasn't sure from where. He turned around to look at the empty walls, until his back was to the middle of the room.

"So you have awoken."

The peaceful voice that sounded like music to his soul should have startled him, but for whatever reason, he felt calm and at ease. He turned around to see a woman hovering just above the ground in the center of the room. Her pale skin complimented the silvery teal hair that flowed down her back in long curly ribbons. Her white dress was as pure as the snow outside of Chill, accented with flowery, silver, crystal-like designs; as well as matching crystal teardrop earrings. Her deep blue eyes met Gavin and gave him a warm smile, despite her chilly appearance.

"Wh-… Who are you?" It was the first question Gavin could utter in the slew of ones that rushed to his mind.

"You may call me… Aurora."

"Aurora?" Gavin frowned. "Like the name the soldiers have for the wall's reflection of light?"

"Who do you think gave them the name?" The ethereal figure's eyes remained locked on Gavin's. "The word for such a concept would have needed to be derived from somewhere. Do you honestly believe that the minds of men alone could have come up with such a beautiful name?"

Gavin recognized that there was some bite to those words behind the smile, and he knew he should have felt some form of resentment and concern, but those feelings were abandoned as again a wave of calm passed through him. As much as he tried to cling to the thoughts that pushed into his mind, they slipped away like water through open fingers, and he looked around the room once more.

"Where are we? Why am I here? Last I recall, I was in my bed in the officers' quarters."

"Rest assured, we are still in Chill. Your body is indeed still lying in your bed."

This time, it was not as easy for whatever magical presence surrounding him to calm his raging mind.

"My body?" His hands rushed to his chest, just now realizing that he was still fully armored.

"Ease yourself, Gavin Stalspar. Your body remains asleep, but I have called your spirit here. For several nights that you have slept, I have been trying to call out, to make contact with you. At first, I believed that my efforts were in vain. Your spirit was brought here, but it remained still, unmoving, and unresponsive. However, I began to notice that with each subsequent time you arrived, you began to become more responsive; a twitch here, a movement there, and then finally your eyes opened. Wide and white, they stared, again unresponsive."

"And now," Gavin shook his head, placing a hand to his temple as he fought an increasing pain.

"And now, here we are." Aurora, as the female called herself, spread her arms out in front of her and then let them fall to her sides.

Gavin shook his head once more; there was some kind of war of thoughts going on internally. His confusion, his anger, an overwhelming alien calm, and a surging of very real pain all fought together on the battlefield of his mind, and he was having a hard time making sense of what was going on, let alone put together any coherent sentences.

"I... Why? Why me?"

"I have reached out to the minds of many that would fight under the banner of this Northern Alliance, and I have seen many reasons and ambitions. I've seen desire forging the paths of most – for money, power, and lust. I've seen those with the most noble of ambitions, and those that would fight purely for themselves. There are plenty of the lost, those that don't know why they fight or know nothing else but fighting and have no other motivation. Then, there are those with darker hearts with mind for even darker deeds." Her eyes had slowly drifted away from him as she spoke, but now they shot back him, almost piercing Gavin with their intensity. "And then there is you. Different from all of the others."

"I am but a man, serving a man's purpose," Gavin said, as he forced himself to straighten under her gaze.

"But there is more to it than that. You do not have desires fueling you;

the things you want aren't guiding your path. You do not know whether fighting for yourself or others serves a better outcome; you struggle to find loyalty. You are lost, but not like the others. You seek purpose, and I wish to give you one."

Gavin snuffed, crossing his arms over his chest. "I am not some puppet that can be commanded to do the will of some... whatever in the Abyss you are."

"I am aware of that. It is that strength and conviction that you call out only when you need it that makes you the perfect bearer of this task. You need a path on which to walk, and I need someone who I can trust to save the very fates of the people of Mantica. I ask you, Gavin, please consider my words. You have every right to decline, but should you, it would take me time that Mantica does not have to find a replacement. Time, in which, the Abyss might rise to swallow the continent whole."

The calm was starting to turn the tide in his mind, but with it came clarity. She had been right, whoever this spiritual entity was. He sought purpose, the kind of which he was unsure if being a soldier in the Northern Alliance would ever give him. Aurora's words sparked something in him that he had not felt in a long time; excitement, perhaps? He couldn't quite put a name to it, but before he could even answer her, the pain pushed to the forefront and rocketed through his senses.

The world around Gavin spun as darkness crept in from the corners of his vision. His hands went to his temples, but the pain was overwhelming. Aurora was still before him, the smile still on her face, albeit somewhat sadder. Her image was fading.

"Think on what I've spoken to you of, Gavin Stalspar."

Blackness overtook Gavin before he felt his head ever hit the concrete floor. His vision returned even quicker than it had faded, and instead of impacting the ground, Gavin stopped himself when he sat straight up in his bed. He placed both hands out to stabilize himself on the frame, even though he was no longer moving. His head swam as reality settled back in; he remembered everything as if it were real life.

It was going to be a long day.

*****

The winds whipped past Gavin's helmet, finding ways into the crevices in between his armor, and sending chills down his spine. He flexed his fingers in the armored gauntlets to keep the blood flowing. Standing on the other side of Chill's walls, behind one of the many snowdrifts created for cover, Gavin missed the warmer climates more than ever.

It didn't matter how closely his squad huddled behind him, he stood at the edge of the barricade, acting as the windshield, as he watched for the enemy. He was loosely aware of the other units around him; Darriel and Hilde were off to his right, with Gorram somewhere to his left, and several other commanders he wasn't so familiar with leading their units scattered between them.

"The scouts sure of what they saw?" Rhynn, one of the Ice Kin elves in his unit, poked his head up to look past the icewall.

"Have they ever been wrong?" Tomas, a large native of the north snorted, patting his dual axes on the ice. "They fled so damn fast, they dropped their bows where they stood – and probably their breeches too!"

The men behind him laughed, but Gavin instead furrowed his eyebrows, staring on a point in the distance where the Abyssals would first appear around the mountain bend. Some time passed and his men began talking more, their laughing becoming a touch below raucous.

"That's enough," Gavin shot a look over his shoulder at Tomas, too often the instigator, and the large man nodded respectfully. "Stay focused. Speak among yourselves all you wish, I don't care what you're chattering about. Just remember the task at hand – those demons will be cresting the ridge at any moment, and I don't want ours to be the last unit astride the field."

It took a few moments, but their talk fell to whispers that ceased in distracting Gavin, none too soon! He heard them before he saw them; the trembling of the earth, the vicious roar of inhuman creations, the banging of rallying steel. The gargoyles were the first around, running on the ground on all fours like dogs instead of flying upon their crimson bat-wings. The beings of gray stone had pointed horns, some with long ratty manes; and a snarl twisted their faces, drool flailing out from their fanged maws. Behind them poured an army of demons, whose red skins were forged from the fires of the Abyss; an assortment of pointed and curved horns accented the long features and the twisted, abhorrent snarls.

The scouts were not wrong. The number of Abyssals was staggering; Gavin didn't even want to think about how many there actually were. All he could see was a sea of crimson, a horned red horde.

He roared as he surged forward, pulling his greatsword out with both hands. Just ahead of him, arrows rained down on the enemy, managing to take out a few of the gargoyles among countless other foot soldiers. He heard as well as felt the thunderous footsteps of the northmen and elves of his unit, and he could see Tomas just out of the corner of his eye. He could hear his men's fury as they bellowed out a war cry at the Abyssal demons; Gavin pushed himself to take wide and quick strides as to not be overtaken by the bigger men of his unit.

His eyes locked with the first charging opponent; the gargoyle snarled as it flung open its mouth. It leapt through the air, using its wings to glide toward Gavin in a pounce. He brought his sword up to stop the two claws, coming to a sudden halt as the beast pushed on the other side of his blade. It remained midair, desperately snapping its many pointed teeth at Gavin's head. Shifting to the left, Gavin pulled the blade out and low. The gargoyle soared past him, but he brought his sword up, cleaving through the body and down the middle of its long spaded tail.

Gavin only had a moment to make sure the torn beast was dead before the rest of the Abyssal forces were on him. The Northern Alliance defenders clashed hard with the demons, blade upon blade ringing out down the line. Gavin found himself against two of the evil entities, both swinging at him at the same time. The former knight parried their blows easily enough, but he found himself unable to work in any offense. He struggled to not backpedal under the offense, but he begrudgingly was being forced back.

He just barely saw the arrow that pierced the head of one of the demons, and Gavin took the advantage to push back against the sole target. His swings were much more aggressive; not having to fear the other adversary getting in a strike, Gavin swung with unbridled intensity. He forced the demon back so much that it hesitated, and then Gavin rushed in with his shoulder. Losing one hand on its sword, the demon had no time to block the strike that cleaved straight through his unarmored chest. It struggled to stay straight, but a swift kick from Gavin put it down for good.

He looked where the arrow had originally come from, and he found Darriel rapidly scanning the battlefield, letting out timed shots. The archer momentarily met his gaze, giving him a wink before he picked his next target.

Gavin heard a howl and brought his sword up before he could see the enemy. The pommel struck home, catching the demon in the chin. It staggered back, shaking its head, but Gavin twirled his sword around and shoved it outward, piercing through the minimal hell-forged armor it wore. Its head shot back down at him, smiling with dark pleasure, blood dripping out its nostrils and down its fangs. It swung at him, but Gavin had no time to dodge. The blade caught him on the forearms and he felt a stinging under the armor. He let the blade go and looked down at his arms. The strike had cracked his forearm guard, piercing through and causing a light wound. The blood was trickling out and it stung, but he could tell it was not lethal. He cursed under his breath and kicked the downed demon in the head as it struggled to rise. He kicked it again and again until it stopped moving.

Gavin bent down to retrieve his weapon, but another screech caught his attention. A second gargoyle was already upon him, its claws hooked into his breastplate. The two hit the ground and rolled several feet, the beast clawing ferociously at the armor while Gavin kept trying to punch the gargoyle in the face. They stopped rolling, but Gavin was pinned under the weight of the winged nightmare. It brought its head back, opened its jaws, and snapped forward. Gavin managed to grab both sides of the gargoyle's face, struggling to keep the maw back from closing on his exposed throat. He could feel the sweat dripping down the side of his head as he fought for his life, but no matter how strong he was, the stony beast was forged in the inhuman fires of the Abyss.

Just as he felt the muscles in his arms would snap, the gargoyle flew off his chest with a yelp of pain. Gavin scrambled to his feet and saw Gorram with his mighty pike in one hand, Gavin's greatsword in the other. The big man stared at Gavin, his look unreadable. The former Varangur warrior tossed over the sword and Gavin caught it with both hands.

"Thanks," Gavin nodded, as he turned to the gargoyle that staggered back to its own feet. Gorram nodded in response, keeping his eyes on the beast.

"Are you hurt?"

"Just a flesh wound from one of the demons. You came before the gargoyle could feast."

"Good. I would not see you die this day."

The gargoyle screamed as it flew through the air, claws out. Both men sidestepped and swung at separate angles; Gavin slashed up across the underbelly and Gorram performed a mighty execution strike downward. As they moved past the corpse of the gargoyle, the two men stood back to back. The demons had surrounded them; Gavin saw the flags of the Northern Alliance standard bearers some distance away, but they were not any of the men in his unit.

"What were you saying about not dying today?" Gavin spat through gritted teeth.

Gorram laughed darkly, the first time Gavin had ever heard, and it unnerved him. "No, we shall not die here, friend. There is much still to be done."

Gorram lunged forward, cleaving into the first foe his pike could find flesh in. Gavin used the momentum of his ally to dive straight toward the enemies before him. The fury he put into his blade was unrelenting as he swung in wide arcs, severing limbs of demons not prepared for the fury, and pushing back the circle that had wound tight upon them. He didn't stop his flurry of strikes, feeling the occasional blade strike his armor. He prayed his breastplate would hold out better than his armguards, that a demon would not get as lucky as the one that wounded him.

His wound began to catch up with him, and he favored putting might into the other arm. But the fury was not as potent as before; his fire began to fizzle out as he began to tire, and the demons could sense it as if they smelled the blood from his wound. They moved to gang up on him, three then four demons pushed on him from different angles, forcing Gavin to recoil into a defensive stance. He cursed his luck as he struggled to keep the demons back, slowly losing the ground he had attained.

The ground beneath Gavin's feet rumbled, and he smiled. Demons flew into the air – not of their own winged accord – but because they had been assailed by a giant spiked club, the size of a battering ram in most men's hands. Snow trolls, arguably more menacing than the Abyssal fiends in their primal rage, tore through the battlefield. The furry white beasts howled with their oversized jaws, the canine teeth protruding on the overbite. Their small blue-white pupils scanned the battlefield as the elite guards of Prince Talannar tore through the Abyssal demons as if they were wading through the sea. This was only the second time that Gavin had bore witness to them, but their fury was impressive!

He pulled himself away, taking several steps to the side, as the snow trolls barreled through the enemies before him. They stopped and stared at him. As if they recognized the colors worn by their master, they snuffed a greeting at Gavin before pursuing the now fleeing enemy; one of them grabbed a gargoyle by the tail and began swinging it back and forth against the ground like some toy.

"Those are some impressive beasts."

Gavin turned to see Gorram standing beside him, arms crossed over his chest.

"You have my thanks, Gorram. Without your aid, I doubt I would be standing here."

"You are a mighty warrior, Gavin," the former Varangur nodded. "I have staked my life on my cause. I just ask that you remember that when the time comes when I need your aid."

"And you shall have it, Gorram. I assure you. It is the least I can do."

As the trolls were clearing out the last of the Abyssals, Darriel and Hilde made their way over to Gavin and Gorram.

"It is good to see you both upright," Hilde nodded, holding her sword low.

"Yes, I have both of these two to thank for that," Gavin nodded back to Gorram and then pointed to Darriel.

"Ho! What's this?" the elf leaned back with his arms out in mock shock. "The former Varangur has become the unlikely hero? I daresay though, Stalspar, it would do you well to stop putting yourself in harm's way. Two of us saving your life? For shame, for shame."

Gavin ignored the archer, pushing past him as he looked for his squad. "How many dead this time?"

"Lotharr had his throat ripped out by a gargoyle," Hilde said gravely. "Shame, Lotharr was a good man and huscarl. A few other casualties here and there. It was good that the prince sent out his ice trolls, or that number would have been much higher."

Gavin stopped when he came to his men. He sighed deeply when he saw the body of Tomas arranged respectfully by the sullen northmen. Rhynn was kneeling by the man's head and closed the dead man's eyes. He looked gravely at Gavin and stood when he approached.

"What happened?"

"He... he got skewered every which way," Rhynn bowed his head. "They ganged up on him, and he, well…"

Gavin placed his hand on Rhynn's shoulder. "It's alright, Rhynn. He died doing what he loved. The battlefield was where Tomas lived, and it was where he died. He would have wanted nothing less."

The elf struggled to meet his superior's eyes, but he nodded and then turned to help the others prepare the body.

*****

Gavin had become so accustomed to being lost in his own thoughts, that most times he found it better to simply block out all of the questions and scenarios that raced through his brain until they faded into a dull buzz. As he wandered the halls of the prince's castle, absently through candle-lit corridors that he had no idea of where they led, a few things crept through the shield around his mind.

Tomas's death was on him. Sure, he could wave a sword around in combat and push creatures like the Abyssal demons around easily enough, but he was not fit to lead men. Not anymore; not since he left knighthood. This had been the second battle in recent days that he had strayed from his unit, unable to give them the commands that they needed. The first had been due to an overzealous urge to scour the Abyssals from the mountainside, but the second had not been his doing; that damn gargoyle had separated him from any friendly units. Had Darriel and Gorram not been there to aid him, he would have met a similar fate to Tomas.

He had taken Gavin's place on the end of Death's scythe. And though, like most humans in their nature, he was reluctant to think of welcoming the cold embrace of forever, Gavin had to feel slightly envious. The northman was at peace – or so he'd like to think. There was hopefully no more fighting on the 'other side', wherever that was, and there would be none of the politics or greed or suffering that the mortals faced on this side of life. Gavin began to wonder what that would be like, but when he realized where he was, he stopped.

He wasn't sure what part of the castle he had wandered through, but there was a snow troll standing outside a doorway. For some reason, Gavin found himself drawn toward it. He walked by it, his head swiveling to gaze within, and he froze.

It was an empty chamber.

The troll growled, standing now in front of the frame and blocking

Gavin's sight. The former knight, in a state of shock, put his hands up and found no words with which to utter; none that the troll would understand nor any that could possibly describe the sensations that rushed through him upon seeing the room from his dreams.

He kept on going through the corridor, hoping it would loop back around to the main hall, but he wasn't really paying attention. Gavin's mind raced back through his dreams, trying to recall every little detail that might help to explain the bizarre connection, and who and how this related to the Aurora woman.

"Strange, is it not?" The voice startled Gavin out of his musings, and he spun on one heel with his hand placed on the pommel of his sword instinctively. Goram stared back at him, snorting in amusement. "Worry not. You have no need to draw your steel on me."

"Gorram, I… I am sorry. I was lost inside my mind, recalling some strange dreams…"

"Dreams? About that empty room?"

Gavin narrowed his eyes as he let go of his sword, crossing his arms over his chest. "No… Not quite. It is just that that room reminded me of something."

"And again, I ask, it is strange, is it not?" Gorram started walking past Gavin, the latter walking beside him. "A castle in the middle of the mountains, with talk of the prince holding some strange mystery that calls forth a million rumors and bizarre tales; and here, in the middle of his palace, is a single empty room, guarded by a lone snow troll."

Gavin nodded. "It doesn't make any sense. Unless… Perhaps it's not empty at all."

Gorram cocked an eyebrow as he looked at the man. "You think that there is magic in that room?"

"Who knows," Gavin shrugged. "Maybe he is hiding something in there. But if he was, then who's to say that he's not hiding all sorts of traps and obstacles guarding whatever secret lay within. Maybe the room is some portal to another realm altogether? Could you imagine if he cast a spell on the room because it secretly led to another tear in the earth, another Abyss altogether? That would be something I would not want to encounter."

Gavin found himself speaking on the subject much more than he intended, his mind moving faster than his mouth, and the former Varangur had his eyes narrowed, clearly thinking deeply on Gavin's words.

"Perhaps you are right, Stalspar. But these are things we must not speak of. Such thoughts might be considered treason. You were already questioned by the prince once, I would not like to be the reason why you were summoned a second time." Through their walkings, they had returned to the entrance hallway and the sound of music and merriment filled the air once more. "I must take my leave. There is much I must still accomplish, and the night grows ever closer."

The Varangur turned to leave, but he came closer to Gavin, their eyes locked and his expression cold. "I must ask you again. Do not concern yourself over such things as that room. The way that this war is going, dwelling on such thoughts will only get you killed." He stepped back and nodded. "Take care, Gavin Stalspar."

*****

Once more, Gavin found himself spiraling through darkness, only this time, he was not as confused when he awoke standing in the empty room in Chill's castle. The icy spirit, Aurora, stood before him again; she still wore a warm smile upon her face, but something in her expression worried Gavin.

"I do not have an answer for you yet, Aurora. There is still much I need to think about and much I need to know. I-…"

"I have not summoned you here because I wish for an answer, Gavin Stalspar." She put a hand up to stop him from speaking. "Of course, I do desire one, but not at this moment. We have less time than I thought – far less time – for me to speak with you and explain. Do you recall how I mentioned that some here in this Northern Alliance harbor dark deeds and desires in their hearts?"

"Yes, vaguely," Gavin nodded. When she did not immediately continue, Gavin felt his stomach tighten in worry. He looked around the room, but everything seemed fine. The calm that overtook him last time was nowhere to be felt, however. "Aurora, what is going on?"

"I am afraid that some of those men have begun to put their plans in motion. They think they have found what they were searching for, and they will be here soon. Gavin Stalspar, I plead with you," her icy eyes locked onto his, her face an expression of pity. "You must help me. Even if you do not wish to take up the quest that I can offer you, you must come back to this room and help me. Or else all will be doomed."

Gavin opened his mouth to speak, but the crippling headache overtook him. As his spirit drifted back to his body, some guttural snarl was let loose, reminding him of a snow troll, and he sat straight up.

He looked around him, and then he remembered Aurora's words. He thought on it for a few moments, but he sighed and stood to ready his armor.

With one hand on his sword, he strode purposely out of the barracks, looking around as he walked out into Chill. Where were the patrols? If something was going on, surely the guards would have noticed and sounded the alarm…

He heard the drawing of steel and stopped.

"Halt, you there." Gavin turned around and saw three hooded men with swords and axes readied. They wore the colors of the Alliance, but Gavin thought he could see some type of warpaint underneath the hood. "Stalspar, that you?"

"Yes. What's going on here?"

"Get out of here while you can," a second deep voice grumbled. "You're not one of them true-blood Alliance members trying to protect the prince. You're an even farther outsider than the rest of them, like us."

"You can walk away from this in one piece," a third voice spoke. "Go on and leave, now."

Gavin slid the greatsword out and held it in both hands, looking between the men. "You're right, I am an outsider, from a distant land, with distant kingdoms and rulers. But justice and what is right is all the same throughout. Whatever is going on here, I will not let it come to pass."

The only sounds were the feet of the men running across Chill's magicked stones, combined with the movement of their light armor, as they came at Gavin. He ducked low under the first one's axe swing, shouldering him in the gut as he stood. The second one pulled back both arms to ready a swing from his dual wielded short swords, but Gavin saw the chance and planted a boot in his chest that knocked the opponent onto his rear. There was no time to fend off the third; he raised his sword to parry the incoming dual axes. The hook of the axe caught on Gavin's bigger weapon and he swung to the side with all of his might, ripping the weapons from his opponent's grasp. Rushing inward, he slammed his helmeted head into the face of his opponent, and he watched as he hit the ground and stopped moving.

There was a loud bang and Gavin was seeing stars as he realized his next opponent had foolishly tried to pierce the helmet with his poorly crafted axe. Gavin could feel his head exposed to the night air, and he ripped it off his head, smashing his opponent in the jaw with it as he whirled around. His foe struggled to rise, and Gavin brought his sword down hard into his stomach, creating a wound he would not get up from, no matter how hard he struggled through the pain and oozing blood.

He whipped around to look into the shadowy hood of the last assailant, who readied his short swords once more. He came at Gavin in a flurry of anger, now screaming as he ran. Gavin, wielding a bigger weapon, was forced on the defense from the quickness of the shorter, more nimble weapons; but he knew it would only be a matter of time before the man ran out of steam. With each attack, the delay in response time and follow up became more noticeable. Gavin sidestepped a swing from the right and swung down low, hooking the flat of the blade against the ankle of the opponent, and knocking him onto his back.

As the man hit the ground, Gavin stabbed down into his opponent's chest as he had done to the other, keeping his blade locked until he stopped squirming.

As he withdrew the mighty sword, he noticed the hood had fallen back and the man's face was exposed. He figured it would be inevitable that he would recognize the man, but the shock hit him hard. He had seen the tattoos and scars before from men from another unit. Hilde had once told him the marks were the easiest way to recognize someone as a Varangur. And this man had served in Gorram's unit.

He didn't have time to wipe the blood off the sword. Gavin turned and sprinted to the castle as quickly as he could. He cursed when he realized that there were no guards on duty; there were always guards on duty. The hall was lit by the same torches as it had been several hours ago, except there was not a single note of music being played. The castle was eerily silent.

He had a thought to check on the prince to make sure he was okay, but for some reason, he found himself more worried about Aurora. As he ran through the corridors, trying to find his way back to the empty room, he found it ironic that he was concerned over a spirit he had only met in his dreams twice, more than the ruler who had taken him in to his kingdom and presented him a title of command without knowing a thing about him. Even stranger, he began realizing, is that no one met him in the hallways; no guards, no sentries, no passing warriors hanging around drunk.

He turned another corner, finally beginning to recognize where he was from yesterday, when he nearly tripped. Catching his balance on the wall, he turned around to see that an outstretched leg had caught him; the body slumped against the wall, bloody and dead. There were no Varangur markings on this one.

Gavin hurried his pace, finding four more bodies in his wake. That made eight dead Northern Alliance soldiers, and combined with the casualties they had lost in the day's battle – as minimal as they might have been – it was a major offset for the already limited numbers. While he didn't have a chance to look at the faces of all of the men, he had recognized the first, a man by the name of Kaleb. They were good men, and even if he didn't fully believe in the purpose of the Northern Alliance, he knew men like Kaleb had. They had died defending something they believed in, even if it was defending against a traitor. At that moment, more than ever, Gavin questioned what he was fighting for.

One more corner turned, and he saw the snow troll that had been guarding the inconspicuous doorway, now sprawled out on the floor. Its head was lying nearly a foot away, its club impaled in its back. He slowed as he came to the doorless room. Gavin knew what was waiting for him, but he dreaded it all the same.

Gorram sat in the middle of the empty room from his dreams, the same room they had spoken about in passing. The same room that Gorram told him not to worry about. He sat with his legs crossed, his eyes shut, and his hand around the handle of the pike standing on its head.

"I thought I had told you not to concern yourself with this room," Gorram spoke without opening his eyes.

Gavin slowly crept into the chamber, his sword held low, but ready. "You did. But what you failed to mention is that you had planned a coup."

The big Varangur let a smile creep into the corner of his mouth, his eyes slowly opening to look at Gavin.

"Since we met, I thought that we were kindred spirits. Two silent outsiders who spoke with their blades instead of flapping their mouths, like the prissy elf, Darriel, or instead of flaunting our pride, like that cur, Hilde. But I was wrong." Gorram slowly stood, pushing up with the head of his pike. He hefted the weapon across his chest with both hands. "You lack conviction. You are lost, drowning in thoughts of the unknown. While myself, I have purpose. My brothers of the Varangur heard the whispers of rumors that stir on the winds around Mantica. The prince of this frozen wasteland has some secret that he conceals because he believes he is protecting the world. He claims to bear this burden alone on his shoulders – and we seek to destroy that burden. I know there is magic here, I can feel it, Korgaan has told me of such blasphemy. And you," Gorrath indicated Gavin with his chin. "You have seen it. You have bore witness to its effects. You empathize with it, or else you would not be here to stop me."

"Perhaps I have seen what you speak of, but I don't stand in your path for the Northern Alliance. I don't do this for the being that has called to me for nights on end, asking me to trust it on its secret quest." Gavin brought his sword up to challenge Gorram's aggressive stance. "I do this for myself. Your death gives me no joy, but I will stop you because too many good men, they themselves believing in their own purpose, have been cut down by your blade. And they were fighting to save lives; not offer them in sacrifice to some god."

The Varangur spit, the phlegm landing at Gavin's feet. "I should have let you die when I had the chance to watch the demons rip the flesh from your bones."

Gorram crossed the room it seemed in a single leap, raising his pike high over his head and bringing it down with a mighty slam. Gavin only had moments to bring himself out of the way, pressing into a roll, and then quickly standing on Gorram's right. Gavin swung horizontally in an effort to catch the bigger man in the arm, but he underestimated how fast he could bring the pike up and around to parry the blow. They exchanged several swings from pike to greatsword in horizontal arcs.

The two blades collided in a deadlock, neither man giving up. The intensity that burned in the Varangur's face was almost more intimidating than the demons; anger flared behind his focused eyes, arched eyebrows, and furious teeth. Gorram was unhinged in his fury. Gavin tried to hook his sword under the curve of the axe head, as he had done to one of Gorram's lackeys, but he could not rip the heavy weapon out of his opponent's hands. Instead, Gavin felt himself being shifted, as Gorram used the hooked advantage to pull the former knight's blade and swing him with both hands.

Gavin held onto his sword and flew across the empty room, rolling as he hit the ground. He forced himself to focus, to not allow himself to rest on the ground from the impact, no matter how hard his body fought to. He forced himself to one knee, his vision blurry and head spinning, he knew Gorram would be on him in an instant and raised his sword with one hand, supporting it with the other. The Varangur hammered his pike down, and Gavin almost buckled from the impact, his injured arm shooting pain across it. Again and again he slammed the pike down. Gavin instinctively moved his head with each strike; he sorely missed that helmet now. But then he realized the man wasn't aiming for his head – he was trying to shatter the blade.

Gavin waited for the big man to recoil, to deliver the blow that he thought would shatter the sword, and he rolled to his left, cradling the big sword as he did. The pike loudly echoed against the floor, shaking the ground under Gavin's feet as he stood. He turned toward his enemy once more, but Gorram was on him, faster than he should have been. He forced Gavin back, pinning him to the wall with one arm against his windpipe. The former knight fought for air; he dropped his sword and clawed at the big arm that was being pushed into him.

"Where is it?!" Gorram's voice took on a darker tone he had never heard before as he bellowed in Gavin's face. "There is magic in this room, Korgaan has told me so! Where is Icekin's foul sorcery?!"

Gavin could feel the world around him darkening and spots dotted his vision. He wanted to curse Gorram and his god. He wanted to tell him to burn in the Abyss. Then he thought about Tomas and the peace he might have found, and all other thoughts left his mind.

There was a noise behind Gorram; almost like a breath of air, but in a very musical tone. All Gavin could think of was that it sounded like ice, as odd as that sounded. Gorram turned his head to look at the icicles forming on the far wall in a spiderweb-like pattern. He dropped Gavin and turned completely to face it, as if it were some sign that he was waiting for. Maybe he thought, like Gavin, that it was a message from Aurora.

Gavin fought with the spasming coughs to inhale deep breaths, but it didn't distract Gorram. Despite the haze that hung over his mind and the cloudiness of his vision, Gavin felt for the greatsword he had dropped, picking it up in both hands. He couldn't see Gorram's face, but he could imagine the look of hate as he stared at the web of ice. That was enough for Gavin. He plunged the sword deep through Gorram's furs and armor, pushing and twisting it through the flesh, until he heard the sword emerge from the other side with a sickening 'pop'. He held it there as Gorram struggled to break free, his pike clattered to the floor as his hands, slick with his own blood, fought to push the blade back.

Gavin closed his eyes and waited until the thrashing stopped and the body fell still. After another few moments, he pulled the blade out and let Gorram's body slide to the floor. He stared into the man's face, the hate still present even in his last moments of life.

"I respected you, but we were never kindred spirits," Gavin said softly, closing his once ally's eyes. "There was always too much darkness in your heart. Even I could see that. I simply hoped it was a life you left behind. Rest easy now, Gorram. Let the hate leave your soul."

"Well said, Gavin."

Gavin spun around, his sword still held ready. He raised his eyebrows and lowered the blade, resting the tip against the ground, when he realized it was Prince Talannar, flanked by two of his elite guards. His hand had a mystical glow around it, and as it faded, Gavin turned to notice that the iceweb did as well.

"The distraction – that was you?"

"Of course it was, who else could it have been?"

"I thought..."

"That there was some other mystical being here?" The prince laughed merrily. "Come now, I would have thought you above listening to rumors."

Gavin held his tongue and Prince Talannar's gaze, unsure of what to make of the whole situation.

"Anyway, this is a shame, to say the least," Prince Talannar waved his hand at Gorram's body. "It would have been a nice thing to boast about, having a unit of redeemed Varangur. Now that is something that could have gotten people below the mountains talking!"

"Your Majesty, I can explain," Gavin stood formally when he realized the weight of the situation.

"No, no, don't worry." Prince Talannar shook his head. "I know exactly what happened. After all, it was I that distracted him. It's unfortunate that a few of the soldiers did not get the orders to leave."

"Leave, Your Majesty?" Gavin narrowed his eyebrows.

"I knew there was a spy among us – I have my sources. We just weren't sure who the spy was. With all of the casualties that we've sustained over the past few weeks, our numbers have reached a new low. I figured if someone were to strike, now would be the perfect night. So I gave almost all of the men the night off; only my most vigilant and trusted warriors watched from the shadows. Unfortunately, it seems there were some that decided that they needed to still patrol the castle anyway." The prince sighed deeply, seeming rather sullen. "The biggest shame in all of this is the death of Uthar. He was one of my better snow trolls. I warned him what would be coming his way though. Had I removed him, I'm sure the Varangur would have been suspicious and not gone through with his plot."

"Thank the gods the soldiers are okay. I feared that the Varangur slaughtered them all."

"I think I have you to thank for that. The guards found the three bodies that you disposed of. They're scouring Chill to make sure that was all of them. Had you not stopped them, they would have certainly killed more of our soldiers and civilians, in sacrifice to their dark god."

Gavin fell silent, looking once more down at the body of his fallen former ally. "They were following their purpose, nothing more than the rest of us."

"Yes, but as you so rightly said, we aren't slaying people for the purpose of satisfying some mysterious dark god. We are saving people. Our enemies are, and always will be, the Abyssals."

Gavin nodded, but he once more said nothing for a few moments. "Thank you for saving me, Your Majesty. If you'll excuse me, I need to sleep and put the memories I shared with this man in the depths of my mind."

As Gavin went to pass by Prince Talannar, the leader put his hand on the former knight's shoulder. He waited until Gavin looked him in the eyes. There was no hate in those oddly colored eyes; there was compassion, understanding, and a great deal of love for life. They were the eyes of a prince that most men would be honored to serve.

"Thank you, Gavin. Should tomorrow morn I not find you among the other soldiers, I want to thank you for all of your efforts with the Northern Alliance. You have fought bravely under our banners against countless Abyssal forces. May you find whatever it is that you're searching for."

Gavin held his gaze for a few moments longer, nodded his head, and then left the room.

*****

Talannar waited and listened for Huscarl Stalspar's footsteps to die away. He inclined his head back, motioning toward Elbis, the guard that stood immediately outside the doorway. The warrior held a hand up as he watched down the corridor. After several moments, he nodded.

"He's gone, Prince Talannar."

"Thank you, Elbis." Four more of his guards filed into the room, standing at attention. "Elbis, stand guard with Hadrill. Oram, see to the snow trolls. Tell them of Uthar's sacrifice and ask them for two more that would be willing to stand in his place. They will understand the words you speak, even though they will not respond. Do not let that daunt you. Percy and Denny, check with the others around Chill. Make sure that no more Varangur roam the city. Check every alley, every house, every dark corner. They are relentless – I'm sure that was not the last of their assassins. Do not forget the stories we heard from the Brotherhood refugees. I will be checking on our friend. Do not allow me to be disturbed under any circumstance."

The five guards nodded; Elbis and Hadrill stood outside the room, weapons at the ready, while the other three disappeared from sight. Content with his orders, Talannar spun on his heel, his cape flowing out behind him, as he came to the back wall. He held up his hand, the pendant around his neck glowing an icy blue, while a similar effect was mirrored on his fingertips.

Prince Talannar Icekin walked through the wall, the magicked effects rippling like water as he passed through, into the stairwell that led down into the lower caverns of Chill. He put his hand down, the pendant stopped glowing, and the wall became whole once more. Talannar walked a few paces forward and took the torch from the right wall.

Lighting his descent, he walked down the spiral staircase and slowly descended into the depths of the mountain.

*****

Gavin stood in the empty chambers of the dream, once more. There was no sign of his combat with Gorram, but he stared at the spot where he had slain him. Aurora stood there as she always did, a smile painted on her face.

"Thank you, Gavin. Had you not come-..."

"You wanted an answer?"

His tone was a bit harsher than before as he fought the calm that tried to permeate his senses. He slowly looked up at her, feeling the fatigue of the last few days settling on him. Aurora closed her mouth and nodded her head.

"Tell me what this quest of yours is – where you'll be sending me, what I have to do, and why this is so damn important. Once I have all of the information, then you'll have your answer. And perhaps I'll have my purpose."

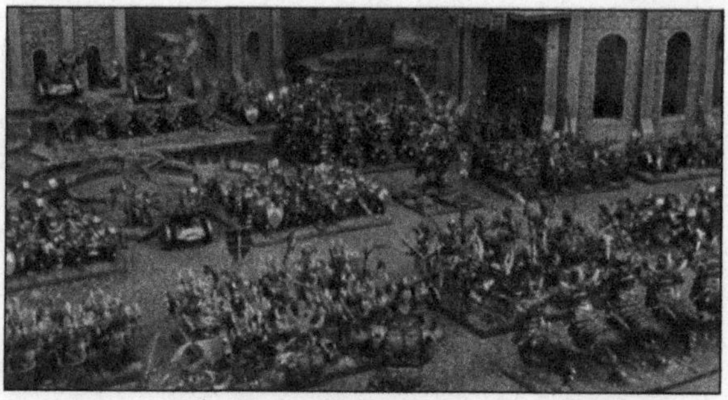

KINGS OF WAR

Look for information on
Kings of War and Mantic Games at:

manticgames.com

BEYOND ANTARES
MARKOV'S PRIZE
ANTARES
MARK BARBER

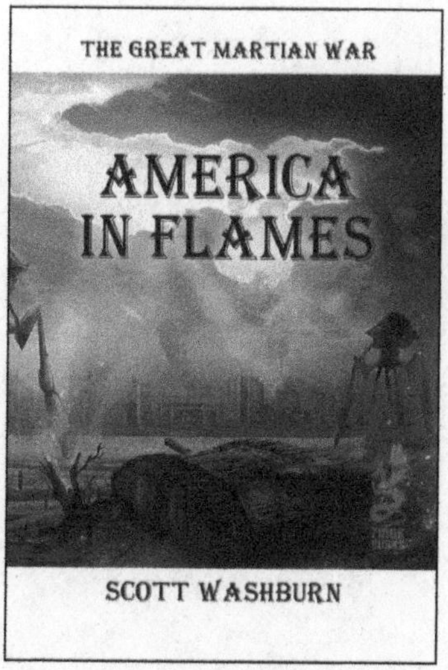
THE GREAT MARTIAN WAR
AMERICA IN FLAMES
SCOTT WASHBURN